About the Author

Jonathan Falla lived in a part of Scotland oddly like Glenfarron, where he inhabited a freezing hayloft while writing a book about tropical Burma. Such incongruities are the stuff of his writing. He is the holder of a Creative Scotland award, and in 2007 was short-listed for the National Story Prize. His previous novels are *Poor Mercy* and *Blue Poppies*.

For more information about the author, see

www.tworavenspress.com

and

www.jonathanfalla.wordpress.com

Glenfarron

JONATHAN FALLA

Published by Two Ravens Press Ltd.
Green Willow Croft
Rhiroy, Lochbroom
Ullapool
Ross-shire IV23 2SF

www.tworavenspress.com

ISBN: 978-1-906120-33-7

British Library Cataloguing in Publication Data: a CIP record for this book can be obtained from the British Library.

Designed and typeset in Sabon by Two Ravens Press.
Cover design by David Knowles and Sharon Blackie.

Printed on Forest Stewardship Council-accredited paper by Biddles Ltd., King's Lynn, Norfolk.

The publisher gratefully acknowledges subsidy from the Scottish Arts Council towards the publication of this volume.

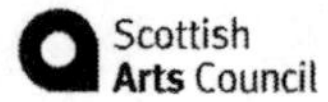

For Rona

Part One

JACKY WHISKY

1940

When war began in earnest, Joyce upped and offed to Glasgow. She was young, she had to get out of Glenfarron, couldn't stand the prying and the nosing, said every time she dropped her drawers she could hear the echo down the village street.

A whorey old joke, even then; she only said it to shock her sister. Sara Dulce was a tad prim, and needed a tease. Sara was to wed a gamekeeper. Joyce was always game and wouldn't mind being kept but she wasn't wedding, thank you.

Photos (those odd little prints with serrated edges) show the sisters together as teenagers on Torbrechan farm. Nothing close up: twenty feet from the camera was the only focal depth Box Brownies could manage. But there is Sara Dulce grinning at Joyce in farm-girl gaucheness, and Joyce pulling a face, always a baggage. So one may readily imagine them in October 1940, side by side in front of the mirror in Joyce's rooms in Glasgow, pinning their hair back, Sara's richer than the conkers in the Farron forest, Joyce's black. They were heading out on the town.

Joyce was piling on carmine lipstick like an overexcited tulip, while Sara eyed her in the mirror fondly, thinking how their parents would shake their heads in dismay. Joyce always knew when she was being looked at. She also knew that her quieter sister was gorgeous. She reached out to finger Sara's nut-brown hair.

'You're a conker, Sara Dulce, you're a red squirrel, you're a knockout!'

'Me?'

'Am I talking to the hairbrush?' said Joyce, leaning forward to kiss her blushing sibling on the cheek.

'Come on. Let's get up to no good.'

◆◆◆

And, not half a mile off, six whisky glasses waited in a ring, five faces watching, one of them (though he'd no notion of it as yet) on his way to becoming a father. Behind the faces seethed a Saturday night pub in Candleriggs, but in this sombre corner, above the racket, rose a soft and solemn voice, intoning:

'Bronski, Maczek, Sikorski.'

A brass lighter moved from dram to dram and the spirit caught fire, *in memoriam*:

'Wachowski, Hojan, Niesiolowski.'

As each was lit, a young man took up the flaming glass. The memory of those passionate Polish officers long endured in Scotland. Their panache set them apart; they clung to their manners, their style, their uniforms, long after they were officially disbanded. The uniforms were blue, and onto each shoulder an insignia was stitched, a red-and-white chequerboard with the Polish Air Force initials: *PSP*. And now they lifted the almost invisibly flaming whisky, gazing at the pale fire with moist eyes. The tongues licked and slid across the surface, shrinking, expiring. Someone said:

'We shall not forget. We shall be back. Poland!'

'Poland!'

They drank. The master-of-ceremonies looked round the table.

'Tomorrow we really fuck Hitler.'

A most solemn oath.

'But tonight we fuck Glasgow.'

◆◆◆

The doors of the City Halls swung wide for Joyce and Sara Dulce. A second of appraisal: they viewed the wide dance floor of springy timber, the upper air sticky with acid smoke, the crowd febrile with time-out from war, the stage gilded with trombones, cornets, flügels, blazing out on *American Patrol*.

'Like it, Sis?' grinned Joyce.

Sara smiled hesitantly. Joyce squeezed her arm.

'Cummon, boil Glenfarron oot yer silly heid.'

So they swept forward and at once young men circled like tugs and tenders about two spanking yachts, two ocean princesses. The boys were in service green or khaki, their ears protuberant below cropped service scalps, their chins polished to an eager gleam, their lumpy boots rubbed to a lustre that could never impart elegance. As they drew near the radiance of Joyce and the softer loveliness of Sara, the young men's approaches were clumpy, gauche and wooden.

'Drinks, girls?'

'Whaddya havin'?'

'Well, you look stunning!'

'May I?'

'Smokes, girls?'

Joyce accepted a Sweet Afton with a regal smile. Sara hung back to admire – but Joyce wasn't having that.

'Relax!' she hissed. 'Get stonkin!'

Sara giggled. An RAF type was nodding at her side.

'I'll say! I'll say! What'll it be? This way!'

He slipped a hand under both girls' elbows and propelled them towards the bar. Sara struggled not to look flustered but Joyce sailed along with her spinnaker out, winking at her sister behind the airman's back. At the bar, thirty yards long and awash with slopped ale, the man shouted a gin for Joyce.

And for Sara?

'Lime cordial…'

'Bugger lime cordial! Have a drink, will you?'

Sara was saved by the bandleader. The players were shuffling the music on their purple stands as the maestro in white turned to the mike and wriggled his shoulders.

'Ladies and gentlemen, take the floor for a two-step!'

'Miss?' hazarded a stocky green infantry sergeant, holding out a hand to Sara. She stood aside.

'Later. Thank you.'

At which Joyce lost her rag.

'Are you playing wet blankets? That's bloody great.'

'Joyce…'

Joyce took her by the shoulders, eyed her straight.

'Listen, this is Glasgow, a wee spot of fun in your tedious life.'

'I'm engaged to marry…'

'So? I'm suggesting you dance, not get pregnant.'

At which Sara coyly smiled.

Her sister stared at her. Sara lowered her eyes with a sly little smirk – and Joyce exploded with delight.

'Sis? You…? Oh, Sis!'

She flung her arms about Sara's neck, landing a wet kiss on her cheek, then pulled back a moment to study her face.

But Sara nodded happily.

'It is Gordon's. He's mad keen. He's made a crib already, his Ma's scandalised.'

'Well, it'll be strong as an ox and a dance'll do it good. Come on, will you?'

So Sara let the infantry sergeant lead her onto the floor. Around they went till the music stopped and they bobbed their thank-yous and Sara was looking for Joyce when…

The doors were flung open.

Five young men in uniform, with red-and-white flashes and *PSP* on their sleeves, made their entrance. It was not that nature had made them more handsome than British boys, but that they knew how to be handsome. Not that they were taller, but that they carried themselves taller. Not that tailors contracted by the Polish government were more concerned with styling than those engaged by His Majesty's War Office, but drape these young men in a potato sack and they'd have worn it graciously. They moved like princes and calmly surveyed the crowd. They were not vainglorious; they were superb.

'Polish Air Force,' Joyce giggled. 'Sexy brutes.'

Sara found two foreign gentlemen right in front of her, bowing. Bowing! The girls' eyes bulged.

The electric voice of the bandleader boomed.

'A great big hand for our friends from Poland who've got Jerry flying in knots!'

To a tumult of clapping, the Poles smartly faced the corners of the hall, snapping off gracious little nods – until the anthem began. At which all five were instantly sober as sober, eyes wistful, hard, and dark with patriotic love and solemn conviction. As the melody concluded, they held a salute as deft and immaculate as their grooming, quite motionless…

Bravo! roared Glasgow.

And then they were grinning from head to foot, beaming at everyone. Drinks were thrust into Polish hands, the trumpets shouted and the young officer in front of Joyce offered his hand:

'Zeman, Stanislaw. Yes, please?'

'Well, now then,' laughed Joyce. She took the hand, and was twirled away onto the dance floor.

'Well what?' exclaimed the RAF type, miffed.

But Sara's stocky sergeant had no sympathy:

'Listen, pal: any Pole could fly up your bum and out again

before you noticed. Pardon me, miss...?'

Sara wasn't listening. A stronger and stranger voice was speaking to her.

'Madame?'

She looked. The second Polish officer clicked his heels. She gawped; she almost asked him to do it again. He said:

'Wysierkierski, Jacek, wishing to buy you refreshment.' His eyes were humorous and soft. 'Your name, please?'

But Sara was speechless.

Below the stage, one of the Poles was calling up to the pianist who nodded and mouthed something at the bandleader. The moment the foxtrot ended, the sheets were shuffled, a pulse was proposed.

The bandleader put out a hand to steady his fat black microphone.

'Boys and girls, a special treat. Don't be shy, they'll show you how, take your partners for ... a mazurka!'

Stanislaw Zeman had spun Joyce neatly back to her sister's side, but now seized her hand again.

'What next?' panted Joyce, wild with fun.

'Mazurka, mazurka!'

Sara noted that Stan had his hand on Joyce's rump. He said:

'You don't know mazurka? Tonight is education.'

He tweaked the giggling Joyce back onto the floor.

'We shall dance,' said Jacek Wysiekierski to Sara. A statement of fact.

'I've no idea!'

'So I teach you.'

Helpless, smiling in spite of herself, Sara was again led onto the floor. They paused, lightly poised. For one moment – Sara bewildered, Joyce exultant – the sisters regarded each other.

And away! The Poles were spinning them, lifting, carrying them a step, whirling them on, stamping and clattering. But soon enthusiastic faces pressed closer, and then Glasgow joined in, women hauling bemused soldiers into the centre, clueless but what the hell, glancing at the Poles for some hint of what on earth to do but dancing anyway.

Jacek Wysierkierski rushed Sara about the floor in exhilaration, his expression a glorious hauteur lit with delight, chin up, eyes sparkling, fierce. She beamed with joy, amazed, breathless. She was giddy, she tottered, he put a hand to her hip to steady her. The crowd cheered and cheered.

'Now then, boys and girls, steady now.'

The bandleader took control: a smooth slow waltz. Jacek Wysierkierski placed light fingers on Sara's waist and she let him turn her gracefully. She looked round for Joyce and saw that all the Poles had girls in their arms and were gently eating them. Prim Sara Dulce felt Jacek Wysierkierski's breath on her cheek, and she recalled that she was to be wed, and was to be a mother.

She pushed Jacek back and stepped free.

'Where's my sister? Where's Joyce?'

She saw Joyce subsiding in Stanislaw's grip, having her ear devoured.

Sara said, 'Actually, I have to go home.'

'To go? Why?'

From the steps of City Halls, Sara Dulce walked swiftly down Candleriggs, the quick click of her hard shoes resonant in the narrow street. The night was dank, the black gloss on the iron bollards misted with dewfall. She heard other steps come after her, a longer stride. By the time Sara reached the corner, he was beside her.

'Did I say I wanted an escort?'

'No,' shrugged Jacek Wysierkierski.

'So? Have you no manners?'

'Oh, some. But have you?'

She stopped, surprised and piqued.

'Meaning what?'

Jacek replied calmly:

'In my country, one does not allow a lady to walk at night unprotected. No gentleman would do such a thing. I am a simple man, Miss Sara, my father has only an electrical shop, but I know my duty, which you reject. Why is that?'

She studied him, and saw he was sincere. She was sorry.

They walked together more peaceably. Jacek smoked a cigarette and spoke of flying.

'In Poland we train on old-fashioned aircraft, tough and basic, so we learn to fly hard. We fought our way out of Poland, then out of France. The French at war you cannot believe. They can fly, certainly, they have good planes, and if one is destroyed a replacement is delivered next day. But they are gentlemen, they do not wish to have war before coffee, and when the Nazis raid at dawn and wipe out the squadron on the ground they are indignant!'

'I thought you said Poles were gentlemen too.'

'But we have lost one country already. We know that Germans do not wait for breakfast.' He let out a sigh of exasperation. 'We are hoping for more sense here.'

'Really.'

'We are the best pilots you have.'

'Are you so.'

'Oh yes. In the Battle of Britain, one in eight of your pilots were Polish, you know that? We have much experience. Young English pilots are very enthusiastic to die.'

'Oh,' said Sara. They turned another corner. An omnibus pulled away from them but she was content.

'What of your family?' she asked.

'Warsaw, where I should be.'

They were nearing Joyce's lodgings. Sara said:

'You seem to be enjoying yourselves in Scotland, at least. Friends with everyone.'

They stopped in the close. He answered soberly:

'Britain is our last hope, Miss Sara. We need friends.'

He held out a hand.

'I thank you for your company tonight.'

She pressed the offered hand, then turned to climb the cement stairway. After a few steps she glanced back. Jacek Wysierkierski had not moved. He bowed to her. She went on up.

◆◆◆

The last secretive crimsons shrank in the small fireplace. Everything was still, save for the gentle ticking of the mantelpiece clock and the soft tide of Sara's breath. She dozed on the floor on cushions from the sofa, under tartan travel rugs and her own long green coat.

Then from the stairwell came a scratch of shoes on cement, and whispers and giggles. When the front door banged wide, two figures lurched straight into the room tripping over their own feet, colliding with chairs.

'Hush, Stan!'

On her cushions, Sara in the darkness wondered if they might fall on top of her. There was a thud, a juddering, an agonised grunt. The corner of the table had jabbed hard into Stanislaw's thigh, uncorking a flood of Polish curses.

'Stan, sssshh!'

Joyce was stuffing her coat sleeve into her mouth to stifle laughs. She dragged Stan towards the back bedroom, clumsily kicking the door shut, heralding a cacophony of a hundred hysterical bedsprings.

Sara Dulce, pregnant before she ought but a proper girl nonetheless, pulled her heavy black coat up over her head. There are, however, sounds you can't blot out; what the ear doesn't catch, the imagination readily supplies – so she heard all about the ensuing conception.

◆◆◆

A thin morning light dribbled in, showing the cramped front room to be tidy: cushions back on the sofa, sheets and blankets folded on the brown armchair. The fire was dead now, and the room cold. Sara sat in her woollen coat at the table by the window, sipping from a yellow teacup and watching the drizzle. Her small suitcase stood in the hall.

She glanced round. The bedroom door was slightly ajar; from beneath a chaos of blankets protruded two feet that did not match.

Sara took her cup to the galley kitchen and rinsed it. She opened the front door – and on the step was a small brown paper packet tied with string. She knelt, and read:

Miss Sara.

She backed indoors. She placed the packet on the table and looked at it. The packet neither moved nor smoked. Sara picked it up again and eased off the string without untying it, as though opening this was illicit. The next layer was a pad of newspaper; she edged this apart.

Inside, there was a coat of arms. It was carved in simple but strong lines from a piece of wood some six inches long by four wide. It showed, in low relief, a two-headed eagle. Across the top, delicately chiselled and touched with a golden paint, were three words:

VIVE LA POLOGNE

There was also a folded slip of plain paper. With reluctance, she opened it:

From your friend, Jacek Wysierkierski.

Sara read this four times, five, before glancing again towards the bedroom. Then she stood the wooden crest on the mantelpiece. She returned to the hall, picked up her suitcase and walked out into the raw day.

1944

No one in Glenfarron could recall a time when the Dulce family had not been there. Everyone knew them. Everyone knew everyone, and they still do: it's a very small world. The inhabitants all get to know every corner, every lane. Some, such as the doctor and the postie, can reasonably claim to know every house. To visitors who say that they have travelled widely in the world, locals reply that they have travelled widely in Glenfarron.

It has changed, very much so in superficial respects. What one sees today is markedly different from the scene in 1942 when little Charlie Dulce, a toddler, first came to live with his Aunt Sara. There are, for instance, many more trees now. In the 1940s the ancient forests were well gone, while few of the great tracts of commercial conifer plantation had yet been established; the Farron woods were a shrinking, though pleasing, mix of Scots pine and oak. One met with capercailzies then, before the new trees were set too close together so that the big bewildered birds smacked into them in flight.

Settlements at the top end of Glenfarron could be very isolated. In 1942 there was no metalled road, although the old way was durable and rain-resistant even in the winter, and the omnibuses crawled up and down the long incline with a gravelly scrunching, a grinding of gears and a doggedness that did them credit. They would reach Brig o'Farron, where the highway leaps up a ridiculous slope and even modern cars strain. There the omnibus would stop. If you wanted to pass over and onwards, you must hire a pony, or foot it. Of those who did set out on foot, not all arrived. Everyone knew of the lass who'd set out one February day to hike over the top to meet her betrothed, and who'd disappeared in the snows. Her body had been found only in May, with the melt. Of course, people say the winters today are nothing on what they were.

Many sections of the road have been bypassed now, with brash concrete spans replacing the stoat-backed stone bridges, and broad sweeps that ignore the awkward twists of the Farron Water. Up and down the glen there are short stretches of what was once the highway but which are now cut off at both ends, a carriageway for ghosts reverting back to grass and purple willow herb, used at most for farm access. There are these little scraps of ghost road all over the improved Highlands.

Mains electricity only reached the top of the glen in the 1970s. In 1942, such power as there was came from watermills, or from oil-fuelled generators that *tug-tugged* their slow cycle, firing once every three seconds – or, at one or two forward-looking homes, from a wind turbine. Joyce and Sara's father had wanted to invest in a turbine and had gone into the matter, sending off for the Lucas Speedlite catalogue. The machine was 'engineered to aeronautical standards', claimed the brochure, and would light half a dozen electric bulbs in the home. But the £23, 9/- was beyond George Dulce's pocket.

There were more smallholdings after the war, and for a while more people. Not a few were Central European refugees; there were large camps of Poles and Czechs to the south near Dundee, and General Sikorski himself had toured these before his death in an air crash. But that population boost did not endure. If you were to explore the glen now, noting certain houses sold to the Dutch for holidays, others dilapidated and beginning to lose their roofs, some open-topped and populated by scrubby sycamores and ivy, you would see that the process of the Highland clearances has continued to this day. For any generation you might think of, from the year 1800 until 2008, you could find a ruin.

Even the grandest houses have had their problems. Halfway up the glen, old maps indicate a Renaissance castle (at least, a fortified house) that has entirely vanished, leaving nothing but bumps in the turf.

Not far off, there is another castle – a Victorian monster.

On a day soon after Easter 1944, you might have seen a military ambulance nosing down the wooded lane banked with dank moss, ferns and feral rhododendrons, passing through a faint steam rising under the April sun that tumbled through budding trees onto a road pasted with thick, slippery leaf mould. The ambulance rolled cautiously between the squat entrance pillars that were once white but now green with mould. There, the driver glanced at a signboard nailed to one of the pillars:

FARRON CASTLE
(*Polish Forces*)

The driveway – little changed today – winds between fine ornamental firs and loops round landscaped hillocks on which sit a rustic creamery and a matching estate office, all their woodwork painted the thick gloss green that factors love to buy in bulk. The landscaping is Victorian, and in the 1940s was already fully mature. As the ambulance moved slowly forward, Farron Castle came into view, framed by a group of enormous Blue Atlantic cedars, just as it is today.

The castle rears up: neither flamboyant, nor gothic, nor French Renaissance, nor even very baronial. Hardly a proper castle, indeed; rather, a massive grey pebble-dashed castellated lump, foursquare in a bend in the river, its one gesture at 'character' being a long glazed gallery looking west over the front driveway and beyond, across a featureless expanse of chilly lawn terminated by a mirthless ha-ha.

Even in its Highland Romantic heyday, when stags' heads were nailed up in the ballroom and every kilted laird wore heather in his Glengarry, even then, few can have thought it beautiful except maybe the commissioning grandee. The architect must have had horrid doubts as it neared completion. It is said that Queen Victoria liked it and would pay visits from Balmoral, that she would cross the Farron Water by the Pugin-esque iron structure known inexplicably as the Chinese Bridge – not looking down, because the water rushing over the shallow stony bottom can be seen through the slats and induces giddiness. In her light open carriage, she'd be driven at a sedate trot up and down the fine avenue of beeches that curves along the bank for a mile and a half and is called the Gallops. The beeches would have been delicate young things in the Queen's day. By 1944 they were ponderous and had Polish names carved into their trunks, flesh wounds that had ceased to bleed and which, year by year, were darkening and shrinking back into the bark, although even today plenty of them are legible and seldom fail to bring walkers to a thoughtful halt.

Around the flanks of the grey harled heap there were, in the war years, structures at which Victoria would have wrinkled her sensual little nose: Nissen huts, brick towers and bunkers, stained concrete things. And on the gravel and the hard standing, vehicles that would have crushed the Queen's landau without noticing the impact: trucks and vans in drab, in greens, greys and blues, all with their headlights blinkered. And, always, two or three ambulances. For most of the war, Farron Castle was a Polish military hospital.

◆◆◆

In that long glazed gallery, as the ambulance approached, Sara Dulce's hand was easing a spoonful of pap between blackened lips in a face swathed in bandages. The lips trembled, and the yellow-grey studge slithered onto the towel draped over the patient's chest.

'Now, Franek, that's a Scottish delicacy, that's dried eggs. You want some milk?'

Sara – who was in fact no longer Sara Dulce, but Sara Meakin – sat on a wooden chair by the bed. She gently wiped away the food, picked up a heavy green cup and eased a paper straw between the burned lips. She wore a stiff and bulky uniform of narrow grey-and-white stripes, and a white pinafore showing the stains of work. The man Franek sucked on the straw – then coughed alarmingly, spraying milk at her.

The tall windows of the gallery were propped open, 'airing' the patients. Not looking up, Sara recognised the growl and scrunch of an ambulance drawing to a halt by the front entrance, then heard steel doors swing back.

Down you come. Steady now. Easy does it. Stretcher, corporal…

Next, a hollow rumbling as wheelchairs were propelled up the new wooden ramp to the castle's front door.

Sara was still concentrating on her patient. Franek was doing better with the straw.

'Enough?'

The man sank back onto his pillow. He'd have smiled his thanks if he could.

The noises from outside were of a sudden more insistent. There was the furious cry of a man outraged by pain and clumsiness. Other voices intervened, a lieutenant trying to soothe, to mollify:

'All right, chum, take it easy.'

Which won him nothing but Polish invective. The lieutenant parried:

'Sorry, chum, we just need to…'

But the Polish voice branded him with vituperation. As Sara moved towards the window, a tall, scowling Matron marched swiftly the length of the gallery, her shoes clacking on the boards.

'Nurse Meakin, come.'

Sara put down the cup and followed.

In the forecourt, wounded men were being helped from the ambulance, on stretchers or chairs or with orderlies solicitous at their elbows, while an earnest young Liaison Officer with a clipboard checked them in. All was care and calm, save for one Polish pilot who was lowering the tone. He looked rough, he looked sweaty and ill-kempt as though he'd been grappling single-handedly with Hitler and would strike you down if you got in the way with your bandages and ointments. One arm was in a sling, the other thrashed at the Liaison man.

'German bastards hurt me less than you. You try to pull my arm off?'

A white-coated doctor intervened:

'Steady on, old man. Lieutenant Baird is doing his best to help. Now, we'll have you inside and give you something for that pain.'

But the Pole was unimpressed:

'What do you know about pain – old man?'

'Jacek?'

Hearing his name, Jacek Wysierkierski twisted in his wheelchair and saw Nurse Sara Meakin gazing at him. For just a moment he returned her stare – until an orderly took hold of the chair and propelled him up the ramp and indoors.

◆◆◆

She deftly withdrew the needle from his buttock, depositing the glass syringe into an enamelled kidney dish while reaching for a bottle of spirit and a square of lint, giving the flesh a brisk rub.

'There we go,' said Sara brightly.

'Thank you so much.'

She hoiked up his trousers.

'My pleasure.'

'Is it so.'

He rolled back on the bed to look at her straight – but she got in first.

'We've met before.'

'I've met half the Luftwaffe,' he replied, 'and they were better dressed.'

'In Glasgow,' smiled his nurse unperturbed, 'before I married.

I was Dulce then. I'm Meakin now.'

'Yes, I remember. Miss tight-arse-won't-dance Sara.'

Her smile faltered, and he turned his back to her with a small grin of victory. Scowling, Sara whisked the screen aside with a tetchy clatter.

So Jacek was left alone.

In spite of the sun, the spring air was chill. His window was open. Through it came a new sound, one which had Jacek hauling himself with his good arm toward the sill, straining to look out, to see the sky. There was a plane circling overhead. Jacek searched it out, quickly finding it in the clear sky, studying the aircraft in a professional light. But, a moment later, he closed his eyes.

At the far end of the ward, someone was watching: a solidly built, crop-headed man with a wide-open, friendly face and white kitchen fatigues. He gazed down the length of the ward at Jacek.

◆◆◆

The watcher's name was Vladislaw Obremski – a name which, decades later, still brought an affectionate smile to many faces in Glenfarron. In 1944, Vladislaw was an airman, or a former airman. He was 'mutilated by war' as the French and Spanish say, and he would never fight again, at least not in an aircraft. He lived and worked at Farron Castle because, like other injured Poles, he had no other home.

Moments after setting eyes on Jacek Wysiekierski, Vladislaw set off an avalanche of grey potatoes that rumbled from a cauldron into battered serving trays obscured by steam. He hefted the pan to a white stoneware sink and unleashed a blast of cold water, scouring off potato debris with the jet. Then he banged it down upon the worktop with such indignant noise that his kitchen colleagues, hardened as they were to racket, flinched and looked up.

Vladislaw was uncommonly excited.

'Best bloody pilot in the bloody world!' he shouted.

He headed for another table, hobbling stiffly (one leg was wood).

'I know that man, I'm telling you. Jacek Wysierkierski, 303 Squadron, he is a legend' (he thumped the table, he couldn't help it, he was impassioned) 'in that squadron of legends. He could land a Spitfire on the roof of a German bomber in mid-air, get out, piss on them, fly home for tea.'

He jabbed a knife at a pallid sausage, from which bled a thin milky liquor.

'How'd you know him, Vladi?' called a lumpish female in a white coat.

'All Poland knows,' averred the potato chef. 'A hero!'

He filled another serving dish with a forcefulness which left the sausages in no doubt that, if they complained, they'd be straight in the pig-bucket.

'Battle of Poland, Battle of France, Battle of Britain. He shoots enemy like Scottish shoot grouse, pam pam pam!'

He swung his wooden leg back towards the potatoes. If there was a grouse or a German in the sky then, by God, Vladislaw would bring them down with potatoes this second, let them watch it! He seized the serving dishes and slammed them onto a steel trolley so vehemently that two small vegetables hopped onto the floor and disintegrated. Vladislaw paused a moment, staring at the little mess at his feet. Then he sighed:

'Jacek Wysierkierski, bloody hero. Bloody hell.'

Along the length of the ward went Vladislaw shoving his trolley, the wheels squealing and wobbling on the wooden floor. Jacek lay facing the other way.

'Sir? Something to eat?'

Jacek did not react, until there appeared before him the broad face of the crouching cook.

'Shitty Scottish potatoes,' says Vladislaw. 'I boil them to death.'

Jacek regarded him in silent agreement: everything is shit.

'Only a Pole can make them edible,' Vladislaw continued. 'For the sausages, no hope.'

When Sara Meakin entered the ward, she saw a kitchen orderly easing a patient as tenderly as a loved one, up into a sitting position with one bandaged arm on pillows. The cook then brought a plate of food to the bed-table, fetched a stool and sat by the bed to cut potatoes and sausages into small mouthfuls.

Sara sat quietly at the desk to watch and wait, hearing the cheerful chatter from the cook.

'You left 303, Sir? I heard Special Operations, night drops, yes? Drop British sausage to the Germans, they'd stay clear of this country.'

Jacek Wysierkierski regarded Vladislaw without expression. The cook tapped his own wooden leg with the dinner knife, *tok tok*.

'Shot off, Sir. Tail gunner in a Blenheim, lousy gunner I was, always day-dreaming, girls and that, and I never saw the bastard come up behind. Now I'm a Pole on a stick, and more use in the kitchen. There you go, Sir.'

He placed a spoon by a pale green bowl of neurasthenic dessert. Of a sudden, his good cheer vanished.

'Very honoured, Sir. Sorry to see you. Bloody hell.'

The wooden leg clumped away behind the twittering wheels of the trolley and out through the far doors. Jacek watched Vladislaw leave the ward. When he was gone, Jacek surveyed the dishes in front of him – and with his forearm swept everything to the floor.

He lay back, closing his eyes. Along the ward, other patients scarcely paused in their own eating to look. From the desk, Nurse Meakin took note.

◈◈◈

A strange activity for two grown men with serious faces: one held up a finger, the other poked it with a sharpened pencil.

'Push,' commanded the doctor, but the finger did not obey. He moved the pencil.

'How about this one? Nothing? I see.'

The doctor sat back and studied Jacek across the ink-stained tabletop.

'This could take a while,' he observed.

Jacek said nothing, but glanced at Sara standing in attendance, hands clasped in front of her pinafore.

'That's all for now,' said the doctor. 'Any questions?'

'How to fly one-handed?' asked Jacek.

Doctor and nurse stiffened, just perceptibly.

'Sorry I ask,' shrugged Jacek.

He pushed his wheelchair hard away from the table, almost running into Lieutenant Baird the Liaison officer who was making little notes on a jotter.

'We can perhaps do something,' the doctor began cautiously. 'Exercises, possibly some reconstruction; it's remarkable what the plastics chaps can do.'

'Take it slowly,' Lieutenant Baird chipped in. 'No need to hurry.'

'No hurry? I have my family in Warsaw.'

'Oh, of course, we absolutely understand.'

But Jacek savaged him.

'No, you do not understand what is happening in Warsaw now.'

'I wasn't suggesting...'

'They are shot, they are raped, they starve to death. No hurry, you say?'

He gestured to an orderly, a tall half-witted lad with protuberant ears who stepped forward to take hold of the wheelchair. Jacek pointed a finger like a pistol at the door: out, out of the hut. By the exit they passed a rack containing two dozen wooden walking sticks.

'Give me two of those,' said Jacek.

The orderly hesitated, glancing back towards doctor and nurse.

'I am Captain Jacek Wysierkierski. Give me two of those now!'

'Sir.'

The double doors of the Nissen hut slammed open; Captain Jacek Wysierkierski tottered out into the spring sunshine. He moved unsteadily, supporting himself on the sticks and any wall he passed. The orderly saw Jacek's knee start to buckle, and reached out...

'Keep off me, damn you!'

Inside the clinic, Lieutenant Baird hurried to complete his medical notes, while Sara swept files away into a green steel cabinet. The doctor was signing a last letter. From outside, there came an explosion of outrage. They all looked up, then at each other.

'Oh dear,' murmured the doctor, whose own brother was in a Japanese prison camp in Malaya.

'I'm told Captain Wysierkierski was an outstanding flyer,' said Baird.

An inarticulate bellow sent them scurrying outside – and there was Jacek thrashing with his sticks at the orderly who was trying to pick him off the ground.

'Get off me, bastard.'

'Just help you up, Sir ... oww!'

A walking stick had connected with the boy's temple. The orderly lurched backwards into the arms of the doctor.

'Now then, Captain!'

'Now then fuck off, I tell you!' spat Jacek.

He beat at the air with the stick, keeping the orderly at bay.

'We want to help...' Baird quavered.

Sara, meanwhile, had circled behind Jacek and was there of a sudden, crouching at his side, too near to have her head smacked.

'Won't you let me?' she tried, her voice soft and low, her hands reaching.

'No!' Jacek was shrill now, near to weeping. 'You can't help, you bloody lots-of-time British, you cannot! *He* can help!'

He pointed: Vladislaw stood in the kitchen door in his cook's whites, drying his hands on a towel, observing the rumpus sadly.

'Polish can help,' gasped Jacek.

'Good idea,' said Baird.

Vladislaw never let anyone down.

◆◆◆

So Vladislaw propelled Jacek in his chair, the solid tyres squealing down the corridor followed by the thudding of a wooden leg. Behind them came Sara, keeping back and out of trouble.

'When the Captain is angry, then we watch out,' said Vladislaw, brisk and jocular.

'In France,' he enthused, 'they see Heinkels bombing refugees, and the Captain has run out of ammunition so he rams the bomber, mid-air, kepouff!'

He took his hands off the chair handles just long enough to slam fist into palm explosively.

'Yes, yes, all right,' muttered Jacek.

'The two airplanes are caught tight. Fritzy is surprised, he stares with a big stupid face and the Captain climbs out, sits on the wing, taps the window, 'Hello, Fritzy!"

'This bit is nonsense,' protested Jacek, grinning nonetheless.

'He gives a wave, he parachutes, they go kaboom!'

Squeal, rumble, thud thud.

'How is your sister?' said Jacek, slithering into a chair by his bed.

'Joyce? You remember her?' Sara wondered.

'Not like my friend Stanislaw remembers her. She was quite beautiful.'

'I'll tell her,' said Sara.

'So were you,' he added, looking pointedly at her uniform.

Sara gave him a professional smile.

'Let's have you on the bed, then.'

'I don't know that I can stand. I fell…'

'So I saw. Knees together, please.'

Directly in front of the wheelchair, she placed her feet so that his were trapped between her shoes. Her knees held his together: his lower legs were secured. She raised his arms and slipped her hands under to clasp his shoulder blades, rocking him forward so that his weight was on his own feet and they were balanced, face to face, very close.

'With me, then,' said Sara firmly.

She pivoted him round with practised ease, then let him sink onto the bed. He nodded.

'You know how to do that.'

She fetched two portable screens.

'I need your trousers off.'

She leaned towards him, hands hovering.

He scowled: 'No, thank you.'

'Yes, thank you. I've to check. You might have knocked the leg wound.'

'Not you.'

'I'm your nurse, Jacek.'

'Captain, if you please. Call someone else.'

She flushed and straightened.

'It's my job.'

'I say who takes my fucking trousers off,' he snapped, 'and it's not you.'

'For heaven's sake,' she blushed wildly.

'Thinking of fucking, send your sister…'

The screens jerked apart; Sara backed out between them, colliding with Matron who stood with nostrils flaring in disgust. Sara flushed, took a deep breath, smoothed her apron in confusion.

'That word,' pronounced Matron, 'is no part of a nurse's vocabulary. You never heard it.'

◆◆◆

Out again into the sunshine, Jacek with a walking stick but on his own feet, lips stretched in a stubborn grimace. At his left walked Nurse Meakin, carrying a second stick. At Jacek's right side, Vladislaw was ready to catch him.

'Give me the other stick,' said Jacek, stopping for breath.

'How do you feel?' enquired Sara.

'Ridiculous. The best pilot in Poland, learning to walk.'

He prodded at the gravel in front of him, set his face and lurched forward once more, then stopped and called over his shoulder.

'You see, Miss Sara, I shall not be a baby so long now.'

'Won't you call me Sara?' she asked.

'Why? So you can stop calling me Captain?'

He watched for her reaction. Sara said nothing.

Jacek straightened and tottered onward, nurse and cook trailing behind.

'You have babies, Miss Sara?'

'Not just yet.'

'But you're married.'

'Oh yes.'

To which Jacek said in Polish:

'What's wrong with her husband's balls?'

Vladislaw snorted; Sara reddened again.

'What's that?' she said.

Jacek switched back to English:

'Nothing in them.'

'I beg your pardon?' She could smell offence.

'What are husbands for?'

'That'll do, thank you.'

But Jacek stomped along chuckling.

'It wouldn't do in Poland. We got more juice.'

He twisted to leer over his shoulder…

But she had left him, walking briskly back to the ward. Vladislaw watched her go, embarrassed.

Captain Jacek Wysierkierski shouted angrily:

'What now? What the fuck now?'

She didn't turn.

◆◆◆

'Never had bad language from a patient before?' Lieutenant Baird enquired gently.

'He used to be so gallant.' She shrugged in dismay.

'But in a war…' He thought for a moment. 'See it as a challenge,' he offered. 'He's grieving. Don't abandon him.'

'There's other nurses,' protested Sara.

'But he has chosen you.'

He looked at her closely. Sara swallowed, and looked out of the window.

Jacek Wysierkierski stood on the gravel forecourt, facing the window, motionless. He stared straight at Sara, not smiling, not scowling.

◆◆◆

Chatter and flutter; woodpeckers marching about on the pines; buzzards circling and mewing at their families, or flapping irritably past crows that wanted to pick fights; jays pulling the young acorns from oaks at the forest's edge; tree creepers spiralling up the chestnuts, then dodging across the glades through sun shafts; perhaps a heavy old blackcock sailing out to sit on a fence post in a potato field. Even, on a very good day, the possibility of a capercailzie. And at dusk, no end of owls.

The art of flight in late summer in the lower Glenfarron woods. Vladislaw adored these woods. When Charlie Dulce was young, Vladislaw would take him mushrooming; the boy would crash about between the trees, and the birdlife startled him with its bursting and rushing. The child paid no great attention, though he might look up and catch sight of something soaring above the canopy and the plods on the ground. For a moment Charlie would feel earthbound and ponderous – until his games recommenced and he lost himself in the moment. Vladislaw would watch with indulgent joy.

But the magic did not work on Jacek, for whom the woods were no relief. Jacek's stick sank into the leaf mould beneath the trees. His leg muscles were still wasted, far from full strength. He was tiring. His left arm was still in a sling. In his right, he carried a saucepan in which he was not interested.

His escort decried the natives:

'Ceps, chanterelles, these people have no idea.'

Vladislaw directed Jacek up a gentle slope through the trees.

'To your left, Sir: a bluette!'

Jacek stopped but did nothing to retrieve it. Vladislaw puffed past him, reached for the fine fat specimen and placed it in Jacek's pan.

'That's it, Sir, delicious, just the job.'

He beamed at Jacek who looked round and, seemingly for the first time, noticed the loveliness of the woods.

'Not bad, Sir?' said Vladislaw.

'Not Poland – but not bad.'

'Absolutely not!' cried Vladislaw. He became of a sudden conspiratorial. 'I'll show you not bad, Sir.'

He was peering a hundred yards ahead to where a thinning of the forest revealed a lane and, just visible, the corner of a cottage.

'Come on, Sir, come.'

The cottage was run down, sold off from the estate, left to itself in a thicket of laurel, viburnam and ivy. The walls were rough lumpish stone, once whitewashed. The porch was supported by two pine trunks painted that familiar dark gloss green, with the stubs of branches left on.

Vladislaw stomped to the door and knocked.

'What is this?' asked the Captain.

'This, Sir,' smirked Vladislaw, 'is Pet and Biddy.'

Through an open upstairs window, just above their heads, a woman's voice yelled:

'It's open!'

Followed by a welcoming giggle, and a stamping of bare feet. Again, Vladislaw grinned at Jacek and had his hand out to push the door when he happened to glance down the lane.

There, coming on foot towards them, was a British officer. As Vladislaw and Jacek gazed at him, the officer looked up, blushed furiously, spun about and retreated in a hurry.

'Is that . . . ?' began Jacek.

'Certainly is, Sir: the good Lieutenant. Pretty much a regular. He's besotted.'

A face appeared at the window above them, pulling her black hair back into a rudimentary bun.

'Hello, Vladi. Come for some physio?' And Vladislaw

sniggered.

But Jacek growled, 'I'm not so sad just yet.'

He turned on his heel – a move that nearly toppled him – and marched off as best he could, back through the woods.

'Sir …?' bleated Vladislaw.

◆◆◆

A cold white stoneware plate, and those interminable potatoes crashing into floury fragments. Then a slice of reconstituted pig slapped alongside, a most peculiar grey-pink colour.

Jacek made no move to eat. He was seated in the hammer-beamed ballroom of the castle, now the hospital dining room. It echoed bleakly. Stags with bullets in their skulls glowered from the walls, brandishing their antlers at the wounded Poles.

An outside door banged open; Vladislaw came in from a cold night. For some reason he was not wearing his woollen overcoat. He carried it in a bulky roll. As he came towards Jacek, he gave a coy nod.

'Hello, Sir,' he said, furtive. 'Late back, aren't I. She gave me a little bit extra, know what I mean?'

He opened the rolled coat an inch; Jacek glimpsed two skinny claws and some long and colourful tail feathers.

'I will have that!' boomed Matron.

Startled, Vladislaw clacked his wooden leg against her shin.

'Oh!' she piped.

'It's something which I found,' stammered Vladislaw, attempting to slip the roll onto Jacek's lap at the table. But Matron seized it.

'You take me for a fool?'

With a flourish she dragged out the pheasant, discarding Vladislaw's coat and thundering at him:

'And you see this as a rest home for poachers. Nurse Meakin!'

Sara in her grey stripes and pinafore came across the ballroom.

'The midden, if you please.'

'Yes, Matron.'

The bird swinging heavily by its feet, Sara set off down the corridor. Vladislaw thumped after her hissing:

'You can't! Miss Sara, don't do this, please.'

'It has to go,' muttered Sara.

'But I beg you – it's for the Captain.'

Sara looked back down the passageway at the stern departing back of Matron. She glimpsed Jacek Wysierkierski still at his table, motionless, his head turned towards them ever so slightly.

Vladislaw placed a hand on her bare forearm.

'A man like that needs nourishing.'

He gazed at her, frank and simple. Sara dithered. Right behind her was the door of the cold store.

'We hide it for him!' beamed Vladislaw, delighted with plotting. 'For the Captain. You and me, his friends!'

Almost without thinking, Sara opened the store and disappeared. When she reappeared seconds later, Vladislaw was gone from the corridor.

But Jacek Wysierkierski was waiting for her, resting on his stick.

'You could lose your job,' he observed.

'Oh, I don't think so,' she smiled. 'Nurses are always needed in a war.'

At which, a command rang out down the corridors.

'Nurse Meakin!'

Sara said, 'She's after me.'

'Can you get us rosemary?' asked Jacek.

'Who?'

'Or thyme, or some Scottish herb maybe? We will make you a pie, or sausages.'

She stared at him uncomprehending. He tried again.

'A little taste of Poland, Miss Sara. Help us, please?'

◆◆◆

Charlie Dulce had by this time been resident in Glenfarron two years or more: not quite all his life. He'd come without fanfare or announcement. The less fuss, the fewer questions.

In later life, as Dr Dulce the GP, his work sometimes took him back to Bellcraig, the keeper's cottage where he first stayed with his Aunt Sara in 1942. The doctor would try his best to recall the house in the 1940s, but was never quite sure of the result, for how could one be sure what was memory and what was imaginative retrospection, filling gaps with information gleaned on later visits?

He would try to let his memory relax, return to the 1940s

and speak to him of very earliest things: to begin with, qualities of light. A pervasive green; that must be sunlight tinged with the green of the lawn and the woods surrounding the house. Also, a soft grey-whiteness above his face, which he thought was the light of afternoon entering a small timber-lined bedroom where he was placed for his afternoon rest – although that may have been not at Bellcraig but at Torbrechan farm, for his grandparents minded him while Sara worked at the castle. And then there was the terrifying light of a room filled with white sheets, billowing.

He could remember smells: the odour of scorched resin from Gordon Meakin's circular saw; the smells of potato scones and burned milk; of gas lamps and of disinfectant, doubtless brought home on his aunt's uniform; a musty smell from old pillows that he used to think was duck's blood, dried on the feathers inside; the smell of clean linen, and of the bakelite of the wireless when it had been on for a while and the valves had made it hot.

Sounds: the singing of that circular saw, and the sudden harsh dip as it tore into timber; the wooden resonance of the confined staircase leading up to cramped rooms; the rattling and scraping of a range being emptied of ash and clinker. But again, though he told himself that he remembered these things from childhood, and though it may have been true – how could he know? He had heard the same sounds in similar places in Glenfarron throughout his working life. It is a consequence of living all one's days in one locality: memory is enhanced by constant reconnection, but also weakened because it is not distinguished from the present. Charlie really couldn't be sure what constituted his memories.

What he remembered certainly was loss, partly offset by the advent of a sister who was not really. And having no say in who minded him. He remembered the nightmares from which, like many small children, he suffered badly – although, again, he may have been confusing nightmares with nightmarish realities. Or realities that persisted as nightmares. He remembered aeroplanes, big and small, destroyed.

He remembered textures very well, and textures often brought back entire scenes: his little fingers digging, for instance, crescents of black dirt under each soft nail, or toying with the tight, crisply curled leaves of French parsley. The herb was past its best, and the wind had bashed the parsley. Sara – to all intents now his mother – looked down at the plants and the boy crouched there, his miniature brown duffle coat discarded on the grass. She held a kitchen knife and a biscuit tin of stems and greenery. She seemed to be thinking, but not about parsley or about the child.

A shadow stirred in the cottage porch behind her.

'Do we get tea now? Sara?'

She didn't move, but idly picked at her thumbnail with the knife's blade.

'Sara, are you in there?' called her husband. 'You planning to cut throats or what?'

She started out of her reverie, called back:

'Coming. Tea, Charlie.'

She reached for the boy's sleeve, raised him, and led him towards the kitchen door with her hands full: child, tin, coat, knife.

◆◆◆

At much this moment, Jacek Wysierkierski attempted to raise his left arm, which lay inert on the table before him. He strained, he sweated, his face clouded with effort and determination, his brows knitted and he scarcely breathed, so focused was he on that one small movement.

'High as you can,' urged the doctor.

Jacek's face twisted with frustration as he attempted to use all the muscles of his shoulder and back as a substitute for the simple function of his arm. His hand lifted a fraction from the tabletop – then fell back.

'All right,' said the doctor, 'just relax'.

Jacek looked away, looked at nothing in a far corner of the Nissen hut, struggling to keep back tears and failing.

◆◆◆

Night, brightly moonlit. The breeze was up, the oaks in the lane shifted and rattled. Vladislaw stood by Jacek looking at the scruffy white cottage fifty yards in front of them. They had been drinking, but whereas Jacek was morose and taciturn, Vladislaw was voluble with excitement.

'Called Petunia,' he bubbled. 'Arse like a carthorse. And her pal Biddy who's tighter. Come on, Sir, it'll do you a power of good. Have a drink.'

He thrust a bottle at Jacek, remembering his rank halfway and awkwardly trying to inflect 'drink' into a deferential offer.

Jacek considered the bottle, seized it and sucked. Then he stopped: the front door of the cottage had juddered open.

'Oops, clientele,' murmured Vladislaw, as they both slid into the moon shadow of an oak. 'The lieutenant, is it?'

Not the lieutenant. A larger man, a purposeful figure, appeared in the porch. He stood burly and defiant as though waiting for some fool to swing at him and then they'd see. Instinctively, Vladislaw moved deeper into the tree's shadow, while Jacek remained very still. The big man paused in the doorway a moment – then strode off.

'He's bigger than me,' remarked Vladislaw.

'Hasn't got a wooden leg either,' Jacek observed, pulling at the bottle.

Minutes later, Jacek was upstairs in that house. The light was off, but autumn moonlight washed into the room illuminating a woman in a dressing gown of yellow towelling. She was perched on the bedside, hands on the mattress edge as though ready to spring. Jacek – dishevelled, drunk and sullen – peered out of the window at the black forest on the broad slopes of Glenfarron.

'Come on, help a girl,' said Petunia, lifting her generous posterior off the candlewick coverlet, reaching up to undo his short buttons.

'No need for that,' he snapped.

'Right, I shan't touch,' she placated. ('Go easy with the Captain,' Vladislaw had whispered).

She returned to her bed that gave bouncy twangs as she sprawled.

'Who's the big man was here?' asked Jacek.

'Boy with a frigid wife,' Petunia laughed. 'Never a problem in this house. Isn't it time you told me your name?'

'Wysierkierski. Jacek Wysierkierski.'

'Bloody hell,' pondered Petunia, 'Can I make that Jacky Whisky?'

He gave her a swift look, then threw the curtains across the moon's face.

◆◆◆

On a bench outside the gallery, he sat unmoving. A sound caught his attention, a sound that would always catch his attention: the sound of an aircraft overhead. He looked up, and saw Nurse Sara

Meakin coming.

'Captain?' she began, but hated the stiffness. 'Jacek? I brought your herbs.'

He couldn't think what she was talking about. She was holding a battered square biscuit tin which was open, the lid in her other hand. She tipped it for him to see: stems of parsley, rosemary and thyme.

'Is it what you wanted?'

Jacek took a pinch of the greenery between his fingers, rolling and rubbing a little, inhaling the scent. He hesitated, then said:

'You call me Jacky. Jacky Whisky. It is more suitable now.'

He held the crushed pinch of herbs under her nose; she breathed in, smiling at him in complicity.

'Nurse Meakin!'

Matron, her blue cloak hanging to her calves, stood in the gallery doorway scrutinising them.

Sara scowled: 'Yes, Matron?'

'Time you were away home.'

The voice was kindly, but held hints of scrutiny and question.

'Oh, yes,' Sara replied breezily. 'Going out tonight. Family do for Da's birthday.'

She hurried away to find her bicycle, Jacky Whisky following with his eyes.

◆◆◆

Four magnificently naked women went striding with legs wide apart, stiletto heels and feathers up their bottoms, like roosters. On their heads, the plumed helmets of cavalrymen. In their arms, gigantic bottles of champagne and overflowing glasses – except for one, from whose outstretched hands dangled on puppet strings a helpless flock of pilot officers in uniform, slavering at her pneumatic bust.

'This is Flight Lieutenant Hulewicz's sister, a figure from Botticelli, lithe and supple, with skin smelling of rosewater.'

October, a rainy late afternoon, the room crowded with men lolling on beds half-dressed or perched smoking in the window bay. They smirked: a brief collective moment of manly smut. The mural of nudes, rendered in broad strokes and purloined War Ministry paints, covered an entire end wall of the room. The artist was an air navigator with a crutch, a man with an angular, weasel face and eyebrows much given to ironic lifts. He used a garden cane to point up his lecture.

'The entire squadron,' he sighed, 'fawned upon Irena Hulewicz. Few were rewarded.'

'You?' called a voice. The Artist flared his nostrils.

'I only draw from life.'

Titters scampered round the room. He turned back to his work. Flittering about the nudes were scores of tiny, desperate servicemen. Between the splayed thighs, miniature fighter aircraft with oversized pilots soared optimistically, crotch to crotch. *Na zdrowie!* cried the banners waving overhead, *Good Health! Kia Ora! Na zdrowie!*

He tapped another nude, a voluptuous lass with a big bum, open lips and pearly teeth.

'Next to Irena, we have a local flower: Petunia. Who here has plucked Petunia?'

More smirks, more titters. The men grinned at one another, sheepish. The Artist raised a black eyebrow.

'No one? Really? Not one that has ever dallied at a certain little cottage up a certain little lane?'

He eyed a beardless boy from Poznan who turned to beetroot.

'Lieutenant Baird!' someone shouted, to cheers.

'Ah, yes, he is deeply smitten, but where the thrusting Lieutenant leads, Poles are proud to follow.'

The Artist sighed again, eyeing the portrait.

'For myself, Petunia is too Rubens-esque, but some enjoy the fuller figure.'

At the far end of the room, the door opened quietly and Jacky Whisky entered. He surveyed the gathering, smiled briefly, and received a broad smile from Vladislaw and a nod from the Artist.

The latter now turned his attention to the left hand corner of the mural. Here, the last of the striding beauties struck a different pose; she had her elegantly shoed foot on the back of a ghastly crone of elongated proportions who was crawling off the end of the wall, as naked as the rest. The Artist jabbed his cane at this creature.

'Gentlemen, you will recognise our Matron, a nightmare out of Goya. Note the shapeless hip, the leathery thigh.'

'Drawn from life?' they called.

'All art is suffering,' parried the painter, winning another cheer. He lifted his stick to indicate the strikingly beautiful nude with nut-brown hair whose foot was upon Matron's back.

'Here,' he proclaimed, 'taking revenge for us all, is our friend Nurse Sara.'

Vladislaw saw Jacky's eyes narrow.

'A figure that merits close study,' averred the painter to a murmur of agreement. 'The breast is understated but notice, please, the exceptionally delicate bottom.'

Jacky frowned. The Artist was fingering her, saying:

'An arse worthy of an artist's touch.'

'You'd be lucky!' someone yelled. Laughter round the room.

'Moving her thigh,' the painter drawled, 'would reveal fine brushwork…'

Jacky felt himself blush. He made to leave – but the door swept open and there stood Matron, on her rounds with Lieutenant Baird in her wake. The smokers at the window hurriedly stubbed out on the paintwork.

'Afternoon, gents…' the Lieutenant began, but Matron cut him short.

'What is all this?' she demanded, then pointed at the mural. 'And what is *that?*'

The Artist gave his smoothest bow.

'Matron, it is the Theatre of Health and Hygiene, a daily drama which we poor flyers watch, shall we say, from the wings.'

'What?' bristled the harridan in the doorway.

The Artist surveyed his own creation, leaning forward to examine plump Petunia. He turned slowly to fix Lieutenant Baird with his eye.

'Perhaps the Lieutenant can assist with our explication?'

Baird turned the colour of Angus raspberries as the men round the room struggled to choke back their guffaws.

'Let me elucidate, Matron,' the Artist continued. 'Our leading lady (*he prodded big Petunia*) plays the part of Ample Nutrition, so very needful. *(Splutterings from the window seats.)* To the right we find *(Hulewicz' busty sister)* the persona of Sanitation, built to withstand any amount of filth. And here *(Matron)* is a Nasty Disease suppressed by *(Sara)* the Angel of Carbolic Soap.'

Three dozen pairs of eyes, blinking back tears of mirth, turned on Matron.

The door slammed shut. Jacky Whisky had left the room.

◆◆◆

'Gravy, please, Janice,' whispered a young man with bat ears, yearning to take off his hot jacket.

'Pass Arthur the gravy, Janice,' echoed unsmiling Mrs Duncan opposite.

'I'll have the gravy after you,' called a hefty young man whose tie was strangling his thick neck.

A birthday dinner in the Farron Hotel; the women were in stiff frocks, the men sweating in tweed jackets by a log fire.

'Mind, Arthur, you're spilling!'

Arthur, his lugs aflame, pressed a napkin onto the brown puddle, then sat his side plate on top of both. He peeked around the table, mortified.

'Lovely gravy, isn't it, Mrs Duncan?' tried Janice, a plump lassie from the Glenfarron Cooperative. 'Will you have another ale?'

So the tinkling, cooling cinders of conversation were fanned a little longer.

Thirty feet away, across the bar, Vladislaw and Jacky Whisky skulked in a corner and watched.

'We picked a bad night, Sir,' remarked Vladislaw. 'This is grim. Poor nursy.'

From the dining table, Sara Meakin glanced over her shoulder and gave Vladislaw and Jacky a fleeting smile.

'Are they celebrating or grieving?' wondered Vladislaw.

'It's the old chap's birthday,' Jacky replied.

A spry gentleman – Sara's father George – small and wiry with white hair neatly combed back and a face red with beer and warmth, sat at the head of the table wearing a dark suit too big for him and a faintly bemused smile, waiting for something to happen.

'Here we go, look!' enthused Vladislaw. 'Oh come on, clap or something.'

A barmaid bore in a tiny horseshoe cake with seven candles. A whisper went round the table: *That's nice*. Janice of the Coop leaned over the table and urged:

'You sing, Arthur: *Happy Birthday*.'

'Oh no!' gasped Arthur, horrified. 'You!'

'I can't sing, I'd crack the glasses,' Janice blushed.

'Tom'll sing,' called Sara. 'Go on, Tom.'

Big Tom picked up his beer in a hurry.

'Forget that.'

Across the room, Vladislaw shook his head in dismay.

'Poor old chap. You ever seen anything so bleak, Sir?'

For a moment, Jacky made no response; he was watching Sara, who gazed into her glass of cordial to let Tom's snub go by.

Jacky said: 'Let's cheer them up.'

He tapped the barmaid on the shoulder and murmured to her. The diners looked up as two men in uniform limped towards George Dulce.

'Sir!' declared Jacky Whisky, 'We like to wish you traditional happiness, Sir.'

He stood to attention and proclaimed (in Polish):

'I sincerely hope your funeral is more fun than your birthday.'

He looked at Vladislaw: '*Tak?*'

'*Tak!*' beamed Vladislaw, adding (in Polish), 'It could hardly be worse.'

'From Poland, we salute you, Sir!'

George's guileless face shone back at them.

'Thank you, lads!'

The barmaid arrived with a tray of three whiskies, and Jacky became more expansive still.

'Yes please, for the birthday toast, Sir.'

He placed a dram in the old man's hand and cried:

'Your very excellent health, Sir!'

They raised their glasses, clicked their heels as best two cripples might, and downed the drink.

'Oh aye!' smiled George, knocking his back too.

'George!' Mrs Duncan gasped.

'Bravo!' Jacky and Vladislaw cheered as one. Jacky was more animated than anyone had seen him for months.

'Now we sing for you a Happy Birthday Polish song. Vladislaw!'

'Sir!'

And they began a Polish lyric to this effect:

Four and twenty virgins
Came in from old Gdansk.

By the time they got down
To Warsaw town,
Not one of them had their pants ... hoy!

They clicked their heels to salute once more.

'Aye, thanks again, lads!' cried George, radiant. The rest of the table sat gobsmacked, but Sara beamed at Jacky and he her, both rejoicing.

◆◆◆

Before a mahogany washstand with a willow pattern bowl, Sara studied herself in the mirror. She was stripped to the waist and the candlelight gleamed on her breast, making her small pale nipples appear to move as the flame and shadows shifted. She regarded her abdomen; she laid her fingertips on the skin by her navel. The candlelight caught the delicate down on her flesh.

Through the doorway, she was intensely aware of her husband. He was too large for the little bedroom. She said:

'There's someone at the hospital I've asked in to tea.'

'Oh?' said Gordon Meakin.

'A Polish officer. He was at the pub tonight; he sang for Da.'

'I'm sorry I missed that,' said Gordon.

'He says he'll make us some Polish sausage.'

'Out of what?' demanded her gamekeeper husband.

She sidestepped.

'He's lonely and he's sad, his family's in Warsaw and he can't fly any more. He's called Jacek, or Jacky.'

She pulled a nightdress on over her head but hesitated to move. She was steeling herself. At last she blew out the candle and passed through into the bedroom. Almost at once, the candle there was extinguished also.

'I still like to look at you,' Gordon objected.

A brittle silence.

'Sara?'

She turned away from him.

'I'm sleepy, pet. Goodnight.'

Again the fragile silence, the room hung with slivers of glass.

He whispered, 'For pity's sake.'

The blackness shook, the bedcovers flumped and the heavy man settled down, unsettled.

◆◆◆

After midnight the sky was brighter; the moon was up, and gleamed on rows of aluminium pans hung along the wall of the hospital kitchen. At one end, a corridor lamp shone through a fanlight over the door. Nothing in the kitchen stirred, apart from a hand-cranked mincer bolted to the end of a long bench. This small machine appeared to be turning of its own volition. Tendrils of mince were falling, glistening in the moonlight.

But no, there was a hand reaching up from behind the bench, cranking. The meat dropped onto a tin tray in lumps.

'Family restaurant in Warsaw, Sir,' whispered Vladislaw, who was sitting on the floor between the remains of a pheasant, a hare and a rabbit, and chopping herbs into a basin. 'Sausages a speciality. We've been in restaurants for three generations… Ssshh!'

Jacky stopped cranking.

A military torch played through the window. The beam came upon the meat that hung from the mincer in swags. The light probed suspiciously, then peered into deeper corners of the kitchen.

Behind the bench, Jacky wriggled a hand inside the hare's pelt, two fingers stuck into the front ankles, one up the throat. The hare nosed up over the edge of the table, its bloodied paws beckoning.

The torchlight passed over – then swiftly returned. The hare ducked down, its little face reappearing two feet to the left, wrinkling its whiskers in the moonlight. When the torch beam swung back, the hare dropped behind the table, only to pop up to the right.

Behind the bench, Vladislaw grabbed the rabbit skin and thrust his hand inside.

The patrolling squaddy peered in through the window, and saw a hare with bloodshot eyes gazing back at him. Then a petite rabbit rose up alongside the hare. They turned to each other – and kissed.

The squaddy turned the torch off, breathing deeply.

'He's going,' declared Jacky. He sat up – and his head met the handles of an inverted stack of saucepans. They rattled, they tipped, they teetered.

'Shit!'

He lunged to catch them; he was off-balance. Vladislaw reached to support him, the pans poised on a hare's whisker. The torch beam came back…

And went off. The patrol marched away.

Vladislaw picked up a length of animal gut and stretched it.

'Right, Sir, let's get stuffing.'

◆◆◆

The wind pulled at his hair as it ruffled the pines, and the sun ducked and dived in the clouds. On the gravel before Bellcraig cottage, Jacky Whisky stood, poking the stones with his walking stick. He examined the sturdy fittings of the trim estate cottage; he glowered at the small windows, the lumpish granite masonry. His uniform was smartly pressed, but his left hand rested useless in his tunic pocket. Tucked against his side was a brown paper bag.

He was taken aback, when the door opened, by Sara's loveliness. She was wearing a light flowery dress that billowed a little as the wind reached for her.

'Jacky, welcome.' He didn't move.

She said, 'Won't you come in?'

A man was reaching to place a shotgun in a rack over the kitchen door.

'Gordon? This is Captain Wysierkierski.'

Her husband turned; there was no mistaking the big man they had seen burst from Petunia's cottage. He gave a civil nod.

'Afternoon. What you got there?'

Three huge sausages rolled fattily onto a dinner plate.

'Gracious,' Sara exclaimed.

'We made them, myself and Vladislaw.'

'And where'd you get the meat?'

'Gordon!' his wife protested, saying to Jacky, 'Never mind Gordon, he's a gamekeeper.'

'Aye, well, sorry.' The man nodded. He yelled through an open door: 'Now, Charlie!'

A three-year-old boy trotted into the kitchen, saw the newcomer and attempted to grab at and hide behind Sara.

Gordon ordered:

'Say good afternoon to Captain Wyshysh…'

But the name defeated him – so everyone laughed and the ice

fissured a little.

'Jacky Whisky is best,' their visitor urged. 'But I only bring three sausages.'

Sara said, 'We'll divide them up.'

The best service was out, dashing in modernist triangles of black, orange and green. (Joyce had chosen this for her sister's wedding, and Gordon had wanted to take it straight back to the shop.) There was Sara's bread – none of the bleak grey wartime matter – with potatoes and the fragrant oozing sausages, with new-mixed mustard.

'You'll have seen different parts, flying over,' remarked Gordon.

'But we fly at night, to resistance groups. We don't see so much.'

'Can you fly?' Charlie demanded.

'Yes,' said Jacky Whisky firmly. 'Yes, I can. I'm a pilot.'

'What's a pilot?' Charlie asked, so that had to be sorted for him.

Jacky surveyed the family room, nodding.

'You are very lucky here,' he murmured. Sara reached out, and for a moment she might have touched his arm. But she was reaching for Charlie.

'Eat your sausage, Charlie. We're certainly lucky today.'

'The sausage?'

'Wonderful and different!' she cried, 'Isn't it, Gordon?'

But Gordon peered at his mistrustfully, pressing it with his knife.

'It's strongly flavoured,' he muttered, embarrassed and cross.

'Polish style,' beamed its creator.

'Oh. I ... if you don't mind, I'll just have potato.'

'I'm so sorry,' breathed Jacky Whisky, and for a moment his dismay paralysed everyone.

Sara said brightly:

'Gordon has to take some fencing up to the loch. Won't you come for a drive with us?'

◆◆◆

'There was a plague pit.'

She pointed to an upright stone out in a field.

'A woman buried all her neighbours, then rode away to

Inverness on a white horse.'

She was proud of her place and its stories. The old estate lorry, dark green with lights like the eyes of a metal toad, growled its way up the stony Glenfarron road. Gordon gripped the wheel, Jacky was jammed against the door, and Sara in the middle held Charlie on her knee.

They reached the loch, where the wind combed the water into sparkling seersucker. At the margin, beech trees were still dressed in brown. Sara stood on a root that heaved out of the ground like a thick snake.

'This,' she indicated with glorious certainty, 'is where Pontius Pilate was born.'

She saw Jacky's face, and laughed.

'And why not? It's historical; his father was with a Roman legion, his mother was a local lass. The camp was over there, they've found remains. Trust a Glenfarron girl to behave like a baggage.'

'At least she was trying,' said Gordon, his back to them.

He moved away along the water, apart and aloof. Sara followed him with angry, hurt eyes.

Charlie had found a battered ring of cork, an old float, thrown up on the pebbly shore. Timidly, he offered it to Gordon.

'What's that?' the boy asked.

'Dirty,' said the towering man. 'Put it down.'

All their exchanges were like that.

'You once said,' remarked Jacky to Sara quietly, 'that you had no children.'

'Charlie is my sister's boy. You remember Joyce? She's not married. Charlie's best with us.'

The child had climbed astride a bleached log, facing the water. Jacky found a length of old cord, curled on the shingle. One-handed, he tied it to the front of the log, placing the other end in Charlie's hand.

'Hold the reins of your horse.'

He sat astride behind Charlie.

'Now, this is a song about a horse rider.'

Over there beside the black water
Sits a young Cossack on his horse,
Saying his sad farewell to his girl,
Saying his farewell to the Ukraine.

'Again!' Charlie demanded.
'There's a refrain,' Jacky smiled.

Hey, hey, hey there, falcon!
Leave the mountain, forests and plain.
Ring, ring, ring the bell,
My little skylark of the Ukraine.

Off went Sara and Jacky along the breezy shore, swinging the boy between them. Gordon did not follow. After half a minute, Jacky Whisky sensed the eyes on his back and he dropped Charlie's hand, letting Sara lead on to the water. Jacky looked away, gazing at the distant purple hills.

He saw them – but they were not his. Over the trees, a light military aircraft climbed towards the sun.

◆◆◆

Vladislaw, in later years, would tell anyone how fine Sara looked in uniform, slim and neatly made. He would recall her cycling in to the hospital, sometimes a little warm with the exercise, and with small dark patches under her arms.

Coasting downhill into the hospital grounds, she always seemed light-hearted, and she threw smiles to anyone she passed. She'd tweak the cycle bell for simple pleasure. The day after that outing, she was humming to herself:

Ring, ring, ring the bell,
My little skylark of the Ukraine.

Over the Chinese Bridge she rolled; the slats rattled but she kept her eyes up lest the sight of rushing water make her sick. She pinged her bell again – then felt self-conscious and put out a finger to still it.

An hour later she stood absently smoothing her pinafore, waiting at the clinic hut window. On the ink-stained wooden table lay a manila folder of medical notes. On the floor nearby were weights and bars. The hut was quiet and still. A bluebottle thrashed in a cobweb. Sara looked toward the door: no one coming.

She walked quickly through the castle corridors, passing with neutral smiles the damaged men. In a silent upper passageway she came to an open door, a dormitory with four plain steel beds and lockers, and one man sitting with his back to the door.

'Jacky?'

She moved round to face him.

'No exercise today?'

He had in his hand a small pouch of red cloth that he weighed and contemplated. She saw that all the life had gone from his face. She sat on the bedside chair.

'What's wrong, Jacky?'

He said, 'Give me your hands.'

Surprised, she held them out. He took and positioned them on his own knee, palms upwards in a cup. Then he eased open the drawstring of the pouch and trickled out a little of the contents: rich dark soil.

'That is all I have of Poland.'

He studied it for a moment.

'The only tangible thing.'

Sara gazed down at the dry soil in her hands. She couldn't bear to look at Jacky; she felt as if she was someone wandering on a misty hill where there might be a precipice. She closed her hands over the soil as though it were a fledgling she'd saved but didn't know how to heal.

She said:

'Come and see us again. Please?'

'Your husband doesn't like me,' Jacky remarked.

She was about to deny it, but he put his hand over hers, which stilled her. So she only murmured:

'Charlie likes you very much.'

He absorbed this, and pressed her hand.

◆◆◆

Charlie Dulce liked Jacky Whisky, but warily. Jacky's voice was strange. And a strange voice suggested a world that the little boy had no experience of, and could not gauge at all. Just as there were things about his Aunt Sara that he could not understand: a bitter-sweetness, a sense that she both clung to him and was reserved; adoring but also cool.

In later life, Charlie Dulce did his best to remember them both and understand them. He sometimes told himself that the effort was useless, that he never would bridge the gap of experience.

But then he became a doctor and, as such, attempted to imagine a woman's experience of childbirth. He could not know how that felt. On the other hand, he could imagine it sympathetically, and since none of us can know the contents of another mind, he decided that no one could say categorically that his imagination got it wrong. Nor, indeed, could any woman be entirely sure that she knows 'just what it was like' for any other woman, since everyone's experience is different and, again, we cannot know the content of another mind.

Similarly, Charlie had never suffered a stillbirth, although as a doctor he perhaps knew more about the mechanics of that horror than many women who had only ever given birth normally. So, when he thought back twenty or thirty years to his Aunt Sara, it was with a sense that he could not know what she lived through at this time, but also with a stubborn conviction that he had the right to trust his imagination.

Also with Jacky Whisky. As a child, there came a time when Charlie sensed something new in Jacky, an excitement that stemmed from that other world from which the strange voices came, and which perplexed him. Looking back later, having learned the history, he decided that there were many experiences that he would never meet first hand, but might still share in. He had never been in exile or 'liberated' either, but events in Poland had a deep effect on his life, and so as an adult he tried – with a 'working imagination' – to relive the effect that the news must have had in Farron Castle. He imagined the patients' mess heavy with cigarette smoke, men listening with heads cocked, staring with fixed, unblinking eyes at the brown radio:

> *The Soviet Army this morning launched an invasion of Poland in the vicinity of Lublin. German resistance is reported to be fierce…*

The listeners scarcely breathing, the smoke curling up their nostrils.

At the same time, on a bench in a nearby shed, an aircraft was taking shape. The shed was a therapeutic workshop. The plane was little more than eighteen inches in wingspan, its fuselage merely an outline drawn onto very thin plywood taken from a tea-chest. This was held in a vice. Shaping it one-handed was not easy, but Jacky had learned to turn the wrist while touching his elbow to the table edge for steadiness as he cut. His walking stick rested against the wall.

He circled his work, bending down, squinting, his concentration intense – until Vladislaw clattered in through the door calling, 'Sir! Sir!'

Now the mess was in tumult. Frantic men quarrelled and stabbed angry fingers at each other.

'Murdering bastard communists!'

'What do you know? It's freedom, for pity's sake.'

'There's Polish brigades with them.'

'My wife's in Lublin, I don't give a damn who liberates…'

'A sell-out!'

'It's freedom, not selling…'

'Bloody hell!'

They were near to blows, their pent-up frustrations uncontrollable. Vladislaw looked towards the door, where Jacky Whisky stood, pensive.

'You hear this, Sir? Lublin, Sir!'

'I hear,' nodded the Captain.

'Sir,' Vladislaw wondered, 'did you leave your stick in the workshop?'

Jacky looked down at his own hands.

Vladislaw said, 'That's wonderful, Sir!'

'Progress,' Jacky returned.

◆◆◆

He approached Bellcraig cottage, the toy plane in his hand. The day was cold and grey, and spitting wet. The front door stood open but he could see no one, until he noticed little Charlie pottering on the far side of the yard. Jacky regarded the boy distractedly, then pulled himself together and called:

'You'd like to be a pilot?'

He crouched and handed over the plane. Charlie took it in both hands.

'Polish, you see?' said Jacky. 'That's Poland.'

He'd painted a red and white chequerboard on the wing.

'Make it fly,' Charlie commanded.

'Let's try.'

The glider sailed away into the long grass.

'Let me!' the boy squealed, pelting after it.

'Did you make that?'

She was there in the kitchen doorway. Jacky said:

'My mother claims I made my first plane before I was born. She swears she could feel me throw it.'

He straightened, grinning cheerfully. Charlie hurled the glider into the ground again and again – and then suddenly it flew true, cruising into the herb bed.

Otherwise, the yard, the sheds, the kennels were quiet.

'Where's your husband?' asked Jacky Whisky.

'Drinking,' she said.

◆◆◆

'Aye, weel, the Russkies'll tak o'er 'n' all the Polaks can bugger off hame.'

The shepherd looked to Gordon for approval; the gamekeeper gave a tiny sharp exhalation through the nose. His pub cronies followed the lead, snorting and nodding their contempt.

Gordon put his beer on the mantelpiece and fished in his pocket for tobacco. He stood warming his shanks by the black iron fireplace, with the best view of the room, the window and door. It was where he always stood.

'Bloody time,' he remarked. 'Had my fill of Polaks.'

'Outlived their welcome, I'd say,' obliged someone.

'Labour Party says they're fascists,' offered another.

To which the cronies chorused:

'Well, they are, aye, they are, fucking fascists the lot of them.'

'Now, then!' The landlord was stern.

Gordon licked his Rizzla paper.

'Fucking something, for sure.'

◆◆◆

Again, the toy glider soared across the back lawn, Charlie in pursuit.

'They have found the graves of many Polish officers, murdered by the Russians in a forest. Every one has been shot in the back of the head.'

Jacky Whisky sat on a wobbly bench, his back to a huge fir tree, while Sara lifted couch grass and dandelions from an onion bed with a kitchen fork. He was not thinking of her. He had a long green stick in his hand, and thrashed the stony ground as he spoke, his voice hard and quick.

'That is Stalin, you see, butchering future resistance. Can you imagine: this man calls himself our ally. Our saviour!'

He cut at nettles, fracturing the stick on a rock so that it dangled stupidly. Sara, tossing a handful of weeds onto her little heap, heard him hiss with self-loathing.

'I would wring all their damn necks, Russians, Germans, all of them. But I can do nothing.'

'Make it fly!' Charlie clamoured, scampering back across the gravel. Jacky adjusted the rudimentary nose ballast of tin and launched the glider again, high and far.

'Yes!' the child squealed.

Jacky Whisky looked quizzically at Sara.

'You don't want your own children?'

She said:

'I lost two babies.'

She continued weeding. There was silence between them until he knelt also, picked up a piece of broken slate and started work beside her, dropping his weeds onto her little pile. She looked round at him in surprise. He picked up a handful of soil, assessing it, rubbing it with his thumb and remarking:

'Not Polish, but not bad.'

'Well, thank you, Captain.'

'My pleasure,' he answered. Then he dumped the handful on the lap of her skirt.

'Oh, now!'

She flicked her skirt to send the soil flying into his face, hers too. They laughed and spluttered, and Jacky put out a hand to wipe the earth from her cheek.

'What are you doing?' Charlie asked, returning with the plane.

'Making a good mess,' declared Jacky. 'Come, you help us.'

He started tugging at weeds with gusto.

'Would you like a job?' she asked. 'Not here – my parents' farm, Torbrechan, up the glen.'

Jacky peered at her, unsure.

She said, 'You can't stay at the hospital for ever.'

◆◆◆

'Mother? This is Jacky, to help you. From Poland.'

Jacky Whisky clicked his heels smartly and bowed to Aileen Dulce who sat beside the range, a merry-faced old lady, immobile and exceedingly fat. She held a tiny piglet on her wide lap, bottle-feeding. Torbrechan farm kitchen was large but crowded, with green painted dressers creaking under best blue-and-white china, a press heavy with pristine linen, guns over the door, work boots and rainwear giving off their rubbery smells.

'We remember you singing at the pub, don't we, George?'

Beside her stood her white-haired husband.

'We've a few beasts,' said George, businesslike, 'the Highland sort. But Torbrechan's mostly sheep. You know anything about sheep, lad?'

'Not so much,' Jacky returned.

'Mother'll keep you right.'

Aileen cackled.

'That's for sure. Will you like to come here, then?'

'I shall be honoured, Madam,' declared the ace pilot turned farm-labourer.

He bowed again and the old lady giggled

◆◆◆

Footsteps; a swaying oil lamp picked out the toy glider lain in the onion bed. The red-and-white chequerboard on its wings gave it away. A large hand seized it and carried it indoors.

'What's this?'

He held out the glider. Sara was taking bread from the oven, and did not meet his eye. She kept her tone busy:

'Jacky made that for Charlie.'

'He was here?' her husband demanded.

'This morning. He's going to work for my parents.'

'How's that?'

'They're desperate for help. There's a scheme, the Liaison Lieutenant was telling us. There's no need for him to be at the hospital now, he's as cured as he'll ever be. He's got to be doing something; now he can't fight, he's going mad with it.'

Tapping and stacking three loaves on a wire rack, she didn't notice how Gordon stared at the glider. She said blithely:

'Charlie thinks Jacky's wonderful.'

'No doubt.'

She heard the ice in that; it hit her in the spine as she crouched to close the range. She composed herself before she straightened, wiping her hands hastily, removing her apron, struggling to put a different note into her voice.

'Won't you come to bed?'

He looked at her in surprise.

His boot fell to the bedroom floor.

He sat on the far side of the bed in a vest only, the pale blue quilted counterpane cold under his immensely strong flesh as he twisted to see her. His hands rested at his side. He observed Sara through the bathroom door where she stood in front of the mirror taking clips from her hair. She wore a creamy nightdress that she prayed was appealing. The very lamplight was chill. She could feel him waiting for her, as she searched her own face for traitors. She licked her dry lips, then went to him.

He noted her every move, logged every sound, the slip of her feet on the boards, the heavy sweeping sounds of cold bed linen. She lay back against the thick pillows. Her husband's pupils were very large and never left her; each face was loud with questions. She opened the front of her nightdress, took his hand and placed it over her breast. She saw that he was excited but mistrustful.

'Come on, then.'

For all his power, he was a gentle, considerate lover, easily pleased and keen to please. But when he lifted himself off Sara, her face was trembling. He pulled himself up against the pillows, studying her turned-away head.

'I'm disgusting, then.'

No response, save that Sara closed her eyes.

'Sexy as a sack o' neaps.'

He was not a sarcastic man, not used to being unkind.

'Or a corpse. Like shagging a corpse.'

'I'm sorry,' she whispered.

She looked at him, saw how miserable and angry he was, how bewildered.

'I've lost two, Gordon.'

'So we give up on family.'

Turning away, she whispered:

'Each time it's like making ready for another death.'

'Well, thank you!'

He stood, lowering over the bed, boiling.

'Gordon, love, I don't like us like this...'

'Meaning me with a hard dick? S'all right, that's away.'

'Please...'

He grabbed at her shoulder, pulling her back to face him.

'You want an immaculate bloody conception?' He roared with pain and she was scared.

'Gordon, hush.'

'Gordon, hush!' he mimicked crudely. 'Don't bloody hush me.'

He slapped her face. Sara cried out, burning with injustice and hurt as she squirmed from him across the bed. Her husband stared at her, incredulous.

'Och, Jesus. Oh, for Christ's sake.'

He thundered out of the room and downstairs, setting the house trembling.

◆◆◆

She slept a deep exhausted sleep, waking to the breeze tugging the curtain out through the open window. The house was quiet. Coming downstairs, she found the kitchen empty but warm; the range was alight. A rug and a pillow – its black-and-white ticking without a case – lay discarded by the small settee. The back door stood open, and through it came the sound of urgent sawing. Sara filled the kettle from the rocker pump over the sink, and put it on the range.

Gordon was hammering now, working with furious energy, the double doors of his shed open, a roll of chicken wire and a half-built crow trap on the ground outside.

'I brought you tea,' said Sara.

He didn't look at her. She put the mug on a bench among the pliers and the jam jars of nails.

'I'm away to Glasgow to see Joyce.'

Still he said nothing.

'You can take Charlie to Ma and Da. I'll put out his breakfast.'

He stopped work, staring at the trap he'd made.

Shortly after, he stood at the kitchen window watching her bump down the track on her bicycle, a small case jammed into the basket. Charlie sat at the table in a high chair, with a cup of milk and a plate of bread and butter. The plywood plane lay on the table also.

'When's my Ma coming back?'

Gordon shrugged.

'Och, soon enough for us. Fine old time we'll have.'

He studied Charlie as he ate, and saw that the boy was unconvinced.

'I'll make you something,' tried Gordon, stabbing a finger at the glider, 'much better than that. You'll see.'

Charlie chewed slowly, considering what might be better.

◆◆◆

A vast railway shed, a din of clanking iron plate, of carts rumbling on the paving, clacking shoes, parents scolding boys in shorts, officious persons blasting whistles at nothing apparent, squaddies in green battledress and bankers in astrakhan, hurrying WAAFs and engines whoofing steam, and out of this emerged Sara with her little green case. She scanned the crowd, moved forward – and then stopped again, surprised.

In the press, her sister Joyce stood face to face with a man in uniform. His face in profile meant little to Sara till she saw the Polish chequerboard on his sleeve. She couldn't hear what was said but it was not friendly: Joyce's chin was thrust forward pugnaciously, her hands on her hips, telling him what for, till the man gave up and backed away.

An instant later, Joyce squealed and ran to her sister.

'Was that Stanislaw?' enquired Sara, disentangling herself.

'Was is the word.'

She took Sara's arm and led her away.

◆◆◆

'He *hit* you? The shite!'

Joyce stood over the shabby, boxy old settee. Over its lumpish brown back was draped a rich Paisley shawl of oriental reds and blues. Sara was curled in a corner with her legs under her, encastled, looking up gratefully at the one person who'd fight her corner without question.

Joyce seized a packet of cigarettes off the table.

'Want one? Go on, don't go pretending it's your first.'

She came to the settee, puzzling and probing.

'Gordon used to be a nice man.'

'He *is*,' Sara parried. 'He loves his work, the countryside, the animals and the woods and me too, I still believe. It's not indecent for a man to want babies, is it, but in Gordon it's an obsession. Sometimes I feel I'm not a woman, more a plant pot. It's what he was born to, I suppose, the crafts of the land and handing them on. He's kind enough to Charlie.'

'How, enough?' Joyce prickled.

'Oh, he's never harsh, but cold sometimes. Confused, I think. He's no imagination, he doesn't begin to understand how sad I get. I had two babies die in me. I'd felt them move, I'd named them in my head and spoken to them, and then they died and I had to carry them about like a tomb on legs. Now, if Gordon wants me, I freeze.'

She tapped off her cigarette ash too frequently, as the unhabituated smoker does. She turned the glass ashtray with her little finger.

'I did want the babies.'

'You've Charlie,' said Joyce.

'Your Charlie.'

'Our Charlie.'

'But Charlie's the child Gordon doesn't have himself, you see. The crib he made is waiting in the back room upstairs, that horrid dark room.'

Joyce pondered this, drawing deeply on her cigarette.

'Charlie okay?' she asked.

'He's just fine. How's Stanislaw?'

'Och, bugger him. Bloody Poles.'

'What?'

'Fascists. Labour party says.'

'They're heroes,' said Sara, blanching.

'Bleedin' spongers,' Joyce grimaced. 'No money, nothing. Stay there.' She jumped to her feet and disappeared into the bedroom.

Sara stood and moved about, restless and fragile. Her face felt numb; she wondered if it was still the slap, or perhaps the tobacco. She felt nearer to tears now than when struck. She tried to focus on immediate tangible things in the room. She narrowed her mind onto the scents in her nostrils; behind the tobacco, she caught a trace of perfume.

On a recessed shelf, she saw something face down and forgotten, and knew it immediately. She picked it up – a painted crest:

VIVE LA POLOGNE

Back came Joyce, hands spilling a cascade of brown nylon.

'I get chocolate too. He's called Russ, he's from Moose Jaw, Saskatchewan.'

But Sara was distracted, her lips open with half-formed, terrifying questions. Puzzled, Joyce saw the wooden crest in her sister's hand.

'You want that?'

'Yes.' It was a whisper. Joyce peered at her.

'Sara?'

◆◆◆

They went hurrying through the evening streets, with only Joyce's high and wobbly heels saving Sara from being overtaken and confronted.

'You're out of your bloody skull!'

'Lay off, will you? Joyce, nothing's happened.'

'But you bloody want it. Look at you!'

'I just said…'

'Bugger that. Listen, you and Gordon may have differences but you've a decent man in your wedded bed.'

'Jacky is a friend. Who said anything about beds…'

'I did, I'm saying it 'cos it's plain as an effing four poster. It's a bitter night but you're all hot and wet down below.'

'Joyce!'

'You're wanting to trade Gordon for a Pole? Jesus.'

'You've got men from all over.'

'I'm not married! Anyway, Russ is one of us. Why'd you have to pick a greasy Pole?'

'I've not picked anyone, I said he's my friend. Keep your dirty mind in order.'

She was so fierce that Joyce laughed, and Sara protested.

'I don't care where he's from. He's funny and gentle. He doesn't stamp on me like I'm a frozen puddle – which how Gordon makes me feel. Charlie adores him. And he sang *Happy Birthday* for Da.'

'Spare me,' Joyce snorted.

She grabbed Sara's arm and stopped her.

'Sis, have you not heard? We're for Joe Stalin now, that's our man. When the war's done, the Poles are going to get kicked back where they came. They're finished.'

Sara looked away, biting her lip.

'Cummon, cheer up,' tried Joyce, 'Wait till you meet Russ. He can do better than *Happy Birthday*.'

She took Sara by the elbow and steered her into the pub.

'Heard a lot about you, Sara.'

The uniform immaculate, the teeth perfect, the voice like orange juice and bourbon, strong and smooth.

'What are you drinking?' Russ enquired.

Sara smiled, cagey, but Joyce was slavering with proprietorial excitement as Russ headed for the bar.

'Cummon, Sis, admit it: he's beefcake.'

The pub was loud and turbulent, as man after man barged towards the bar for drink. The blend of scent and cigarette that Sara had caught in the flat was thick here. Sara looked round, and a table of three men returned her look. They wore tired uniforms; one was an airman with a red-and-white chequerboard on his sleeve.

'Joyce ...?' began Sara.

'Shit! What's he doing here?'

Two of the men regarded the sisters with simple curiosity, but the other, a skinny dark creature, stared piercingly at Joyce. All three were down at heel, skulking in a corner.

'Christ, I'm not here,' Joyce spluttered. She turned her back, hissing to Sara: 'That's your heroes, Sis. Nobody wants them. They're losers, they speak peculiar, they're weird and I don't like them.'

She saw dismay in Sara's eyes, relented a little and took her hand.

'Oh, Jeez, sis, stop this before it starts, I'm telling you.'

'Something bothering you ladies?' Russ asked, putting down the glasses. He straightened and eyeballed the Poles in their alcove, who glared back at him for a moment – then returned to their drinks.

'Drowning some eastern sorrow,' mused Russ, mildly surprised that the rest of the world was not as content as himself. 'Well, drink up, girls; we're meeting Tom and Ritchie in ten minutes.'

Of a sudden, the three sad men across the room stood, pulled their coats about them and headed for the door. Sara looked away, not wishing to watch a small death.

◆◆◆

They walked out, the Dulce sisters with Russ upright as a great sequoia. They were making for the city centre.

'Remember Angie Ferguson, Sis?' began Joyce. 'From Drumcullen?'

(Had they had eyes in the backs of their heads, they'd have seen three figures appear noiselessly from an alley, and follow.)

'I remember,' said Sara.

'Well, she's only marrying a naval bloody Commander.'

'Commander Dave McCleary.' Russ nodded with approval. 'Coming coming home to his Scotch roots.'

'There's Tom!' Joyce piped, waving.

'And Ritchie,' said Russ. 'Ritc…!'

He staggered, clutching his head, then fell in a heap, consciousness leaving him in a sigh.

'Russ!' Joyce screamed. 'Russ!'

She was shoved aside as they closed in, two of them dragging Russ to throw him head first against a wall, where the third swung a boot into his kidneys.

'Bastards!'

Joyce went for them, her claws out to tear, but she stumbled and slipped on the wet cobbles. Russ was a sack of rubbish by the wall, the kicks knocking his head from side to side.

'You shits,' Joyce raged. 'You shits you bastards!'

Seventy yards ahead, the crew of a Canadian destroyer turned to see – and now the assailants were outnumbered, mouths split, eyes jabbed, men grunting and falling on the cobbles, faces torn, blood in the drains. Someone ran into an alley, was tripped and knocked to the ground. Someone else stamped on his face. Russ was moaning and broken. Joyce rushed to lift his face clear of the pavement.

'Russ, they've bloody killed you!'

She looked up; a figure in a long coat was standing over her.

'Stanislaw, you fucking shite!'

She was about to go for his throat.

A squealing of tyres and brakes: redcaps now. Stanislaw turned and ran, as did any of the combatants still on their feet.

'You bastard! You Polish *coward!*'

A few steps away, Sara stood frozen, shoulders hunched, rigid, silent.

◆◆◆

In Bellcraig kitchen, Gordon screwed a blue wheel onto a wooden lorry. He examined his workmanship, then passed it across the table to Charlie.

'There you go. You like it? Take it to Torbrechan, show your Nan.'

Charlie regarded the lorry coolly, fingering it without great enthusiasm. It was nicely made, but it never travelled very well; the wheels didn't turn easily.

'That'll loosen up,' said Gordon. 'It'll go nicely.'

But Charlie had heard bicycle wheels. He was out of the door.

◆◆◆

Within a short space of time, Jacky Whisky became almost a son to George and Aileen Dulce. Jacky's gratitude was so intense as to be slightly odd. He did anything he could to repay them for their trust. He made Aileen a wheelchair, of a sort.

There was, in the late autumn of 1944, a short spell of wonderfully warm weather. Torbrechan responded to the warmth. Birdsong bubbled, chaffinch and siskin flitted in the blackthorn. Chickens followed the sun sneaking in through the open kitchen door, and their beaks *tick ticked* off the flagstones. Aileen watched them, neither calling nor shooing, for the fat old lady's heart could scarcely manage the pumping any more; there were just too many miles of vein in her to be filled and flushed. She sat by the scrubbed table, her breath shallow and panting, her skin clammy.

Into the sun-filled doorway stepped Jacky Whisky, framed in a golden aureole. He studied the helpless farmwife who returned his look with mute pleading.

That afternoon, Jacky ransacked a junk heap behind the hospital where rusted bed frames, fencing wire and angle-irons, rolls of rotten carpet and broken light fittings lay, together with a wheeled contraption once trundled across the interminable castle lawns by a groundsman, though to what end was anyone's guess.

Here with his one good arm Jacky heaved at the wire, cursing the scratches as he struggled to retrieve his prize: a porter's barrow, the upright sort with small wheels, for shifting sacks and heavy boxes. He dragged it clear, then trundled it to the workshop where Vladislaw lashed on a wooden chair.

'Neat!' Jacky demanded. 'Tie it neat, and strong.'

Vladislaw grunted that he was doing his best.

Half an hour later, with a rhythmic squeaking, Jacky headed for the Chinese Bridge, bumping his barrow over the slats and out through the rhododendrons beyond.

At much the same moment, the green toad-eyed lorry was chugging up the lane under the beeches.

They'd been discussing Joyce.

'You best not tell your Da how she carries on,' Gordon ordered.

Sara, with her arm around Charlie, did not reply. Gordon's hands were clamped onto the steering wheel.

'I can't stand that,' he added. 'We're raising a whore's boy.'

'Gordon, that's enough. There's no call for that.'

Charlie hadn't a clue what it meant, of course, but Sara reddened with anger, her hold on him tightening defensively. Her vehemence stopped Gordon short.

'Aye, well,' he mumbled, abashed.

Sara nudged the boy, pointing to a figure in the distance leading a horse and cart into the farmyard.

'There's Grandpa, look, Charlie.'

There was, at Torbrechan farm, a broad yard behind the old house. The kitchen facade glowed with five-fingered Boston ivy that in autumn dropped in rusty drifts to the cobbles. To the north and east were the steadings for beasts, machines and wagons. The steading doors were huge and heavy, the roof a broad sweep of coarse slate. In the 1940s the southern side was open. At the far corner, where yard became garden, a fine Douglas fir gave a pool of shade from the sun. Here stood a rickety card table, and an oak armchair with a cushion.

There came that rhythmic squeaking again, and from the kitchen doorway Jacky Whisky emerged with Aileen Dulce perched on the chair on the porter's barrow, clinging to her skirts in alarm and delight. She was massively heavy: to manoeuvre her over gravel took two. George Dulce had one handle and Jacky the other, using all the strength in his good arm with some use of his hip and sometimes a shove on the axle with his foot. They reached the table by the Douglas fir where Aileen shuggled across to the armchair, panting, then waving merrily to Charlie at the farmyard gate.

'Charlie! Did you see?'

'There's your mother howked like a sack o' neaps,' Gordon told Sara.

'Jacky is very kind,' she said.

'Oh, so, that's me told.'

He went in through the gate. Sara saw her mother glowing with happiness, out in the sun. Back came Jacky with a glass of water, nodding to Gordon like a deferential butler, smiling at Sara as everyone gathered to admire the trolley.

But George was calling from the kitchen door.

'Jacky?' he beckoned urgently, 'Jacky, lad!'

There was a brown bakelite wireless in the kitchen, on the sideboard. The volume was high and the newsreader booming:

General Komorowski has ordered all units of the Warsaw Home Army to attack German positions in the city.

Jacky stood by the table, rigid, at attention, staring at the radio as though expecting an order.

Partisans have seized key installations but are lightly armed, while German tank regiments are thought to be preparing a counter-offensive.

From the doorway, George watched, anxious.

Heavy fighting is reported.

◆◆◆

Just imagine, Vladislaw would urge him later: imagine the scene. And Charlie, touched by the fierce sadness he saw in the old Pole, tried his damndest, for it was, in a way, his own history too. Throughout his youth he longed to identify with this story, and would strain his powers of visualisation. Indeed, he tried all his life, even in retirement. Although the freshness of experience had fled along with the all-pervasive reek of rough 1940s tobacco, and although the faces were long faded, in certain respects he could perhaps visualise better as an old man than as a teenager or a medical student, when he had no spare brain capacity for learning anything more than the order of the cranial nerves. He had little notion of Poland. He never went there, although it could be called his paternal home. But he did, in due course, do some reading. He knew what happened to Jacky, Stan and Vladislaw's country.

So he imagined: the hospital mess, crowded; a Polish voice, stiff with the formality of radio and with the overwhelming excitement of the news, but carrying a tremor of apprehension.

General Komorowski has vowed that the Home Army shall not sleep till the last German is swept from Warsaw.

A roar of applause! The men press around the radio, shaking hands, clapping each other on the back, embracing, whistling and stamping, banging their crutches.

Yes, Charlie could imagine. Vladislaw told him much; he worked with Vladislaw's memories. Vladislaw seized Jacky by the shoulders, shouting, 'Damn and hell, we stand tall again, Sir!'

A ridiculous confusion of salute and laugh. He stamped his wooden leg thunderously, again and again.

'Steady, friend,' smiled Jacky. His mind was already travelling to Warsaw.

◆◆◆

That blue lorry. That lorry troubled Charlie all his life – the little wooden lorry that Gordon made for him. The fact that he had kept it, albeit hidden away, told him that he felt guilty. He persevered in this guilt for six decades. Why had he, aged four, always rejected Gordon's clumsy offers of friendship, his coarse gifts? There wasn't much; Gordon was a repressed, taciturn, bottled-up sort of man. If Charlie had responded to the small gestures Gordon was able to make, would that have averted any of what followed?

But was Gordon offering friendship, in fact? Was it not just a sorry attempt at manipulating and controlling a child, in the face of the altogether more seductive Jacky Whisky? Was he not just trying to buy Charlie as a partisan?

Nonetheless, there was guilt and pathos. Charlie kept the lorry, but couldn't bear to look at it. When, in later life, he thought of it, a knife turned in a wound – but whose wound, he could not be sure. He remembered a professor of medicine quoting Dickens, a scene in which someone is asked if they are in pain, and the patient replies that there is a pain in the room, but they are not sure if they have got it.

So Dr Charles Dulce kept that toy lorry in a cupboard, and from time to time would scourge himself with the memories it evoked: his own tiny guilt, and Gordon's pain.

There, now: it lay on its side on the gravel, ignored. Gordon saw it there, its blue wheels dulled by grime and rainwater. He crouched by it and set it upright just as Charlie, the fostered son, tottered by him with a plane held high.

Gordon heard: *Cracckk!* from the shed.

The logs fell apart, dropping to left and right. Jacky placed each on the execution block, steadied himself and hefted the splitting axe.

'Aren't you very pleased?' she asked.

He pursed his lips. *Cracckk!*

'Warsaw will be liberated,' she said. 'That's wonderful, surely.'

She could not understand why he didn't sing and dance.

Jacky paused. He looked past her at the weak daylight outside.

'The Home Army has pistols,' he said. 'The Germans have tanks, heavy machine guns, mortars and flame-throwers. My parents are in Warsaw.'

'But the Russians …' she cried.

'The Russians are waiting to see.'

He rested the axe on the springy woodchips, his hand light on the long haft. A small shadow ran across the doorway, holding up a glider.

'You have a family here,' she murmured quietly. 'Charlie, my parents, they are so fond of you.'

She could not look him in the eye, but slowly extended a hand and touched his, lain on the top of the haft.

'Sara? Sara, where've you got to?' her husband cried.

She grabbed at split logs and chucked them noisily into the fraying wicker basket. Gordon appeared in the doorway, eclipsing the daylight. He saw his wife lobbing wood for all she was worth and the Pole leaning on his axe gazing at her.

'Everything all right?' Gordon enquired. 'We'll be away home, then.'

'I'll take these in to Da,' she said.

She hefted the basket and went out, lurching under its weight. Gordon didn't move, but remained studying Jacky, who said:

'Should we help her?'

Gordon raised an eyebrow:

'Sara's got two good arms.'

Jacky made no response, but returned the stare.

'Right,' said Gordon. 'I'll be leaving you.'

◆◆◆

Clustered around the mess radio, the mood of the men was quite changed. They were silent, smoking with nervous intentness.

> *... continued heavy fighting in Warsaw. German radio claims that the partisans are surrendering but the Polish Home Army continues to broadcast and reports that they are holding firm.*

One or two sneaked glances at their companions' faces, but there was nothing to read there.

> *Soviet Army groups are reported to be twenty miles from the city but are not, at present, advancing.*

The men went their ways without speaking.

◆◆◆

A delicate strip of pale golden pine in the workbench vice, lightly gripped. A short smoothing plane passing along it slowly, set to a very fine cut.

He was concentrating. After every pass he crouched and inspected. He pushed again at the plane, striving to balance the force he applied to the resistance offered by the wood, using his body's tense stance to control any slip. It was so difficult, one-handed; the hours ran away from him. He pushed gently but now the blade was sticking

He paused and straightened, aching. On the bench, the fuselage of an aircraft was under construction, much more elaborate than the first glider. This new one had a delicate frame of tiny spars trimmed with a razor blade; it was a model of a fighter aircraft, a type that had been obsolete before it ever saw combat. Jacky pushed at the smoothing plane; it stuck, and jerked, and something snapped.

'Shit.'

◆◆◆

From the slopes behind Torbrechan farm, the panoramas of Glenfarron were such that even old George Dulce paused sometimes, gazing at the distant loch gleaming, at the fragments of the ancient Caledon forest rising from the waterside, at the spectral glimpses of far West Coast peaks.

But it was not George up on the steep pasture now, mid-September. A creaking came over the swell of the hill, preceding a battered cart hauled by a pony and the pony led by Jacky. The cart was heavy with turnips and the sheep dogged its progress, until Jacky dropped the back flap, climbed up and began heaving off their dinner. He was instantly mobbed.

The pony, normally quiet and biddable, had caught his mood and was skittish. As the sheep milled and pushed, the pony started kicking, almost throwing Jacky off his footing.

'Behave, damn you!' he bawled in Polish. 'Keep your stupid arse still.'

He saw Sara below, arriving in the yard on her bicycle, Charlie in a black metal seat up behind. She opened the gate, wheeling the cycle towards the kitchen door.

The pony tweaked the halter from Jacky's hand and shambled forwards.

'Stand!'

The pony stilled, biding its moment. Jacky closed his eyes and sighed, trying to blow away the tension. When he looked again, Sara was climbing the field towards him.

'Polish horses do what they're told,' he informed her.

'And Polish wives?'

'Make wonderful horsewomen.'

He knelt by the pony. Sara smiled, curtsied, put one foot on his knee and turned lightly onto the pony's back. He gave her the halter.

'Like a Polish peasant,' he remarked.

'Thank you so much.'

They moved off across the field, Jacky walking beside the cart and sweeping off more turnips as they went, so that the sheep scurried behind like gulls after a trawler.

'Yes,' Jacky asserted, 'fine strong women they are. They make good lovers.'

'Of which you've had plenty.'

'Half Glasgow.'

He came in front of the pony and stopped it.

'I have to leave here soon.'

'Why?' she whispered.

'Because I am not sick, just useless.'

'Useless? You work so hard.'

'The hospital needs my bed.'

'My parents can't do without you.'

'But, I'm afraid...'

'Nor can I.'

They could not look at each other. She took a grip on her voice, and asked less shrilly:

'Where would you go?'

'They may send me to Leeds.'

'Leeds!'

'Some Polish have gone there,' he murmured.

'You can stay here,' she burst out again, 'stay right here.'

'With you? Nurse Sara, that is not smart.'

'With Ma and Da.' She rushed on in spate. 'They have a bothy, a bunkhouse for the working men. It's empty now.'

Before he could reply, the sky cracked open. An aircraft sprang over the brow of the hill. The pony shied, kicked, thrashed, rolled its eyes in panic. Sara was thrown, landing on her feet but stumbling and falling, her face grazed by the hooves, till Jacky grabbed and dragged her clear before he too fell.

The outraged pony yanked the cart in a circle with a clatter of wood and ironwork, until the plane was away over the loch and the din with it. Glenfarron fell silent. The pony shuffled and dragged a few yards more, then stood still.

Sara lay beside Jacky Whisky on the grass, jangled with fright. She remembered to breathe, and looked at him propped on his good arm, watching the aircraft. Slowly she lowered her cheek onto his chest. She murmured:

'You're not to go.'

She lifted her face over his; he touched the streak of mud on her cheek. They kissed hesitantly, with a sudden sly chill in the hillside air and a roaring in their heads. Sara grabbed at him because the moment might cool, it might not carry her far enough. She seized Jacky's hand and pushed it under her clothing onto her breast, gladly. She remained there, her forehead poised against his shoulder, feeling the hard chill of the ground through her hip.

In the farmyard below, a dog began to bark. Sara pulled herself upright, straightened her clothes and ran from Jacky Whisky, down the hill.

The aircraft, a twin-engined Mosquito, loud and powerful, returned to swing over the loch, reclaiming Jacky's attention. So he did not notice two men from Parkneuk, the farm downstream, walking on the Glenfarron highway, or that they had slowed their stride a little and were peering up the hill.

◆◆◆

Again the sombre-faced Polish men (warmly dressed for deep autumn) in a knot around the radio, curls of tobacco smoke rising like distress signals.

> *...and that partisan resistance is now confined to isolated pockets of the city. Warsaw Radio has insisted that there will be no surrender.*

Jacky Whisky lifted his head as he might a leaden hundredweight.

> *Allied aircraft have attempted to drop supplies and ammunition but have been hampered by smoke.*

'You sit here, you do nothing!'

They all looked round. The speaker was in a wheelchair, a grey hospital rug hanging empty over the front: he had no legs.

He raged at them.

'Look at you! Some little scratch, some little scar on your arse and you sit the war out here while Warsaw dies.'

Another man hobbled away, kicking at a wooden chair that skidded across the room before catching on a board and toppling.

An hour later, Jacky Whisky glued a paper skin onto the tail of the model plane. That the paper adhered in the right place was miraculous, for his good hand was trembling badly and the tears that streamed down his face were blinding him.

◆◆◆

He hovered irresolute in the lane to Bellcraig cottage, bearing an awkward shape loosely wrapped in newspaper.

In the kitchen, Sara looked up from the sink, and hurried out.

'You unwrap it,' he said. 'For the boy.'

'Will I? Gracious, Charlie!'

Out it came: a fighter aircraft in Polish Air Force markings, with a shellacked skin and a scarlet-and-white chequerboard on its tail.

'I didn't do the paintwork; I've a friend at the hospital, a real artist. It won't fly like the glider, it's too heavy, but maybe Charlie will like to have it hang over his bed.'

But Charlie hung back, overawed.

'Well, now,' Sara demanded. 'What do you say?'

'Why can't it fly?' the boy blurted out, and Jacky looked sorry.

Sara said:

'Jacky, walk with us up to Torbrechan. There's something to show you.'

◆◆◆

Clear October light dropped through the trees at the margin of a stubble field. In those days, the forest in the upper glen was mostly old Scots pine with some small new plantings of spruce. Near the road, there was beech and ash also; the brushwood snapped and the white rumps of roe deer flashed. Occasional fat pigeons cruised between the trunks, while the little crossbills held down pine cones, and prised them open to insert their tongues after the seed. A blackcock, perched on a gate, took fright and scudded low over the field.

A broad track ran just inside the forest edge. Here scampered a boy with a stick that he whacked on the wire fence. Behind him, a man who was far away, and a woman who glanced at the man frequently and at last took his arm. They walked in silence some minutes until she stopped him.

An old stone barn stood jutting from the forest into the field, half in the woods, half out. Beneath the arch was the usual forgotten clutter of bale and bucket and broken tool, all encrusted with grey dirt. At the forest end, a stone stair led up to a wooden door; there were small skylights along the roof, and a chimney pipe protruding.

'The farm boys stayed here,' she said.

At the top of the stone steps, the snick of the door clicked sharply. Within was a long chamber under the slope of the roof, lined with plain boards. The colour had gone from the wood, and everything was cold but clean, though with a musty scent. There was a small cast-iron stove and a neat wood stack. A strip of worn carpet lay between four wooden cots with tidily rolled mattresses.

'If they're damp, we'll bring one from the house. And you'll get your meals at the farm.'

But he said nothing.

'Do you like it? It's yours if you do.'

From the barn below came a rattling of stick and wire.

'Charlie? Charlie, what are you doing?' she called, but she couldn't go down. Jacky Whisky sat slowly on one of the cots.

'Jacky, please talk to me.'

He seemed not to see her.

◆◆◆

...while Soviet ground forces remain twenty miles short of the city. Efforts to supply the Polish Home Army by air have been discontinued, and broadcasts from Warsaw Radio are infrequent.

◆◆◆

Jacky Whisky, alone in his wooden bothy, lying on his bed. Beside the bed stood a whisky bottle, empty. He rolled off the cot, and kicked the bottle flying into the eaves. Then the wind rose and attacked one corner of the roof, putting long fingers under the endmost slate to tweak it up a fraction; it drew its cold claws over the whole roof, slate by slate, till a rattle passed across the building, as though the devil scratched it.

Jacky looked up: in front of him, there was faint handwriting, in pencil on the ceiling boards. He put a hand out to the wood to steady himself, peered and shifted to catch candlelight on the graphite. It was a list of names:

G. Henderson
A. Gilmartin
Alexander Aitken
S. Kilpatrick
1916

'They all enlisted,' she'd said.

Jacky half-tumbled, half-jumped, plunging down the stone steps outside. And ran along the forest lane.

He neared Farron Castle as the light failed, the stuccoed battlements silhouetted against a washed-out sky. Hurrying through the wet rhododendrons and across the Chinese Bridge, he was breathless; he hung his head and was dizzied by the scudding water glimpsed through the slats. His toe caught on an iron nail head and he fell, banging his weak shoulder painfully and streaking his clothes with green slime from the timbers. He picked himself up, shaking his head, trying to toss out the alcohol. The dusk was cold and there was no one about save a car picking up nurses as the shift changed. Jacky closed in, unsteady, would-be-furtive, blundering. To the south of the hideous main building stood the Nissen huts: workshop, patient's mess, clinics. And a guardroom, with a cluster of military vehicles parked untidily nearby.

He edged closer. Through the window of the guardroom, he glimpsed uniforms, steaming mugs, cigarettes, men laughing.

A diesel fired; the guard barely paused from laughing when a truck bellowed and raced past their window in some ridiculously low gear that shrieked. The truck swayed, swerved and charged at an oncoming Morris, the night-sister blaring her horn furiously till she veered off onto the grass, bumping to a stop as the truck careered past.

Through the open door of the office, Sara Meakin saw the thin back of Matron rigid with anger as she spat at the telephone:

'Flying to Poland? So? He is no longer my responsibility.'

While, at the airfield, a young duty officer nodded, 'Of course, Matron'. Next door, a man lurched in circles bellowing incomprehensibly in tearful Polish, kicking at the furniture, the man they'd pulled from the cockpit of an Anson that maybe he'd not seen had both motors out, and where he'd sat pounding at the control panel weeping and shouting *Warsaw! Warsaw!* till his fist bled.

◆◆◆

This morning, German High Command announced that the last units of the Polish Home Army in Warsaw have surrendered, and that all resistance is at an end.

◆◆◆

December: thick snow, and freezing. Trucks and cars had compacted the snow to ice. Salted sand had been shovelled onto the castle steps and the wooden ramp. Here, the dark bulk of a heavy man, a drinking man, reached the door where, in gross defiance of blackout regulations, a candle hung in a jar over a handwritten sign: *Welcome!*

He wrenched at the door handle.

Hogmanay. In the dining hall, at a broad horseshoe of tables sat Poles and doctors, wives of British personnel, local noises, RAF and WRAF and the nurses, Matron with a sprig of mistletoe in her cap, Sara Meakin with a twist of golden tinsel held with hairclips round her collar. There had been an effort at cheery decor: the stags wore paper chains on their antlers, with Union Jacks and Polish flags and *Happy New Year* banners. Glenfarron girls served dinner; everyone had a beer. But the jollity was forced, the British faces apprehensive, the Polish dark and strained.

Jacky Whisky sat with Vladislaw, scowling as plates of something grey were placed in front of them.

'What's this?' said Jacky.

'It's called haggis, Sir.'

'What's in it?'

'Anybody's guess, Sir.'

The door banged open; a few heads turned. Gordon stood grim in his long coat and his boots dropping snow. Sara stepped toward her husband.

'Come to join us?'

'I'm not invited.'

'You were, Gordon, but you said…'

'No room, is there.'

'We can find you a place.'

'But am I welcome?'

This was too loud. Jacky Whisky watched unmoving; Vladislaw watched Jacky. Sara bit her lip.

'No welcome for me, then.' Gordon nodded, his voice nasty.

Sara said:

'I'll be home by eleven. Ma and Da are expecting us, Charlie's there, why don't you go…'

'Why don't you go to hell?'

'Gordon, please,' she whispered.

'I came to say I'll go where I bloody like.'

'Ma's made your tea,' she protested, 'you can't…'

'Don't tell me what I can do!' he snapped, taking her tinselled collar in his powerful fingers.

Jacky pushed back his chair, took five quick paces and bowed:

'Sir, this is a festivity.'

The big gamekeeper regarded him, looking pointedly at the left hand lifeless in Jacky's pocket.

'Which hand are you going to hit me with, Captain?'

Now half the hall was listening. The voices stopped, only a clatter of plates and cutlery as the girls bustled and looked away. Jacky felt his friends shrinking, his countrymen who had once broken the Red Army on the Vistula, who had defied Hitler, now cowed by a winter drunk.

An English Wing Commander exchanged looks with Matron, discreetly checking that his officers were ready to move and watching for his instruction. Lieutenant Baird was rising to his feet.

Gordon sighed, whistling through his teeth.

'Och, fuck it.'

He released Sara, in the process dislodging her tinsel which he tossed idly in Jacky's face.

'Happy Hogmanay.'

And he departed, leaving a trail of frost.

'Okay, okay,' Jacky Whisky nodded. He strode back to Vladislaw.

'We're on,' he commanded.

A minute later, as the debris of Utility Haggis and dried egg trifle was swept away, they stood in the middle of the floor, a double-act with a lewd Polish ditty:

The mountain boys, they planted their oats
From one end of town to the other,
Oh yes!

The room brightened, the pinched pallid faces filled out with laughs of gratitude. Before the song was ended, they were shouting: *More*! *More*! *Encore*!

'Another, please, absolutely!' cried Lieutenant Baird

'We'll do *Four & Twenty Virgins*,' Jacky hissed.

'Sir, we can't, it's filthy!'

'Here goes.'

Shoulder to shoulder they paused. An expectant hush. Vladislaw looked shifty, Jacky looked mischief:

Four and twenty virgins
Came in from old Gdansk...

On they rollicked in gutter-Polish; the crowd of airmen sniggered and turned puce, then they all joined in. As the sordid refrain roared about the room, their British guests looked ever so pleased.

The Wing Commander waggled an eyebrow at the Consultant Surgeon:

'Spirit in the face of adversity, Doctor?'

'Admirable. What say, Matron?'

'Very jolly,' she returned, dour as death, deeply suspicious. She scanned this gang of cripples shrieking with laughter in a foreign tongue while the locals clapped along happily. She saw Lieutenant Baird beaming at Captain Wysierkierski, and Nurse Meakin gazing at the Captain...

The Lieutenant asked his neighbour, 'How do you say Happy New Year in Polish?' The man nodded seriously, and told him. Baird struggled to his feet, raising his beer.

'Friends,' he stammered in Polish, 'I fancy a bit of slap and tickle!'

'Hurrah!' they yelled. 'Hurrah for the Lieutenant. More!'

'Go on, Sir,' Vladislaw prompted Jacky, prodding him and stepping aside, and everyone shushed as Jacky sang:

Over there beside the black water
Sits a young Cossack on his horse,

> *Saying his sad farewell to his girl,*
> *Saying his farewell to the Ukraine.*

Now all the company was nodding mournfully.

> *Hey, hey, hey there, falcon!*
> *Leave the mountain, forests and plain.*
> *Ring, ring, ring the bell,*
> *My little skylark of the Ukraine.*

He ended, and there was a silence in which Sara Meakin and Jacky Whisky gazed at each other, though their eyes didn't meet.

He grabbed a glass from the table, shouting for attention.

'Now my friends! Honoured guests! A toast. We drink to Poland.'

Every eye on him, every hand reaching for a glass, *Here, here…*

Jacky continued:

'Not Mr Stalin's Poland.'

('Oh dear,' the Wing Commander murmured.)

'Not Mr Churchill's Poland.'

Jacky looked straight at the Wing Commander, raising his glass.

'Our Poland. Yes, Sir? Our homeland, free. Free Poland.'

The Wing Commander stood, lifting his drink.

'Poland.'

'*Poland!*' they roared.

Music, thank Heaven; Lieutenant Baird scurried to supervise the pushing aside of tables. Then the fiddle, accordion and drummer drew a military-hobble and a none-too-quickstep from the walking wounded.

The fiddler called:

'A Pride of Erin waltz.'

Sara Meakin stepped up to Captain Wysierkierski. Jacky sensed her coming and faced her, and she took his hand.

'Time I taught you to dance, Jacky Whisky.'

Was it really a Pride of Erin? That was what Vladislaw told Charlie long afterwards, though how would an old Polish sausage maker know one Gaelic waltz from another? Somehow, the name lodged in Vladislaw's mind, and he recalled it as the most graceful of waltzes: the couple move together and apart, taking two hands, mirroring one another, turning and returning.

Vladislaw was entranced: a tune that sang to him, and Sara dancing around a bemused Jacky Whisky. Her steps were gently elegant, he striving to keep time as she passed about him, guiding and prompting, her eyes joyous, her delight defying the time and place, quite forgetting the room.

The village girls, clearing the tables, saw and exchanged looks. The mood spread like a scent. A nurse collared another Polish flyer:

'Rightiho, Radek, on yer feet. S'rude to refuse.'

'I'm wounded...'

'Aye, an' I've seen your wound at close quarters. Stand up.'

In a moment, a dozen pairs were dancing after a fashion, even if some had a crutch to cope with. The Consultant Surgeon coughed:

'Ahem ... Matron?'

She simpered: 'It's been a while.' But she was game.

Vladislaw, led to the dance by a dumpy maid, clumped about on his wooden leg. He beamed all around the floor, and saw Jacky Whisky leave the hall. Then, a few moments later, Sara Meakin following.

◆◆◆

From Torbrechan woods, through a fringe of beech and ash, they glimpsed her parent's farm hunkered down in the snow, moonlit.

'Your family expect you,' Jacky Whisky told her.

'They'll wait awhile,' she replied.

They stood in their heavy coats at the wood's edge. The forest was sombre but, to their left, the fields shone, and drifts had formed against the fence. The cloud cover was gone and the small wind made them shiver. From the great arch of Jacky's barn, a compact shape with a white face hurtled above them, and out across the field. Jacky began to sing:

Hey, hey, hey there, falcon.

She reached for his hand and squeezed it tight.

'It's an owl,' she said.

'Oh, thank you, silly me,' he replied.

'Now,' she said, 'we've to dance again.'

Or ride perhaps, as he'd said the peasant women ride, with the doors of the iron stove ajar and the fire furious, projecting across the ceiling boards fantastical shadows of Sara Dulce riding as she'd not done in a long while, her breast sheened, her breath sharp and snatched and her thighs gripping hard, and beneath her the song turning around in Jacky Whisky's head:

Ring, ring, ring the bell,
My little skylark of the Ukraine.

◆◆◆

Wrenching open a drawer, Gordon plunged his hands in among Sara's clothes, searching for something, anything, he had no idea what but there would be something.

Only blouses, slips and woollens.

He sat on the bed, near to tears. The room was bitterly cold; the day outside was white.

He went to the linen cupboard and dragged a sheet out by one corner; he stared at it, then with an angry jerk flung it across the room so that it billowed like a loose sail, catching the snow light.

This flash of white, Charlie saw. Climbing the stairs, carrying his little glider and humming engines to himself, the child stopped, frightened. Through the door, he saw Gordon surrounded by a chaos of bed linen, all across the room. He had something in his hand, he had found something, buried under the linen. It was a painted wooden crest saying:

Vive la Pologne

Gordon was studying this with the puzzled disbelief of a man reading his own death certificate. Charlie fled, taking with him the sight of that room filled with terrible, blowing whiteness.

Gordon did not notice the boy. Downstairs, the fire door of the kitchen range opened with a gritty scrape; Gordon shoved the crest inside and watched as the paint caught. Then he slammed the door shut and looked round. Over the door, a 12-bore and a game rifle rested on the rack.

◆◆◆

Jacky Whisky stopped in the doorway, surveying the ward. Nurses worked from bed to bed with dressings and white enamel bowls.

'Hey, how's the farm worker, Sir?'

Vladislaw pushed the meal trolley with wobbling wheels.

'You're busy,' observed Jacky.

'Not much longer, Sir. It's nearly over.'

'What is?'

'The war, Sir.'

'Yes. Yes, so I hear. Listen Vladislaw, I need something really tasty, a pie maybe, can you do a pie? Hare? Duck, how about duck?'

Vladislaw peered at his idol, the matchless fighter pilot.

'It's for friends, Vladislaw. I need to have this.'

◆◆◆

Standing by the bed in a cold greeny dusk, Sara Dulce regarded the chest of drawers, feeling the first touch of fear. A corner of moss-green wool protruded from the second drawer, which had been shoved shut carelessly.

She looked about. The door of the linen press was slightly ajar. She crossed the room making her footfall on the boards as quiet as possible, for Gordon was in the kitchen below. Sara opened the linen cupboard – and froze in fright.

It was a shambles, sheets bundled back inside with no pretence.

Gordon was shouting for his meal.

◆◆◆

Jacky passed out through the kitchen door, wearing his long coat with the collar up. He set off across the icy yard, but stopped midway.

The farm truck with toad eyes had appeared in the driveway, creeping towards him on the ice. Entering the yard, it slowed to a cautious stop. The door opened; Sara stepped down wearing her uniform under a blue cloak. He saw that she was pale and nervous and he almost spoke, but she fixed a look of warning on Jacky as she walked straight by him with a nod.

'Captain,' she said, unsmiling.

She went in by the side door of the hospital.

Jacky looked towards the truck. From the cab, her husband studied him.

◆◆◆

'I don't know what she's at.'

Gordon shook his drunken head, his clothes hanging off him like the rigging of a defeated man-o'-war. Petunia lolled fleshily on the eiderdown, slightly bored, tugging at his shirt tails.

'You know fine what I'm at,' she purred.

He wasn't listening to her.

'What she's thinking of?' he said. 'I just can't imagine.'

That's just it, thought Petunia; he can't see it. He hears talk of 'imagination'; he tries imagining but nothing comes. The frustration is making him nasty. Well, at least she could do something about frustration.

She pulled at Gordon's belt.

'Come on, help a girl.'

'Sent us more sausages,' growled Gordon. 'I'd not have them in the house. Gave 'em to the dogs.'

Petunia was shocked: 'You did what?'

'Wouldn't have them in the house,' he repeated.

'Well, when the duck pie comes, you just pass it over.'

'What pie?'

'Polish duck pie. Vlad told me. Going to make you all a duck pie.'

Gordon's eyes narrowed, and he paid attention.

'Where's he thinking to get ducks?'

◆◆◆

Turrets, like party hats, topped the house they stared at. It had been built as a miniature French chateau but named *Mandalay* by a Victorian teak merchant whimsical with his money and careless of congruity. Through the pines at night it appeared like a storybook silhouette. In the war years, it was the home of a retired Inverness banker.

That night, the wind blew a thin veil of snow cloud over the stars. The chill was piercing, the forest dead, and the lochan iced over hard.

There was a wooden duck house on the shore. From within

came scratchy rustlings, the ducks unable to sleep for cold, and jittery, sensing someone creeping about outside.

A hand reached for the door bolt: it was iced solid. More vigorous attempts produced only agitated clucks.

'It's frozen!' hissed Vladislaw.

'Mind out.'

Jacky motioned him aside, stood directly in front of the door and pissed on the fastening.

Vladislaw nodded approvingly.

There was, however, in the avenue of firs sixty or seventy yards back from the water's edge, the barrel of a shotgun that gleamed softly, and a gloved thumb waiting on the safety catch.

Jacky freed the bolt. He glanced round at the turrets of the house, then jerked the door open with a crack of ice.

'Go on!'

Vladislaw climbed inside and was met by outraged hissing, clattering and quacks. At the door, Jacky held out a sack into which Vladislaw bundled a duck with a limp neck and kicking feet.

'One more, Sir?'

'No more.'

'For the pot, Sir.'

'Quickly!'

It was done.

'Let's go.'

They stumbled away down the rutted drive, a light snowfall beginning. Between them swung the bulging sack, they were moving quite fast – until the shotgun crashed out twice.

'Ahh! Fuck, fuck ahhh! Shit!'

Vladislaw lay on the snow twisting in pain, clutching at his thigh. As Jacky knelt at his side, he saw a bulky figure lope away, unhurried.

He searched frantically for Vladislaw's wound.

'Where'd he get you? Christ, where'd the bastard get you?'

'I'll kill him, I'll kill him!'

'Later, Vladislaw. It's your leg, he's got your leg, let me see... Jesus!'

Vladislaw's leg had come off in Jacky's hand. Horrified, both men stared at it.

'Vladislaw,' said Jacky, 'he's shot your wooden leg.'

'Bastard! What'd he do that for?'

'Scaring us, my friend,' said Jacky Whisky, peering down at his hands. There was plenty of blood.

'Fine, well, I'm scared,' moaned Vladislaw, 'and hellish cold, Sir.'

His voice was trembling, was thinner.

'Wait a moment,' said Jacky, and he set off back towards the duck house.

'Sir!' wailed Vladislaw.

'Wait!'

There was a plank of wood on the ground, a passable crutch.

'Here goes,' said Jacky.

'Am I bleeding?'

'Yes. Come on, will you.'

'I can't do it, Sir…'

'Here we go.'

He hauled Vladislaw upright, his arm about his friend's waist, tucked the timber under his arm and dragged him away hopping, stumbling and whimpering down the snowy track. Behind them lay two dead ducks tossed aside for the foxes, and Vladislaw's wooden leg in the ditch.

◆◆◆

'Easy now.'

The doctor had been dragged out of bed; he was crumpled, his breath was rank and his hair stuck to his scalp. He pushed into Vladislaw's arm a large needle to which he attached a length of red rubber tubing. Beside him, a glass bottle in a cage swung knocking on a steel pole. The doctor thrust a second needle through the rubber bung and opened taps, till a foaming fluid washed down into Vladislaw.

He lay on his back on a steel stretcher. The room was white tiled and brightly lit, crowded with glass-topped trolleys, spirit-sterilisers and shelves laden with brown bottles of disinfectant, salves and emetics. Vladislaw saw none of this; he was moaning and barely conscious. The doctor glanced across to where Sara Meakin worked on the wounds. The old amputated stump she had freed of shredded fabric, covering it with a large gauze dressing that was already red. Now she was cutting cloth from the other knee.

'Some damage here, Sir.'

Jacky was leaning in the doorway, filthy and wet.

'You sure you're all right, Captain?' asked the doctor.

Jacky nodded.

The doctor wondered, 'Who'd want to shoot our old cooky?'

'A gamekeeper,' Jacky told him, 'aiming at me.'

Sara's hand wavered. She raised her eyes to Jacky, but he had nothing more to say, and left the room.

◆◆◆

For a brief hour at daybreak, they clung to each other on the narrow cot in his bothy, the fire sinking, Sara's head on his chest. She was so still that he was not sure if she was sleeping. His head propped on a bolster, he gazed through the window in the gable-end.

If she says, 'I don't love you,'
The cavalry are recruiting, I'll sign up.
They'll give me a flask filled with spirits
So that I won't long for my girl.

Outside, the snow fell steadily.

◆◆◆

She slithered along the street, heading for the post office.

Across the way, in the Farron Hotel, men drank together while their shoes puddled the linoleum. Near the fire, Gordon talked shop with the forestry foreman and the wartime rump of estate staff. At a corner table, a group of Poles were getting methodically drunk. By the bar, a Flight Lieutenant and a Pilot Officer from RAF Bomber Command tried to unwind after a long tour of duty, their effort undermined by the Poles' tense murmuring.

'Not happy chappies,' observed the Flight Lieutenant.

A man clattered his crutch and got up; it was the Artist, creator of lubricious murals, a fop gone to seed. He began loading empty glasses onto a tin tray. Disaster threatened; the barmaid swooped.

'I'll take those, then.'

'No!' he snapped at her. 'I am a gentleman. Go.'

He shooed her out of his way, picked up the tray and, teetering on his crutch, made for the bar. He pointed to each glass in turn.

'There: fill, fill, fill. I pay, because I am honourable.'

The barmaid hesitated.

'Fill!' commanded the Artist.

The barmaid pumped; for a moment the rush of beer was the only sound.

'Your Mr Churchill,' the Artist informed the Flight Lieutenant, 'is not so very honourable. Mr Churchill has given Poland to Mr Stalin. Poland was not his to give.'

The RAF men peered into their ale.

'Can't comment on that, my friend,' said the Flight Lieutenant.

The Artist's eye glittered.

'We fought, yes? Poland has fought.'

'No question,' the Pilot Officer agreed.

'Battle of Britain,' the Artist demanded, 'top score, which squadron?'

'303, I believe,' replied the Pilot Officer.

The Artist nodded, '303 Squadron, Polish Air Force.'

From his place by the fire, Gordon glimpsed above the frosted glass his wife returning from the post.

The Artist continued to interrogate the two pilots.

'Why,' he said, 'did we shoot Germans? We should have shot Mr Churchill, who gave away our country.'

The Flight Lieutenant breathed, 'Take it easy, chum.'

'He betrayed us,' insisted the Artist. 'A stinking traitor.'

'That's enough now,' the barmaid began, but the Artist blundered on:

'I think I am going to employ a British servant, so I can call him a damn traitor every day to his face.'

A forestry worker placed his beer glass carefully on the narrow mantelpiece, crossed the room, turned the Artist by one shoulder and, equally carefully, drove a fist into his face. The Artist collapsed across a table of drinks.

Slowly, all the Poles stood up. The Artist struggled to lift his face from the floor as blood streamed from his broken mouth and a gash on his forehead. One of his compatriots crouched and dabbed with a handkerchief. The forester returned to the fireside where Gordon handed him his glass of beer, nodding to him with a curious, cold elation.

The door flew open. Sara went straight to the Artist, crying:

'What in God's name is happening?'

'Leave it alone,' someone behind her said.

'But what happened?'

'He asked for it.'

She turned on them.

'He asked for a safe refuge, not to be hit in the face. This is a wounded man!'

'Whose side are you on, then?'

'Side? These are our allies!'

Somebody sniggered.

'Gordon!' she cried.

Gordon put down his drink and stepped across the shambles of broken glass and tumbled chairs, one of which he set upright. He stooped, and with easy strength hoiked up the Artist like a sack of nothing much and plonked him onto the chair.

'Tuck him up in bed, Sara, why don't you.'

He left her and went out into the snow, and everyone in the room stared at Sara.

◆◆◆

A thick, milky darkness, the moon struggling to make an entrance. By this poor light, Jacky Whisky found his way to the Chinese Bridge and crossed into the castle park.

In the patients' mess hut there were voices raised.

'If we object, if we make trouble, they'll throw us out.'

'They might anyway.'

'So? Don't stand for it.'

Jacky, entering, saw a visitor who held up both hands for calm.

'Just a minute...'

'This is crazy!' spat a man with a liverish face. 'I have to stay here, I have nowhere else to go, damn you.'

'Listen to me...' the newcomer began.

'You think I don't want to go home? You think I have no pride? But you start fighting the British and we lose every damn thing.'

The visitor almost laughed.

'Please, let me... '

'No, I want nothing to do with this.'

He marched to the door. They turned to see him go – and the

visitor smiled:

'Jacek!'

'Hello, Stan.'

A face once so charming, thought Jacky. And now haggard, but full of resolution.

'Please, let me finish,' Stan repeated. 'The British say that our armed forces are now illegal. *(Cries of protest, which he stilled.)* Yes, the heroes of Westerplatz, and the dauntless Air Force and the glorious Cavalry. Mr Churchill says we're illegal because we do not serve the new government in Poland – that's to say, Stalin's bumboys. *(Obscenities.)* In Glasgow, I have heard shipyard conveners telling union men that we are potential traitors *(bitter oaths and groans)* because we oppose the lawful and popular demand for Russian Socialism. *(Incredulity, contempt.)* The Glasgow men say we will take their jobs. They even say *(a portentous lift in Stan's voice)* that we might take their women *(followed by an ironic smirk)*. A bit slow there. *(Laughter.)* The British Socialists say we must have no pay, no pensions, nothing. We, who have lost everything else. *(He surveyed the intent faces.)* Some of our people have been beaten. It's time to organise, friends.'

Around the room, his listeners nodded soberly.

◆◆◆

'That's where my boy is?'

'That's it.'

They stood in the black, frozen lane just fifty yards from Bellcraig cottage. A lamp burned in the kitchen, but the shadows were upstairs, lurching and swaying across the curtains.

'Are they good to him?' Stan whispered, loneliness catching in his throat.

'No problem. Take it easy, heh?'

'You watch out for my boy?'

'Sure.'

'I have to disappear now, there's a difficulty with the police. Come and see us in Glasgow.'

'Sure.'

They embraced clumsily in their thick coats, scuffling round on the snow in the lane, all at sea in sentiment.

'What happened to our British friends?'

'No friends now, enemies and lovers only. See you, Jacek.'

They cuffed each other on the shoulder, and Stan slunk off into the darkness. Jacky stood a moment longer, but it was cold, and he headed for his bothy.

◆◆◆

There was in Glenfarron in those days a seed-and-feed merchant's office. It was a large, gloomy room lined with dark tongue-and-groove, with enamel lampshades and traders' calendars, box files, ledgers and chits on spikes.

Here, a gathering of farmers, estate managers and the older forestry men left behind by conscription were being stirred up by Mr Livingstone Robertson, Glenfarron's NFU convener. He stood before them ruddy-faced in a tweed jacket with elbow patches, the sinews taut in his impassioned throat.

'So, when the lads come home, they get their jobs, their livelihoods back, am I right? *(Aye!)* Their cottages. *(Aye!)* It turns my stomach to see so-called Allies cashing in. *(That's right.)* I won't have them at Parkneuk. *(Nae chance!)* I say to you farmers, factors, gentlemen: whoever tells you to take 'em on – Czechs, Poles, Colonials, any of 'em – I say to you, don't stand for it! You've the full support of the NFU and our brothers in Congress.' *(That's right!)*

The men were noisy in agreement. Leaning against the iron safe, Gordon Meakin was liking this talk. His satisfaction caught the eye of Livingstone Robertson. The convenor looked straight at Gordon; his voice of a sudden dropped an octave, became soft and darkly personal:

'They're just cuckoos in our nest. I say, chuck 'em out.'

And every face in the room turned on Gordon, who had his pride.

◆◆◆

'It's not their fault.'

Sunday lunchtime at Torbrechan, and Sara persuading herself, lecturing herself, pacing the woodshed while Jacky split more logs in his angry one-handed way.

'They're just farm boys,' she went on, 'but they left to fight willingly…'

'Poles have to be pushed, yes?'

Cracckkk!

'I didn't say that.'

'So, they come home, they get my job.'

'Nobody's mentioned your job.'

'My friend's job.'

Cracckkk!

In the kitchen, Gordon sliced a loaf as deftly as Jacky did logs, but quieter, thinking.

Charlie was there, eyeing the buttered bread.

'Go tell your Nan,' said Gordon, 'dinner's about ready.'

As the child trotted away down the corridor, Gordon glanced out of the window, then crossed the kitchen to the narrow back stairs, and slipped up to the landing. He entered the front bedroom, an old couple's room of bulging counterpanes and mahogany furniture: wash-stand, tallboy, and a chest of drawers on which sat a rosewood jewel box.

Cracckkk!

'Anyhow, they've a right,' Sara persisted, crouching again for the logs, 'to come home.'

'Yes, we Poles should like that.'

'You *can* go,' she murmured miserably.

'To be shot by Mr Stalin? Thank you, Scotland. Legend is right: Pontius Pilate, born right here. Shit!'

The head had flown off the axe, wobbling past Sara to thud off the wooden wall.

'Let's stop this,' she breathed. 'I won't fight with you.'

He lowered the axe handle, contrite.

'For a little while,' he said, 'you have made this our home. It is all we have.'

She took his hand, and clung to it tightly. He saw that she was trying not to cry. She slipped her arms around him, coming close up, and he touched the nut brown hair.

'Oh Sara, Miss Sara ... wait, though.'

He was frowning. There was a livid bruise on her neck.

'What is this?'

'Nothing...' She squirmed free, trying to cover it. But he searched again, strong and insistent.

'What has happened? He did this?'

'Please, forget it.'

She twisted away. Jacky picked up the axe handle with no thought of logs.

'I will settle with that shit.'

He glared at the fading daylight as though he would bludgeon the entire winter. But she grabbed him by both arms, crying:

'You stop that nonsense!'

She was furious with him.

'You think I need more fighting? We've been brought misery by proud fighting men. I'll not love that in you, I tell you, I'll not love that!'

Jacky Whisky stood redundant, with nothing to strike at.

'So what can I do?'

Again, he lowered the axe haft.

There was a call from outside, Sara's father.

'Sara? Jacky, lad? It's on the table.'

Jacky and George came easing Aileen Dulce through to the kitchen, the three of them moving like an articulated crab in the passage, knocking elbows and shoulders on the cream glossed doorway.

'All right now? Here's the step.'

'What a bother I am…'

She huffed and wobbled on her bulbous legs while everyone talked at once, and Sara and Gordon backed round the table to let her pass. At last she was settled in the stout captain's chair at table's head.

'Thank you, Jacky dear.'

The business had diverted Jacky from cracking Gordon's skull. Sara served a thick pea soup, and they were settling to eat.

Gordon, still on his feet, kept glancing at Jacky.

'I've those feed prices for you, George,' he said to Sara's father. Gordon closed the door, revealing the coats on pegs.

'You'll find they're a better buy than Robertson's. Where's my coat?'

He thrust out a hand, dived into a pocket, then proclaimed his mistake.

'Ah no, that'll be Jacky's.'

He stirred his hand in the pocket. There was a muffled clinking.

'Collecting pebbles, Jacky?' Gordon smiled. 'What you got in here?'

He pulled out a string of pearls.

'Well, now,' he frowned. 'Hit the jackpot, have you?'

He peered narrowly at the pearls.

'What is that?' enquired Jacky.

'I'm asking you.'

'Jacky?' said Sara, uncertain.

'I do not know what this is,' said Jacky.

'This is pearls, laddy,' Gordon told him. 'Question is...'

'Pearls?' said George Dulce, bemused.

'Aye, pearls. Question is, George, how'd he come by them?'

Sara faced Jacky directly.

'What's this about?'

But he shook his head: 'I don't know about this.'

'Let me see those,' requested the old farmer. Gordon lowered the pearls into George's hand while addressing Jacky Whisky.

'In your pocket, pal.'

'They are not mine.'

'That's rather what I thought.'

'Those are Aileen's,' murmured George. 'Aileen, these are yours.'

'What's going on?' Sara's voice was brittle now.

'How can they be mine?' puffed the old lady in the captain's chair.

Her husband demanded:

'Why were they in your coat, Jacky?'

'That,' nodded Gordon, 'is what we'd all like to know.'

Sara was frightened.

'Jacky, what is this?'

'I don't know.'

'Well, I think I know,' said Gordon inexorably. 'I think I know light fingers when I meet them.'

'Stealing?' The old lady stared about the room bewildered, while her husband shook his head.

'Oh, Jacky.'

'I have never seen these before!'

'Jumped into your pocket, did they? For warmth?'

Her face pale, her voice coldly steady, Sara asked it again:

'How did they get into your pocket, Jacky?'

'You think I have taken these?'

'I'm asking, how did they get there?'

They were all staring at him.

'Someone has put them there.'

Gordon scoffed. George said:

'Steady, Jacky lad. Perhaps you should step outside while we see about this.'

So Jacky Whisky went out, and Gordon didn't miss the opportunity to push him through the door. Stumbling on the gravel, Jacky rounded on him.

'I have nothing to do with this. You are crazy!'

Gordon, in the doorway, sneered and folded his arms in satisfaction.

But in the kitchen, the debate was not going to plan.

'I'm not saying I know what happened…'

'Da, you do not think, honestly…'

'I can't think ill of Jacky.'

'That's fine, Aileen, but I'll not see this family hurt.' George Dulce sighed. 'Gordon's your husband, Sara.'

'Da, you believe this nonsense?'

'Which nonsense is that?' demanded Gordon from the doorway, triumphant. Yet they would not look at him.

'Which nonsense?' he insisted. 'Stealing?'

An awkward silence. Aileen Dulce began quietly:

'Gordon, dear, I think there's some mistake.'

'I'll say!'

'I don't think there was anything stolen, exactly.'

'What?'

'I'd just like them put back,' the old lady told him, 'and all this forgotten.'

Her husband nodded. Gordon's look flickered about the room, nervous.

'You don't believe what you saw? What I found? You believe that Pole, but not me?'

'Now, Gordon,' said George. 'Least said, you know.'

For an instant, Sara studied her husband. Then she ran to the door.

Gordon snapped, 'Sara!'

She was already outside.

There was no one in the yard. She saw Jacky hurrying along the edge of the field in the direction of the forest and his bothy.

'Jacky? Jacky!'

She heard a foot on the step behind her. Gordon said nothing, but his face was weak with pleading. She regarded him with open contempt – and the pleading vanished.

◆◆◆

In the bothy above the barn, Jacky Whisky in a rage stuffed his few possessions into a kitbag. He was livid, mad with the injustice, it made him boil in a way that was strangely worse than war: he had never been angry with Hitler; that was a matter of cold hate and steely revenge. But this was an outrage.

His service clothes, a book or two, that little bag of Polish soil: in they went. He seized the kitbag and stamped outside, slamming the door but taking no notice when it banged open behind him, flailing in the wind.

He appeared at the top of the stone steps. Looking west, he saw Torbrechan farm and a large figure standing out in the yard, the posture strangely diffident even from this distance.

Jacky Whisky clattered down the steps and hurried away along the forest edge.

◆◆◆

'Cat got yer tongue?'

She did not reply. She was perched on the edge of the bed, quiet but not cowed, head up and staring at the back of the door. Gordon paced about the room that seemed to him too small for this betrayal.

'I'm saying, if I see him near you again, I'll kick his face in.'

He came very close to his wife, leaned forward and breathed at her:

'A thief's bad enough, but if I thought anyone was laying hands on my wife, I'd kill him. Say something, will ye?'

She could hear the tinge of desperation, and she grew defiant.

'No point, Gordon. I've nothing to say that you'd understand.'

'Has he touched you? If he's so much as touched you, I'll cut his hands off.'

'Then you'd best cut mine off first,' she retorted.

He peered at her, unwilling to believe.

'You?' He grew pale, he was shaking. 'You'll regret…'

'I'm going out,' she announced.

She headed for the stairs but he followed her, grabbing at her wrist to spin her round. As she cried out in fright, Gordon pushed her fingers into the door jamb and pulled it shut on them. She screamed, falling to the floor at the stair's head.

That scream, ripping out of the cottage, reached Charlie. The little boy was in the yard outside, in the winter dusk, throwing his glider which nose-dived into the gravel. He squatted, staring fixedly at the plane like some who believes that pain can be thwarted by tightening every muscle. He put his hands over his ears and began humming a loud motor note. Through the bedroom window above him there came, from somewhere deep in his home, a cry that thickened into a deep sobbing.

He pressed his hands tighter over his ears and hummed louder.

◆◆◆

Dusk at Petunia's cottage also.

Jacky Whisky with his kitbag, seeking a refuge, tramped up her slippery, slushy lane. His pace flagged; he was weary and stiff. Before he could see the house, he heard shouting. He moved circumspectly, coming forward between two sycamores.

There was Petunia, fists clenched, lips curled, glaring and cursing two village men who stabbed at the girl with accusing fingers.

'Shaggin' anyone ... Fuckin' filth ... Bloody hypocrites, you needn't come back ...'

While these confronted Petunia at the door, two more were busy with a pot of black paint and broad brushes with which they daubed the harling of the gable-end:

POLES FUCK OFF

The paint dribbled down the whitewash, as Jacky slipped away.

◆◆◆

In the yard at Farron Castle, along the carriage sweep, rolling in and out of the gates went growling green trucks, much larger than before, and each with a blazon of a single large white star.

In the ward Vladislaw lay asleep. He was the only patient.

'How is he?' asked Jacky, pausing in the doorway. The Artist rocked upon his crutch and shrugged:

'He'll do. Our Vladislaw is as tough as the mutton he cooks.'

There came a clack of heels behind them.

'Excuse me, Captain.'

Matron led two male orderlies pushing a flat trolley. They began to strip every bed except Vladislaw's, and to fold and stack the blankets and linen, trundling everything outside.

'Closing down,' remarked the Artist. 'Vladislaw is to be transferred to the City Infirmary.'

'Closing? Why?' breathed Jacky.

'It seems, Captain,' called Matron, rather shrill, 'that we've outlived our usefulness.'

'What she means,' remarked the Artist, 'is that there is not much war left, and no Polish Air Force to speak of, so what's the point of a Polish Air Force Hospital? Hence the Yanks in the yard; they're taking over.'

The Artist watched Matron disappear down the passageway.

'There'll just be a shrinking handful of us convalescents,' he continued. 'The Yanks bring their own nurses, their Harley motorcycles, everything. Every room is to be repainted, even my mural. I dare say Petunia and Biddy will be welcoming a wealthier clientele.'

He sighed the unmistakable sigh of regret.

'I myself once paid visits to that address – but nothing came of it.'

Jacky said, 'I thought I could sleep here, in the attics maybe.'

'Not for long. They'd arrest you.'

'Then I must go back to the bothy,' Jacky said, deflated.

'That is what we have come to, Captain. Lie low.'

'Listen to me,' said Jacky, urgently. 'You tell Sara.'

Now the Artist raised an ironic brow.

'You wish me to tell her of Poland's plight?'

'Tell her where I am,' Jacky snapped, 'when she comes to work, damn you!'

The Artist frowned.

'I am so sorry, Karol. I need your help. Oh God, Karol.'

◆◆◆

Light snowfall among the trees: in the middle distance, Torbrechan farm in monochrome, a silver-grey roof on a black house surrounded by snow-heavy trees. Only in the ploughed fields was there any colour, the rich loam striped with snow.

A figure hurried along the forest track, splashing to the barn and climbing the bothy steps. A click of the iron snick; a moment later, a face peered out across the bitter fields.

Meanwhile, behind the frosted glass of the Farron Hotel, Gordon and his cronies were by the fire and deep into afternoon pints, elbows on a damp table. Across the room, there was Lieutenant Gideon Baird sitting alone with a glass that grew warm in his grip, for he was moping, contemplating his future as Liaison between His Britannic Majesty's Armed Forces and those of Poland, now that the latter were to be disbanded.

Round the corner of the bar, deep in shadow lurked Petunia and her friend Biddy. They did not look happy, lighting and stubbing and lighting fag after fag. The men by the fire eyed the women, and smirked at sad Lieutenant Gideon.

'Christ,' breathed Petunia. 'What a fan club.'

Biddy nudged her, indicating the window.

'Another friend of yours: the paintbrush cavalier.'

The Artist stood outside, trying to survey the bar without being seen by the men. Petunia grimaced.

'The boy with the limp brush – like stuffing a caterpillar into a keyhole. I've had enough, I tell you. I'm set to flit to Glasgow.'

'I'd join you,' sighed Biddy, 'only Ma would make me look after the twins.'

Petunia supped her dregs and stood up.

'Right, that's me. Be seeing you.'

She marched out past Gideon Baird without looking at him.

Emerging from the hotel door, Petunia glanced along the street. A few villagers, shapeless in thick clothes, stomped about in the snow. A coal lorry rolled past her, its exhaust as black as its load. She was about to move when she heard a tapping on the corner bricks just by her knee; she peeked down and saw the tip of a crutch waving feebly.

'For pity's sake,' she muttered, stepping to the corner and facing him with her hands on her all-accommodating hips. 'Yes?'

'I came to your house.'

'For what, a repeat performance?'

'I beg of you...'

'We're off limits to you, pal.'

'Please! I only ask you, take a message.'

'Take yer own bloody message.'

'I cannot.'

It was a hiss, a nervous whisper. The Artist looked round anxiously. He backed behind the brick corner of the pub, reaching out and tucking a slip of paper between her fingers, saying:

'Please, go to her house. I am afraid.'

Petunia studied him.

'Catch her at the hospital,' she said.

'No, not today. I beg you, it is urgent.'

His breath smells foul, she thought.

'Why the hell should I?'

'It is to a woman in need.'

'We're all in need, petal,' she grimaced, holding the paper as though it might be infected. 'You more than most.'

He said nothing, regarding Petunia with his pale blue eyes unflinching, dignified even. But to her, besieged and bitter, they seemed to glitter with mockery, how bloody dare he...!

Before she could think of another thrust, the Artist teetered off down the back lane.

Petunia watched him hurry away, seeing little dollops of snow fly from the end of the crutch. She seethed: a poor day, a very poor day, humiliated and insulted by every blasted man... She glanced at the scrip in her hand, the few pencilled words.

'Pimp for bloody Polaks?'

She pushed back in through the hotel door.

Biddy looked up questioningly: Petunia had paused, her eye on Gordon who stood patiently as his next pint was pulled. He sensed her and looked round, warning her off: *Not here, for Christ's sake.*

But Petunia came close and murmured:

'News for you, pal.'

◆◆◆

As his fire took hold, Jacky Whisky relaxed just a little. He went to the window; the long, low room was warming but the afternoon light had begun to weaken. Restless, he found two candles, set them in empty bottles, lit them, and then blew them out again. He sat on a wooden box in front of the stove and sang quietly:

Over there beside the black water
Sits a young Cossack on his horse,
Saying his farewell to his girl…

He thought of her, of that cottage, of her receiving his message.

Sara, however, was not where he imagined. She was leaving the hospital, pushing her bicycle round from the kitchen yard because she was unable to ride it through the slush with one hand bandaged. The bell jingled timidly of its own accord.

Ring, ring, ring the bell…

When she reached the main driveway, there was the Artist staring at her in dismay.

'Karol? Why do you look at me like that?'

'Miss Sara … but you are not on duty.'

'I swapped shifts. Matron asked for some help, so I've been here all day.'

The Artist mouthed stupidly, gazed at her bandaged hand, then found his words. Sara set off in the direction of her parents' farm.

◆◆◆

The spars crumpled, the fuselage collapsed, the papered wings splintered and tore. Gordon dropped the wreckage onto the table, glaring at the Polish chequerboard he'd ripped through. Many days later, when George Dulce came to fetch away their things, the ruins of Charlie's plane were still there.

Across the table, two of his cronies watched. Gordon moved to the back door where, from the rack above, he lifted down his game rifle. He opened a dresser drawer and scooped shells into his pocket. He stepped outside, glancing at the lean-to where her bicycle should have been. Then he walked through the dusk to the sheds.

Sara had reached the open road. Between her and the forest edge was a broad field and, in the distance, Torbrechan. Several hundred yards ahead of her, half in the shadow of the trees, was the barn she hardly dared look at. She cycled on – and saw, pulled into a gateway, the toad-eyed truck.

Jacky Whisky crooned before the fire:

I grieve for the green Ukraine,
I grieve, my heart cries,
I'll not see her again.

Sara ran plashing through the snowmelt on the forest path, stumbled, fell gasping on her poor hurt hand. She caught her breath, picked herself up and ran on.

She stayed there alone,
My little quail.
And here I am, far away,
I long for her night and day.

Jacky stopped singing, hearing a sound, a boot on the stone flight outside his bothy. He looked round, started to rise, started to smile.

Sara was still seventy yards away.

'Jacky!' she screamed her head off, 'Jacky!'

She screamed and screamed.

On the steps, Gordon hesitated. At the far end of the barn, glass and woodwork smashed and splintered: Jacky had kicked open the window, had jumped. Landing clumsily in the snowy mud, he picked himself up and moved towards Sara, but two silhouettes broke from the trees and pounced on him; there was a confusion of flailing, of cries. He threw off the first attack, scrambled to his feet. He felled one man with a fist, lashing out with his boot and catching the other in the stomach.

So the one-handed hero stormed back, his enemies there before him at last.

'Stop it! Stop it!'

She howled, ignored by the fighting men. Jacky had seized a broken bough, was jabbing it at the eyes of his two attackers who looked to Gordon for help, suddenly half-hearted, minions doing a jealous man's thuggery.

But Gordon stood on the top step, rifle in hand, gazing down on Jacky Whisky and his wife.

'Leave him alone!' she cried out. 'Gordon!'

Then Jacky Whisky looked up at Gordon Meakin, and loathing blazed between them. He prepared for his own attack, stick against rifle, tearing up the steps into his adversary.

'Jacky!'

He gasped, something thudding across his back. Sprawled, he saw the crony raise a plank to bring it down on his face. But Jacky rolled aside, took only a glancing blow on the shoulder. He staggered to his feet, skidding towards Sara.

There was a single shot, and around them rooks exploded from the trees. He tottered two paces, falling.

'No!' she screeched, 'No!'

Gordon looked down from the steps, the rifle sinking slowly. The cronies froze. Jacky Whisky raised himself from the slush onto his working arm, his fighting arm. He dragged and hauled and kicked his way towards Sara as she stood with her head bent, hands over her eyes, shaken with sobs so violent that she near vomited. In front of her, Jacky's strength failed, the muddy snow beneath him turning to a red stew.

'Jacky…'

She took her hands from her face and stumbled forward, slithering and kneeling, quite beside herself. She cradled his cold head in her lap, patted his sodden hair, stroked it eagerly as though it were the warmest fur.

Gordon from the top step watched. His hand worked the bolt of the rifle, but he did not notice what he was doing. Jacky looked up at Sara, shivered, and died.

She stuck her arms out sideways like a scarecrow in a storm, clenched her fists and beat the air. She twisted a knot in her face and bawled. Gordon stared, bewildered; he couldn't imagine what she was at. His cronies stood futile as he came down the steps, came forward as though to comfort her, take her home. But Sara didn't see him. Her face was pressed to Jacky Whisky's.

Gordon turned and walked away down the snowy track, into the falling darkness. The rifle trailed from his hand till the stock bumped on the rutted ground. He dropped it, walked on.

◆◆◆

Polish forces in Britain were disarmed in 1945. At the Victory Parade in London, Poles were excluded so as not to offend Stalin. Someone who, in the newspaper reports, was named as S. Zeman and was almost certainly Stanislav, Charlie's father, led a small group of former airmen attempting to gatecrash and join the parade, but they were detained by police.

Vladislaw and his generation never forgave this.

Gordon Meakin paid the common penalty of that time for murder. Sara Meakin, née Dulce, did not long outlive him; she died of post-partum septicaemia shortly after her daughter was born. But the girl did well, and was named Claire. The children were raised together, Claire and Charlie, cared for by Joyce who, against all expectation, returned from Glasgow and settled at Torbrechan. Joyce had grown curiously muted, and never married. Two years later, after her parents had both died, Joyce let part of the old farmhouse to Vladislaw, who had become a pie and sausage maker by trade. The rent quickly fell in arrears, and was soon forgotten.

Part Two

LOSING TOUCH

1971

Charlie Dulce was haunted by memories that were not his own. One might imagine that he'd have sufficient personal stock: the tumult of his early childhood, the loss of Sara when he was just four. Those troubles were little spoken of; Charlie did not hear Gordon Meakin's name again until he was ten years old. His mother never spoke of Gordon but, as the boy grew, Vladislaw took it upon himself to relate the tortured family history, bit by bit.

Later, however, as a young doctor, Charlie found that the memories that preoccupied him, that he dwelt upon, often belonged to other people. Some of these were his patients; others were closer to him. For instance, he wilfully and needlessly preserved in a cupboard the little blue wooden lorry made by Gordon. With the aid of that toy, he would inflict on himself Gordon Meakin's pain.

Once, in a bookshop in Inverness, Charlie Dulce pulled off the shelves a book about the complicity of ordinary people in the crimes of the Third Reich. He flicked idly through the photographs until he came upon one that he could not forget.

It showed three people. To the right of the picture, and facing off to the right, stood a young mother. The wind was pulling at her skirt, and in her arms she held a small child. They were Jews. On the left, a dozen paces behind the mother and child, was a Waffen-SS soldier in his coal scuttle helmet. He had his long rifle raised, and was aiming at the young woman. Another second, and a bullet would smash her skull, followed doubtless by a second shot from close range that would kill the child. Charlie – or, by now, Dr Charles Dulce – was reminded, grotesquely, of that painting of a tiger leaping through the air upon a man, with its coy title, *He is quite safe, it's only a picture*. But Charlie could not think this way about the photo of the young Jewish woman with her tugging skirt, with her warm young life, with her love for her child that she clasps in futile protection. And he asked himself over and over, what was going through her mind at the instant before she died. And through her child's? And through the mind of the young man who was about to kill them? And through the mind of the photographer? Whatever it was, the next few seconds would alter all of them.

That soldier, and the photographer, might have been still alive even as Charlie stared at the picture in the book. How would they remember the moment? Had they managed, perhaps, to expunge it?

Charlie never did. He had not read the photograph's caption, and would later wonder: was that in Poland? He knew he could have only the remotest connection, believing in a vague way that such things had occurred in his father's homeland. But, as with the wooden truck, he would continue to inflict this suffering upon himself, quite unnecessarily. If he was ever in a bookshop, his eye would seek out that title on the shelves. He would never open the book, but he would stare at the title on the spine, summon up the image of the mother, child and rifleman, and he would hurt himself with it. At the time of the murder, he could only have been an infant. He knew of that war second-hand, largely from stories told him by the Polish sausage maker who raised him, tales of conflict in a distant country.

But Charlie had a certain gallumphing gift of empathy. His patients and neighbours never suspected this; from the time he returned to Glenfarron as Dr Melhuish's trainee, people thought him a decent but somewhat unimaginative young man, stolidly respectable, a tad pompous. Perhaps to mitigate his family history, he cultivated that image. It was quite wrong. Charlie might not always understand what people told him, but he dwelt on what they said. For one young woman in particular, he came to feel an alarming fascination.

Charlie did not believe that he was directly related to Anna Baird – although given the goings-on in the 1940s, he wouldn't swear to that too fervently. Their family stories, however, overlapped at many points, and she had a knack of drawing others into her situation. As Dr Dulce, he visited her often over the years – more than was quite necessary, for she was unlike any other patient. She came to trust him, and in her curious fragmented way she told him a good deal. So he felt the kinship of intimate knowledge – kinship and pity. Some of Glenfarron's incomers arrived from distant countries, others from our own cities. The latter, he realised, were just as lost.

◆◆◆

At the top end of Glenfarron, you are fifteen hundred feet up; at this altitude, on this latitude, in this climate, farming is a slog. The aesthetic pleasures are austere, the pecuniary returns meagre. If you enjoy floundering through snowdrifts after sheep that have value only by virtue of subsidy, this is the place for you. If you're an estate factor by trade, you'll be wondering how to discreetly bump off the local raptors before they annihilate your grouse. Either way, you'll probably conclude that you could do better with a few thousand acres of Sitka spruce. Charlie Dulce enjoyed the stark beauty on a sunny day, but as Dr Dulce he couldn't help noting that the more remote his patients, the more cussed they could be about demanding home visits, or refusing to go into hospital when medicine ordained it.

Not that he had many patients up here. If you were to take off up the side glens that debouch into the Farron Water, looking for a melancholy picnic spot, you might appreciate that these empty hills were once populous. You might note the scabs of habitation, of 'lazy bed' cultivation (that most back-breaking of livelihoods), and indeed of entire abandoned villages, cleared, burned, gone. You might survey the low green cicatrices in the turf, outlines of a score of houses and byres; you might readily fill the mind's eye with smoke seeping through rotten thatch, and the ragged, tubercular urchins that scampered there. But still you might not grasp the sheer numbers that have vanished.

Higher still, near the Farron's source in a squashy peat bog, tough Blackface and Cheviot ewes crop the grass close. Here, where a few last cottages hunker down, small vegetable plots are possible but the growing season is cussedly short. The Farron Water begins as innumerable, infinitesimal rivulets trickling into the bog, which then drains into a stream that rushes away downhill, east towards the Moray Firth.

That upland bog lies in a lopsided basin. To the north, high hills do their best to block the way to Sutherland. Rumour of riches – iron ore, manganese, gold and latterly ski slopes – has time and again lured optimists up there, but they never last long. The southern rim of the basin is much reduced; indeed there is hardly a rim at all but an expanse of moorland, treeless and shelterless; at 1500 feet, the winds scour it pitilessly. Over that high-level moor, keeping its head down, creeps a tributary stream that enters the marsh. On the Ordnance Survey map this stream is called Purgatory Burn.

At Brig o' Farron, where the marsh becomes a river and is thus bridgeable, the Glenfarron highway hops over one of General Wade's smaller humpbacks. Leaving the tiny hamlet, the road turns up behind the little Brig Bar, climbing into the hills towards the distant ski-centre. Its route is marked with orange snow-posts which can be useful even in May. In summer, a few tourist cars stop at the pub for a beer and a toastie before heading uphill in low gear. In winter, the day-glo snow gate is often closed.

So much for the main road. There is, though, another track which not many feel the wish to explore. It parts from the road at the bridge, skirting the rear wall of the kirk and the cemetery with its single wind-bullied yew. The track then turns south over the moor. In a quarter of a mile or so it meets that tributary, Purgatory Burn, which it crosses by a wooden footbridge, heading off across open ground towards an area marked on older maps as 'Elrisch of Lipperlaund'. A handful of walkers go that way. Otherwise, apart from the sheep, it attracts very few, and fewer still in March.

◆◆◆

Except for the girl waiting in the car. It was an ancient and muddy black Peugeot estate – the old model with steering wheel set slightly skew – laden to the gunnels with luggage and stopped half a mile above the pub. She sat in the passenger seat, pale and thin-faced, staring across the marsh. She took in the whole hamlet of Brig o' Farron, peering at the kirk (why here, with so few homes? But there had been many more once). She noted the diminutive pub and the hump-backed bridge. She saw one sizeable house with all its shutters closed tight, screened by a beech hedge and with an odd turret on its roof. Nearby, she saw a clutch of other cottages, several of these topped with tin and red oxide, and she looked again at the narrow way that set off across the moor, over the metallic trace of Purgatory Burn and beyond.

Then the car rocked and jerked. A rattle and a scrape, and a face appeared at the window, a bespectacled young man grinning at her, holding up a well-rotted exhaust pipe.

'Bloody typical,' he yelled, for she hadn't wound down the window. 'A mile from home.'

At which she looked once more at the larger house among the trees, with its curious roof.

◆◆◆

A wooden outhouse door stirred in the wind, two rusted notes squeaking like some bereaved bird. For a moment the call was overwhelmed by the belly-aching of the Peugeot. Then a stop, a silence, a stiff car door, a foot on thin gravel.

'Well!' cried the young man, staring.

In a horseshoe of beech hedging stood that shuttered house, two storey and four-square, harled, with scalloped bargeboards painted a flaking grey-blue. Nothing out of the late Victorian ordinary, save for the curious turret above one corner, a small wooden thing with a green copper dome. Like a miniature lighthouse, except that it stood beside a moor fifty miles from any sea, and had no lamp.

The pigeons blew off the roof with a clatter. Then all was still and silent save for the two notes squeaking and a faint *tick tick* of the cooling car, from which the pasty girl peered out.

'Cummon, woman.'

The young man reached in, seized an outsized iron key, then ran to the portico step, turning to wave both arms theatrically.

'Ours! All bloody ours!'

He vanished inside. At last, she stirred and followed.

She found him flicking dust sheets off threadbare green upholstery, off a lustrous mahogany sideboard, and a small French-polished cabinet whose lid he lifted with trills of delight.

'A grannyphone. Records, too.'

He looked hopefully at her.

'Anna? You like it?'

She gazed at the stained green flock wallpaper, at the mangy red velvet drapes, the glass cabinet of leather-bound books, the horsehair chaise longue.

'It's a museum,' she whispered.

She wrinkled her nose at the fustiness.

'Open the shutters, Pauly, quickly,' she cried, and light poured in.

And so they saw the portrait. It hung over the fire, an ancient gentleman in a black velvet gown and cap:

KENNETH BAIRD OF FARRON
OBIT. 1572

'Well now,' breathed Paul, 'it's Great-great-great-very-great-Granpy.'

He peered closer at the painting.

'Shouldn't have him over the fire, though. They used bitumen to get those sombre brown-black backgrounds, and it can melt in the heat. It's not unknown for paintings to slither down their canvasses.'

'He has a kind face,' Anna said.

In the dining room, a huge table on clumpy spiral-twist legs was matched by a ponderous sideboard.

'You could feed an army at this table,' she exclaimed.

'It's a shooting lodge,' he said. 'A band of Victorian hearties would barge in here to gorge on claret and venison pie, then stagger off to kill some more. There's three loos off the hall, did you note? Three.'

He beamed around the room.

'It's hardly changed in a hundred years. Uncle Gideon's done us proud.'

She considered this a moment.

'Shall we look upstairs?'

It was a mean staircase, after that epic dining table. But who'd come up here? Not the Duke and his lunch-party guests, the iron and shipping magnates in their blood lust and Norfolk jackets. No, just the housekeeper and her ghillie man. The stairwell walls were patterned with leafy bamboo, as though the Victorian marksmen were stalking pandas.

Through the first bedroom door there was a surprise: an excess of Art Nouveau, with a wrought-iron bed under a princess canopy and pink satin drapes.

'What the buggery's all this?' said Paul.

'Gideon's nest,' replied Anna.

She stepped inside tentatively, as though entering a garden made of glass. She sat on the edge of the bulging bed, looking at the flounces and valances, the swags of pink curtain and the briar rose wallpaper, the curlicued mirror and the pair of silver-backed hairbrushes, the kidney-topped dressing table and the heavy dark wardrobe all jammed into this ridiculous room.

By the window hung a framed photograph of a soldier, an officer in uniform.

'Is that Gideon?'

'That's our boy, Lieutenant Baird the fearless.'

'But look at his bedroom,' she breathed. 'It's a bordello. You really have to laugh.'

She was grinning. Paul beamed at her: that easy, universal smile of his.

'Have to laugh?' he said, coming to her side. 'I'll say you have to bloody laugh. You, my girl, have no choice in the matter.'

He pounced, knocking her back to squirm on the billowy eiderdown. His fingers went under her sweater to climb the staircase of her ribs.

'Ah! Stop it,' she shrieked and giggled, 'Please, Paul, stop it … you'll pay, youbastardIpromiseyou'llpay …!'

But his hands were all over her flesh; she thrashed like a martyr on the rack – till they subsided and lay apart. The moment ebbed and she did not sustain it, as though an overture had been played but she had cancelled the remainder of the concert.

He was watching her. Dishevelled, she peered into his eyes which were as strangely bland as ever, as though he was waiting for something and was able to wait for a long time; it was no problem, it would come. She looked up past him at the flounces of the princess canopy, felt for his hand and whispered:

'I do like it. Gideon *has* done us proud.'

◆◆◆

She walked on a threadbare maroon runner along a landing which turned left towards the rear of the house, ending in a window. This overlooked outbuildings and the sheltering beech hedge, and then the upland moor to the south. Half a mile distant she saw again the burn, the path crossing the wooden footbridge and then the peaty, windswept emptiness. The sky was heavy with rain or maybe snow cloud. Anna realised how cold the house was.

She was about to retreat and find Paul, to ask him to light a fire, when she noticed the doors to left and right of the window. That to her left was secured with a brass padlock.

Who, she wondered, would padlock a door in a house in which they lived alone?

But she speculated no further, for there in the yard below was

Paul, poking and rummaging in the outhouses, and he looked up, saw her and waved with his ever-childish delight.

He lugged cases and boxes up the stairs, roaring:

'Out the road, woman, there's a man at work here.'

He had established an empty bedroom as his domain, and was heaping cardboard cartons and plastic bags of power cables in the corners.

The day was fading fast. She clicked the brass light switch and nothing happened.

'Hah!' Paul scoffed. 'We live in a Victorian paradise in the Scottish Highlands; who needs electricity?'

He surveyed his technical jumble on the floor.

'Okay, I do.'

He pointed at Anna and snarled like a secret policeman.

'You – into the treadmill.'

She gave a rueful huff.

'You'd not get much power out of me. It's bloody freezing, Pauly.'

'Never fear,' he countered. 'I'll get logs. There's a shed full.'

In the kitchen, by the light of candle stubs he set about the moribund Rayburn like an officer kicking wounded and exhausted soldiers to their feet. He riddled and raked, jamming the stove with paper and kindling, making it roar. Anna, meanwhile, stirred soup on a camp stove.

'You look like old man Steptoe,' he observed.

She'd wrapped a rug around her middle; she wore fingerless mitts even while she slurped her broth.

'What if it freezes?'

'We'll keep each other warm.'

Her soup spoon hovered a moment, but she didn't look up.

'Ach, well,' he continued, 'there'll be a boiler somewhere for the central heating. Gideon was no Spartan, he did himself all right.'

His eyes lit up.

'And I lay odds there's a wine cellar.'

He was up at once.

'Mind you,' he hesitated, 'digging a cellar in this landscape would be a non-starter. Either it's granite or it's bog.'

He glanced at the rear window, now black with night. On a ledge by the back door stood a rubber torch.

'The outhouses.'

'Pauly,' she protested, 'finish your soup. Wine'll wait till the morning.'

'I prefer my claret in the evening,' he replied, setting out towards a large building across the yard, leaving Anna on the step. 'It'll be out here, though how he stopped it freezing, I'd like to know, because… Good God!'

He had the steading door open. As the torch beam poked about inside, Anna caught fractured glints.

'Anna? Come and see this.'

It had been a stable for the ghillie's ponies. But in each of the loose boxes there was now a dark gleaming slag heap from which Anna recoiled, for as the beam crossed and recrossed, the shadows shifted and the heap seemed to stir and creep like cockroaches. It was empty wine bottles. Thousands of them.

'Oh, yes,' breathed Paul, 'Gideon did himself all right.'

He lit the fire in the drawing room, and set more candle stubs on saucers. But perhaps the logs were damp or too green, or the draught was poor, because it was a feeble blaze, a fire that couched reluctantly in the grate.

She castled herself with legs drawn up in an armchair upholstered in faded green.

'Will we get heating, Pauly?'

'Quit bleating, woman,' he parried. He scrutinised her for a moment – and she had the odd impression that he was making a calculation about how spontaneous to be.

He lifted the lid of the gramophone, peeked at the disk that lay there, cranked the crank, lifted the tone arm.

He cocked a raffish eyebrow at her, like a rutting *caballero*.

'You want heat? I show you heat.'

He seized her by the wrists – '*Pauly!*' – and swirled her to the middle of the carpet.

A tango. For an instant, they were alight, arching and strutting navel to navel, and her thick-socked feet were black patent pumps, while her slacks and baggy Norwegian sweater were a blazing scarlet gown with a fantastical flounce.

'Pauly, please.'

He lowered her gasping into the armchair, from where she gazed up at him in near-panic, gulping and reiterating:

'Pauly, Pauly, Pauly…'

He whipped off the needle and stopped the turntable. In the

silence, he sank to his knees beside her.

'Easy does it.'

She blinked at him wide-eyed, and felt yet again his patient scrutiny, waiting for something. Waiting for her.

'I'm sorry,' she said.

'Tomorrow,' he announced, 'we make enquiry of the local quack.'

She did not reply; her eyes lost their startled lustre, and drifted away from him.

'Hey, cummon now.'

But it burst from her:

'What are we doing here?'

'Doing? We've inherited a palace.'

'A freezing heap of stone on the edge of a boggy moor.'

'It was Gideon's home, poppet; he left it to us and so it's ours. We've no other, Anna; we're all sold up, we've nothing but a clapped-out car and a stack of boxes.'

She considered a moment, then shook her head.

'I'll never belong here.'

'You've got that the wrong way round,' he replied. 'You don't belong to this house – it belongs to you.'

He stood up, kicked the dilatory logs in the grate, dropped on another billet and sent up sparks. At long last, a little enthusiasm appeared in the fire, and the flames licked with a pretence at purpose.

'There, you see,' said Paul. 'Welcome to Brig o' Farron.'

◆◆◆

In the morning, they walked arm in arm in a brisk grey breeze across the caterpillar-humped bridge to the red phone box outside the Brig Bar, imagining a snow-bound traveller who had struggled through blizzards into the warm pub, only to be sent out again to call for assistance.

'Bloody typical,' growled Paul.

They jammed themselves both into the phone box, to plead with the Hydro-Electric Board and Post Office Telephones. Then they took the wallowing Peugeot (its shock absorbers were long gone) down the glen three miles, past the loch and the Victorian castle which – in spite of new paint and a smart signboard, gold on royal blue, trumpeting 'Country Club' – they thought as dour as a cloutie dumpling.

They went into a pokey shop – *SPAR, prop. A. Hulewicz* – selling bashed tins of Tyne Brand chicken curry and UHT Granny Smiths.

'Who's the nearest doctor, please?' asked Paul.

'Now, Dr Melhuish is on holiday,' beamed Aggie Hulewicz, 'but his trainee Dr Dulce stays in the village. The main surgery's down at Drumcullen, but there's a clinic here Tuesday and Friday mornings. We take the appointments.'

So they were booked in.

When the power came on at last, they went into another outhouse and Paul did battle with a rusting boiler and an iron tank that sweated paraffin from its joints. When the old leviathan squirted rusty bilge at him, she laughed and dabbed it off with a rag.

The boiler fired; he shouted '*Yes!*'

It went out.

He dinged the fuel pump with his spanner and it fired again.

They sorted their workrooms. In a shed they found a utility table which, washed down, would serve for Anna's woodcuts, her chisels gouges blades and ink, her little things. Paul set out his keyboards, his tape decks and scores. They looked into each other's rooms, the brave displays of work soon to commence.

'Are we going to be all right?' she asked, standing at her curtainless window staring out at the chilly moor.

He put his arms around her from behind.

'We've cash for a while, and I've stuff coming up for Grampian telly. The piano quartet's going well. Will you give it a year?'

She nodded, squeezing his hands over her belly, stopping them straying.

◆◆◆

He forced the padlock with a jemmy, splintering the wood, but Paul said, we can't live in a house with padlocked doors. There was a narrow flight of stairs, bare wood and steep, hardly more than a ladder. At the top, another door of pine boards, bolted but not locked. Inside, nothing they had expected.

The chamber was small and cramped, eight feet across at most, octagonal and panelled in pine stained dark brown. A scrap of daylight entered through a dirty window no more than eighteen inches square and fitted with a wooden shutter that was at present fastened back. The furniture consisted of a curious circular table, slightly dished. The top had once been painted white, but was now thick with dust and bird-droppings. Suspended over this were two rods of black iron tipped with handles and brass cranks. The eye followed these upwards to become stickily entangled in cobwebs around mechanical fittings under a small skylight.

'This an observatory?'

Paul wiggled one rod, and brought feathers and acrid bird shit powdering down on his head.

'It's a camera obscura,' she said.

'You what?'

'There's one in Edinburgh; I've seen it. It's got mirrors and lenses. You twizzle it and look all round, and everything's projected onto the table.'

'What's projected?'

'Whatever's outside. Whatever it sees.'

Paul peered up the rods at the dusty drapes of cobweb overhead.

'See up a crow's arse,' he grumbled. He looked around the chamber at the trim panelling, the solid table and its dished plaster top, the purposeful brass fittings.

'It's beautifully crafted. The Duke of Watsit must have put it here to amuse his shooting chums. Maybe they scanned the moors for stags. Like a U-boat: up periscope!'

He gripped the two rods – and more guano cascaded onto his face.

'Pwaaagh!'

He wiped the filth from his eyebrows.

'Why was it locked?' asked Anna.

◆◆◆

On the flat lead roof between two slated ridges, the wind cut into her until her whole body shrank inside her heavy sweater. Light dustings of snow flew past; low, massy clouds watched her like an assailant, waiting. To the north, the hills were decapitated by cloud. To the south, distance and visibility were impossible to gauge; there were few landmarks even in clear weather, and now the snow came and went, blurring the view, then whirling clear again.

She looked back at the wooden tower of the camera obscura,

at the tight little door through which she'd emerged, at the narrow iron ladder that curved over the coppered dome to give access to a protuberance – the viewing lens, she supposed – on top, in a small rotating cap. Paul had climbed up to see. There must once have been a cover, he'd called down; it had been tweaked off by the wind, and that's how the crows or pigeons got in.

Then it moved. The top of the dome scraped and squeaked and the lens rotated a little, but seemed to stick. From inside, she heard frustrated thumps, a curse – and a more excited shout:

'Hey, Anna. Anna!'

He was grinning, pleased as hell.

'Look at this!'

He'd swept the accumulated filth off the dished table with his hand, leaving dirty streaks across the semblance of a white surface.

'It works, look.'

He tugged on an iron lever, and at once a thin light washed over the table top. There, to one side, was a dim image of the bridge and a cottage beyond.

'It's dim because it's filthy,' he declared. 'Best if I close that wee shutter.'

'Don't...' she began, but he had flipped the window closed.

With another tug on the rod, and a twist of the brass crank, the image shifted and the horizon swivelled. They both moved a few steps around the table to look again.

'It's historical,' said Paul excitedly. 'I'm gonna fix it, it's bloody brilliant.'

'Perhaps we should lock it up again,' she answered.

He peered at her.

'Why?'

But in the house below them a phone rang.

'Hah!' he cried, 'we're connected. That'll be fame an' fortune wanting a word.'

He clattered down the wooden stairs. She heard him hurry down through the house, the ringer stopping, some muffled words. Turning back to the table, Anna took hold of the mechanism and the view rotated stiffly; she must follow the horizon, walking around the table. Here the crank handle stuck, and she examined the new image.

It was a view out to the south. There was the flat expanse

of moor. There was the burn that crossed it, and the wooden footbridge. There was cold sun sparking off the water. There were blowy patches of sunlight on the heather and hardy grasses.

Anna stepped to the chamber door and opened it. Outside, the damp snowy grey was as grim as before. She retreated inside to the camera table where, on the distant burn, was sunlight. It seemed to her very clear, very sharp, like the super-bright image in high quality binoculars. It had no warmth.

◆◆◆

He said, 'This won't tell us a thing that we don't already know.'

In 1971 Charlie Dulce was medically qualified, but needing experience in order to become a GP. He'd persuaded Dr Melhuish to take him on, so that he could come home to work in Glenfarron. Charlie rather venerated Dr Melhuish, and aped his manner: tweedy and paternal, even at the age of thirty. It was all bluff; Charlie was far from confident, and that particular week was near to panic because Dr Melhuish had gone off to visit his sister in Largs, telling his trainee to telephone some chap in Inverness if he had any worries. Charlie could have been on the phone twenty-four hours a day.

But here he was in the satellite surgery in the former seedsman's office: Dr Charles Dulce, acting the old-fashioned country GP, courteous but condescending, and now doing old-fashioned things with a blood sample that wouldn't reveal anything but which would please the laity, even while he made believe that he knew the answers already.

'You have, without a doubt, a post-viral malaise,' he declared over his shoulder while filling out a laboratory form. 'Time, just time,' he counselled loftily. 'Sit it out. None of your Glasgow rushing about. Maybe think about getting some help with the house.'

This was addressed to Anna, but she was away with her thoughts. Charlie peered at her over his reading glasses.

'Promise me you'll do that?'

No reply.

'Anna?' prompted Paul.

'Oh yes,' she breathed, embarrassed. 'Yes, of course.'

The doctor regarded her doubtfully, then shifted his scrutiny to Paul.

'And you can fill in a New Patient Registration form, if you please.'

He took one from a steel cabinet and placed it, with a ballpoint, in front of Paul who scowled at it mistrustfully.

'It's not a mortgage,' said Charlie.

To which Paul returned the smile of someone who is going to be obstinate.

'I'll drop it in next time I'm passing,' he said.

'Very well. Leave it with Julie at the shop, and I shall read with interest in due course. You Bairds go back aways in Glenfarron.'

He was holding the door open. Waiting outside sat an elderly body in a brown woollen coat clasped with horn buttons, who beamed at everyone through thick, scratched glasses. She stood up, and was not fat but very broad of hip, as though she had been compressed, beaten down with mallet blows upon the head and spread sideways. By the Glenfarron winds, perhaps.

'Call in any time,' said the doctor, although surgeries were only Tuesdays and Fridays. For some reason he felt it important that Anna should keep in touch. 'If you want a chat, maybe. You hear me, Anna Baird?'

Anna nodded vaguely. She was looking at the old lady.

'Would you know who could show me the kirk?'

◆◆◆

It was a building less formidable than the key which Miss Petunia Forbes, bending over in that wide brown woollen coat, took from a plastic box behind a stone. The kirk having been built on a low outcrop, there was a flight of three steps to the west door. The lock clunked; Miss Forbes pushed the heavy door wide.

She stood aside for them.

'Thank you,' said Anna, passing in. As Paul followed, the old besom made something like a curtsey. He beamed at her, charmed.

Not that, within, there was so much to see; in the Highland manner it was very plain, the walls washed in a cream now distinctly sour. On one wall, to the left of the altar, hung a wooden board painted in crackling black on which the white lettering was fading away like a story that was being forgotten:

MINISTERS OF THIS KIRK

It listed them a long way back. One name had been erased from the mid-16th Century, scratched till the bare wood showed.

To the right of this board, in the corner, there was a small lancet window.

'A squint for the sick, ye ken,' said Miss Forbes at Anna's elbow. 'They'd view the altar frae oot the kirk, seeing as they were unclean.'

She's batty, thought Anna. The old lady was fixing her with a watery stare, bubbling on.

'Difficult fer a body to be clean, d'you no think? They'd be taken oot an' awa.'

'Out where?' asked Anna.

'Beyond the burn, miss, oot the moor. See fer yesel.'

Anna did so. She went to the squint through which the sick had once peeked in at Holy things, and found that it was cut through the wall at an angle. She peeked out. A glimpse of flat brown heathers. Oot the moor.

'Difficult for a body to be clean,' Miss Forbes repeated.

Before Anna could ask what she meant, a wheezy chord bubbled and gasped as though from emphysemic lungs.

'Get a load of the music centre,' grinned Paul, perched on a tapestry stool in front of an ancient harmonium. He pumped his feet on the brown linoleum pedals till the bellows creaked and hissed; the old instrument groaned but could not altogether oblige.

'Feeling the years,' he announced, running a sympathetic hand over the oak case and reading out the name: '*Alexandre Père et Fils, Rue Richelieu, Paris 1869*. A centenarian, this.'

'It makes a horrid noise,' said Anna.

'Well, sorry I'm sure. I thought it was doing well for its age. I'll get this working again.'

'When you've got our own house working,' she returned tartly.

There was a discomfort, an empty beat – into which stepped Miss Forbes.

'I used tae love the hymns.'

'Did you now,' said Paul. 'And you played?'

'Not me!'

'Cummon, sing with me.' He was being puppyish; the old lady blushed.

'No, no!'

'Let's see,' he said. There was, above the harmonium, a single wooden bookshelf with half a dozen volumes, each faintly bloomed with white mould. He tweaked at one with his forefinger, an austere volume in a brown cloth binding. Paul started to turn through it.

'Here we go. Which was your favourite?'

He beamed at Miss Forbes who was no longer blushing, but regarded him with seriousness. Paul offered the open book up to her.

Miss Forbes took it; she peered at the book and began pushing at the leaves. Then she stopped, and stared at the page.

'That one?' asked Paul.

He held out his hand and gently took the book from her; she watched intently as Paul placed it on the harmonium. He peered at the music in the poor light, then put out his right hand, fingering the first notes of the tune. It was a sombrely sweet thing, with an archaic dignity.

'Mmm,' murmured Paul, interested. 'It sounds very old.' He lifted his left hand to try the harmony.

But before he could do so, Miss Forbes was speaking to Anna, rather loudly.

'I could help you, in the house. I know the house.'

She was staring at the pale girl.

'Well now,' said Paul, beaming at everyone, 'how about that, Anna? Miss Forbes could help. Anna?'

For Anna was staring back at the old woman with unexpected hostility.

Paul, with a touch of vexation, said again:

'Anna?'

◆◆◆

On the kitchen table stood a cardboard box.

'Polish country wine?' she said incredulously. 'Does that say, from Poland?'

'It was a complete bargain,' he enthused, standing a bottle on the Rayburn to simmer, 'like she was waiting for me. The moment I took one off the shelf, Mrs Hulewicz was saying I could have a whole box for a fiver, less than £1 a bottle. She was dead keen, I couldn't disappoint her. I'll lay it down.'

'To die,' said Anna.

'Oh, boil yer heid. We'll try this one an' I'll lug the rest out back.'

'Allow me.' She picked up the box, heading for the back door.

'Put it on a shelf or it'll freeze,' he called after her.

She stepped out into the chill afternoon and crossed the yard, clasping the none-too-sturdy box to her belly as she lifted the latch of the steading door and went in. The pallid daylight made no effort to reach the back of the loose box, and the bottle mountain gave no glint.

She groped round the doorframe and found a light switch, but it was dull and dead, not even clicking properly. She moved forward, kicking herself for not bringing a torch. A shelf, he'd said. Did she remember a shelf? Yes, to the left of the loose box. For tack, it must be, wide enough for hats and suchlike; she'd barely noticed it. She steered left – and almost dropped the wine in fright when she kicked an empty bottle on the floor, sending it in a gritty spin to bump against the timbers. Pausing, giving her eyes more time to adjust, she made her way past the loose box to the rear wall where there was indeed a solidly fitted bench, onto which she placed the wine. From under the cardboard came a scrape of dirt and droppings.

Another case of wine, she thought, alongside the sorry mountain of Gideon's empties. Will we go the same way?

At which point, behind her, the heavy door swung shut.

She turned smartly to face that way, feeling for the edge of the bench, putting her hip against it for security.

Shit shit shit.

Straining to see, searching with the corners of her eyes, still she could make out nothing. The darkness was thick and palpable, an intense black. She listened: had someone come in? Not a mouse, not a thing, except a rhythmic rush that she realised was her own heart whooshing.

After a moment, she could make out a faint trace of daylight at the door's bottom edge. It gave her a sort of horizon by which to keep upright, a landmark to steer for. At her left hand she found the wooden wall of the loose box. She edged forward, patting along the timbers. She moved by inches; nonetheless, when her foot again made contact with the empty bottle, it swung and thudded gently against the wood. She realised that, heavy Norwegian sweater notwithstanding, she was thoroughly chilled.

She came to the front of the box, her hand finding the stout corner post that rose up to the roof beams, the wood smooth but faintly sticky with grime or dubbin or some horse-exudate. Now that she was nearer, she could no longer see the thread of daylight under the door; she thought it must only be four or five steps from the box corner across the stone floor. There were no obstacles, surely. She stretched one hand out before her and one to the side; she inched forward, but because she was not taking proper steps she could not gauge how far she had moved and the door seemed impossibly far away, it must be there now but no, where was it, it was retreating from her…

Something stroked her cheek. She gasped, flapped at it, gave a small shriek…

It was a piece of plastic cord, very old, coarse and thready. It must hang from a rafter above her, put there god knows when and god knows why. She pulled at it angrily but it was fixed firmly and didn't give way, and merely hurt her hand. So she circled round the dangling string until she realised that she now had no clear notion of her way to the door. She stretched her hands out all round like a child playing blind man's buff, and she felt nothing. Her eyes registered no difference open or closed, though she waved and strained her head to catch the faintest gleam. She shuffled nervously a foot or two in one direction, but thought the floor felt unfamiliar. She changed tack, heading off to her right with her hands flailing about in every direction, no longer to protect her face but to find something, anything at all onto which to fasten her by now utterly failed orientation.

She kicked another empty bottle. Or was it the same empty bottle? Or were dipsy old Gideon's empties creeping out under her feet…

She screamed: nerves, humiliation, all at once:

'Pauly! Paul! Fuck it, Paul!'

The door banged wide. The daylight, that had seemed so feeble, was now a white wall against which stood a broad silhouette.

'Now,' said Miss Petunia Forbes, 'no need for upset. Just swung in the wind, the old door, nothing more.'

◆◆◆

She tried to work, aware that Paul had set to cheerily. But nothing seemed to come to her.

She had taken up residence in a small bedroom, a place with a central island of dusty pink carpet whose edges were fraying out white fibres. By the window was the plain table with a small vice clamped to the front edge. Along the window sill was her gallery of miniatures, fixed with masking tape. They were woodcuts, proofs and trials on scrap paper, all of a rustic, sub-Bewick charm: a sleeping mother fox with cubs gambolling, reapers in the corn, throstles among roses. And a few copies of Bewick himself, the master's darker aspect: a suicide hung by the neck from a bough over water; a blind man led across a marsh by an unlettered boy who cannot read the warning sign, *Keep on this side.* Not quite the tone for cards.

Anna sat motionless, staring vacantly at a blank page, a virgin block of wood, a box of chisels unopened. If her eye was empty, her ear was not, for in it a tune circled, angular and insistent. She'd heard it just once, in the kirk, but it had seemed different then, not like this at all, not so intrusive, so sternly forbidding, so harsh.

She cocked her head slightly; the sound came from somewhere outside herself. She frowned with annoyance, then rose – but remained there between chair and table, as though clear about what must be done but reluctant to pick a fight. She looked at the door but it gave her no help. At last she moved out into the corridor.

Paul's room was open; she stood on the threshold observing him. He was sitting at two tables arranged in an L-shape, heavy with keyboards and their attendant boxes, devices, switches, loops of green cable, spools and cassettes of tape. Beneath the table squatted two fat loudspeakers with black metal grilles. On the other worktop, pencils and rubbers and a glass of water crowded about a spread of music manuscript paper. And a book, a hymn book that she recognised, with a faded brown cloth binding. From the kirk.

Paul was engrossed; he didn't notice her. He was swivelling between the two tables, between the score and the keyboard, picking out notes, scribbling and rubbing, going back to play. Not a note could be heard; he was wearing fat black headphones – but she had heard, surely. Had he only just now plugged those in? As he played, stopped, annotated, played again, the only sound was a delicate clicking from the keys.

She studied his back, puzzled, before retreating. Out in the corridor, she turned the corner and went towards the distant window. On the left-hand door, the padlock hasp still hung broken. She put her hand to the latch, and climbed the narrow wooden stair.

In the upper chamber, the window shutter was open, the cobwebs still dangled in swags, the control rods hung motionless, and a pale shaft of light struggled down from the grimy apparatus above. On an impulse she tugged the sleeve of her heavy sweater over her hand and swept more filth from the dished tabletop, then regretted this, patting at the woollen cuff to clean it.

She reached out and closed the shutter, so that the projected image on the table stood out brighter in the darkened chamber. There was a view of the hills to the north, with the road rising up and away. She reached out and grasped the brass control crank.

She stood a moment as though waiting to be electrocuted: nothing happened. She began to wind the crank; a small squeaking came from somewhere overhead and the image started to rotate anticlockwise, obliging her to follow round the table. She saw the Brig Bar, lifeless, and the stone bridge itself. She saw the kirk and kirkyard. She cranked more vigorously and the horizon swung dizzyingly about as it might for a pilot turning on a wingtip. And then the expanse of the southern moor came into view, with the wooden bridge over the burn.

She studied the distant flowing water, which gave out that curious cold sparkle, intensely clear in its focus. It was a strange thing to see: an image, but moving. Not a still photograph, not a home movie nor a cinematic fiction, but an image of immediate, present truth, projected and laid out in front of her. She put out her hand and, where the shaft of light fell across it, she saw the water in the burn flow over her knuckles. She could lift the image up, lower it, take her hand away and leave the stream running across the table top.

She eased the other control rod towards her, and the picture on the table jerked downwards. The footbridge disappeared and she could now view the path much closer, at a point only half way out towards the bridge, or less, quite near to the house.

She froze, startled.

Figures had come into view, a line of four, walking on the path that led to the wooden bridge. Men or women? Perhaps both; she couldn't tell. Some appeared to limp. All carried sticks. She peered closer and was puzzled to see their clothes: brown, loose and tattered. In single file they marched away from her – or shambled, rather, for their movements seemed clumsy and reluctant – deeply reluctant. All except the figure at the rear. He alone (Anna was sure this was a man) wore a long black cape, and sturdy but elegant black boots. He too carried a wooden staff, but not the rough thing of those before him; his was straight and black and the top glinted, capped perhaps with silver. And, although he did nothing to coerce the others – he carried no whip, he did not goad or appear to threaten – yet she sensed that, without his presence at their backs, they'd not have gone forward at all. By some means, he drove the walkers on.

Then, to Anna's astonishment, this person in black stopped on the path, turned about and looked up at her.

They seemed to be gazing straight at each other, though Anna was peering down at a dished white tabletop and the distant walker could not possibly see her. She leaned closer still, and examined him: he was tall, he looked quite young and well-made, but stern. Before she could tell more, he had spun on his booted heel and was pursuing the line in front. A few seconds later, they all reached the edge of the image on the table, and had stepped into nothingness.

She grabbed at the control rods, rattling and tugging. The view remained fixed; something overhead had jammed.

She stepped round the table and pulled open the outer door, startled by the cold that smacked into her. She stepped onto the roof leads and crossed quickly to the side overlooking the moor, blinking a little into the wind, gazing at the distant bridge, the burn winding away and the path following, on its farther side.

Empty. All quite empty.

◆◆◆

Miss Petunia Forbes was sorting the cutlery. She stood with a motley collection of tarnished electro-plate and cracked bone handles heaped on a tea towel after a collective bath. Some she laid back in the scrubbed plastic compartments of the table drawer. The split or corroded she dropped into a cardboard box. She was doing this (Anna decided) with as much noise as possible, in order to be intrusive.

Anna watched her from the doorway, wondering why she disliked the woman so much.

There were, in the passageway, several boxes of books not yet unpacked. Anna rummaged, countering Miss Forbes' clatter with the bump of books onto carpet. She found what she wanted: a large-scale Ordnance Survey map. She came into the kitchen and spread the map on the table opposite Miss Forbes and the cutlery.

'Planning your holidays, pet?' asked Miss Forbes.

Anna thought, the stupid cow doesn't know what an OS map is.

She said aloud, 'Purgatory Burn.'

She was tracing its course across the moor with her finger.

'That's it,' said the old woman, not looking up.

'You didn't tell me it was called that.'

'No.'

'That's where the sick were washed? In Purgatory?'

'That's it. Crossing the burn.'

Still the woman did not return her look. This, thought Anna, is to make me feel ignorant and stupid.

Miss Forbes dropped a last broken butter knife into her discards, picked up the box and headed for the back door.

'You'll no be wantin' these.'

And went out, with Anna's dislike beating on her back. Miss Forbes was so wide in the hip, thought Anna, that she must turn sideways to pass through the door.

Paul came downstairs, to forage for biscuits and instant coffee.

'Was that Miss Forbes?'

'Who else,' Anna murmured. 'Since when can we afford a housekeeper?'

He paused, the jar of powder open in his hand.

'For you. Doctor's orders.'

'Free prescription, was it?'

'Oh, cummon, two mornings a week cleaning, five quid.'

He was studying her. She thought: he's changed, he's not quite as he was; there is something calculated. But a moment later, Paul had reverted to his usual bland smile. He focused on stirring a mug of grey effluent, bearing it away upstairs. She could feel his eagerness for his work, and caught herself begrudging it.

Miss Forbes returned; Anna made an effort at amiability.

'Shall we stop for coffee?' she offered.

Miss Forbes did not even meet her look.

'I'll get on just now, pet.'

She was filling a large pan with water, setting it with a resonant clang upon the old Rayburn and slamming on a lid.

'There is hot water,' said Anna. 'Paul fixed the boiler.'

But the old woman took no notice.

Miss Forbes left the kitchen, leaving the pan hissing on the hotplate. Anna stood, purposeless; she made herself another mug of that revolting coffee and gazed out of the window. Fine, hard snow was in the air, scratching at the glass, like coarse sand.

She folded the OS map. She wondered about crossing the burn.

She poured the coffee down the sink.

She drifted upstairs.

From her work-room doorway, she regarded the desk with its vice and unfinished woodcuts, unable to find any reason to go inside, to take up pen or chisel. Then she was back at the door of Paul's room; as before, he sat engrossed, his skull enclosed by the squashy headphones, jotting on his manuscript paper.

She flushed; she wanted to rip the phones off him, to haul him out of that secret world of his. Then she was coldly furious with herself: how petty and envious and jealous she was being. Dear Paul, he was wonderfully happy…

She looked to her left, towards the far end of the passage where the door to the camera obscura was. And then she looked at the door opposite, which she had never opened.

A few steps down the worn carpet and she was there. She tried the plain white ceramic knob, almost wishing to find it locked so that she'd have to fetch Paul to help. But it swung open freely.

It was a child's bedroom. It was small, but it didn't seem crowded because the furniture was miniature: a wooden crib painted eggshell blue with delicate yellow beading; a low, square table with two seats; a toddler-sized chair, and a sturdy stool for nurse. There was a divan also; the precious infant would never be alone. There was a diminutive wardrobe in that same blue and yellow, and a chest of drawers with a raised front edge, to make the top into a safe nappy changing surface. The floor was of hygienic linoleum. Shelves held a few wooden toys: a ship and a dark green racing car with fat wheels; a merry-go-round with red and gold horses. There was an anthology of nursery rhymes.

Everything looked pristine and untouched but old nevertheless, and faded. The walls were papered in a pattern of steamboats and rocking horses, in blues and yellows also, and there was not a trace of crayon scribbling, but the colours were washed out wherever they faced the daylight. There was no clutter, nothing to suggest that any child had ever inhabited this space.

'Gideon wanted children, it would seem,' said Paul. He was at Anna's shoulder.

'But there were none.'

'So we get the lodge. Bad luck Gideon, and lucky us.'

She didn't reply, but moved into the room, her imagination supplying the life in here, the cooing and cradling, the little smells. She stood looking down into the crib. It was not made up; there was only a kapok mattress with black-and-white ticking. She thought, if I open one of those drawers, there will be all the sheets.

But then she remembered:

'He never married.'

'Feels as though he came close, doesn't it?'

Paul turned away. He headed back to his desk and she followed him, not knowing why. Before she could speak, he grinned at her and held up his hand for quiet.

'Listen!' he said.

He pressed the play button on his tape deck. There came a plastic music, complex and angular, as though the components were not complementing each other but pushing for supremacy. Somewhere in there was an antique and melancholy tune that Anna recognised, and disliked.

'You hear how it fits?' said Paul, pleased with himself. He replayed it, but with Miss Forbes' kirk melody enhanced and protuberant.

Paul beamed with satisfaction.

'That's bordering on talented,' he crowed.

'It's twisted,' said Anna. 'I think it's a horrid little tune.'

'Well, I beg your pardon, I thought it was charming. Darkly sexy, in fact.'

He flicked controls and the tune died. He looked hurt.

'Oh God,' she cried. 'I'm sorry, Pauly. I am sorry!'

She threw her arms round him and squeezed.

'You're doing so well,' she mumbled into his neck, 'and I just can't seem to settle.'

◆◆◆

For an hour or two, a wintry sun came out and, before she knew it, Miss Forbes had the yard full of swaying laundry. But then the sky changed again; at mid-altitude, something clotted. The weak sunlight turned grey and the wind returned and there was Miss Forbes with a basket gathering the washing in.

Knowing that this was just another excuse not to work, Anna went out to help. She found, as she dutifully held the damp corners for folding, that the old woman was unaccountably chatty.

'I've been to Glasgow, and Edinburgh for the Tattoo but I'm Glenfarron at heart, born an' bidin'. That's the best, no need for all this comin' and goin' of folk.'

To which Anna, the arriviste, could say nothing.

'Och, I'm no meaning yourself, pet,' said Miss Forbes, 'you've the connection and that's fine, to see the house stay in the family. But we've had an awfy lot of newcomers. There was all them Poles in the war, they were a slippery lot, not safe. I knew them, but we had trouble with some.'

Miss Forbes stopped folding the sheet in her hands and contemplated it, uncharacteristically thoughtful.

'I like a clean village,' she said. She looked up at Anna. 'Do you no like a clean village, Miss Anna?'

'Well, surely …' Anna began, but was interrupted.

'Sometimes,' said Miss Forbes, 'a place needs purged, like, with syrup o' figs.' She blushed at her own absurdities. 'Och, what a thing I'm saying!'

'Purged of what?' Anna asked.

'Sin and decay,' said Miss Forbes.

'What sort of sin?'

'What sort have you got?'

Anna stared at her dumbstruck. She felt Miss Forbes' scrutiny fixing her like a specimen to a board. But the old woman looked down at the sheet, dropping it into the washing basket.

'Some things just won't come out. Some stains. Like, you've just the one blue blouse and all your whites are spoiled. You'd think that something that washed in would wash out as quick, but it disnae. Stained for good.'

She gave a deep sigh.

'Aye, there's lessons in every wash. I knew your mother, dear. I used to work with her.'

'You worked with her? Where?'

'We worked from home,' said Miss Forbes.

But before she could expand on this, an electric shrilling from the roof caused them both to look up. It was Paul with his drill, halfway up the iron ladder on the outside of the camera obscura, fixing something.

In the kitchen, he had brass bits all over the table, and lenses that he carefully washed and polished.

'The optics were seized up,' he enthused, 'but nothing broken. It's not complex, and it's beautifully made.'

'That's wonderful, now,' said Miss Forbes, bustling away to vacuum somewhere.

'If it's going properly,' continued Paul, squinting through a gleaming prism, 'I expect you could survey the whole glen right down beyond the castle. You'd see what was going on, all right. If you looked across the moor, you'd see…'

'Purgatory Burn,' said Anna.

Paul looked at her through the prism, seeing her in rainbows.

'What's that?' he asked.

'The stream. We saw it in the distance the day we came.'

'You might have. I was on my back under the car fighting the exhaust.'

'We should throw this out,' returned Anna, looking at the scattered optical parts.

He looked around, unable to believe what he'd heard.

'Why?' he mouthed.

'I don't like it. It's spying on people, intruding.'

'Only if they've got something to hide,' he countered sanctimoniously. 'I think it's beautiful. I'm bringing it to life.'

'We should lock it up,' she said, leaving the room.

◆◆◆

That afternoon Anna began behaving very oddly.

She'd been asked to give a demonstration of woodcutting in Glenfarron primary school; the teacher, Ronnie Christie, told everyone afterwards what a success she'd been. She had her portable vice screwed to a table; she had her chisels, inks and rollers ready, and a dozen tiny souls watching from a ring of little red plastic chairs. Her fair hair was held back with a green velvet scrunch and over her old grey denim work shirt and trousers she wore a cook's apron, red and white striped. She sat before the vice, teasing a design out of a woodblock with her sharp blades, talking easily about how she loved to make these blocks that not only printed charming pictures but were themselves pretty.

'It must be very hard wood,' she said, slicing and lifting, 'with a fine, even grain, so that your picture comes out cleanly. Now then: ink.'

She rolled the block carefully with her gel roller.

'And paper ... and print. There!'

A man riding a pig; a comical nonsense. The man wore a stovepipe hat and his legs stuck straight out before him, like an Edward Lear. The children tittered happily.

'Okay?' Anna smiled. 'Your go.'

So the children made a grand mess with potato cuts, digging with chunky craft tools, squidging on red poster paint, stamping and pressing and holding up sheets of sugar paper with little faces and flowers, rockets and stars. Even one that was recognisably a pig.

'Well, don't they just love you?' purred Ronnie Christie. 'Eating out of your hand.'

He was a dapper man, Ronnie, with a trim silver beard and a smiley face. Anna blushed.

'It is fun, isn't it?' she parried.

'You're fun,' the teacher insisted, a light hand on Anna's shoulder. 'And we're very happy to have you here.'

Anna's blush spread delightfully.

'Though their mums mightn't love us so,' Ronnie added. 'I wish I'd bought better painting smocks, with sleeves. Stains are not popular.'

'No,' breathed Anna.

She cleared up, washing off her roller, tucking her chisels into their cloth bag, while Ronnie laid the children's work to dry on a radiator: 'We'll pin them up tomorrow.' Together they discarded a heap of rubbish, swilled out the jam jars, binned the sliced tatties.

'Are these . . . ?' Anna began, glancing through proofs and prints. But only one person could have done this: a finished woodcut on a small square of handmade paper, in crisp black ink. It showed a man standing on a small bridge, a man wearing a black cape, holding a staff.

She stared at it frozenly. She had no recollection of this at all. After a moment, she screwed it up tight and dropped it into the waste bin. Then she rummaged through the blocks that she'd brought with her – cuts of throstles, a phoenix, a padding tiger – to examine the original. But there was nothing of the sort.

She felt an anxious thrill, as though something had got very close to her before being noticed, something not understood. But she resolved not to let it interfere with her pleasant afternoon, and she left the building.

Anna crossed the schoolyard to the lane, carrying her kit in an old maroon duffle bag on one shoulder. The brisk wind tossed her hair across her face. She climbed into the Peugeot, now so rusted that she had the curious sensation, each time she sat there, that the seat had subsided a little further towards the tarmac and would one day drop clean out. She wished Paul would get rid of the car but he always laughed that he could cure its ailments, that he wasn't going to collude with the throw-it-away culture. She hated the Peugeot; she felt unsafe.

Paul had come with her ('Gotta get out!') down to the village for a walk and to shop in Aggie Hulewicz' SPAR, which Anna thought meant 'savings' in Danish. Or was it Swedish? And run by a Pole's daughter. Heavens, what a cosmopolitan glen. She backed the car gingerly onto the road and coasted the hundred yards downhill, drawing onto the dirt verge at the side of the shop next to a grimy red Hillman Imp. She couldn't see Paul. She stood in the lee of the building, gazing absently up and down the village street, feeling the wind trying to push her home uphill.

Inside the shop, Paul had worked his way through a modest list when he met the doctor. Charlie Dulce was congratulating himself on taking every opportunity to get to know his patients, rather than sending the receptionist Julie round to buy coffee. The shop door opened; out they came, chatting, but at first neither saw Anna some yards down the road.

'So, how is she?'

'Och, full of beans,' said Paul, but it sounded forced. 'Can be a bit down, now and then. There's days she gets quite nippy.'

The doctor was about to press for more, but they were interrupted: Julie's bright little voice rang across the road.

'Doctor, will I open up surgery?'

Paul raised his hand in greeting.

But Julie, coming towards them, saw Anna and waved: 'Hi there!'

Paul and Charlie turned to look, just as the Peugeot pulled out onto the road in a small flurry of grit, accelerating up the glen and leaving Paul standing.

◆◆◆

She did not look, not once, in the rear-view mirror. She drove steadily the three miles home, up beside the Farron Water, up through the forest and then open country, between grassy spurs that rabbits had honeycombed. She knew as she climbed that the wellbeing she'd felt at the school was dissipating with every turn, thinning with each foot of altitude.

At Brig o' Farron she slowed, turning onto the potholed track that led to the lodge, skirting the kirkyard's granite wall. She realised that, although she'd explored the kirk interior, she'd not yet read the stones.

She left the car standing in the lodge drive. Instead of opening the front door and taking that first hit of stony cold which the house would breathe at her, she deposited her duffle bag in the porch and returned to the iron gate of the kirkyard. Between the stunted yew and the grey-green headstones, she drifted up and down as though searching for something with inadequate clues. As she went, a flash of light reached her, striking down into the kirkyard from the house: it was the optics of the camera obscura, catching the sun. The brief white blaze stopped her dead, and she stared back fiercely as though daring it to say that again.

Then, with a tetchy spin on her heel, she burst out of the kirkyard through the wooden side gate. Without thinking, she headed out towards the moor.

The wind was rising, a flat sheet of cloud dragging over the sky. She felt the chill but decided that the answer was to move energetically. Touched by a sense of being watched, she glanced back. She saw the Brig Bar in the distance, looking very closed. The kirk was there, of course, but turned in upon its own thoughts.

She noted that the camera obscura would have a clear view of her out here. She turned her back on it, moving swiftly towards the wooden bridge.

Pausing on the single wooden step, she looked across the bridge; the far side of the burn looked even colder. A thin but tenacious crust of snow covered the path, and hung on the colourless heather.

Despite the cold, she remained still. There was a tune in her head that blocked out the sound of the wind, as if she was wearing those fat, soft headphones. But no, it wasn't a tune, not a whole tune, only two notes repeating and repeating. As she puzzled over this, she glanced upstream and saw a small structure, a sheep pen, a wonky thing of galvanised gates and corrugated iron sheeting that the wind was pushing, so that it shifted and creaked two notes.

She shook her head crossly, to toss out that endless encore. Stepping back off the bridge, she moved down to the stream's edge, and peered into the burn. The water was fringed with ice that stood out from the bank in delicate jagged shelves always an inch or two above the flow. She crouched and extended her hand, reaching out her index finger to touch the surface, creating an arrowhead of ripples. She realised that she could feel nothing – but it was numbingly cold. The two notes were gone from her head, displaced by the gurgle of the stream in its recesses, a strange, hollow sucking. And by another sound, a light wooden *tap tap*.

Reflected on the water, a black cape waved. And someone had a stick, was knocking on the rail of the bridge. She started up with a gasp of fright.

The cape was a ragged remnant of black agricultural plastic, nothing more. It was caught on the rail at the far side of the bridge, and was twisting in the rising wind. The tapping was only the sheep gate at the far end of the bridge, shifting an inch to and fro within its snick, knocking the bridge timbers.

She turned for home. She began to run.

As she neared the house, she saw the red Hillman swing onto the road and set off downhill. When she entered, Paul was there in the hallway.

'So why did you do that?' he began at once, his chin jutting belligerently. 'Why did you leave me there? I had to hitch a ride from Julie, who put herself out. I was humiliated. I want to know why you did that.'

She had no idea of the answer. Then she thought of Julie who, she decided, was a little bitch on high heels.

'Don't flirt in public, please,' she said frigidly. 'It's indescribably vulgar.'

She left him, staring, and went upstairs.

An hour later, she returned to the kitchen and saw him at the table. He had the box of optical bits spread out again, and was tinkering in a half-hearted way that made him look little and lonely.

I've hurt him, she thought. I've hurt him needlessly.

'Pauly?' she said, and saw his hands stop their restless fingering of the brass components.

'I'm sorry, Pauly, I'm really sorry. I was all stressed up.'

Which was a lie; she'd not been so content for weeks as she'd been that afternoon at the school.

Paul got to his feet and came to her with a wistful smile.

'Okay, just don't make a habit of it; that's a long uphill walk, you know.'

He took her narrow hips in his hands and they stood silently, Anna picking at the fluff and bobbles on his jersey. She felt her tenderness rising in flood, felt herself swirling in towards him. She heard in her head the deep sucking of the water in the icy burn.

She looked over Paul's shoulder at the brass fittings spread on the table.

'What are you doing?' she asked, an edge creeping back into her voice.

'Putting it back together,' he said, taking his hands from her sides and moving to the table. 'It's terribly simple, just a few cogs, lenses, mirrors, look...'

He suddenly held up a mirror – and she recoiled.

'Don't do that.'

He smiled.

'You're not so hideous.'

'Get it off me,' she protested, as though the mirror were a leech. 'Get it off.'

But he wouldn't put the mirror down.

'Get a grip,' he laughed. 'You've seen a mirror before. You're acting like a fuzzy-wuzzy.'

'It's not safe.'

He blinked.

'It's a mirror, what's it going to...'

'Gideon locked it up,' she said, angry at his obtuseness. 'He must have had reason.'

'Well, I think it's great...'

'Just jack it, Paul.' A demand, her voice ever harder. 'Please, shut the bloody thing away.'

But now he too was angry, and defensive.

'For fuck's sake, can't I have a bit of fun and interest? I work day and night, I'm struggling to make a shite career that nobody wants to pay me for, and you won't let me play with a wee mirror.'

'I just ... I just really hate it. I hate that whole chamber and everything.'

'So don't go up there.'

He pushed past her, swept all the brass assemblage into its cardboard box, then marched out of the room and away upstairs.

◆◆◆

In the kirkyard, she found that half the inmates were Polish. Foreign casualties from the wartime hospital had been buried at Brig o' Farron, not down at the village. She looked: Reysowski, Mieszala, Wysierkierski. Strange, quarantined up here. Other stones bore her own name, Baird.

She passed round to the south of the building, away from the road, and moved towards the far end. Near the corner was a lancet window piercing the stone so that it looked forwards to the altar: it was the squint that she'd seen from inside.

She went up to it, glimpsed the interior and was about to turn aside when she drew back with a start. There had been a shadowy flourish of black.

Or perhaps not. Maybe a curtain inside, nothing more. Though she knew that there were no curtains.

'Will you come in?' said a voice behind her. She spun round.

'I've the key,' said Petunia Forbes, holding it out for inspection.

They went in together.

Inside the kirk it was still, and quiet and chilly. Anna moved in that half-speed walk that people use in kirks. Miss Forbes seemed to have even less determination or direction, and drifted among the pews.

Anna drew near to the altar table, raised on a single stone step. To her left she saw the lancet window. Above it, there was the black-painted board:

MINISTERS OF THIS KIRK

And the name, near the top of the list, that had been scratched out with the point of a knife.

'Murdo,' said Miss Forbes at Anna's shoulder. 'Reverend Jacob Murdo, 1570.'

'That's when he died?'

'That's when he left here. You're all of a tremble, pet.'

Anna was shaking all over.

'Why am I getting like this?' she whispered.

'Must be something, mustn't it?' said Miss Forbes. 'Something needs to come out.'

'What did he do?'

'Reverend Murdo blessed the sick and cleaned our village.'

'I see.'

'What do you see, dear?'

'I can't tell…'

Anna went to the squint window and peered out at the moor, at its frosting of snow, at the reassuring emptiness, with no figures walking into the distance.

'I have to work,' she blurted, and fled the kirk.

◆◆◆

Gideon Baird had not been a well man. His constitution had always been delicate, which was why, during the war, he'd been assigned to liaison with the Polish military at Farron Castle. His propensity to melancholy had not been helped by amorous failure; he'd methodically poisoned himself with alcohol and had become a hypochondriac to boot. But Gideon's obsession with illness was not wholly self-centred. There was one malady which had fascinated him, which he had not infrequently discussed with Dr Melhuish, and which was the subject of a book of no small value in his collection.

Anna had often scrutinised, but had never yet opened, the book cabinet in the sitting room. She had supposed it to be locked, but when she now put her hand to the tiny dangling brass handle and gave a tug, with the satisfying air-resistance of a snug fit, the glass door sighed open for her.

The little collection had an amiable, serendipitous feel. There was Douce's *Illustrations of Shakespeare,* 1807; when she opened this, an engraving of unfriendly Morris-men and fools leered at her. There was Tasso's *Jerusalem Delivered,* "done into English by Edward Fairfax, gent." and a tacky two-volume Boccaccio, with lubricious Edwardian etchings. There were flower engravings, of course, and a bound set of etchings of the castles of Northumberland, *circa* 1800; also hand-coloured plates of the costumes of the clans. An 1815 Bewick in a library binding; that was lovely, but familiar. She had wondered if there might be some new source of inspiration here, but she wasn't finding it. She gave up. She was on edge. She ran a hand over the spines, then closed the cabinet. She looked around the room, realising that there were any number of drawers, crannies, cabinets, and hiding places that she'd not yet prised open or pried into.

Directly alongside the book cabinet, there was an occasional table of delicate workmanship, finished with butterfly-veneer walnut. It was tall for a table, and of unusual design: she saw that the top divided in the centre, with ebony knobs on the front edge which meant that the two halves could be opened out to the side – as she now did.

Inside, beneath an inner cover of glass, was a tray-like recess lined with green baize, on which lay a book. It reposed, she thought, or nestled; what was the word for a book snug in green baize? The glass would be for safe display, so that you could have a precious volume open at some wonderful illumination and let people view it without fear of careless splashes of tea. But the book under this glass was shut. It was quite small, but she thought the proportions odd, squarish. She struggled to recall those peculiar names for paper dimensions: was this, perhaps, quarter-of-an-imperial-elephant? She noted prosaically that it was about nine inches along the top, and maybe eight down the spine, a small landscape folio in calf and marbled paper, with the title gold-blocked on a leather label:

McCorquadale's Relicts
or, Leprosy in
Caledonian Antiquity
1773

She stared at this for fully half a minute before wondering at herself, at the frozen state it put her in. She supposed that the notion of leprosy in Scotland had never occurred to her. If she thought of the disease at all, it would be in Africa or India, hot places where limbs dropped like rotten fruit. Then she corrected herself: wasn't the leper a common sight in the Middle Ages, the Dark Ages or whenever? Haunting the dirt highways of feudal Europe, clanging a bell in warning. Bands of ragged folk with ghastly collapsed faces traipsing from Aachen to Cologne.

In Scotland too.

She tried to open the inner glass but it was locked, held by a chromium clasp at the bottom edge. She studied this helplessly, surprised by how disappointed she felt.

She was drifting pensively out of the library when she was hit down the stairwell by a blast of music so ferocious, so raucous, so appalling that she thumped the wall several times in incoherent rage before she rushed upwards, her face dark with hatred.

'Turn it off!' she screeched. 'Paul, turn it off!'

She stumbled where the stairs twisted at the top, half-sprawling onto the landing but at once pushing herself forward so that she hurtled towards Paul's open door hardly in control of her movements. Then she was inside, where he sat with his rubber headphones about his neck and the huge PA speakers throbbing at her, and she was shrieking:

'Off now, Paul, turn it off now!'

She leaned past him, stabbing frantically at buttons on the recording deck, while the startled Paul tried to stop her, to protect his work, only to have Anna snatch the cassette from his hand and try to break it, turning her back on him and attempting to snap it in half, then catching the tape with her fingernail and hoiking it out in a loop, fragile…

'Anna, cool it, Anna, shit, Jesus!'

'It's everywhere, it just gets everywhere, it's in every corner of this bloody house!'

She threw the twisted wreck of the tape onto the floor.

'In God's name, Anna, that's hours of work! Shit!'

She lurched away from him and subsided, stunned, onto a wooden chair by the wall. Already, he was frantically scanning his equipment, a damage control exercise.

'It's okay, I think, okay, it's there, it's copied. Jesus, Anna, what are you doing?'

She was still staring at the ruined tape that lay gleaming brown like a dead cockroach. She was mumbling:

'I'm sorry, I'm sorry, I'm sorry.'

Her face was pasty white and covered in little beads of sweat. He crouched by her, quick in his concern.

'Hey, listen, it's all right, it's not lost, I'd made a copy.'

He put a hand to her damp face – and she turned away.

There was a sound from the doorway; both looked up. Miss Petunia Forbes stood there with a tray in her hands. There was a pretty jug of milk with a lace cover, and there was a plate of shortbread, but only one cup.

'Hey, coffee!' Paul cried, ever so jolly, as he stood up.

Miss Forbes hardly glanced at Anna. She came into the room and placed the tray on the end of the trestle table.

'I'll be away home,' she announced, and they heard her descend the stairs.

'I dislike her pretty seriously,' said Anna.

'What don't you like?' Paul enquired; the habitual steady cool was back, that blandness that she found so unsettling.

'She gives me the creeps,' Anna said, getting to her feet and starting downstairs herself. 'She behaves as though we're house guests. In fact, I think she's mad. I want rid of her.'

Paul followed, calling:

'I can't sack her without reason.'

'Why not?'

'You need the help, Doctor Dulce said.'

From the turn step, she rounded on him, ablaze again.

'Why do I need help, Paul? Am I incapable of looking after my own home? Perhaps you think I'm terminally feeble?'

'I've not said that,' he replied, calm as calm.

'Well, I've said I want her out of here. Paul, I don't want her in the house. Will you tell her to leave us alone?'

They were in the hall now. They could see Miss Forbes moving with her heavy gait along the driveway.

'To leave us alone?' Paul mused. 'Just the two of us.'

She stood with her back to him, facing the window but not looking at anything. In fact, she had a knuckle in her mouth.

'The two of us,' she breathed.

She felt his steady gaze piercing the back of her skull.

'Right,' he said, 'if you like, I'll speak to Miss Forbes just now.'

The latch clicked; she heard the interior timbre of the house altered by the front door standing open. She heard his footsteps on the gravel going after the old lady. Anna stepped into the porch and saw Miss Forbes overtaken, and a discussion, and she saw Paul gesture towards the house. Then he was returning. Anna felt relief, a dead weight taken off her, felt gaiety tapping at her heart – but before she could rejoice, she saw Paul's face as he re-entered.

'Change of plan. Just temporary, but we agreed that she should get the curtains cleaned.'

Bewildered, Anna turned white with apprehension.

'Cleaned…? Why, Pauly?' she whispered.

'And she'll need help getting them down, being quite a weight. So, instead of interrupting our work – yours or mine – she's going to bring her niece Julie.'

'Julie?'

'You know Julie, the doctor's receptionist. She's Miss Forbes' niece.'

'Here?'

'That's right. She'll come to help, just for an hour or so.'

He left her. And it was as though Anna had placed her foot on a landmine and now couldn't move. To lift her weight, to step clear, would be to detonate it beneath her.

◆◆◆

When, at evening, she stood wrapped in a towel before the bathroom mirror, again she felt frozen with anxiety. It was bedtime; she was going to bed with Paul. She peered into the glass at her own face, bony and almost translucent in the delicacy of her skin. Was there any emotion there? She could see none. She searched minutely for sensation within her facial muscles: was anything tense, or pulling, or resisting, or striving to grimace or grin? Was anything tingling, or rising or swelling? She could feel nothing.

She looked, by reflection, across the hallway to the bedroom. She could see Paul in bed, thumbing a music magazine, waiting for her. She thought, I am full of dread. How many women feel this, going to bed?

She put on her blue flannelette pyjamas, slid between the sheets and lay beside Paul staring at the ceiling. He put down the magazine and turned on his side towards her, smiling pleasantly.

'Well, hello,' he said.

He did not touch her. And yet, in every corner of her skin, she felt as though he was touching her, as though his fingers were walking lightly over her. Her skin was reacting, her breasts flushing delicately. She was not sure whether she felt weightless or crushed; it was both at once.

She didn't move.

'You're exceptionally still,' said Paul, in that cool voice of his, rather close to her.

'Please ...' she began hastily.

'I didn't touch you,' he said.

Which was true. He was waiting for her to touch him, waiting until she must. 'It's not,' she began weakly, 'that I don't ...'

She paused, almost gave up, tried again.

'I don't want you to feel ...'

'I wouldn't dream of it,' he said.

'It's rather, I'd like not to feel ... I ...'

She despaired of her own meaning. She felt him ready for her, making no effort at physical contact. She thought, he will wait forever, or for as long as.

She rolled to face the wall. There was the hanging portrait of Lieutenant Gideon Baird in uniform.

'Poor Gideon,' she whispered.

'Why poor?' asked Paul.

'He was very lonely, wasn't he? All those bottles – that's a lonely man. He should have married.'

◆◆◆

She managed little in the morning, but in the afternoon returned to her workroom. She had an order for posh Christmas cards, tasteful things to be sold in those shops that trade in corn dollies, mock-Victorian nighties, clocks (battery-driven) purporting to have been made in some cathedral town and decorated with faux-naïf pigs, spice racks in limed wood and birdcages artificially patinated with blue, such that you might imagine yourself in a Thomas Hardy novel. Her cards sold well.

But she wasn't concentrating. Her mind drifted out of the house, along the path onto the moor, to the people that she might meet heading for the bridge.

She came out of her reverie, and frowned. She had supposedly been designing woodcuts of market scenes, but that was not what she'd produced. On the worktop in front of her lay half a dozen sketches in black ink, all of that same stern, black figure. She swept them into a ball, casting them into the cardboard box that did duty as a waste bin.

She felt light-headed, needing something to eat.

As she came downstairs, she heard voices. Carefree voices.

'Now, watch yourself,' said Paul.

Through the drawing room door she saw a billow of maroon: swags of old curtain were coming down. Anna saw the ample rear of Miss Petunia Forbes who, bent double, was folding the drapes on the floor. She was receiving these from Paul who was taking the weight of the curtains as they were unhooked and lowered by Julie. She was at the top of an aluminium stepladder, stretching prettily, teetering…

'Careful,' Paul was saying, 'you'll do yourself an injury. Come on, I'm taller.'

Anna saw him gesturing the girl to come down, offering his hand.

But Julie insisted, 'You just hold me steady.'

Paul raised his hands and placed them on Julie's shapely hips.

Miss Forbes had stopped folding and was looking not at her niece, nor at the curtains, but at Anna in the doorway.

'Paul?' Anna said loudly.

'Yes, Anna?' he responded, in an entirely unsurprised tone.

'I'll get the tea – seeing as you're so busy.'

She backed out of the room in a cold rage.

◆◆◆

He came in, sat and was still, observing her movements about the kitchen with his strange dispassionate gaze that she found more and more unsettling. She cut bread busily, dumping it on his plate without asking. She did not sit down.

'Productive day?' he enquired.

'Hardly,' she replied, clattering about in the fridge for more butter.

'Excellent soup,' he remarked.

'Let me give you some more.'

'I've plenty…'

But she ladled out more regardless, splashing him. He didn't flinch, but considered the soup a moment before taking another spoonful. He seemed about to say something – so she pre-empted him, asking:

'Will there be any hot water?'

'Should be.'

'I'm going to have a bath. See you later.'

At last he seemed mildly surprised.

'What about your own meal?'

But she headed for the door, pausing only to say:

'I'm going to move my things into the little nursery.'

He lowered the soup spoon. She thought: I've shocked him just a little. But Paul's voice was unfalteringly calm.

'Oh,' he said. 'Why are you doing that?'

'Give you more room,' she replied over her shoulder.

'Do I need more room?' he called.

After her bath she took fresh sheets from the linen press on the landing, and two mothbally goose-feather pillows with thick, striped ticking. She made up the nurse's divan in the blue-and-yellow nursery, with its cot and the ship-and-pony wallpaper. She fetched her book, her towel, her underwear, her glass of water, her clock...

He came upstairs to watch, not interfering.

She was dressed in the pyjamas that she always wore, but now even these seemed adolescent as she scampered to and fro.

Now he came right to the door – and looked concerned.

'It's freezing in here,' he said.

'I've a hottie,' she replied. 'We'll both sleep better.'

She stood in the centre of the little room in her pyjamas and bare feet, waiting for him to do or say something. But he just remarked:

'I don't believe this in you, Anna.'

'Good night,' she replied hurriedly, closing the door. She looked back at the handle, wondering if he would enter to drag her out. But he didn't come.

Whether she slept or not, she couldn't say. But at some point in the night, she became aware, as she lay still, of something pulling at her. Possibly it was her own anxiety.

She sat up, putting her feet onto the cold linoleum. There was a tune in her head, of course. Had it been there all along – or only on raising herself to an upright position? This was something to do with blood pressure and posture, wasn't it… No, she decided angrily: it wasn't in her head at all.

In the corridor she found that there was moonlight enough to navigate by. The light was cold; Anna was cold. She moved down the passage thinking that the music must be coming from Paul's workroom. But when she reached his door and put her ear to the panels, the sound did not alter.

Is it in my head after all? No – she fought it – no.

She retreated along the corridor; the tune remained with her, unchanging. She shivered, and wondered if that was merely the cold, or the touch of the sinuous, archaic melody. She reached the far end of the passage, stopping by the door of her little bedroom. But she did not open the door; she stood motionless feeling the meagreness of the worn wool runner under her feet, and the general chill.

Then she did at last turn, to her left. She put a hand out to that other door, behind which was the narrow wooden stair. As she was about to press the latch, she glanced back along the corridor.

He was there, in the moonlight at the far end of the passage, observing her.

'What are you doing, Anna?'

She didn't reply, but remained with her hand on the latch.

'It doesn't work at night, surely you know that. Not even in this moon. It needs daylight.'

She lowered her hand slowly, otherwise not moving.

'Go to bed, Anna,' Paul said, his voice sweet.

◆◆◆

She wanted a vegetable garden, and she designated a rough, neglected plot beside the drive. She put on overalls and began to clear it, saying that the soil should be turned in the winter before the hard frosts came, which would then break up the clods. He didn't ask where she'd gathered such horticultural lore. The grass was thick and tough, and there was rusted stock wire embedded. She was struggling, and worked up a frustrated sweat, at last jabbing the fork into the ground and leaving it standing.

She didn't want to go into the house. She walked to the kirkyard and wandered up and down, eyeing her own surname on many of the stones. Then she headed for the side gate, that gave onto the path across the moor. She went out, walking only a few yards before realising that the blue cotton of her overalls did nothing against the winds of upper Glenfarron. But when she turned to go back to the warm kitchen, she saw that there was a gravestone on the outside of the kirkyard, facing out towards the moor. It was old and sinking down, as though half-ashamed to be found there. Still, there it was.

MARGARET BAIRD
WIFE OF KENNETH BAIRD
OF FARRON
DROWNED 1570

◆◆◆

'Leprosy,' said Dr Dulce.

'In Scotland?'

'And why not?' retorted Charlie, as though contracting leprosy was an inalienable human right. 'It was very common in the Middle Ages. The Scots version of the Troilus and Cressida story has Cresseid dying a leper. The disease persisted in Shetland into the 18th century.'

(If Charlie sounded marvellously learned for such a young practitioner, this was entirely thanks to conversations with Dr Melhuish.)

They thought about this a moment, sipping the Polish country wine for which Anna had apologized repeatedly, and nibbling the pecan pie she'd made. Such fashionable snacks were comforting; one couldn't imagine noses rotting and fingers falling off, not by the Rayburn over pecan pie and socialist merlot, late on a Friday when the doctor calls.

'I suppose it carried fearful social stigma,' Paul suggested.

'Fearful indeed,' Charlie replied, 'and leprosy was no respecter of person. To be denounced as a leper was to be condemned to a living death, in a curiously literal sense. You'd be shunned and ostracized, but also seen as nearer to God, being half-way to the tomb. There was a certain doomed sanctity about it.'

'What happens when you get leprosy?' Anna asked quietly.

'Well,' said the doctor, toying with his glass and resting his forearms on the table (a comforting, confiding posture that patients liked). 'It attacks the nervous system, destroys nerve fibres. You lose the sensation of touch, so you damage yourself repeatedly; cuts, burns, you don't feel anything.'

'Oh dear,' she said, peering into her glass.

'Meanwhile, billions of bacteria invade the skin of the face, making it swollen and lumpy. The front of the jaw rots, the nose collapses inward, you croak like a raven.'

'Charming,' Paul remarked. 'Anna, you've gone white.'

She gave a silly laugh.

'We need more country wine,' she said.

'I'll get it.' Paul jumped to his feet. 'It's outside.'

Off he went. Charlie Dulce was watching Anna. She had begun to feel that everyone was watching her all the time.

'Medieval medicine took little interest in leprosy,' Charlie said, to restart the conversation. 'It was seen as a matter for priests.'

'And what happened here?'

'A colony, out on the moor. On some maps the name is still marked: Elrisch of Lipperlaund. At least, a colony is what it was called; I can't imagine anyone survived many winters out there. Before going, lepers were brought into the kirk. It was the only time they were allowed in, and they knelt under a black cloth before the altar and heard the Burial Service.'

'Like they were dead?'

'Halfway to God. Not much consolation for being driven out to die of exposure.'

Driven out, a man with a silver-tipped stick at your back. Crossing the burn.

'With music?' she asked. 'There'd be music at the service?'

'Oh, doubtless some queer old tunes. They were led across Purgatory Burn, to wash away their moral decay, and were then abandoned to their physical decay. There were a good number of the wretches at one time. You've to remember that there were a lot more people living here then.'

'Not very Christian,' said Anna.

'Hah, kirkmen! Thought they were doing the Lord's work, driving out impurity.'

But some things, thought Anna, jes' willnae wash oot.

'Zealots and bigots,' the doctor mused.

'Reverend Murdo?'

Charlie looked at her in surprise.

'You've been doing your homework. Well, you're quite correct.

Not a nice man, condemning sick folk to death.'

Dr Melhuish had told him all this one day as they drank mid-morning coffee, adding that deep local knowledge is good in a country doctor. The patients feel that you understand their world.

Back came Paul bearing wine, busily opening it, pouring for the doctor, for Anna.

'Who's Murdo? A hanging judge?'

'He was a minister here,' said Anna, 'in the 16th century.'

'And what happened to him?' Paul enquired.

'He got thrown out,' Charlie said, 'by none other than your ancestor, Kenneth Baird of Farron; you've his portrait in the sitting room.'

'Good for great-great-great granpy.'

'Oh, there was a fine stushie. Murdo had gone too far, so Kenneth petitioned the bishop to have him removed from the ministry. But it all went wrong. Kenneth went off to Edinburgh to find the bishop but, of course, it was really the duke he should have been seeing and he wasted weeks. By the time he realised his mistake and got back here, he was too late.'

'For what?'

'To save his wife.'

'From what?'

'She drowned.'

Charlie sipped his wine demurely in the silence that followed.

'Well,' said Paul at last, 'what a business. I've never heard of him.'

'His name's gone,' said Anna. 'It's been scratched off the board in the kirk.'

The doctor put his hand over his glass to stop Paul replenishing it.

'I expect Petunia has been enlightening you,' he smiled. 'Priceless, is she not?'

'She's unreal!' Paul chirped, 'but great value.'

'Good – because frankly, she's not got many friends. She's long lived alone in a cottage up a lane. She has a bit of a history, let's just say. There was a scandal way back, just after the war, and because of it the great love of her life rejected her. So she turned to the Lord.'

Paul grinned at that.

'Who was the big passion?'

Charlie dabbed at his lips with a napkin.

'Your uncle Gideon.'

◆◆◆

She was in the bedroom – the 'master' bedroom – sitting on the bed that they no longer shared. There was no heating; though Paul had got the boiler working, they'd run out of oil and could ill afford to refill the tank. So she wore two sweaters, tucking the inner layer into the elastic waistband of her slacks. The heavy mattress and quilted bedding were too thick to sit on easily, and she tended to slither off the edge. She perched precariously.

She peered at Uncle Gideon in his uniform, his naïve and honest face filled, she thought, with indecision and sadness. And yet – this decent man, smitten with Miss Petunia Forbes? Farcical. Revolting. She felt a wave of disgust; it was grotesque, mere lust, surely, that he mistook for something better, for what could there have been about Petunia Forbes even forty years ago? An intellect, a talent, a magnetism? Hardly – but you never knew. And if you thought of Miss Forbes' face, well, she had good bones. Maybe, once.

She looked at Gideon Baird, and she shivered.

She went out onto the moor, walking slowly with her eyes cast down. The springiness of the turf, its resilience cushioned her footfall, letting her brood undistracted. She walked slower and slower, absorbed in herself. Sometimes she would come to a halt, poking with her foot at the thick decaying heather, heavy with winter rain.

The wind had died; the afternoon was quiet and still, earth and air. Few birds lingered out here; the pipits, ouzels and ptarmigans were absent. On she drifted, stopping and starting, pondering and musing, hardly aware of ground she covered until she had gone half a mile and was almost upon the wooden bridge, where there was a single ambient sound that filled her ears: the sound of water, the chatter of Purgatory.

She felt senses prickle. The cold, that had not touched her before, now stabbed through her two jerseys and her waxed jacket, and she drew breath at the suddenness of it. She must not stand still or she'd suffer, but she could not (yet again) turn back short of the stream that she'd never crossed. So she stepped onto the boards of the bridge that were wet with damp and topped with chicken wire against slipping.

It was hardly a grand bridge. Nevertheless, because of the unevenness of the ground, the threat of boggy subsidence and the need to reach across to a firm, rocky footing, it did extend for some ten or twelve paces. Anna placed both hands on the timber handrails. She took several steps until she was over the water, just beyond the halfway point. She stopped, peering at the opposite bank.

What would have happened in the lives of poor souls who came this far, at the moment of crossing the burn? No return, no hope, no charity. Did they not protest, or rebel? Why did they not turn on their persecutors, pummel them, strike them down, then flee away to the lowlands? But where could they hope to escape recognition, with their noses collapsing and their voices like a raven's caw? Did they go forward meekly, with just one tormentor at their backs?

Across the burn.

Anna told herself tetchily: you cross over or not, as you please.

She began to go forward…

Until sounds from behind struck her with such sudden fear that it was like a blow. Heavy footsteps, a knocking of sticks. She spun about, her eyes popping, her face ashen and her lips blue and pencil-thin, opening to protest at the figures coming in procession over the bridge with long sticks in their hands.

'Brisk old day,' said the lead walker amiably.

The man in a red anorak stopped two paces from Anna, puzzled: would this person blocking the centre of the bridge not move to let them cross? The walking companions slowed, hesitated, halted, resting their sticks, one of them tweaking at the padded shoulder straps of his blue daysack.

But Anna didn't move. She stared boggle-eyed until the man in red must speak again, however ludicrous it might seem to request passage over a footbridge.

'Excuse us.'

Anna leaned back against the handrail, never taking her eyes off the man who finally made a vague gesture, raising the hand that held his walking stick to indicate that he was coming by.

'Thank you,' he said, easing past this curious woman.

So they all came on, their sticks tapping, their heavy rubber soles clumping on the timber, each of them giving her an instant's scrutiny and a curt nod, as though uncertain how to address someone so awkward, so startled. Each face passed close to hers; she saw with clarity the skin pores, the running noses, whiskers and downy lips and wind-watered eyes. She leaned back as far as she could against the handrail, though the walkers' synthetic coats still brushed against the lower part of Anna's body with a slippery sound.

When they had all pressed by her, she straightened and came off the bridge, hurrying back to the house in a stumbling run.

Entering the yard, she stopped to listen – but could hear nothing except her own blood swishing in her temples. She knew she should go in and try to work, but she was too edgy. She went towards the stable door; at first she had no idea of her intention, but by the time she laid her hand on the latch, she knew that she wanted a drink. She closed her eyes to the deep green winking that came off the mountain of empties in the loosebox, and she came out with a bottle of wine.

She opened the bottle in the kitchen, just stopping herself from filling a coffee mug, reaching instead for a smeary tumbler. The wine was very cold and harsh, so she drank some more. She wondered where Paul was; his study door had been open and the room empty when she passed downstairs. A twinge of pride decided that she did not want to be caught drinking alone, so she downed the second tumbler of wine quickly. She rinsed the glass in cold water, leaving it on the draining rack more smeary than before. She found a roll of foil, tore off a scrap to close the bottle, and placed the wine in the refrigerator. Then, with an uncomfortable tightness in her head, she went upstairs, thinking to wrap herself in blankets on nurse's bed, and sleep.

But when she reached the nursery door, she stopped. That fragment of pride was needling her; she wouldn't like Paul to discover her curled up and foetal under the covers mid-afternoon. So, without thinking, she opened the door opposite, and climbed the wooden stairs to the camera obscura.

She opened the hatch to let in light, and stood quietly. She had not been up here for weeks, not since their first days in the house, not since she had first seen people moving across the dished table. She wondered if the figures she had seen projected that first time had not been today's very ordinary walkers – but she knew better.

Hadn't she rushed onto the roof to peer across the moor with her naked eye, and seen that there was no one there?

Then she forgot the past, because everything about the camera obscura was different. That's to say, it was clean. Her feet noticed the change first; previously, any movement had produced a gritty scrunch and a smell of dust and droppings. Now it was swept smooth. When she reached for the black iron levers, the mechanism clicked and slipped readily, and a strong beam of daylight poured down. The bat and bird filth had been washed away, the tabletop whitened so that it positively shone. Above, the brass handles were polished.

Paul had been busy.

She looked down at the projected image. At first she could see little but sky and a clip of the high ridge to the north, but the view was sharp, with colour even in that distant fragment of hillside. Touching the control rods, swinging the optics too fast, she sent the image scudding across the tabletop, swirling through her wine-heavy brain. She stilled the controls, and moved around the table to make sense of the scene. There was now a view down the length of Glenfarron, with half of the Victorian castle and a corner of the loch. She touched the levers more gently, controlling things better. She inspected the castle, then swung left to view the kirk and the village street three miles away, with tiny figures moving in and out of the shop, and a car pulling to a halt in front of the primary school, in silence.

Tipping a lever brought the picture closer; she could travel up the glen road, lingering to examine each house in passing. People came in and out of doors, or stopped in gardens or driveways, to chat or put out the compost. It was disconcerting, these people projected and inspected, examined in the shallow dish. Observing neighbours like this felt intrusive, ill-mannered, and compulsive.

She shuffled further round the octagon. Her view swept over the Sitka plantations on the northern slopes of Glenfarron, then the open heather and the road taking off for the ski slopes. At the Brig Bar, two – no, three cars: who was drinking? Whose was that car, that red Hillman Imp?

Pushing the rods, she dipped her inquisitive lens closer to home.

And there, past the kirk, from the direction of the pub walked her Paul.

She held out her hand, under the streaming light. She reached out to Paul, his miniature simulacrum walking towards her across the white surface, sharply focused, living and immediate. She opened her palm so that Paul stepped onto her hand. She kept him walking there, in the cup of her hand.

At which there came over Anna an aching, tender protectiveness; and heartache, because she kept him at bay so; and a bodily ache to take him, seize and absorb him. As she stood, with Paul walking up her hand and then her wrist, she began to tremble. Her mouth fell open and her breathing was short and quick. She wanted him to climb her forearm, and in a hurried movement she flung off, both together, the two thick woollens that she was wearing, leaving only a green T-shirt. She thrust her arm further out across the tabletop, and Paul was walking up her arm, seeming to skip lightly across the blue veins as though they were rivulets on the moor.

'Oh!' she whispered.

She turned her arse to the hard edge of the table, and let herself sink backwards. She lay her shoulder blades and spine onto the chill white surface, and pulled the T-shirt up under her chin so that her breasts were naked. She lifted her head awkwardly, to peer down at her own flesh; Paul walked there, going across her abdomen, his living image stepping across her navel in a torrent of light. In a moment she had loosened her jeans and wriggled them down under her buttocks, taking the underpants with them to hang foolishly about her calves. As the little figure strode gaily down the fine road of hair from the navel to the *mons pubis*, she spread her knees and opened the way for him with her hands.

When she came to herself, she was breathing peculiarly, and was chilled and aching with the discomfort of her frigid white bed. She lay blinking up into the stream of light from the optics above. Paul had been walking towards the house; he might be coming up the stairs right now. She raised herself, knocking the control rods as she moved, having to wriggle her thighs up the slope of the table till she could make an ungainly flop off the edge. She seized her clothes, diving into the double layer of sweaters, then reaching downwards. As she pulled at her pants, she saw a rusty red stain: her period was starting. She looked across the table and saw to her dismay a red streak, garish on the white surface onto which was now projected a distant view of the moor.

Even as she stared, a new figure came into view, coming to

stand alongside the slash of blood. This person stood looking straight at her. Not Paul. A man in a black cloak of antique cut.

She dodged round the table, flung open the door and rushed onto the roof. She ran the few paces to the parapet and stared up the path, along the burn to the wooden bridge – where there was no one to be seen. She looked round hurriedly: no one, neither on the moor nor on the road – nowhere. Until she lowered her gaze, and there was Paul coming into the yard.

There was movement behind him; he glanced back to see the grubby red Imp that had followed, and Julie getting out to speak with him.

A jealous rage gripped Anna. She wanted to shout insults, to stamp her foot, to hurl bricks. Paul glanced up, and noticed her. In humiliation, she turned her back on them and stood trembling…

Then she saw it: the dome of the camera obscura, the green copper cap in which was mounted the optical device, this was rotating. It was turning towards her, and within the mounting she saw the lens and mirrors tip down to look at her.

She screamed, and screamed and screamed.

Paul burst out onto the leads.

'Anna! Anna, for pity's sake…!'

But he got no further, because she crouched, grabbed a long jagged triangle of fractured slate and hurled it at him. It buried its point in the wooden wall of the camera obscura, some eight inches to the right of his face. Still she shrieked. And again she shrieked.

'Shut it!' shouted Paul. He slapped her face. 'Just bloody shut it!'

◆◆◆

'Will you tell me what's going on, Anna?'

Charlie Dulce was doing his best to be very kind, very doctorly, very calm – although he was rather uneasy, because Dr Melhuish (back from his holiday in Largs) had decreed that, having started, Charlie should continue to see Anna as his patient.

'You need some help. I'm going to refer you to a colleague, a clinical psychologist.'

They had lain her down under rugs on the chaise longue, and Charlie had given her a large and potent injection. Her eyes drooped.

'Don't speak just now. I'll come back when you're awake.'

They tucked the rugs about her shoulders. Then Paul and Charlie retreated into the hallway.

'I must tell you that I am pretty much at a loss,' the doctor admitted. 'Dr Melhuish likes the notion of referring her to the psychologists.'

It had in fact been Dr Melhuish's proposal.

At that moment, they believed Anna to be asleep, or as good as. They had no idea that she could hear them, but she did. She heard Paul, the anxiety sharp in his voice.

'I'm not keen on this shrink.'

'Oh?' Charlie raised a stern eyebrow to nip rebellion in the bud.

'It's not necessary. I can look after her.'

'I suggest that it is urgent and essential.'

'They fill your head with notions that aren't yours at all…'

'Oh, please! Do you think I'd refer Anna to such a person?

'I wouldn't want…' Paul whimpered unhappily.

'I assure you, this man is trustworthy.'

That seemed to stop his nonsense. Charlie said more gently:

'There's something in her mind that needs out, that's all. Have no fear: she'll be the better for it.'

He pulled on his heavy woollen coat. The weather had turned bad again, the sky was sombre.

'I'll call you in the morning, see how she's been overnight.'

The heavy front door thudded closed behind him; Paul returned into the room. Her eyes were wide open, gazing at him.

'I don't want you to see this shrink person,' he said.

'I don't want you to see Julie,' she replied.

He blushed, then nodded. She gave his hand a squeeze.

'We should get out more,' she smiled. Then at last she fell asleep.

◆◆◆

At about this time, Anna and Paul discovered the best sausages in Glenfarron. Which is to say, they discovered Vladislaw.

He was about sixty years of age by then. He was still tall, not stooped; indeed he seemed almost abnormally upright in his posture because of the wartime wooden leg. He had a beard and a wild Polish look about him. But Vladislaw was not the ebullient figure he had been in the 1940s; he had been touched by too much sadness of his closest friends and of his homeland. He had become reserved, and rather gruff. He lived with an old crone (Charlie's mother Joyce, only fifty-three in fact, but quite batty) at Torbrechan farm, the Dulce family home. It was nothing like the pristine, rather austere Highland place it had been in time of Charlie's grandparents. Torbrechan – so Paul declared with amusement – was a madhouse. There were ramshackle huts everywhere, ancient railway wagons with chicken wire over their windows doing service as drying sheds for searingly spiced continental sausages. There was a slurry scraper fashioned from a steel I-beam crudely welded to a tractor, and a hen-house contrived from a plastic water tank shaded from the sun with a thatch of heather. It had vents made by heating air-bricks in the fire and pushing them into the walls.

Paul loved it.

'Part of the lore of Glenfarron,' he'd say. 'A little piece of Poland.'

And, indeed, the old farmhouse had a huge mural covering the end wall: a coat of arms and a big brash legend:

VIVE LA POLOGNE!

The paint was decades old and flaking, but clear enough.

If anyone held a bash or a do – a wedding, a 21st, a village ceilidh – Vladislaw would appear with his barbeque (a 44-gallon drum torched in half lengthways) and set up his stall outside, selling his excellent sausages, pies and burgers. When Glenfarron Primary School held its winter dance in the corrugated hall behind the Farron Hotel, Vladislaw was there, generating fatty smoke and meaty stink.

'I have seen you before,' said the old man, flipping his rich, paprika-charged burgers on the grill. 'You are at the lodge.'

'Yes,' agreed Anna, who stood before him in a brown wool coat wondering why he made her nervous.

Paul appeared in the hall door, clucking after her.

'Hey, there you are. It's too cold for you, cummon!'

'I'm not an invalid,' she demurred.

Paul looked as though he might dispute that.

'It's bitter…'

'Don't fuss over me, Paul.'

Vladislaw watched the young man retreating.

'You have Petunia to work?' he asked, as he gutted rolls with a carving knife.

'Miss Forbes? Yes.'

Vladislaw said no more. Eventually Anna had to ask:

'You know her?'

'You want onion?' he parried.

'Yes – a little.'

He stuffed her roll with oily brown onion, adding a squirt of strong mustard.

'So,' he said gruffly, 'now she is mistress of that house.'

'What do you mean?' retorted Anna. 'It's my house.'

'Ninety-nine,' said Vladislaw, wanting money.

'What do you mean?' she persisted.

'For the burger.'

'Anna!' Paul, standing in the bright doorway.

Vladislaw, glancing from under his brows at Paul, muttered something foreign.

'So,' he smiled fleetingly at Anna, 'you will treat our Petunia better than Gideon Baird has done, yes?'

'Come on, Anna.' Paul was at her elbow, tugging. 'Your pal Ronnie the teacher's asking for you.'

She followed meekly towards the door, the warmth, lights and music, Ron Christie and a drink. But, as Paul passed in among the crowd, Anna turned and hurried back out to the smoky glow of the barbecue. She stood in front of Vladislaw with her fists balled in her coat pockets.

'What did Gideon do to Miss Forbes?' she demanded.

The old exile pursed his lips and peered down at his sausages.

'What he didn't do,' he said. 'Bloody waste of a good heart.'

'Is she…' Anna hesitated, 'a friend of yours?'

The old man studied Anna as though debating whether she was fit to be told anything. 'You look after Petunia, please,' he said.

And then gave his attention to another customer.

Anna went into the hall, shedding her coat and chewing on her meat.

As she entered, she could see Paul looking about, confused, puzzling as to how she'd given him the slip again. Ah, she'd not meant to snub him, to hurt him. How he cared for her; who else would ever care for her so?

Thinking of snubs, she saw Julie eyeing Paul from near the band. Julie was wearing, over very tight jeans, a babydoll top of lacy white cotton that pressed her pert little bust into a cleavage, into which her crimped black locks dangled with calculated abandon. There were some present (Charlie Dulce among them) who found the effect rather marvellous, but Anna saw matters differently. Julie was on the verge of swanning up to Paul and accosting him, so Anna got in first. She cut between the Dashing White Sergeants, slipped her arm into Paul's and steered him away. She could feel Julie's daggers in her back, and very pleasant too.

'Hey, hello!' Paul smiled.

The music ended; the caller called:

'Right folks, we're taking a breather.'

'Bugger that,' said Paul. 'I was planning to warm you up.'

'I'm eating.' She touched his hand. 'Go up and play yourself.'

'You reckon?'

'Do it.'

So Paul went to the dais, spoke to the keyboard man and slipped into his place. He gave the plastic keys a casual glance, leaned towards the microphone and spoke in a mealy-mouthed falsetto voice.

'Ladies and gentlemen, take your partners for a slow waltz.'

The crowd regarded him indifferently as he played a languid chromatic introduction. But before they could drift away, he unleashed a hard driving blues:

Sugar Mama, Sugar Mama,
Please, come on back to me!
Bring me back my Sugar Mama,
Please, ease my misery!

The band drummer, still in his seat, couldn't resist joining in. Glenfarron put down its beer and streamed back onto the floor to dance.

Ronnie Christie moved to Anna's side.

'Ease my misery, Anna?'

'Well now,' she smiled, for both Julie and Dr Dulce were glancing her way. 'I don't mind if I do.'

She danced the teacher's socks off.

When at last they slowed, Ronnie looked admiringly towards Paul.

'Does he do this for a living?'

'A living would be nice,' she replied wryly. The punchy blues ended and, without a whiff of hesitation, Paul shifted into something slow and easy:

I got a right to love my baby,
She treats me just like a king.
Yeah, she's my mind, body, soul,
She can do most anything.

Ronnie offered a chaste clinch. Off they went across the floor.

She's my doctor when I'm sick, people,
She's my all around standby.
She's my lawyer when I'm in trouble,
She's my mother when I wanna cry.

'Did you know Gideon at all?' asked Anna.

'I had a lot of time for Gideon,' he replied.

'What happened to him?'

Didn't she know?

'He drank.'

'To death?'

'Well…'

Ronnie's grasp on her stiffened just slightly. But she persisted.

'Something to do with Miss Forbes, wasn't it?'

'I believe so.'

They turned some more, not speaking.

'He was a gentle chap,' Ronnie suddenly added, 'who died of unrealised love. A waste.'

A waste. A waste of love. Anna drifted on in the teacher's hold, listening to Paul sing.

She's my mind, body and soul, people,
She can do most anything.

'He's a natural, your Paul,' said Ronnie the teacher, and he saw that Anna's look was fixed on her Paul.

Oh, yes: mind, body and soul.

◆◆◆

The wood fire lit, the room warm as warm, the mellowest fiddle music playing and Paul working hard to please, wheeling in a butler's trolley with the late night gourmandising that he'd assembled: brandy bananas, cream, and Gideon's best malt in crystal rummers. He had a tea towel over his forearm in butler-buffoonery. She laughed at everything, purring as they ate:

'Will you bathe me?'

He paused in his whisky sipping.

'Please?' she added coyly

She had imagined it all in advance; she had been seduced by her own vision, and now she let it happen. She had him sponging and soaping the curve of her creamy back in a cloud of fragrant steam; she had him carrying her, wrapped in green towels and giggling into his neck, laying her down on the billowing nonsense of their bed in front of another bright fire, powdering her as she beamed up at the flouncy pink canopy. Submissive and delighted, she remembered, as she lay back, how his little projected image in a shaft of light had walked boldly across her abdomen till she opened for him, even as she did now, with him bigger and brighter still.

◆◆◆

She dreamed that, in nightclothes, she stepped from the kitchen door into the yard that was ice-bound and treacherous. Though her feet burned with the cold, though she shivered in the wind-still crystalline night, she continued down the frost-set gravel to the main road which was lit by the unkind orange gleam of sodium lamps. Under one such stood Paul and Julie; the minx mouthed something obscene, his hand came up in slow motion and he slapped Julie hard …

A slow, hollow thud: the big kirk door slamming shut. All three turned to watch it close and rebound, and slam shut again.

When she looked next, Paul and Julie were gone. Anna had a powerful torch in her hand, a long chromium thing with a strong, sharp beam. She played this left and right over the kirk interior, which was piled with snow drifts. She moved forward, swinging the beam until she saw, arrayed high on either wall, all the headstones from the kirkyard pinned up like pictures, all the dead of her own name, one after another:

Baird, Baird, Baird. Dead.

In one corner, a light was burning, a single candle in a red glass on a small table. She came close to it, and she held out a hand, right over the flame. She felt no heat.

It attacks nerves. You don't feel anything.

She turned to the source of the voice. It came from the squint window left of the altar. A face – Charlie Dulce, her doctor – soaked in orange sodium light, was leering at her through the squint. She stepped hurriedly back. As the orange face disappeared, she looked up and her torch lit the cracked and flaking black board of the Roll of Ministers.

Jacob Murdo – newly painted.

At this moment, Anna heard the thin, reedy notes of the harmonium, and an alto voice singing to a familiar tune:

And on Him tuke our vile nature,
Our deadly woundës for to cure…

She was trembling; she crept back to the corner and peeped round.

'Paul…?'

It was not Paul. When the figure stopped pedalling, when it twisted round to confront her, it was Anna herself except that the face was hideously deformed, the brow puffy and swollen as though the skin was packed with bacteria, the nose gone entirely leaving only a ragged pit, the mouth twisted in a sorry leer – yet it was herself, it was herself!

She screeched and collapsed, striking her head against an oak lectern, slithering down to the stone flags.

◆◆◆

When Paul woke, she was sitting up in bed, gazing out of the window (they never drew the curtains). Her hair was stuck to the back of her neck as if with glue, and she smelled of inundations of sweat, dank and sweet.

The wooden window casements were shifting and knocking. Any improvement in the weather had been postponed; there was now a brisk wind nudging the panes. He was about to reach out and touch the nape of her neck – but thought better of it.

'Morning,' he said pleasantly.

'Gideon wouldn't marry Miss Forbes.'

'What?'

'Gideon. What was he scared of? It would have been something appalling.'

'I'm saying good morning here ...'

Anna had not in fact been looking out of the window, but at the portrait photo of Gideon in uniform that hung just alongside. Now, however, she did stare out at the cold day.

'Perhaps he'd come back,' she murmured to herself.

'Who?' asked Paul, quite bewildered. 'Gideon?'

But now she didn't seem to be thinking about Gideon. She was frowning, concentrating, as though assessing a threat.

'He'd still be wanting to come back. He'd come back again.'

Again, she scrutinised the photograph.

'Why did Gideon lock the camera obscura?' she asked.

'How would I know?' Paul replied. 'To stop housebreakers from entering via the roof, or to stop thieves swiping the optics? Could be anything. Why make so much of it?'

He no longer felt like touching her neck.

◆◆◆

Mid-morning, she needed coffee.

She was alone; Paul was outside stripping down some stubbornly malfunctioning part of the heating boiler: a Quixotic gesture, given that they rarely turned it on. Cradling the hot coffee mug, which seemed to pass no heat at all into her hands, she drifted from kitchen to drawing room. She looked yearningly at the cold, grey ash in the fireplace; they had few logs either. The whole house felt stiff with cold.

Turning about the room – as much to keep moving as anything – her eye fell upon the display cabinet. She went to it and opened out the walnut-veneered top; inside, beneath the protective glass, lay the book with its gold blocked title:

McCorquadale's Relicts
or, Leprosy in Caledonian Antiquity 1773

She felt, with sudden urgency, that she must examine this book. She pulled at the edge of the toughened glass with her fingernail but it was just as locked as before. In frustration she put both hands on the cabinet and shook it.

And was rewarded. With a little rattle, something lodged underneath fell to the floorboards: a small key.

She retrieved this, and of course it opened the chromium clasp.

She lifted the glass, and for a second or two stood still, as though to let foul air escape from the case. Then she put out a hand and opened the book.

She read the table of contents:

There was a black silk bookmark sewn into the headband and lying between two pages halfway through. She lifted this, thinking that the binding would be stiff, but these pages at least fell open readily.

She looked – and felt her skin prickling.

There was a woodcut (cruder than her own) some six inches across and four deep, within a black border. It showed a kirk; below the steps at the west door, a small crowd was gathered, one of whom, a woman, was casting herself to the ground in extreme despair. There was a text:

Margaret Baird named a lipper.

A merciless figure stood before her, barring the door, and raising one hand in blessing, command, or damnation. This man was tall, and wore a long black cloak. Anna recoiled, dropping the glass cover which, when it fell, cracked right across from the bright hinge.

◆◆◆

She tried to work, but her nerves were shot to pieces. She might have blamed the cold but Paul had installed in her room an old convector heater that ticked and sparked with an odour of singeing dust.

She'd drawn a Victorian fisherman by a mountain pool, hoiking a splendid trout from the water. But as she tried, two handed, to control the fine chisel cutting into the pear wood block, her wrists trembled. The wood was resisting; she did not have her usual control, her touch, her feeling for the infinitesimal variations in the texture. She bit her lip and persevered, trying to coax and wiggle the slim V-shaped blade across the grain – until there was a thump as her hand shot forward and her wrist struck the table edge.

The chisel had broken, the snapped end gouging deep into the fisherman's head.

She stared in dismay at her hand. Her left ring finger was bleeding freely at the knuckle, where it had struck the steel of the vice.

She went to the bathroom, washing the bleed, watching the pink rivulets of blood swirling in the stream.

It attacks the nervous system. It destroys the nerve fibres. You lose the sensation of touch, so you damage yourself repeatedly, cuts, burns, you don't feel anything.

She couldn't feel her finger at all.

And then billions of bacteria invade the skin of the face, making it swollen and lumpy. The front of the jaw rots, the nose collapses inward, you croak like a raven.

She peered at herself in the mirror, touching her face, feeling for lumpy swellings.

The last streaks of blood tailed off down the drain. The house was quiet: Paul was outside, Miss Forbes was not here. Anna had the bizarre realisation that she missed the old lady's bustle.

Petunia Forbes.

Anna hurried downstairs.

'I'm going shopping,' she shouted from the driver's window.

Paul had heard the car reversing on the gravel and had appeared from the boiler shed. Anna did not stop.

She drove down alongside the Farron Water, turning off into a lane where a decaying wooden board read, ***Torbrechan***.

There were the railway wagons with chicken-wire windows, the tractor with its home-made slurry scraper, the hen-house under its thatch of old heather, and the fading script: ***Vive la Pologne!*** And there was the old man with his wooden leg and his deep black eyes. He peered at her from the doorway of his 'office' in an old caravan.

She got out of the car feeling ludicrous. Every noise she made, from the scrape of her shoe to the creak of the ancient Peugeot's door, sounded tinny and unconvincing.

'Good morning,' she said. 'I'd like some sausage.'

He said nothing, but reached inside the caravan, taking a key off a cup hook and then marching stiffly across to another shed. Inside, from the ceiling hung dozens of long sausages, hard and dry, knobbly, all covered with a thick white bloom. Anna indicated: she would have this sort, and maybe that sort. He unhooked them, and took her money, unspeaking.

'I wanted to ask you…' she faltered. He made no reaction, continuing to wrap the sausages without looking at her.

'I wanted to ask you about Gideon Baird.'

He looked up at last, patient and expectant.

'To ask, if you know, just why it was that Gideon wouldn't marry Miss Forbes.'

'Because,' said the old man, 'everyone knew she was the bloody whore. Now she's in the kirk but then she was whore. Half the Polish Air Force got in there, okay, but she was nicest, kindest whore in all bloody Scotland, though not good enough for *swinia* like General Gideon.'

Anna stood clutching her plastic bag of dry sausage.

'He was afraid,' she said. 'But, of what?'

Vladislaw shrugged.

'For his big soldier career, his life, his old family name, his house. His repute. She was the biggest whore.'

He said the word loudly, roughly, laughingly. Then he was thoughtful, speaking with startling tenderness.

'No one in this damn place spoke to her then, and no one speaks to her now. Only me.'

'I speak to her, and Paul. And the doctor,' said Anna.

Vladislaw considered, then nodded.

'Yes, you and also Dr Dulce. But for most, she is a leper,' he said, 'a rotting thing. You behave bad, you are a leper. People get shunned, you know? They get turned out.'

'Turned out by who?' she demanded.

'There's your sausage,' he said.

◆◆◆

With hindsight, Dr Dulce's next contact with Anna was particularly revealing, had he been able to read it correctly. But of course, hindsight…

She had been into Aggie Hulewicz' shop to buy a bumper pack of soap. Having paid and left the shop, she'd gone back in again and bought disinfectant and medicated shampoo. Finally, she came round to the surgery and, in her frostiest voice, asked Julie for an appointment with the doctor.

Julie smiled sweetly; there was a cancellation: was Anna free just now?

Charlie listened to Anna with astonishment.

'You? Leprosy? You're not serious.'

'You said it was slow developing,' Anna replied.

'Not several hundred years slow.'

'That it could be infectious within the family.'

'By close contact. It's not inherited.'

'Or couldn't it be in the house? Things lie dormant, don't they? What if…'

'Anna, you really cannot…'

He stopped, because there was a little tap on the door and Julie came in, holding out a buff folder.

'Mrs Baird's notes,' she said, popping them on the table and heading for the door.

'Thank you,' said Charlie. 'Oh, hang on.'

Julie hesitated. He was examining the folder.

'These are Mr Baird's,' he said.

Julie took the file back, puzzled.

'I'm sorry,' she said, 'it's the date of birth… I'll get the others.'

She clearly wanted to ask something – but thought better of it and went out again.

'Now,' he said to Anna. 'What is all this?'

'It is in the family,' she insisted doggedly. 'Margaret had it.'

'Who?' Charlie was bewildered.

'Margaret, Kenneth Baird's wife. She was denounced as a leper by Reverend Murdo. She was ostracized and cast out.'

'Oh, good heavens. The poor woman was denounced because old Kenneth was away to the bishop to get Murdo expelled. It was Murdo's retaliation. It was vicious nonsense. It was also four hundred years ago!'

Julie re-entered. She had in her hand another, identical folder. For a moment, she did not hand it over, but stood by the desk staring at Anna as though she had never seen her before. The doctor glanced at his receptionist in mild surprise.

In the silence, Anna said:

'Margaret drowned herself.'

◆◆◆

Can you cease to feel moral imperatives, she wondered – literally, cease to feel? Can you lose moral sensation? She had realised rather to her surprise that sometimes one did indeed *feel* moral impulses physically: obligation, compulsion, or boiling anger. But she herself? She often thought that something she did was wrong, at least by common standards, but without feeling anything at all. Did she not believe in morality, or in social norms? Or was she just sick?

The following day – having told Paul nothing of her visit to the surgery – she went back to the village and into the post office.

Why was the postmistress staring at her like that?

When she came out, she saw Julie and two other women standing on the opposite verge, smoking. They saw her. Anna saw Julie give one of her friends a nudge. They all looked away.

Anna walked round to the school.

'We were going to fix a day for me to come back to work with P6,' she said to Ronnie Christie.

Why's he not giving me a straight answer?

She went home, and drank more coffee. She knew it was a bad idea, knew she was too tense and nervy as it was, but she needed coffee. She wanted to go upstairs to speak to Paul. But then, no, Paul was the last person she wanted to see. Miss Forbes was due this afternoon. Did she want to speak to Petunia Forbes? To the whore? What would she feel then? What does a whore feel, in her body? Did she want to be a whore? Did she know what she wanted? She wanted out.

She put on thick clothes, for the wind-chill was acute. Out she went into the cold blast, positively striding to the kirk. The door was locked. She walked twice round the graveyard, the chiselled names sneering at her: *Baird, Baird, Baird.*

She was buffeted by gusts coming off the moor. For a split second, she saw a line of gaunt and ragged figures bearing long staves coming in through the gate off the moor, driven towards her by a man in a long black cloak. She saw them!

Only for a split second. Her mind's eye in overdrive. Nothing at all.

There, near the corner of the kirk, was the slight bulge in the masonry where the squint was. Uncertain but compelled, she went towards it. She put a hand to the stone embrasure, pressing. She could sense the general resistance to her pressure – but the cold, abrasive grittiness? Where was that?

Perhaps she was just too cold to feel.

She looked though the glass of the squint, in towards the altar as each leper had done, looking for salvation. But the interior was dark.

She went back to the porch. She remembered the key behind the stone, and slipped inside, closing the door carefully lest it slam and crack from its hinges right across.

After the roaring air outside, in the still interior she could hear her heart beat in her ears, very quickly indeed. Could her heart really beat so fast? She put one right finger to her left wrist, but she couldn't feel a pulse.

You lose the sensation of touch, you don't feel anything.

She walked slowly forward towards the altar.

Lepers were brought into the kirk, the only time they were allowed in, and they knelt under a black cloth by the altar and heard the Burial Service.

She stopped herself; she wasn't going to imagine that, to see herself kneeling. She dragged her eyes up; the black painted board was as normal, no Murdo there. Something had been replaced, however. On the shelf over the harmonium stood a familiar volume in a faded brown cloth binding. She took it, and opened it. It was Victorian edition, a scholarly reprint:

Ane Compendious Buik
Of Godlie and Spirituall Sangis
(1567)
Edited with the melodies by E.F. Dalziel
Scottish Historic Publications Society
Edinburgh 1893

There was a scrap of newspaper placed as a bookmark. She opened, and read:

Let us rejoice and sing
And praise that michty king
Whilk sent His Son of a virgin bricht,
And on Him tuke our vile nature,
Our deadly woundës for to cure…

She thrust it back onto the shelf. She moved along the wall to the squint, to peer out at the moor.

A dark, bearded face swam into view right in front of her.

She screeched and stumbled back. She fell, she crawled in front of the altar. She heard the kirk door open, a heavy, uneven tread, she shrank away…

'Miss? Miss Baird?'

The voice was dark, was warm and concerned, human, nothing vile or wounded or dead.

Vladislaw looked down at her.

'You are unwell? You have fallen! My goodness, you are sick?'

She looked up at him in bewilderment.

'I was looking for you,' he said anxiously. 'I see you go round the kirk and I have followed you, but you come inside. I was at the shop. You left something and they said I should bring it, I was coming this way. Here, you left something.'

He offered her a crinkling plastic bag. She got to her feet, blushing furiously. Oh God, she thought, you can still feel a fool. She took the bag and peeked inside.

Three bottles of bleach.

◆◆◆

She felt a fool, she felt a traitor, she felt disgusting. Yet she felt nothing. Inside, in her heart, in skin – nothing at all. Not even when face down on the eiderdown of Gideon's princess bed with her face in goose feather pillows and a thick cushion under her hips so that her naked arse was in the air and she was being screwed ragged by Paul, her Paul who had waited and said nothing all those long cold months, and was now exultant.

Nor did she feel much in the shower afterwards, scrubbing at herself with the loofa and the loo brush, scrubbing and scrubbing until she heard Paul calling to her:

'What are you doing in there, Anna?'

Soaping and cleansing, wading in suds and bilge, running the shower hotter and hotter till it suddenly went cold on her. She stood dripping in the bath, looking at the three large plastic bottles on the windowsill.

Later, she appeared in the kitchen. She rattled the old Rayburn, the iron noise thundering in her head. She was on edge, supersensitive. She found bread and jam, attempting to eat a little, and she dragged the heavy kettle onto the Rayburn. As it seethed, she stared out of the window. Across the garden, she could see the corner of the kirk, the small yew cowering against the wind and, above the stone dyke, the tops of certain gravestones taller than the rest.

Baird Baird Baird. Vile woundës.

In the corner of her vision, something shifted. Scarcely daring to move, she watched the handle of the back door turn slowly.

What little colour there was in her face drained away.

The door swung open with a clatter, and a stout figure was bundled inside by the gale. Miss Petunia Forbes placed her basket on the floor and pushed the door closed, huffing at the weather.

'What a windy old wind,' she began, 'it just blows and blows … Oh!'

Wide-eyed, she pointed.

Anna's right hand was resting on the open hotplate of the Rayburn, and was smoking.

Anna wrenched it away, sending the fat brown kettle clanging to the floor in a scalding cascade.

◆◆◆

'That'll be sore,' declared Dr Dulce, as he piled on layers of white gunk. He was watching Anna's face. She mumbled something inaudible.

'I beg your pardon?'

'It was an accident,' she said expressionlessly.

'Well, indeed it was, Anna,' he agreed, 'an accident of some sort. How on earth did you manage to drive here?'

But she seemed hardly aware of Charlie, or of the plastic bag he was wrapping around her right hand, taping it over the burn cream. She was staring into the middle distance.

'Margaret,' she said quietly, 'must have been mad with fear; that was no accident. She thought she'd be marched out over Purgatory Burn, without seeing her husband again. Never to return.' She lifted her face to look at Charlie. 'Murdo scared her to death.'

He stopped strapping, and studied her.

'Anna,' he said patiently, 'your hand was resting on the hotplate. Why didn't you move it?'

She seemed to consider this as an academic problem.

'I didn't feel it,' she said dryly.

He sensed that questions would get nowhere, so he drew himself up and spoke with traditional medical severity.

'I want you back in the morning. We'll look at it again, and we'll need to discuss it again. I'll write you up something for the pain.'

'It's quite all right,' said Anna.

He peered at her in surprise – but Anna was now gazing at Petunia Forbes who sat immobile in the corner of the consulting room. She was scrutinising Miss Forbes with an expression of extraordinary pity and compassion, as though it were she, not Anna, who was wounded.

Petunia Forbes looked steadfastly at the floor.

Charlie sighed, the measured professional sigh of the baffled, silently berating Dr Melhuish for insisting that the trainee see this through.

'Well – Julie'll run you home.'

Anna sat still as a stone.

'Anna…?' he queried, cocking his head.

'There is something else,' she murmured.

She got to her feet, crossed the room to the examination couch and lifted herself onto it. She lifted her hips, pulled her denim skirt up to the small of her back and slipped her washed-out yellow pants down below her knees. Then she lay back, letting knees and thighs fall open.

'Anna, what is this about?'

Charlie was an innocent young man; he had not faced much of this sort of thing. Astonished, reddening, he again looked to Miss Forbes for help, but the old lady still stared at the floor. Flustered, he pulled a wheeled curtain forward to screen Anna from the door. Then, reluctantly, he stepped forward to his patient. He stiffened, and his eyes widened in horror at the flaming, blistered, excoriated mess in her crotch.

'Oh, my dear girl…!'

She gazed up at him, and for a moment he saw both desperation and contempt for his denseness. Her eyes filled with tears and fear, pleading with him to understand.

'I don't feel a thing,' she whispered.

◆◆◆

He summoned Paul, sending Julie to fetch him since the Peugeot was already at the surgery. When they were gathered, the air was full of awkwardness and a great deal that was unspoken. Perched on the examination couch, Anna sat mute in her black woollen coat. By the desk sat Charlie Dulce, feeling quite out of his depth. He hissed urgent things to Paul who was sweating freely, eyes fixed upon the doctor as though he didn't dare look across at Anna. She gave no sign of listening anyway, but she caught the conversation:

'… self-harm … the chemical burns … colleagues in psychology…'

Paul was insisting that there was no need, he didn't want poor Anna subjected to that prying, that humiliating interrogation; she wouldn't be able to stand that.

And Charlie, conscientious but dreadfully lacking in experience, didn't know what to do, didn't know what he was dealing with, and was beginning to bluster.

Anna watched them. She would let them fight it out, the men.

After a minute or two, she stirred slightly and they both turned to see.

'Anna?' said Paul, speaking too fast and too much. 'Shall we get you comfy at home? I'll light a fire in the sitting room, Doctor, and look after her there. It's partly the cold, how can one feel things properly in that freezing house. You always love a wood fire, don't you, Anna, to smell the wood smoke…'

Anna's hand suddenly flew to her face.

The nose collapses inwards. You croak like a raven.

She stared back at him, opening her mouth, and the sound that came from her was a splintered croak, a disgusting caw:

'Don't want a thing! Don't want a thing!'

◆◆◆

She'd been left to sleep by the fire, but it didn't happen. She heard Paul creeping upstairs to his work. Restless, she got up from the chaise longue and went to the window.

Snow was falling; the high hills to the north were no more than faint silhouettes, and the road up to the ski centre vanished within a hundred yards into a swirling whiteness. The police would soon be shutting the snow gate. From this downstairs window she could not see the moor at all. She felt trapped. She could not stay here, even with the fire.

When Paul appeared in the kitchen some while later, he found her cooking.

'Well, hello…' he said, astonished. Then he became aware of a delicious hot fragrance.

She stepped round him, reached down and opened the oven door. With her good hand she lifted out a tray of lightly browned wholemeal rolls.

'Look at this!' he gawped.

'You want one?' she returned. 'Sit yourself, then.'

'Your hand's okay?'

'It's fine.'

'Terrific.'

He sat obediently, as she plonked plate, knife, butter and jam in front of him.

'And I'm fine,' she added.

'Well, that's great.'

'Come on, while they're hot.'

He scoffed eagerly.

'Have one yourself,' he urged, mouth full. 'You've eaten damn all lately.'

Which was true: not a meal in days. She sat opposite, nibbling for show, watching him.

'How's work?' she asked.

He shrugged cheerfully.

'Could be worse. I should finish the score for the crappy cop show today. Then I can get back to the quartet.'

She smiled to hear it. He studied her face, hoping but hardly believing.

'You're really feeling better, are you?'

'Absolutely.' She glanced down at her heavily bandaged hand.

'But, I mean, in yourself. You look…'

'Normal?' She laughed. 'Oh, yes, back to normal.'

'Great!'

She was still examining her hand.

'But I can't drive.'

There was something else coming, something difficult. He paused in his chewing, half the roll held in mid-air. She said:

'I know it's a pain, but can you take me into Inverness?

'What for, hen?'

'To Raigmore hospital.'

'You've an appointment, then?'

'I need to speak to someone,' she said. Now there was a brittle edge to her voice. 'I need to see someone in the skin department. Or the infections department, it doesn't matter which.'

He glimpsed a precipice.

'I don't know that you can, sweet, not without Dr Dulce referring…'

'I don't need referring, I don't need crap, I just need to see a specialist.'

'Anna…'

'I'm fine, all right? I'm okay – but I need to get this thing sorted by someone who'll take me seriously.'

'We all take you seriously, of course we do.'

'Then do what I ask, please. Just drive me.'

'I don't like to… Anna, I don't think you're so well…'

'Well enough to be fucked though? I mean, last night, you thought I was well enough last night.'

'For pity's sake…'

'Okay to be poked but not worth curing? Sure, driving to Inverness is a bother…'

'I never said that.'

'Fine, I'll cure myself.'

'Anna …!'

But she had grabbed her coat and was out of the back door into the snow, leaving him hunting frantically for his boots.

Down the drive she went in a loping run, scrunching the new snow under her shoes, onto the moor path but twisting to glance back at the kirkyard and the stone outside, half-obliterated by drifts:

MARGARET BAI
WIFE
O
DRO

She ran full tilt into the floating snow, screwing up her eyes and flailing the flakes away from her face. She wore no hat, no coat, but could thus move at a reckless, slithering speed. She could hardly make out the way, and was following instinct and memory; she'd walked or stared at the path often enough. She skirted the edge of the marsh, heading along the burn towards the wooden bridge. Behind her, the house receded and faded in the snowy dusk.

On she floundered, and now she could make out – she'd swear she could make out – a shadow, a form, a woman moving steadily in front of her along the path.

'Wait, wait!'

She was frightened, losing her direction as the snow deepened, but soon stumbling if she strayed off the path into the heather. She was panting, her hair and the shoulders of her jersey sodden, and the cold biting. The wind had got up of a sudden, coming in gusts that beat on her back, propelling her forward. Even so, she was close to exhaustion and would not have been able to go much further – but then she was at the wooden footbridge on which the snow was building, almost whiting out the horizontals but leaving the upright posts dark and clear.

She came nearer, studying the bridge intently as though expecting to see someone standing mid-stream or even coming towards her. She saw the margins of the burn thickened by white drifts closing over the water from either side, like swollen lids drawing over an infected eye. By the bridge, she knelt down in the snow and plunged her bandaged hand into the stream, holding it there still and deep. Then she dipped her good left hand, to scoop and splash water over her face and head, gasping at the chill.

Then her eyes widened, her cold and starved brain swam, and she almost plunged forward in a faint at what she saw.

Drifting into view from under the fringe of ice below the bridge, came the white, puffy face of a young woman, a sweet and simple face, staring but unseeing, open-mouthed.

Anna gagged, she gasped, she stumbled to her feet but fell again, sprawled in snow. There she lay, peering into the dancing storm. As she looked, out of the whiteness came a line of dark shapes moving with sorrowful deliberation to pass within feet of her, stepping onto the bridge one by one, and across Purgatory Burn – then vanishing again into the snow.

She jumped to her feet, shivering violently. She began to run headlong back into the wind, into the blizzard away from the bridge.

And stopped short. There had been a sound, surely, a thin sound on the wind, a cry.

Ahead of her, she glimpsed someone new, at first fleetingly in the white swirl, but then more certain, swaying towards her in the dark outline of a cape. Panic-stricken, she took a step or two backwards, then spun about to see whether the terrifying line of figures was behind her, coming at her. She couldn't tell, the light was almost gone, she could barely see the bridge at all, they might very well be there. She looked downhill again – and the single oncoming form was close. Frantic with fright, she dithered, she attempted to move off the path but was snared by the heather and fell.

'Anna!' The cry again, thinly, blown apart by the rising gale.

She began crawling off the path to thrust herself into some refuge in the snow.

'Anna!' Almost upon her. She stood, trying to run out across the heather, falling at once.

'Anna, Jesus wept, Anna!'

His hands seized her, dragged her upright.

'She was all right!' Anna screeched.

'What?!'

'She needn't have done it, she needn't. She wasn't sick, she was quite all right, she needn't...'

Again, Paul slapped her.

'Get a grip, Anna!'

He'd dragged off his snowy waterproof and draped it around

her shoulders as she stood sobbing. He shook her again.

'Are you trying to get us both fucking killed? You get the fuck down that path or I'll fucking thump your face in. You hear me?!'

◆◆◆

A strange little scene followed, which Anna related to the doctor some time later. When he heard what she had to say, Charlie Dulce was disinclined to believe it, and decided that it must be another product of Anna's now seriously overheated imagination. But by this point, his own personal situation was on the point of changing, and that clouded his judgement. He was reluctant to take the matter up with Julie, and so it remained between them, a memory which Julie and Charlie both carried, but which they did not share.

Brought in from the storm, Anna was back on the chaise longue under two rugs. The fire was blazing, heaped with dry wood and throwing out a ferocious heat. She wondered if that was the sensation she could feel in her cheek, the side that was towards the fire. Then again, it could have just been snow-scouring. Or perhaps she couldn't feel anything at all – she could no longer tell. Perhaps she only hoped for, and therefore imagined, sensation.

She could hear voices out in the hall. The doctor had returned, summoned by Paul. He had Julie with him; she'd declared that she was coming to assist, and wouldn't be dissuaded even by the snow, though Charlie did wonder why she was so keen. There was a policeman there also; he'd brought them both up through the storm in his Land Rover. They wondered, should they be sending Anna to Inverness by ambulance? Paul was having none of it, said the roads were lethal, said he could warm her up as well as anyone. They were still debating the point when Julie re-emerged from the kitchen. She was carrying, on a tray, a mug of something that steamed. She opened the drawing room and went in.

In Anna's account, Julie came on quiet little feet over the worn Turkey carpet towards the chaise longue.

'Anna?'

She found a stool and set it beside the chaise longue, placing the mug within Anna's reach. Then she knelt down.

'Anna?' she murmured again, her face close. 'There's your milk, good and hot, with honey.'

Julie leaned over the mug, worked her mouth a moment and carefully spat a large gob into the contents.

'Plus a little added something,' she said, picking the teaspoon from the saucer and giving the milk a stir. Anna watched her without expression.

'You'll like that,' Julie continued softly. 'It'll be absolutely squalid, like you and your squalid brother.'

She stood up, smiling.

'I worked it out,' she said, 'from your medical notes. Twins. It's pretty obvious: date of birth the same, and the place. I made a phone call. Not surprising Paul doesn't want any shrink digging too deeply.'

She leaned down and whispered, 'I *know*, Anna.'

Then she retreated to the door.

'Night, night,' she called back as she left.

Anna heard the policeman's voice, the doctor and Paul, then the front door and the Land Rover starting.

Paul came in, grinning anxiously.

'Can I try a sip of your milk?' he asked.

She said, 'Finish it.'

◆◆◆

She woke again, in bed. Their bed.

Midnight, or later. The wind had dropped, the snow stopped. The moon was out, and the uncurtained room was full of moonlight reflected off the snow, and then off Gideon's briar rose wallpaper.

Her Uncle Gideon, and Paul's Uncle Gideon.

Paul lay beside her with the eiderdown tugged round his ears, breathing noisily. Not quite a snore; more tuneful.

And then she heard the music. In this room, or next door, coming from somewhere. Possibly from the moon.

She turned her back to Paul, and closed her eyes firmly. But her eyelids were not thick enough to exclude the snow-bright moonlight.

And the tune was hurting her. She tried thinking of other music, but anything else was overwhelmed. She tried putting her hands over her ears, but you cannot sleep with your hands over your ears. The tune was like a sharp steel augur, drilling inexorably through her skull to get a firm purchase, deep in her grey matter.

She freed her legs from the eiderdown, and the hot water bottle flopped onto the floor. Paul's breathing paused – then restarted, quieter.

She stood by the bed. The room was not as chilly as usual, because Paul had brought in that extravagant electric convection heater. The moment she opened the bedroom door, however, she felt the cold. It slipped into her pyjamas and caressed her. It took especial notice of her calves, and made the hairs there stand erect. It had chilled the nails in the floorboards, and the worn fibres of the runner.

I can feel all that, she thought.

Still the tune played.

She moved along the passageway with quick, small steps, glancing at the door of Paul's room wondering, but only for a second, if the music came from there. She turned the corner; a few steps more, and she reached the stairs to the camera obscura.

Up she went.

When, at the top, she opened the plain timber door, the octagonal chamber was filled with pale light, so much light that she thought for a moment that a bulb was burning. But it was the same moonlight on new snow, collected and refracted by the prisms, mirrors and lenses over her head and cast streaming down onto the round table before her, whose white surface gleamed.

The tune in her head had stopped.

Anna looked at the table top and at first could not understand it, since the entire image was white. Of course: it was an expanse of snow. She touched the controls, swinging the image until she could see – with huge relief at its banality – the pub, the Brig Bar by the Wade bridge, firmly shuttered against the night.

Curious to examine her world in this strange light, she gripped the handles again and rotated the lenses. She looked right down the valley, seeing the forests of Glenfarron heavy with white, the village draped and muffled. She caught moonlit reflections on the Farron Water and the distant loch; she saw the castle beyond, that hideous castle, much improved by a clean white shroud. She saw the surrounding hills, hard and clear against the black sky.

Everything was very clear. She saw pale glints off the windows of sleeping cars three miles away. She saw Parkneuk farm on the hillside, and Torbrechan where Vladislaw lay. She saw, at the very edge of the forest, a stack of builder's gear by a barn that was being converted into a house. And a dark gash in the trees that must be the lane leading to the home of Miss Petunia Forbes, the whore.

She turned the lens further, skimming over cottages and byres. As she completed the circle, bringing the view back to the pub, she depressed the angle and brought the view closer, until she was looking down at the kirk.

And there he stood, looking up at her.

He stood out, stark against the white field of the kirkyard, the severe lines of his cape making an unmistakeable geometry, his long staff a harsh black vertical stroke. He was waiting, and looking up at Anna.

She lowered her hands slowly, as though fearing to provoke him with sudden movement.

They stared at each other for an eternity, both immobile. Anna stopped breathing. Then he stirred; at once, her hands flew back to the control rods. She pulled and manipulated, keeping the figure in view as he walked across the kirkyard past the stunted yew. She was unpractised, she was unskilful, and as he came through the gateway into the lane she lost him, and gave little gasp of fear. With tweakings and twists she found him once more, moving up the driveway towards the house. He was striding briskly. Frantically she sidled round the white table top, swinging the optics to keep track of him as he approached. He passed behind a stand of trees, and panic seized her as he failed to reappear and she thought she'd lost him again – but he was only now coming out from behind the trees – there he was! Still coming, still gazing up at her, so brightly illuminated that she believed she could see the black of his eyes seeking her out.

Then he was in the yard, and the optics would not depress further. He was lost to view; he was too close.

She released the control rods, listening, sick with terror. She put her hands out behind her, touching the wooden walls of the chamber to keep her equilibrium. She glanced at the little door that gave onto the roof leads, but what safety could there be out there? She looked at the door to the stairs, but there was no lock that she could secure, nothing moveable in the chamber that she could barricade it with.

For half a minute, nothing happened. Then she heard the click of the latch on the landing below.

She screamed. She screamed again and again, screeching as

though screeching itself was a weapon. Even above her own screams she heard – or felt, through the wooden structure – footsteps rising. She reached up and grabbed at the iron-and-brass control rods, using her weight to wrench at them with a weird strength, even as the footsteps came up the last wooden stairs. Something above her snapped and gave way; a cascade of glass and fittings smashed onto the white table. As the door opened, she lifted the iron rod in her hand and she swung it, she swung it again and again at the figure that staggered at her, at the hands that reached out to seize her, she swung at the head, the face. As the figure sank to the floor she flailed at the skull that after many blows felt less resistant, felt softer, pounded...

Until she stopped, and nothing moved in the chamber.

◆◆◆

The house was sold, though not without difficulty; all attempts at letting had failed, the allure of Gideon's princess bed notwithstanding. After the sale, and the auction of contents, Anna was in theory quite a wealthy woman. But as she was hospitalised for a very long time, this was a matter of indifference to her, if she even understood what it meant. So the substantial estate lingered in her name for many years.

Young Dr Dulce, married and looking to settle in Glenfarron, had for the space of two minutes considered offering for the house; the asking price was a lot less than *Mandalay*, his first choice. But he thought better of it.

Charlie went to visit Anna several times in hospital, and from the outset felt unsettled by something that he could never quite put a finger on. At first he talked of Glenfarron trivia, to which she made little reaction, and may or may not have paid any attention. But even as he spoke and she stared distractedly out of the window, Charlie had a feeling that some part of her was watching him shrewdly, and knew very well what he was saying. And then she began, in a disjointed way, to tell him this story.

He thought about her a good deal (more than he ever let on to his wife), and pondered the matter often: how we may, perhaps unconsciously, take on a second-hand memory or a distant history for our own purposes. Charlie once hazarded a few thoughts with Dr Melhuish, just speculative notions about Anna 'seeing a way out of a dreadful situation'. But the old practitioner didn't take him on, and Charlie's occasional remarks to the psychiatrists were not followed up either. So he kept those notions to himself. In time, he came to realise that in Glenfarron he was appreciated as a conscientious doctor, but that few people regarded him as particularly shrewd or perceptive. This reputation has its advantages – people put more trust in a GP who is not going to see through them too readily – so he did nothing to dispel it.

At the lodge, the camera obscura was cleaned in a perfunctory manner by the estate agents. They sent a young woman who swept up the glass and left the various metal fittings in a heap by the stairs. As for the horrid stains on the floorboards, she certainly wasn't going to start scrubbing off blood. So she resorted to the expedient of pouring a bottle of bleach (she'd found several in the bathroom) over the stains, and then walking out and shutting the door.

In later years, visitors were occasionally taken by the new owners up the narrow wooden flight to see the camera obscura chamber; they would always talk, in a desultory way, of repairing and restoring the device.

But it's not possible. You can no longer get the parts.

Part Three

MUNGO'S PARK

2006

There was a warrior on the hillside; they had him clear in the binoculars. They could see him flourishing a shield of zebra hide, his steel assegai glinting in the first light. Hefted high in the warrior's fist, the broad shield was caught and tugged by gusts of wind that thrashed the dry uplands. The spear blade swung and dipped, grazing the tussocks, and the old man stamped his feet, shaking his greaves of waterbuck skin, shuddering the knotted calves of his legs and the leather apron at his waist. Again and again he lifted the shield to the east, to the new day.

And in answer, the sun shouldered the clouds apart, streamed down upon him, sparking off the razor edge of the blood-pocked blade.

The watchers glanced at one another, not unimpressed.

So, with their field glasses lowered, they missed his next move, which was to drop the shield and take from a leather pouch a tin of small cigars and a purple plastic gas lighter. He lit, he puffed, his face filled with contentment. He surveyed the landscape: the kirk spire, the trim stone cottages, the river and the rushy burns, the time-share chalets clustered about the distant castle, and the bus emerging from the roadside conifers – the school bus to Inverness. If he also saw the glint of glass as the two men raised their binoculars once more, if he noticed the watchers standing by a tractor in the farmyard half a mile off, he gave no sign of it.

'That's him, Doctor, he's away home.'

They saw now the old man stoop to pick a green anorak off the heather, then tramp down the hillside.

'Was I right to call you, Doctor? Hardly normal, is it?'

'Is Mr Robertson barmy?' said a small boy at their side.

'Go on, son, you'll miss the bus.'

'But is he barmy?'

'We're just wondering,' said Cameron.

But Charlie Dulce only shrugged, non-committal. As Dr Dulce, he was obliged to point out that such pleasantly harmless eccentricity is quite untreatable. And if Cameron Geddes was suggesting that they should be bundling Mungo Robertson off to the asylum, Charlie would have had to say: eccentricity is not grounds for custody. Since his return from Africa, Mungo had not pestered Dr Dulce unduly, and Charlie Dulce had no intention of pestering him.

◆◆◆

Each day, after his morning ceremony, Mungo in his anorak and leathers would lope down to his own yard, past a painted wooden sign – *Parkneuk* – appreciating the durability of things: the buildings well-settled in the hillside, the house and steadings of grey granite flecked with glittering quartz, everything old but in good repair, apart from the rusting skeleton of a motorbike in the log shed.

But what of that skull above the front porch: an eland, or a wildebeest? And the disturbing design of eyes framed in red-black zigzags on the steading doors? And the ghastly fetish swinging in the rowan tree, a thing of bone, feathers and nails sticky with antique blood? And the animal skin, stretched upon an ash frame, crusted with salt? And there, hanging over the goat pen: a desiccated monkey! Mungo lived in another world, a world in which some Glenfarron folk – notably Julia Dulce, the doctor's wife – would not set foot.

Bending to riddle the tepid Rayburn, Mungo would feel the years in his spine. His was a one-chair kitchen, cluttered with the usual Highland junk: vests drying on the pulley, wet shoes packed with newspaper by the stove, a wireless with specks of gravy on the loudspeaker. But there were black men on the mantelpiece, a row of prognathous pottery figurines, their scalps tufted with wool stuck into the clay. There were coil pots in terracotta patterned with black ash; there were woven baskets, and curious leather strappings. There were blades of all sizes tucked among the marmalade and coffee jars, and porcupine quills jabbed in patterns into the wood-chipped wall.

Dr Dulce knew these collections. On a rare house call some months before (Mungo had broken his ankle pursuing a ptarmigan for the pot), Charlie Dulce had asked him the use of these things, and Mungo had grinned and confessed that even he had forgotten. Charlie – who had never travelled – had surveyed the exotic paraphernalia, and after a morning clinic which had seemed to him an endless queue of whingeing middle-aged women with lists of little ailments, he had felt a fresh, vicarious excitement.

Hobbling in his plaster, Mungo had led Charlie through into the parlour. An interesting room; above the fireplace, a portrait of a young gentleman looked down at the doctor. He wore a high-collared coat with flaring lapels and the buttons straining somewhat over a manly chest. He had a white stock knotted right under his chin, and his hair was brushed back and powdered. *Circa* 1800, Charlie had guessed. The face was delicate, the cheeks high; the eyes were large, and a little vulnerable.

'That's very fine,' nodded Charlie. 'I admire that. But look at this, now!'

In the window bay hung another face, painted on bark fibre: a regal dance mask, conical and fringed with a skirt of grey-green grasses, and with staring spiral eyes. Mungo had seated himself between the mask and the painting, in an armchair of mangy magenta velveteen, staring out at the dank and breezy Glenfarron morning. Charlie had asked how he would cope with not being able to get out, with shopping and so on, and mentioned that the village store would deliver. Mungo had nodded without replying; there was a moistening in the old eyes, not so much self-pity as frustration. It is one thing to remember a far-away land, quite another to live there in your memory.

As the doctor was leaving, Mungo had struggled to his feet and teetered towards the bookshelves where a massive old open-reel tape-recorder perched. The window was open; as Charlie crossed the yard he had heard the house behind him fill with exalted singing, a hymn to the cattle, a choir of shrill women's voices pulsing and ululating. The women of a warmer continent were calling to Mungo.

And as he drove down Mungo's track, Charlie had felt a stab of envy, but also of poignant sympathy for the old man on his hillside, wallowing in lost love.

◆◆◆

Cameron Geddes, the neighbouring farmer, had been the first to come to Dr Dulce with concerns for Mungo's sanity. Then, young Constable Reid was obliged to call at Parkneuk, and felt distinctly uncomfortable.

They were standing in the yard studying the shrivelled

monkey.

'It improves the milk yield,' said Mungo. 'I kept goats in Africa and it was a herdsman of the Pinwa tribe who recommended a dead monkey over the compound gate. I saw an immediate benefit.'

PC Reid took a step backwards, wishing he were in his Land Rover and far away, while Mungo tweaked the remnants of the monkey's genitalia.

'This is known as a Nail Monkey because, when erect, the penis has a flattened head that resembles a household nail. Its proximity stimulates lactation in the nanny goat; I daresay it excites her.'

'Excuse me, Mr Robertson,' the constable coughed, 'but have you been threatening sheep?'

'I've no time for sheep,' retorted Mungo, strictly a goat fancier.

'I've had reports,' persisted the officer, 'that you've been seen in the vicinity of sheep with an offensive article.'

'Ah,' said Mungo, 'you'll be referring to this.'

He clumped across the yard to the front porch, and produced the spear with which each morning he invoked the rising sun. This spear was almost eight feet long, its blade a broad steel leaf.

'I do carry it up the hill,' he admitted, 'but the last blood upon this blade was that of a warrior slain in a cattle raid. I was not handling the weapon at the time.'

'You wouldn't be worrying the sheep?'

'They seem unperturbed to me,' observed Mungo mildly. 'Will you view my collection of Pinwa artefacts? I'd be delighted to elucidate…'

But moments later, the police Land Rover was thumping away down the Parkneuk track to the main road below. Mungo observed thereafter, to anyone who would listen, that it was a wonder crime was ever solved, since the Constabulary lacked curiosity. He might have been amused to know that Reid drove straight to the Glenfarron surgery, only to be told by Dr Dulce, politely but firmly, that an interest in shrivelled monkey genitalia did not make Mungo a sociopath. And perhaps Mungo would have appreciated, in Charlie's reply, a certain warmth – not of irritation, but of regard.

◆◆◆

There was also the pub.

Lunchtime often found Mungo at the bar of the Farron Hotel.

This was an unglamorous Inverness-shire place (B&B £15, no ensuite), but clean. In the bar, a coal fire burned slowly and folk were civil, though you might still see a farmer's wife sitting patiently in a car in the yard while her husband took a pint within. Miss Claire Dulce presided, sixty-one years and with a haughty beauty still, and hair that retained a hint of chestnut amongst the silver. She had been married once, to the licensee, but (in spite of Dr Dulce's best efforts) he was in his grave and she'd put all that behind her, reverting to her maiden name in honour of her mother Sara Dulce of Torbrechan. She was known for her courtesy and her excellent rabbit pie. She was also a gossip, though few suspected this because the only person to whom she gossiped was Dr Dulce. Claire regarded it as a service to public health to keep Charlie well informed. They had been brought up, after all, as brother and sister.

Here in her bar, Mungo liked to perch upon a stool, his grey corduroy leg draping to the floor. He was sometimes a tad drunk; he waved his small cigar and held forth to the occasional tourist, or a passing sheep-dip salesman needing a dram, or a certain farmer's wife in a synthetic panda-skin coat who favoured a coconut-flavoured liqueur. This particular year, Mungo's talk had returned repeatedly to a favourite topic: the great explorers, the bicentenary of a death, and an epic journey.

'The Moors,' averred Mungo, 'wouldn't let him draw water. They said, how durst an infidel pollute a well hewn by followers of the Prophet.'

Marion Morrison, in the panda skin, swayed at the very notion.

Claire from behind the bar enquired: 'This was a relative of yours?'

'Distant, Miss Claire,' confessed Mungo, 'only distant, and I wish it were closer. Of all the Caledonian explorers, Park stands out. Noble of spirit, without bigotry, generous and open minded.'

This was addressed in a melancholy tone to his empty beer glass. But then Mungo looked up with a flash of pride.

'I take the name Mungo in his memory.'

'Oh aye?' said Gordon Morrison the farmer, one ear following the rugby on Claire's kitchen radio. 'Dead now, is he?'

Mungo peered at him, then said curtly:

'Drowned.'

'Oh, there's a shame,' Marion sympathised.

'In 1806.'

Mungo placed his empty beer glass carefully upon the mat, not noticing the glances among the company.

'Two hundred years ago this summer,' he added, pretty much to himself.

'What are you drinking, Mr Robertson?' Gordon offered, but Mungo did not respond. He leaned a long elbow on the bar, his voice grown maudlin.

'It's too late for us. We can never look at Africa with such innocent eyes.'

'Oh dear,' Marion commiserated, regarding him with dismay.

Mungo had begun to weep. Claire Dulce made a mental note to tell brother Charlie.

◆◆◆

Mungo's farmhouse, Parkneuk, was downstream from Torbrechan. His father, Livingstone Robertson, seed merchant and farmer, was once a power in Glenfarron agriculture, and the local NFU convenor. But Mungo went to Africa, because Glenfarron has always had outgoers just as it has incomers. Mungo was not greatly interested in farming. He preferred hunting.

This was how he met the shepherd, one spring morning.

On the hillside, there was a ragged gap in a stone wall; the stones had been shouldered aside by a growing rowan. From this gap, Mungo peeked. Thirty feet away crouched a rabbit.

Slowly, Mungo extended one arm. He held a cord two feet long with a knotted grip and a flat length of wood tied to the other end. He started to swing this over his head as he rose, staring fixedly at the doomed rabbit. A low humming note began: whirring, beating. The rabbit did not move, though Mungo now filled the gap in the wall and the wood swirled and throbbed above his head. The poor creature huddled into the short, wet grass, hoping to be spared.

Two thuds to the neck with a stick ended the matter. Mungo hoiked his twitching victim into a cloth bag.

'You're no proposin' tae eat that?' said a gruff voice.

An ancient little figure in a Gannex coat and a cloth cap was scrutinising Mungo from beside the wall.

'I also use the skins, of course,' Mungo assured him.

'And fits a' this?' queried the shepherd, with a gesture of twizzling.

'An African technique,' said the hunter. 'The sound transfixes the prey.'

The shepherd stepped forward, took the bag from Mungo's grasp and peered inside.

'It couldnae see ye. Blind wi' myxy.'

He stalked away shaking his head, leaving Mungo solitary on the hillside with his bag of diseased rabbits. And the next morning, attending surgery for his blood pressure, Alec Aitken the shepherd described the scene, and told Dr Dulce outright (where Cameron Geddes, PC Reid and sister Claire had merely hinted) that someone should be sending Mungo to the funny farm. No, insisted Charlie, his warmth now of irritation: no indeed! As long as Mungo harmed no one, we'd leave him be.

Charlie never understood why people always wanted him to interfere. Charlie was due for retirement. He couldn't wait.

◆◆◆

In his loneliness, Mungo was not the easiest of men to get close to. Apart from Charlie Dulce, one of the few to persist was Molly Anderson, the school head-teacher.

The doctor and Molly were in regular contact; between them, they monitored the well-being of the forty-odd children at Glenfarron Primary, and Charlie had the warmest regard for her kindness and her tact. They often compared notes. Charlie, indeed, called at Glenfarron Primary more often than was strictly needful, for there was in Molly such enthusiasm (albeit scatterbrained), such ingenuous adoration of the children, that when he thought back to the stiff proprieties of *Mandalay,* his home, it was invariably with a pang. This pang he did his best to tread down, but it would rise up and get him soon enough; he lived with guilt.

Often, during Charlie's visits to Molly Anderson, they would speak of Mungo. Between them, the splendid old African became a favoured topic, around which they could themselves draw closer.

But even Molly found Mungo strong meat. The very day that Alec the shepherd voiced concerns to the doctor, Molly encountered

Mungo at the village shop.

In the drizzle-darkened forecourt, a child in a yellow mac was drifting and mooching. This little girl now climbed onto the back step of Mungo's Land Rover to peer inside.

'And who is this small yellow person peeking into my car?' asked Mungo, appearing at the same instant from the Post Office.

'I'm Katy,' she said.

'And what is Katy looking for?'

'Pesty-side. My teacher says it's wrong to use pesty-side because it kills animals but my Da uses lots on our farm.'

The child spotted something else through the car window.

'What's that wood and string?'

'A magic wand from Africa.'

'Can I see?'

He opened the door, lifted out the bull-roarer and twirled it dramatically. The deep note sounded, and the girl beamed at him, holding out her hands for a try.

Inside the shop, Katy's father had brought trade to a halt. When Mungo entered, he saw Gordon Morrison confronting the teacher.

'How would you feel, Miss Anderson?' Gordon roared at Molly. 'I send my girl to you for an education so that she can help manage the farm, and you tell her I'm a poisoner!'

Behind the chest-freezer, Mungo pretended to read a newspaper.

'We had no trouble with your predecessors,' continued Gordon. 'Mr Christie and Miss Wallace had respect for country ways. But you – you don't give up stirring, do you?'

'I'll never give up on Katy,' replied Molly. She was a determined body.

'But she can barely read!' the farmer raged. 'She knows more about Greenland than Scotland. You're schooling illiterate gypsies.'

'Ah, but Mr Morrison,' Mungo interposed, 'there is a world beyond Glenfarron.'

'Oh? And how will she get to see it, if she cannae read nor write? I'm warning you, Miss Anderson.'

He banged out through the door. Molly glanced gratefully at Mungo.

'Now, there'll be words at the school board,' predicted Aggie

Hulewicz from behind the till, shaking her locks. Aggie's hair was once plain mousey, but with advancing years she'd taken to dyeing it a remarkable ginger.

'Shame on them,' Mungo remarked. 'The young must have broad horizons.'

'Mr Robertson worked in Africa,' Mrs Hulewicz confided to other customers. 'He's not long back after years and years. I remember you in your school shorts, Mungo Robertson.'

She wagged a finger at him; whatever great things Mungo may have done in Africa, his Glenfarron school reports had been mixed. But Mungo smiled peaceably.

'And I recall you in a pinafore, Aggie Hulewicz. I believe, also, that your aviator father saw the world before he became a shopkeeper. He would have shared my sentiments.'

Molly, meanwhile, smoothed her hair, took a breath and sallied outside with her shopping. Mungo was not far behind. In the car park, Katy still twirled the wooden twizzler.

'Don't knock yourself on the head,' called Mungo.

Her father was bellowing: 'Katy!'

'Do you have more magic things?' the child asked Mungo.

'A whole heap, but your Pa's wanting you.'

'Will you show me?'

'Yes, another day.'

Katy skipped off and departed in farmer Gordon's car.

'Would you show me?' a voice called.

'I beg pardon?'

Mungo looked round, and saw Molly Anderson, battered but undaunted.

'Your things from Africa: would you show me?'

And so she invited herself to Parkneuk.

The very next afternoon, having done with the children at school, she went and sat on a plain wooden chair in the middle of Mungo's yard. Drumming, proud and warlike, a sound that once spurred Cetshwayo's Zulus to souse the Transvaal in the blood of British columns, poured from a loudspeaker balanced in Mungo's kitchen window.

Across the yard wobbled a bizarre figure of grass and bark fibre: the mask that usually hung by the parlour window. It swayed and lurched, the spiral eyes spinning in a frenzy. The grass fringes rustled malevolently, swishing about the dancer's legs. Looking closer, Molly saw corduroy trousers and sensible shoes below – but what a dance, shimmying and blood-crazed.

The tape ended, the dancer shivered to a stop. Molly beat her hands for joy.

'That's fine, now! That's really fine!'

Slowly, very carefully, Mungo lifted off the mask. He smiled, a mite sheepish.

'What a glorious thing,' said Molly, touching the painted bark face gingerly lest those extraordinary, swirling ochre eyes should flash at her.

'The mask is royal,' Mungo replied, 'a most powerful icon, symbolising the spirit world's leadership of the tribe.' His voice darkened. 'It was entrusted to my care in a time of crisis for the Pinwa people.'

'Well, it's wonderful,' Molly crowed once again, 'Just wonderful.'

'Hold out your hands,' said Mungo.

She obeyed; he placed there a little group of terracotta figures, three characters forming a tableau, and none too pleasant. One figure was kneeling, hands tied behind him. A second pulled the victim's head back by the hair, and the third thrust a spear into his eye.

'I witnessed such scenes,' Mungo remarked.

'That's terrible,' she trembled. 'Terrible. Who are they?'

'Rival tribes. TaBunte warriors murdering a Pinwa.'

'I had no idea.'

'Few have. It is a sorry land with a terribly familiar story: two peoples forced by colonial ineptitude to occupy the same space.'

Mungo took it from her.

'I have lovelier things: beauty and barbarity in equal measure.'

Behind them, the double doors of the steading stood open to reveal the common farm jumble: rusting implements, tangles of orange twine, plastic drums, dirty bales of inedible hay. But on the ground beside Molly, Mungo laid out his treasures, the cream of an African collection spread in the sunshine: drums, sculptures, headrests fashioned from twisted roots, wire toys and wooden flutes, jagged weapons and joyously colourful fabrics.

Molly surveyed them in wonder.

'How will you display it all?'

'Display it?'

'Here!' She was fired up. 'There must be a display, an exhibition. I'll bring all my children.'

'Good Lord,' breathed Mungo, struck. 'Good Lord…'

So the museum was Molly's notion. But even the sort of schoolmistress we encourage nowadays, bursting with novelty and initiative, cannot sweep past the authorities, nor can we suppose that such breadth of vision will necessarily be welcome.

◆◆◆

The first Glenfarron heard of all this was at the Community Council. The Secretary did not approve.

'There'll be no provision for African museums in the Rural Planning Strategy, Mr Chairman, so I really don't see that…'

They were in session in Glenfarron hall, the trestle tables laden with plastic cloth, paperwork and self-importance. The Secretary looked uncertainly at the chairman, Dr Charles Dulce. The latter's brow clouded; he tapped the order paper with his fountain pen and glanced round the assembly. To one side, on chairs of grey polypropylene, the observers and petitioners sat, Mungo among them. Beside Mungo – Charlie was acutely aware – sat Molly Anderson.

'It's simply a matter of Council support,' urged Mungo.

'Which is not very usual,' demurred the Secretary.

'Well, it's not altogether simple,' Charlie rumbled, playing for time.

'I've made enquiries,' Mungo persisted. 'There's money at regional level, if you'll back me as an educational and tourist amenity.'

Charlie peered at him, and at Molly. He sensed the new alliance between the two, and – he could not help it – he was jealous. He longed to agree, to back the plan, to join their party.

At the Committee table, however, and at the doctor's side, sat the person formerly known as surgery receptionist Julie Forbes, now his wife Julia Dulce, Medical Practice Manager, chatelaine of *Mandalay*. She was sitting bolt upright, wearing a green quilted body-warmer and a smile to freeze Vesuvius.

'I am not clear in my mind, Mr Robertson,' remarked Julia, 'that the people of Glenfarron feel the need of a display of primitive tribal paraphernalia so very acutely.'

'Primitive?' Mungo parried. 'There's not an item in my collection that does not reflect a thousand years of science and artistry.'

Julia looked at her husband and raised an eyebrow that was both world-weary and warning. Charlie winced – but Mungo warmed to his theme.

'The Pinwa are the most skilful herdsmen in Central Africa, and the finest potters. They know seventeen forms of lethal vegetable poison. A Pinwa arrow flies so true that it can split the skull of a parrot and pin it to a tree from seventy feet. I have tiny, exquisitely made cockroach traps which they place…'

Julia immediately objected.

'I should certainly have taken note of any reports of cockroaches in Glenfarron, Mr Robertson, but there have been none, leastways not since I took up post.'

No, thought Charlie Dulce; the poor little beasts will have drowned themselves.

'That is not the point…' Mungo began.

'Then I fail to grasp what the exact point is,' Julia snapped. Charlie shrank miserably. He tried to interpose a more measured tone.

'Can you, Mr Robertson,' he ventured, 'give us a little more idea of the relevance to Glenfarron?'

Mungo looked stunned.

'Relevance? It's … for goodness' sake, it's interesting, it's another world,' he raised both hands in helpless passion, 'and it's dying!'

'I daresay,' Julia retorted, 'but I don't think we want it dying here.'

The Secretary leaned near to Charlie, murmuring: 'Excuse me, Mr Chairman, a procedural point…'

As Charlie half-listened, he was pained to see Mungo regarding him, personally, with profound disappointment. Worse: at Mungo's side, Molly Anderson looked confused and embarrassed.

But on Mungo's other hand sat Alec Aitken in his Gannex coat, hands resting on a tall crook. The old shepherd declared for all the hall to hear:

'Most a' them are no really agin it, they've jes no idea fit ye're bletherin' aboot.'

Mungo shook his head: 'Dulce is an educated man.'

Charlie heard and appreciated that, at least. But Aitken spoiled it:

'The doctor's a thrawn cuss who keeps his batty ol' mither in a tower.'

Which was sheer provocation; Aitken knew the doctor could catch every word.

Molly, meanwhile, squirmed and blushed. She had seen the thin smile of determination on Julia Dulce's lips; she'd seen Charlie flinch; she felt for her friend's torn loyalties.

'Ssshh, Alec,' she murmured. But Aitken scarcely dropped his voice as he leaned toward Mungo and Molly.

'Dulce disnae ken the world, he's nivver been beyond Peebles – though, mind, he were merry-begotten by a Polak hisself, all the wrang side o' the blanket. As for that Julie Forbes, she's an ignorant crabbit wyfie, an' she disnae ken a-thing aboot a-thing. Ah doot she kens where Africa is. Noo, ah ken weel.'

'Do you?' replied Mungo, depressed.

'I was there in '42 wi' the Argylls.'

'Were you, now?'

'Oh aye, an' we saw some recht peculiar folk in Africa, Italians an' a' sorts, but nane as weird as…'

He turned his baleful eye in the direction of the Committee table – where Charlie had had enough.

'Mr Robertson, I'm afraid we cannot proceed without a much more detailed written submission. In the meantime…'

He fixed the old shepherd with his stare. Aitken braced for battle:

'That'll be me. They've a mind to close down my caravans.'

◆◆◆

Community Council decisions are by no means always popular, but the formality of proceedings keeps resentment under control at meetings. Not outside, however; as soon as the public reach the car park, grievances overflow.

Mungo Robertson was fuming.

'Miss Anderson, tell me true: was not the quintessence of the parochial on show in that hall?'

Molly poked at the tarmac with her shoe. She saw Charlie Dulce departing with his wife and manager, the doctor eyeing Molly in a puzzled, hang-dog way, Julia Dulce ignoring them all. Molly sighed inwardly. The doctor was a good man; she would even say that she was fond of him – but if he would not stand up to Julia in a worthwhile cause...

She said to Mungo: 'Don't expect too much from us, not all at once. You're privileged, you know, to have seen the things you have. Be patient.'

'Och, the thing is hopeless.'

'No, don't write us off,' Molly protested.

'Forgive me, Miss Anderson, but I see no grounds for optimism.'

Molly did, though; she saw a flyer in the shop window.

'Show interest in the village,' she said. 'And come to the dance.'

Mungo guffawed: 'Hah!'

'I mean it,' she persisted. 'We've a midsummer ceilidh on Saturday.'

'Oh no, not at all my style.'

'Come now, it's none of your boiled shirts, just a village fling, right here. Do you have a kilt?'

'Get away!' Mungo laughed.

'Highland dress, why not?' Molly smiled. 'I shall expect you – seeing as you dance so nicely.'

◆◆◆

Parkneuk is one of Glenfarron's colder farmhouses, with fine views, but windswept upon its hillside. Its previous inhabitant – Mungo's father, Livingstone – was an unpleasant individual who was widely believed to treat his wife brutally. He was not much mourned when his tractor toppled over in a steep field and squashed him. Old Livingstone had formed a strong aversion to foreigners, especially Polaks and blackamoors, and it was in rebellion that the young Mungo departed for West Africa, only retiring and returning after his father's demise. Mungo then turned Parkneuk into a little corner of Africa, exemplified by the music one often heard trickling from his Land Rover, the music of the *kora* or lyre, a sound as sweet as tropical rain on the fabric of umbrellas carried by women walking to market, swinging and plashing gaily through the puddles.

The Friday after the Council meeting, it was raining hard on Glenfarron. In the yard at Parkneuk, the fetish in the tree was bedraggled, while water was sluicing down the zigzag patterns on the steading door, dribbling off the eland's antlers, and dropping through time's punctures in the tin roof of the sheds.

Mungo, however, was sitting in the bar of the Farron Hotel reading a *Scotsman* which was open at the Foreign page. Claire Dulce did not disturb his reading, but heard him mutter in disgust:

'Oh, dear God.'

The news from Africa was bad. It so often was. And thus Mungo accepted that he needed cheering up.

The next day, Saturday, brought a cool but pleasant summer's evening. From the Land Rover cab, Mungo watched the people squeezing between two dozen parked cars, making for the door of the hall where Dr Dulce sat at a card table, taking the cash. As yet, Mungo was observing, making no move. Two days of downpour had left the air fresh and encouraging. Into the humble hall came Glenfarron – apart from, to one side of the car park, a clutch of youths in black leathers, perched on beefy motorbikes. As Mungo watched, a monstrous Honda Goldwing arrived also, followed by two (seeming) children perched together on a diminutive Vespa. Six riders in all, glowering half-heartedly from the side of the car park, loathe to be left out, disinclined to be included.

From the hall came a sharp electric stabbing as the band plugged themselves into the wrong socket. Mungo stirred at last. He stepped down from his Land Rover dressed in sandals and goat hair, a long cape of rough beige that covered him from his leonine beard to his hairy calves. He crossed the car park, not to the hall door but toward the bikes, his eye lighting with admiration upon one in particular. This was no upstart Japanese, but a British classic, a big single, gleaming like a Stubbs racehorse.

'That's a rare machine,' said Mungo.

The owner glanced at him, pleased but disdaining to show it. A friend, however, buxom and scraggy-blond, now piped up defiantly in a strongly foreign accent – Polish, in fact:

'Brian has restore this. Brian can to fix anything.'

She looked proudly at the heavy-set Brian who spat and grunted. Mungo studied the old bike.

'A Matchless, 1957 model if I'm not mistaken, last in the series; they only made a few hundred.'

'You know that?' another voice demanded, Polish again.

'Had one myself,' Mungo explained. 'Rode it all over West Africa: desert, scrubland, right up through Chad once. Chewed up more tyres than I did tobacco.'

'Africa is bad for bikes?' asked the Polish girl, curious in spite of herself.

Mungo sucked his teeth.

'Roads of rock or dirt or both; ground temperature near a hundred degrees. I had to double the air filter.'

'Oh?'

'The old Matchless, though – tough as a tank. There's some great memories in that, now. Are you folk not dancing?'

The bikers snorted at the very idea. The little ones replied in unison.

'Nae chance. That gang o' snotbags, they dinna want us, ye ken?'

'Aye, well,' Mungo nodded, adding, 'That's fine, that bike.'

He approached the card table, dropped a fiver into the doctor's cash box without a word and stalked through to the hall, unaware that Charlie had gazed up at him in a mute offer of friendship, or that his long cloak had dragged the raffle tickets onto the floor. The fiddle and the accordion were poised, and the drummer was rolling up the sleeves of his cardigan.

Mungo hesitated by the improvised bar – beer in cans, tots in plastic cups – then saw Molly Anderson, and they made a beeline for each other.

'That's fine, now: you came.'

'A very good evening, Miss Anderson.'

'Molly will do fine. You have a kilt under that cape?'

'Oh, some tasteful garb.'

'And will you be dancing?'

'I do strip a decent willow.'

Children skidded about the dance floor as the band struck up a summons:

'Now, take your partners please, for a Gay Gordons.'

'I'll be asking you for a wee birle or twa,' said Mungo, cod-Scottish, to which Molly laughed and simpered:

'I'll no be refusing.'

But at this moment, Mungo spotted the doctor's wife pausing at the door to instruct her husband with regard to the raffle.

'If you'll excuse me just now,' Mungo said, 'I see Julia Dulce speaking with the doctor. I'm anxious to have the Gay Gordons with her.'

Molly breathed, 'That's good, you make your peace.'

Mungo crossed the room.

Still wrapped in his cape, he bowed to Julia. The dance was formally requested, the request stiffly accepted. Mungo took Julia by the hand and led her (as she was not often led) onto the floor. The opening chord sounded out from the accordion – at which point Mungo at last removed his cloak, handing it to Molly.

He wore a leather G-string, goatskin flaps over his buttocks and his pudenda, waterbuck leggings, a necklace of small rodent skulls on copper wire and armbands bright with bee-eater feathers. Julia was trapped in his enormous hands, her eyes bulging and her face twisted in disgust as, before all Glenfarron, Mungo propelled her into the dance.

Four minutes later he stepped out of the door, grinning fit to bust.

A salvo of wolf-whistles and clapping came from two oil drums under the high windows, where the bikers now perched, observing. Mungo smiled up at them and lit his small cigar.

'That is so nice dancing!' cried the Polish girl.

'They dinna like your leathers, ye ken,' cried Pam, one of the little ones, pointing at the goatskin skirt, 'nae mair 'n they like oor leathers.'

'Ah like to dance, mind,' remarked her brother Sam.

'Aye, we can dae it.'

'Ah likes a fling, aye.'

'Well,' mused Mungo, 'let me teach you something new.'

In the hall, the more presentable inhabitants of Glenfarron waltzed, trying to suppress their giggles. The doctor was dosing his wife with a sedative dram when Molly approached.

'Julia,' Molly asked, 'did you notice which way Mr Robertson went?'

'To the Deil and damnation, I trust!' spat Mrs Dulce.

'Oh, come now…'

'When I left home this evening, Miss Anderson, I was lightly perfumed with Nina Ricci. I now reek like a goatherd.'

She thrust her forearm under Molly's nose in evidence. Then she turned to her husband, hissing:

'And, Charles, if you ever allow me to be humiliated like that again, I promise you I shall not readily forget it.'

Charlie, even as he blushed, smarted at the injustice: what

had he done? He looked towards Molly, longing for some small kindness...

That very instant, the sedate waltz was blown apart. From the car park came a thunderous drumming. The band faltered, the dancers dithered. Outside, clanging blows were answered by a rhythmic clapping. The uproar battered its way through the thin wood walls. The waltzers struggled on a few more bars, till they and the band were overwhelmed – and everyone went to the door to see.

It was Sam and Brian who were making most of the din. They hammered on an oil drum, two chunky sticks apiece, black leather fringes thrashing at their elbows. The others shuffled in a ring, clapping. Mungo conducted a ferocious rhythm: rapid strokes, three claps, a stamp, a shout. He urged the Polish girl into the centre to face her boyfriend, each of them clutching a long spear, shuffling and prowling, clacking the shafts.

'God in Heaven,' Charlie murmured, staring at the bikers, for one of them was Lewis, his very own son.

'Bloody savages,' his wife growled.

But Mungo was beaming, applauding the dancers as they leapt.

'Highland dancing, Doctor,' Mungo bellowed, 'from another world!'

◆◆◆

Thus were Molly Anderson and Lewis the doctor's son drawn into Mungo's peculiar universe. Mungo had a knack of fascinating the most disparate people.

Charlie Dulce, however, felt bereft and left behind. He feared that Molly was furious with the Community Council. For some days, there were no conversations, no telephone calls from Glenfarron Primary. When he considered another thinly-justified visit to the school, he was shy of it. When he wondered about dropping in on Parkneuk, where only a few weeks before he had been gushing friendly admiration, Charlie could not imagine that he would now be welcome. When he pondered these changes, he felt cross, and could not resist blaming Julia. In rare slack moments at the surgery, he would gaze out of the window at the sombre green of the Farron woods, and he was saddened.

There came a change in his mood, however, when the young

Polish bikers arrived at his surgery.

He knew a little about them, because they had entranced his son. Julia cursed them for corrupting Lewis, though the fact was that, well before the Poles arrived, the doctor's son had already blown his trust fund on the Honda Goldwing. The Polish boy was the great-nephew of Aggie Hulewicz at the shop. He had a near-unpronounceable name – Czcibor – and so was called Fly. His girlfriend Zdzislawa, for company, was known as Zippa. They stayed in Aggie's back room, and cruised the Highlands on their Kawasakis when they weren't harvesting organic chanterelles at the Drumcullen fungus farm to pay for college in Krakow.

As they sat before Charlie in the surgery, he found himself entranced also. The young Poles wore their fringed leathers: in Julia's eyes, costume for cannibals. But they were clean, attentive and scrupulously polite. They travelled where and when they wished; they were slaves to no one. They thought their own thoughts, and seemed entirely untrammelled by the collective memories of a downtrodden Poland. Towards each other they beamed simple adoration, and they filled Charlie Dulce with yearning.

Their reason for coming was a surprise: Zippa was pregnant. Charlie realised that he hoped Julia – just yards away in the Practice Manager's office – would not find this out. He filled in the result of the test and, instead of leaving it in the tray for filing, he gummed it onto a report sheet and filed it himself.

'How do you feel about this?' he asked them, recalling that Poles are Catholics, and wondering if they would be ostracized when they went home (and then wondering if 'ostracized' was a Polish word, because it rather looked it).

For answer, the boy Fly took his girlfriend's hand, smiling first at her and then at Charlie, and nodding. Charlie looked at the girl in black leather, and saw that her eyes were filling with tears, and that they were tears of joy.

Through the surgery window, he watched them walking away. He felt a sudden identity with them; he wanted to throw up the window and call them back for *zubrówka* and paprika sausage. He wanted to rush to Torbrechan farm, to paint red-and-white flashes everywhere, to restore the Polish coat-of-arms and *Vive la Pologne* on the gable wall. But what did such old symbols meant to Czcibor and Zdzislawa? In the car park, the two Kawasakis stood;

different priorities, thought Charlie – until, with a little laugh, he looked again at the twin motorbikes, parked neatly side by side: they were identical models, but one was red, one white.

Charlie smiled happily. He felt quite affected. They were hardly the first couple to whom he'd announced a pregnancy, yet they touched him; it was their freshness, perhaps. He felt suffused with a generosity he'd been losing track of lately. He thought of Mungo, and of Molly, and he resolved to put selfish jealousies aside.

◆◆◆

The day after the ceilidh, Molly went back up to Parkneuk. Mungo gave her coffee, and played her a few minutes of favourite *kora* music, of which she showed appreciation. Then they wandered outside together, aimless, Mungo paying her courteous attention. They went into the steading.

In shafts of hay-dusty light slanting through the broken shutters, they drifted. Molly picked up items of Africana as she went, feeling their grittiness and keeping her voice steady.

'I'm separated, as it happens. In Edinburgh; a mite messy.'

'My dear lady,' Mungo breathed, lumbering beside the slightly-made woman, 'I don't wish to pry.'

'Oh, it's years ago. And I've my hands full with children, haven't I? At the school.'

She picked up a small clay statuette of a young African kneeling with her hands crossed on her lap. It had a personal, from-the-life look.

Both regarded the figure; Molly and Mungo stood very still.

But the moment broke, and he went to an open window.

'So,' she said breezily, 'where are all the Robertson clan?'

'Plenty of us in Glenfarron kirkyard.'

'Did you never ...?'

He pre-empted her.

'Marry? I regarded Africa as my consort – a common colonial error.'

He was gazing out of the window, his mind on other hills. She took a step nearer, about to speak when Mungo cocked his head and held up a hand: *Listen!*

They came streaming up the dirt drive towards Parkneuk yard: three superbikes, then the Vespa, and Brian's dignified Matchless coming at the rear.

'What's all this?' Molly demanded.

'My contractors,' Mungo announced. 'Am I to be deterred by a mere Council?'

The posse rounded the gateway, and stopped.

'Morning,' he nodded, as they raised their visors.

'We brought the twins,' Lewis pointed out.

'The deal is on?' Fly wanted to know.

'It is,' Mungo replied, 'if Brian is the builder you say.'

'He can do it,' said pregnant Zippa, slipping off her Kawasaki, 'and we can help.'

The taciturn Brian peered round the yard.

'In the goat shed,' Mungo told him. Brian grunted and the rest followed him, each patting the goat in passing.

'Now, explain,' Molly demanded.

'A deal. I've a vintage motorcycle, wartime Harley-Davidson. My father purloined it from our American cousins at the castle in '45. It's a wreck now, but restored it'll be worth a fair bit. So, they get the bike to work on in the evenings, but weekends they work for me.'

Anyone will work, given the right incentive.

From a spur above Parkneuk, after school, a small boy watched, the wind tweaking at his hair. He peered downhill to where, in the yard below, motorbikes were neatly arrayed. Something was going on. Tousled by the breeze, outlandish music whipped about; it came from loudspeakers in the kitchen window. But there was no one in sight.

Until Mungo, that first afternoon, appeared from the steading, pushing wide the black-and-red zigzagged doors. Out behind him marched a procession: all six bikers with farm junk in their hands. Fly had a wheelbarrow heaped with half-bricks; Zippa lugged an ancient tractor battery; Brian dragged two rolls of stock wire; Lewis bore a boxful of old paint tins on his head, coolie fashion; the twins hauled on little squeaking wheels some iron device with teeth and drive chains. Mungo pointed to a far corner and the dumping began.

As did the dance. Freed of their loads, the twins and Zippa bowed and bobbed their heads, shuffling round to the music, wiggling their hands behind their bottoms like ducks' tails. Lewis clapped and waved them back into the shed, back to their work. Mungo strode into the house to reappear with a broad broom and shovel. Brian slouched across the yard, seized a long wooden ladder with a rung gone, propped it against the steading wall and climbed to inspect loose slates.

The child on the heather hill looked up at his father.

'Fit they dein'?'

Cameron could only shake his head.

'I've no idea. No idea.'

Next afternoon, the boy saw a van visit Parkneuk yard:

D. HULEWICZ
PLUMBING AND ELECTRICAL

Mungo received several cardboard boxes, pulled up a thornwood stool, sliced open the lids, and rummaged in the paper straw: lamps: small, glittering, modern things. On a packing case nearby knelt the African clay girl; he pointed a lamp at her speculatively, sucked his bottom lip and looked to Dougie Hulewicz. The tradesman nodded: that would do fine.

Again, the African tapes thundered through the window. Again, the dust and noise of labour. On the steading roof, Brian at full stretch nailed down a slate. In front of the doors, Fly paddled concrete, his close-cropped head shining with sweat. Lewis cut timbers on a sawhorse. Kneeling on an old tarpaulin, Zippa painstakingly outlined black letters on a white wooden board. And from the house came Pam and Sam, she with a tray of tea, he going before with a twirling assegai. Wonderful, how they had spontaneously created ritual.

Late in the afternoon, the bikers were usually still there. But now they huddled round the ancient Harley-Davidson, murmuring respectfully while Brian lifted off the cylinder head or repacked a bearing.

Each day they were observed from the hillside by young Callum from Torbrechan, perhaps with Cameron his father or his little brother Tom, and sometimes Alec Aitken the shepherd, all gazing down. Lewis Dulce would wave to the boys and they waved back. Mungo saw them too; he returned their stare without animosity. Little Tom beamed with pleasure at the drumming, Alec chuckled to himself, and Callum loved to see a bit of madness.

'It's a queer thing,' the shepherd remarked to Claire in the pub, 'Polaks an' bongo-bongo in the glen. Robertson's faither, now, he were an auld bigot. He tried to have a' the Polaks banned frae Glenfarron, said they were takin' jobs frae the ferm loons.'

'When his son went off to Africa,' Cameron enquired, 'did Livingstone not object?'

'He did,' Claire recalled. 'He wasn't pleased at all.'

'Old bastard'll be turning in his grave now,' Cameron smiled.

'Right enough,' old Alec agreed. 'He thocht blackies no better than slaves. Houseful o' bampots, that.'

Not long after, the watchers on the hill observed another ritual. The sawhorse was dragged to the middle of the yard and a camera balanced on top. Lewis took aim, pressed the shutter-delay, then scuttled to join Mungo and the rest striking a pose in front of the zigzag steading doors, above which glistened a newly painted sign:

PARKNEUK MUSEUM
OF THE PINWA PEOPLE

◆◆◆

Mungo summoned Molly.

Silence at evening. A pristine display stand waited, finished with terracotta paint, a sharp little down-light making it bright. Onto it, out of the gloom, the exquisite figurine of a young African woman was lowered into place by Mungo's enormous but tender hands. His shaggy visage appeared behind the statuette, gazing at it with deep concentration. He inched the figure with his pinkie, just a hint, to its best position.

Car noise swept under the steading doors.

'All done?' Molly called.

Mungo grasped her hand with a bow, saying with the greatest courtesy:

'Come, see what it is you have inspired.'

He took her arm and escorted her into the dark steading, to where a single down-light picked out the little statuette.

'Oh my!' Molly exclaimed, 'isn't she glorious.'

She hurried forward.

'So lifelike. It's just perfect.'

Mungo concurred quietly: 'A perfect woman.'

Molly looked up, surprised.

'It's a portrait,' he said. 'She was killed.'

Molly absorbed this carefully. She straightened and peered round at the darkness.

'Is she in solitary splendour?'

Mungo smiled; an electrical *clack,* and the new hall was brightly flooded. Two dozen miniature spotlights picked out the exhibits: on brick columns, on plinths washed in ochres and umbers, on shelves, or free-standing: statues, fabrics, fine grass-work baskets through which black geometries threaded, pots and farm tools, their forms elongated by a tall people reaching across a broad landscape.

All very simple, plain but not crude. Cement and brick, softwood and a lick of paint.

'Michty me!' Molly exclaimed. 'It's lovely.'

Mungo nodded slowly.

'The finest flower of Pinwa material culture, gathered just before Africa's pre-rusted consumerism trivialised it. And before the last craftsmen were butchered.'

They came to a pedestal, where the clay tribesmen skewered their enemy through the eye.

'I saw that one before,' Molly grimaced. 'Not so nice.'

She moved on briskly.

'I have here,' remarked Mungo, 'artefacts that no longer exist in Africa. In Glenfarron, at least, they are safe. The presiding genius is over there.'

He pointed to the far wall where the portrait of Mungo Park hung, brought from the parlour, and seeming now to smile upon them.

'It's fine,' Molly exclaimed. 'It's all so fine.'

'Glad you like it,' the proprietor breathed.

'We must get everyone in to see this. Will you have an opening?'

He looked startled. 'You think I should?'

'Oh, I do! Open their eyes.'

Mungo regarded her thoughtfully. He'd not considered this – but yes, he'd like an opening.

◆◆◆

It should have been so festive: a pleasant, sunny Saturday, the breeze teasing the woods and ruffling Loch Farron beyond. On the hillside, rabbits chased in diminishing circles, while the sheep drifted at summer's pace across the field. In the forest, a blackcock clucked. But in the yard at Parkneuk, all was gloom.

By the shed, with the goat as scrutineer, the bikers watched Brian fiddling with the Harley's carburettor, which gleamed with oily promise. Pam came to her friends with a tray of white wine; the bikers took a glass each, raising these in salute across the yard. The museum door stood open, and between two trees hung a banner:

Kolukwe! Welcome!

Below the banner stood a table under a white cloth, with goblets from the Drumcullen off-licence and three boxes of Cape chardonnay. Mungo sat there with Molly to his right. To his left, Alec Aitken nodded bucolically, his smeary glass a witness to his afternoon's work. No one else was present.

Molly was embarrassed. Mungo was not smiling. No one spoke. The banner stirred, restless. Mungo glanced repeatedly towards the open gate, then down the long track to the main road – but there were no cars coming. He placed his wine back on the table untouched, and peered at his watch.

Molly ventured: 'Are you not taking any wine?'

Mungo did not reply.

She tried again. 'I daresay they'll be along…'

'One,' murmured Mungo. 'Out of seventy households, one old shepherd.'

Alec Aitken lifted his sozzled pate.

'No, it disnae pay to cross Mrs Dulce.'

'Are you telling me, this is all that woman's work?' Mungo growled. 'A boycott? A telephone campaign?'

Molly protested:

'She'd never be so vindictive.'

'Would she not.'

'Though I'm afraid,' Molly admitted, 'that she was not the only one offended by your dance attire.'

A mechanical parp, a whoop of excitement from Lewis: the Harley fired for the first time in decades – and died again. Mungo regarded the bikers sadly.

'Oh, give me the enterprising young. Pinwa children can skin jackals by the age of five.'

'I'll make it next term's project,' Molly announced. 'Native Culture and Colonial Oppression.'

Mungo peered at her. 'In a primary school?'

'They're Scots, they'll understand. And they'll listen to you.'

'You want me…?'

'Life in Africa,' said the schoolmistress, excited now. 'Teach them what it's *really* like.'

'What it's like is carrying water five miles on your head.'

'Show them! The school has a camcorder; we'll make a video.'

Mungo considered – and slowly nodded his great bearded head.

'We shall show them. We shall educate them.'

He lifted his face, revived, determined. By the goat shed, the Harley fired and the bikers capered.

◆◆◆

Dr Dulce would certainly have gone to the opening, had he ever received an invitation; he would swear that no such thing ever reached his residence at *Mandalay*. When Molly reproached him later, he could only protest that things do go astray in the post.

Of course they do, she conceded – but Mungo's invitations had not gone out in the post; they were taken to every house by the bikes.

The doctor asked his son Lewis, who was adamant: yes, he'd brought one home himself.

Charlie asked his wife: Julia averred that she'd not seen it. Or rather, she said that she 'couldn't think where it could have got to'. She buried her gaze in her magazine; was it Charlie's imagination, or was she avoiding his look? He peered at her across the sitting room, and saw that it was true.

Thus, Dr and Mrs Dulce missed the opening, and Lewis was furious with his parents. Charlie was mortified and dismayed, and only wished he could convince Mungo of that. But it was too late, and he feared that Molly would not readily believe or forgive him either.

◆◆◆

Mungo was not a man to place much store by regulations. Molly will have insisted, however, that he go through all the proper 'disclosure' checks and procedures. Otherwise her job would have been on the line.

No amount of checks prepared Molly for Mungo's first stab at teaching.

An apple sat upon a sawn log by a wooden wall in Parkneuk yard. To its right, a second fruit, then a third, each on its own log. The day was still and bright, the apples warm, the children waiting in silence.

The first apple was large and green, with a red flush. Suddenly, with a delicate fluttering sound, it was transfixed. A long sliver of wood pierced the flesh, ran it through. Yet the apple hardly stirred, so sharp was the needle point that now just touched the timber boards behind. The tail of the needle was bound with a plug of wild cotton: it was a blowpipe dart.

The middle fruit waited in the sun. Mungo put down the blowpipe and picked up a bow and arrow. *Thwack!* – the apple fell apart, split in two by an iron arrowhead that slammed into the wall. The halves tumbled to the ground.

Molly was about to speak to the watching children, when Mungo said:

'Just a moment.'

He reached into a blue plastic sack and pulled out a shotgun. Before Molly could protest, he'd blown the last apple to wet smithereens.

'Mungo!'

Across the yard, a child whimpered, clinging to teacher's coat. Molly stared aghast at Mungo while patting the small head rather too hard. A dozen other children in solid little duffels looked to her for reassurance as Mungo broke open the shotgun, handing the reeking shell to a small boy.

'Mungo,' Molly hissed, 'we never said guns…'

But Mungo didn't hear.

'Hold that, Callum,' he said. 'Now, let's look at our apples. Which can we eat?'

He strode across the yard to the three logs.

'Come and look,' Mungo called.

'Go on,' Molly prompted, white-faced, and the children obeyed. Mungo prodded the sodden, shattered remnants of the shot-blasted fruit.

'Katy, would you eat that?'

Katy and her friends giggled, shaking their heads. Mungo tugged the iron arrow from the wall, picked up the halves of the second target and offered one to wee Tom.

'How's about this? Will you eat this, Tom?'

Tom grinned, grabbed half and gobbled it, to laughter.

'That's a bit better, is it?' Mungo remarked. 'The arrow doesn't smash the apple like the gun. Doesn't mash it up and you don't get lead in your teeth. We'll have to finish it, though, because it's been cut and it'll spoil.'

Callum took the other half, and devoured that.

Now Mungo reached for the last apple that sat upon its log with the dart through its core.

'Can we eat this one?'

'Aye,' the children chorused.

'Can we keep it till tomorrow? Will it be all right?'

'Aye!'

'That's right. The blowpipe doesn't hurt it much. Not like the arrow or the gun. Who was frightened when the gun went off?'

'Callum!' Katy shouted.

'Was not!'

'Who else? You, Katy?'

'No…'

Aye, she was… He was… She cried… Didnae!… Did!

'Everyone jumped a wee bit,' said Molly, smoothing little feathers.

Mungo pointed to a stand of firs beyond the gate, with rooks circling overhead.

'Did you see the birds? What did they do?'

'Flew awa'!' the class cried.

'They did.' Mungo nodded. 'If you were hunting birds with that gun, you'd only ever get one, because the rest fly off. But when I shot the blowpipe, did they fly off then?'

'Didnae hear it!' yelled Callum.

'No, and I could have hunted all those birds one by one, without them knowing what was happening. The people who made that blowpipe knew what they were about, eh? You see what I'm saying?'

'Aye,' the children agreed, considering the rooks.

'Right,' said Mungo, hefting the blowpipe. 'Now then: who

wants a shottie at an apple?'

The African classes took wing.

They made papier maché globes, slapping glue-sodden newspaper onto plastic footballs; passing villagers could see the product through the window, hanging on strings to dry. The older pupils then helped Molly cut with a craft knife, taking each dried globe off in two halves, to be taped and gummed together. They daubed on brown paint and blue paint, land and sea, copying the continental outlines from an atlas. So far, so familiar.

'So where's Africa, Mhairi?'

'On the side of the world.'

'About here,' said Molly, and pencilled it on. 'Where Mr Robertson lived was in West Africa, up a big river here. Imagine: you could go there by water all the way from Glenfarron. You could get in your boat at our bridge, down the Farron Water to Inverness, across the sea, round to West Africa and up that river to visit Mr Robertson's house, without ever getting out of your boat.'

After break, Mungo took over.

'Hamish, if I ask you to fetch me a cup of water for my juice, where do you go?'

'The kitchen,' replied Hamish.

'What if there is no kitchen? Suppose there's no tap in the school?'

Hamish looked at him blankly.

'The river!' shouted Callum.

'That's a long walk.'

'The kirk,' said Katy Morrison. 'There's a well in the kirkyard, behind the old tree.'

Fifteen minutes later, in the shadow of an ancient yew, a falling bucket banged onto black water and the sound clattered back up the mossy stone shaft. A rope gang hauled, with Mungo pulling at the rear.

At the wellhead, Molly wrapped a towel turban about Katy's blond hair. Mungo balanced a coffee tin on top and half filled it from a plastic jug. Katy put one hand to the tin and turned slowly for the gate. Never did a small girl concentrate so. Behind her came Callum and Tom, a bucket slung from a pole across their shoulders.

'All right, now, back to the school, and you've not to lose a single drop.'

They were being watched; from the shop door and from the petrol pump, Glenfarron observed the procession of children, wobbling, shrieking, spilling and squealing, running back to the kirkyard for more, Katy determined and serious as she passed through the school gates. From the surgery window, Julia Dulce scowled.

'Think about that!' Mungo called over the classroom hubbub as the orange juice was poured and they laid into their biscuits. 'A country where you have to walk to a well miles away, just for a cup of juice.'

'And remember,' Molly called from his side, 'it was once like that in Glenfarron.'

Katy, grinning fit to bust, munched on her hard-earned biscuit.

'Did you see her concentration?' Molly murmured. 'She was not going to spill a molecule.'

'Like a Pinwa child,' Mungo remarked. 'Tough as a wee jackal. Fine girl.'

'The sort of daughter men like,' Molly ventured.

But Mungo set his jaw, and Molly was embarrassed. So she said, to cover the silence:

'Has Dr Dulce seen the exhibits yet?'

Mungo snorted.

'Dulce? After he wanted to block the project?'

'It's not easy for him,' said Molly. 'He has all that Council on his back. But he's very interested in the children. Give him a chance.'

Mungo considered – then gave a little nod.

'Very well. We can suggest that he visits tomorrow, if you like. I've a laddie coming from the papers. I'll be telling him about Mungo Park.'

◆◆◆

Charlie Dulce was surprised to be called, and delighted. If the pipe of peace was on offer at Parkneuk, he would certainly not decline. He was, however, uncomfortable to realise that he had not told his wife where he was going.

He reached Parkneuk after morning surgery. The wind was up but it was bright, the forest and the grasses moving, vivacious and pleasant. Charlie drew into the yard just as Mungo stepped out from the porch with a cub reporter in tow, the modern sort that mutters into a dictaphone, who was being given a lecture on the great explorers:

'Mungo Park was a Selkirk doctor, hired in 1795 by the Africa Association in London to map the River Niger. Not to conquer, not to colonize, but to gather knowledge.'

'Scot, doc, Nigeria,' the newshound confided to his machine.

Mungo peered balefully at him, then nodded curtly to Charlie.

'Welcome, Doctor. Here to see the displays your committee tried to obstruct?'

'Oh,' Charlie began, 'we had no intention to…'

'This way,' called Mungo. All three moved toward the steading doors.

'He found himself,' Mungo continued to the reporter, 'in a war zone of petty kingdoms squabbling over slaves. He was robbed, spat upon, starved, nearly died a dozen times, but he walked on across West Africa till he found what he was after.'

'War, royals, slaves, got the dirt,' the scribbler breathed.

Mungo stopped again, gazing over the glen and the Farron Water below. He gestured broadly, and declared:

'Park was the first to know whether the mighty Niger flowed west-east, or east-west.'

'Home's best,' the hack rejoined. 'Didn't the natives know?'

Which won him daggers. The reporter grinned at Charlie, shrugging.

'This way,' said Mungo, terse.

They followed him inside.

'My goodness, Robertson!' Charlie said.

Actually, the first thing they saw was little Katy Morrison, standing in awe before a pedestal. Here knelt the tiny pottery girl, hands on thighs and a brilliant spotlight on her head that made the terracotta glow. Katy reached out a finger to touch.

'She's lovely,' Charlie Dulce said, thinking gently to forestall her.

Katy hadn't heard him coming; she looked round, startled.

'She looks alive, doesn't she?' Charlie added.

But at this moment Katy saw the reporter, and she scarpered into the gloom at the back.

'*Mungo Park*.'

The newsman was reading the portrait's label. Mungo, the explorer's descendant, fingered the great grassy dance mask that now hung from the roof in dramatic half-shadow, a thin raking beam of light catching the striations in the bark. A vague memory stirred in Charlie.

'Wasn't there some argy-bargy out that way lately? A coup?'

'In March,' Mungo growled. 'Not a coup: a blood-soaked pogrom. The provincial government was murdered by TaBunte gangsters. They were shot and dumped in a mass grave.'

From the rear of the steading came a warm light, with the twitter of busy children. The back third of the building was now an 'educational resource', separated by a blackthorn entanglement. There was a small opening in the brushwood, a tunnel through the spines.

Mungo pointed: 'After you – and you, Doctor.'

The reporter went down on his knees and crawled, thorns snagging his suede blouson. Emerging inside, he looked up…

'Fuck that!'

Two vicious iron blades waved close to his eyes, spears held by little savages dressed in nothing but leather aprons, their limbs and faces daubed with red and brown splodges. Behind them stood a witch-doctor in black leather trousers, copper bracelets gleaming on his naked forearm. The reporter scrambled clear.

'Och, cummon,' said Sam, 'Gemma'll no skewer ye. She's only seven.'

Reporter and doctor stared in disbelief. Before them, two dozen children, scarcely clothed, were busy with the domestic chores of the Pinwa day. Two were making pots from worms of clay; onto hers, Katy was incising zigzag patterns with a twig. One little girl was in a tangle in a back-strap loom, while another ground corn upon a stone, the grits cascading onto a tea towel. Three boys were winding cotton wool onto new blowpipe darts, then dipping the points into a jar of something sticky and black, supervised by Lewis Dulce, whose torso was decorated with menacing eyes painted in ochre.

The reporter picked up a dart and tapped the sharp point with his finger: 'What's all this?'

'Deadly nerve poison,' Lewis scowled. 'Dinnae prick yer pinkie.'

He looked up at his father.

'Well, Da,' he beamed, 'I'm doing drugs, ye ken.'

Brian was sawing slabs from an old car tyre. Children stood on the bits, drawing round their feet.

'Making their own shoes,' Molly called, 'just as so much of humanity has always done.'

'Squeeze her tits, then!'

Reddening, the reporter spun round – and there was Mungo's stoic goat, with Pam clasping Mhairi's little hands to the udders:

'You've to squeeze it all out, ken? Or she'll get sair boobies.'

The last milk rattled into a gourd. Pam flicked the stopper off a leather bottle with her thumb.

'Now,' she told the press, flashing a melodramatic eye, 'tae mak it fine, we've tae add a drappie or twa o' bluid.'

She drizzled cochineal into the milk, twizzled it with a finger, then politely offered the gourd of gore to the reporter.

'It's what they have in Africa,' urged Molly, 'for their tea. A good diet, isn't it, Doctor?'

'I daresay it is.'

'And good fun, you agree?' purred the dark deep voice of Mungo.

Charlie was about to agree again, but the young journalist stammered in protest:

'It's all ... it's all so ... so ...'

'All so what?' said Mungo, one brow rising.

'So primitive!'

'I don't know,' Charlie Dulce said. 'It's making me wish that I'd travelled.'

He thought a moment, excited by an idea, by a chance for redemption.

'Robertson, have you thought of wider publicity for this?'

'Such as?' Mungo queried.

'Well, I've a few contacts in London,' said Charlie. 'People I was at college with. Would you allow me to make a couple of calls?'

◆◆◆

They had been speaking of marriage.

She'd been telling Mungo of her own wedding, which had never happened because her fiancé had decamped to run sailing holidays off the Dalmatian coast.

Molly was half-swallowed by an ancient armchair in Mungo's parlour as the log fire subsided comfortably.

'I was a bit stuck,' Molly said. He sat opposite, perched on a gnarled stool, leaning towards her with a concerned and intimate look; this came easily to that rugged face. They were best allies now. Watery *kora* music trickled from the tape recorder in the kitchen, firelight bathed their cheeks, and in their fists they clutched whisky rummers.

'Stuck?' Mungo prompted.

'Stuck was how it felt. It's like that in these glens, isn't it? Life partners identify each other early. By the time I returned from Edinburgh, I'd rather missed the boat.'

Mungo placed a huge consoling hand on hers. She 'bucked up'.

'One is, of course, very involved with the children in a professional way.'

The phone rang and Mungo went to the hallway. Molly stood, drained her glass and scrutinised her own reflection in the uncurtained window, then picked her coat off the floor.

'I must be away,' she said when Mungo returned. 'It's the School Board at eight. They're not going to give me an easy time, and your reporter will be there. Now, what's so droll about that?'

Mungo was beaming.

'You just tell your board: they may not be interested in my museum, but thanks to our doctor, there's other folk now are.'

'Oh? And who?'

He laughed: 'The British Council.'

◆◆◆

Mungo's influence, meanwhile, was permeating the glen. It was felt, for instance, at Torbrechan.

Torbrechan Farm. Landlord: Charles Dulce MB, ChB, MRCGP. Struggling tenant: C. Geddes, since 1995 and the death of V. Obremski (sausage maker). On Vladislaw's demise, Charlie had removed his mother Joyce, installing her in a quaint little tower at *Mandalay*. He'd had Torbrechan farmhouse whitewashed, obliterating from the gable end the Polish insignia; Charlie felt that they'd all moved on. Now the excellent Cameron worked not only Torbrechan but the Parkneuk land also, which Charlie had bought up when Livingstone Robertson died. Charlie knew nothing about farming, and left Cameron to it.

In the yard (neat, good ewes and decent muck, no effigies or shrivelled monkeys), Cameron was welding a broken baler. At the back of the steading, Callum and Tom had a rubber car mat on the ground. Tom stood on the mat and Callum scratched a mark round his foot with a rusty nail.

'Callum!' their Da shouted. 'Fit ye dein'?'

He turned off his welding torch, and shouted again.

'That's frae ye mither's Subaru!'

Callum was about to carve up the mat with a Stanley knife.

'Callum's making me new trainers,' his younger brother announced. Their father strode up and inspected the footprint: 'He what?'

Callum sensed a difficulty.

'Mr Robertson showed us, at school.'

Cameron straightened, and glowered across the hillside. Half a mile away, fetishes stirred in the Parkneuk breeze. He was beginning to find Mungo Robertson a nuisance.

That very day, trouble appeared. It came by road.

Lewis Dulce was in Aggie's shop, buying a packet of Rizzla papers. Mungo was there, scanning the local rag. His nostrils flared at the headline:

SCHOOL BOARD SLAMS AFRO ANTICS

'Narrow-minded dullards!'

He dropped the newspaper contemptuously, and marched out to his Land Rover.

Aggie shook her head.

'Miss Anderson will have to watch her step.'

While Lewis was peering at the paper to see what had got Mungo so excited, the shop door opened and two suited gentlemen entered. One was white and fortyish; the other was slim and black, and carried symmetrical scars on his cheekbones, like the gills of a shark.

'Excuse me,' the white man said, 'I'm needing directions. Can you point me at Parkneuk farm?'

Lewis scrutinised the newcomers.

'If it's Mr Robertson you're wanting, you've just missed him. You'd best follow me.'

'I'm sure we could find it if you...'

'No,' Lewis insisted, 'you follow me.'

Ten minutes later, Mungo saw the Goldwing leading a white Rover into Parkneuk yard.

'Mr Robertson? I'm Tony Edwards, British Council.'

But Mungo ignored Edwards' offered hand, staring instead at the black man who returned a smile carved from ebony.

At which Mungo marched past them both, taking keys from his pocket and unlocking the Museum's doors, while Edwards tried to murmur in his ear.

'Mr Achule is cultural attaché at the embassy; they asked if he might come along. We'd have called first except that I didn't imagine...'

Mungo heaved open the door, then looked witheringly at Achule who stood gazing out across the Farron Water.

'Mr Robertson, please! The F.O. is *very* keen to restore relations. We're all putting the coup behind us now. It's a goodwill visit.'

'Goodwill? He's not Pinwa, he's TaBunte,' said Mungo.

'Well, indeed he is,' Edwards conceded.

'*Ergo*,' said Mungo, 'he's a genocidal thug. So, show him round, and then remove him.'

He strode into the steading. Achule sashayed towards the double doors followed by Lewis Dulce, dying of curiosity. By the time they entered, the lights were ablaze. While Edwards picked at his fingernails, Mungo and the African stalked each other through the exhibits, and in Achule's voice rang a lofty disdain, a cultivated scorn for the products of a lesser people.

'You lived among the Pinwa, Mr Robertson? How very difficult for you. Could it be called "living" at all?'

'Living very well, I'd call it,' Mungo growled, his eyes never leaving this adversary.

'Oh, but difficult,' Achule insisted. 'Difficult and quaint.'

He picked up a small carved object: a piece of wood with hot-poker patterning.

'Now, what is this? A significant cultural artefact, or a tent peg?'

'It's for lockjaw,' retorted Mungo, 'in childbirth. They use it to hold the mother's teeth apart, so that she can drink.'

He took the item from Achule's hand and replaced it upon its brickwork plinth. Achule glided away, chuckling.

'Our new government,' he declared, 'favours trained midwives and tetanus vaccination.'

'Oh?' Mungo inquired. 'How so, Mr Achule, given that most Pinwa health workers were butchered during the coup?'

Again, they faced up – and Achule moved on, fingering the displays and leaving each one slightly awry, so that Lewis must trail after, setting them straight.

Achule said to Mungo:

'You inform the local youngsters about Africa, is that right? What are you telling them about, I wonder?'

'The realities of rural life,' Mungo replied.

'And you know about that?'

'I do. And Lewis here assists me.'

'What do you teach?' Achule enquired of the biker.

'Ethnopharmacology,' said Lewis.

'Where were *you* born, Mr Achule?' Mungo snapped. 'Some luxury Lagos clinic for the urban rich? Africa is as much in my blood as in yours.'

'In a most interesting sense,' Edwards twittered. 'Aren't I right in saying that you're descended from Mungo Park, Mr Robertson?'

'Aye,' Lewis broke in, 'and there's the portrait to prove it.'

Achule regarded Park's gentle features.

'Is that the truth? I daresay you teach the children all the wonderful adventures of Park's first journey.'

'Pretty much,' agreed Mungo.

'But you don't say so much about his second journey?'

They glowered at each other. Lewis scanned the faces: what second journey?

But Edwards squeaked to attract their attention.

'Good heavens, this is fun!'

He was standing in front of the great mask that hung in pride of place with a spotlight to itself. Achule came to Edwards' side – and of a sudden his expression was surprised, and intent.

'How did you come by this?'

Mungo winced; a difficulty he'd dreaded had arrived. And he cursed Charlie Dulce for his so-called 'help'.

◆◆◆

In the Farron Hotel, Gordon Morrison was denouncing Mungo's

contribution to learning.

'Last Sunday he had them skinning rabbits, and curing the skins!'

He was so incensed that he slopped Heavy onto his wife's panda coat. She tried to scrape it off with a beer mat.

'That'll be handy, rabbit fur,' Cameron remarked, watching foam slip down the luxury garment.

'Handy? Fit's handy? Katy's seven. Robertson and that damned school-wyfie'll mak her a poacher.'

In the porch, with room for one copper-top table, Katy the poacher had been parked with a tumbler of juice and a metalised pack of prawn crackers. There came a Land Rover scrunching; Mungo entered. He paused a moment with Katy, who at once demanded:

'If the pottery lady was very beautiful, why did they hurt her?'

Mungo looked away. He lifted a hand, helpless – then let it lie upon the table.

'They hated all my friends,' he murmured.

'Because of you?'

'No, no, it was a raid – a sort of fight. They hurt everybody.'

'And children?'

'I'd not have let them touch you,' said Mungo, recalling friends slaughtered despite his protests.

'Can I come and see her?' Katy said. 'The little statue? Tomorrow, can I come on my bike?'

'We'll need to speak to your father,' he answered, with a nod to the open bar door and the voices.

Gordon Morrison was growing vehement.

'For God's sake, I'm no against fun at school, but I want the wee brutes to learn manners and spelling.'

Cameron, emollient as ever, shifted uneasily.

'As long as they dinnae molest ma sheep…' he said.

'You filthy man!' Marion cried.

But Gordon wouldn't have it.

'Dammit, Cameron, I'm serious. My Brian's lost to the farm already, he's awa wi' the motorbike fairies. Am I to lose Katy as well?'

For hadn't half the farms in Glenfarron lost their children? Town jobs and colleges had got them. Inverness is far enough;

what need Timbuktu?

Alec Aitken, perched on a stool, warmed the soles of his boots at the coal fire.

'Ah was awa' once, in Port Said,' he sighed. 'Ah wanted to be a Whirlin' Dervish.'

He slipped off the stool and started to shuffle in an oriental travesty, his stick held over his head. The farmers grinned, egging the old rustic on, stomping and clapping. Marion slapped a beat upon the bar:

'Show us yer leg, ye daft loon!'

Gordon guffawed:

'Bloody jungle bunny!'

They stopped short. Mungo filled the doorway. His eye lit on Cameron, who blushed.

'Pleased to find you here, Mr Geddes. I've a favour to ask on behalf of the school.'

Cameron peered into his beer.

'Oh, aye?'

'I was wondering if we could get a loan of your pony.'

◆◆◆

His arm well twisted, Cameron took himself off home. He was just in time: Callum and Tom were in the milking byre.

His trainers scrabbling, Callum clambered onto a splintery wooden partition, the Galloway belty regarding him with deep suspicion. Tom passed up a hammer, and the beast began shuffling and stamping, rolling her eyes.

'Hush, will ye, coo?' Callum pointed to a rabbit in a shoebox at his brother's feet. 'Give it, then. No the whole box, ye bam!'

'Dinna like tae …'

'It's dead!' Callum snapped.

But Tom would not touch the contents; he opened the box and offered it up. Callum extracted the dead rabbit and stood unsteadily on the partition, holding the rabbit by one leg against a wooden beam, over the cow's head. They heard their father calling from the house.

'Callum? Tom! Come in for your tea. Where are ye?'

'Quick, gimme the nails,' Callum demanded.

'Find its todger,' his little brother urged. 'You've to bang the nail through its todger.'

'Dunno,' Callum muttered, searching the matted fur, the nails now held in his teeth.

'P'raps it's a wyfie, 'n' has nae todger.'

Teetering on his perch, Callum took a nail from his gob, held it to the rabbit's groin and pounded with the hammer…

A rat on the beam! Callum started, he teetered, his foot slipping…

And Cameron was there to catch his son.

'Steady, loon! Fit ye dein'?'

He clasped his boy in an awkward armful, hauling him away from the startled, stomping cow. Then he looked up, and saw the rabbit.

'Jesus, Callum, fit's that?'

Callum, in his father's grip, was too winded to speak. So Tom piped up.

'Mr Robertson says, if we bang the nail through the rabbit's todger then the coo will have mair milk.'

'What?'

The rat dropped to the ground and scurried for the open. Cameron sighed.

'Callum, can you no turn Robertson's juju on the bloody rats?'

◆◆◆

The afternoon post brought a letter to Parkneuk farmhouse, bearing the insignia of Her Majesty's Foreign and Commonwealth Office.

'What now?' groaned Mungo. 'More assistance from that bloody doctor?'

The postie, wanting a signature, had found Mungo in the steading. Nearby, the great mask of the Pinwa kings gleamed in a shaft of halogen light.

Mungo opened the letter there and then. He waved it at the postie like an item of forensic evidence.

'This is from Mr T.A. Smallbone, Permanent Secretary… Good Lord!'

The postie, meanwhile, saw to his bewilderment that the mask was moving all by itself, shimmering and rustling, turning about in the light, twizzling to and fro so that the skirts swayed and swished, sending up dust from the steading floor.

Mungo read aloud:

'*Dear Mr Robertson ... blah blah blah ... the Ambassadress therefore requests that, in view of the significance of the Royal Dance Mask, we ask you to return this item, as part of the heritage of the Gabunte nation.*

Well!'

He stared at the letter in outrage. The mask itself said nothing, but tottered away down the steading. Mungo read on:

'*The Foreign Secretary views the Embassy's request in a favourable light, and trusts that you will feel able to co-operate.*'

He looked up at the perplexed postie, then at the mask whose ochre eyes seemed to spin in outrage. The mask was twirling between the displays.

'They're telling me to send it back to Africa,' he cried indignantly, 'They've no business!'

He intercepted the mask, lifting it gently. Katy, emerging, looked up at Mungo's huge face and cinder-grey beard which would be regal too, were it not for the tears of fury in his eyes.

◆◆◆

They were shooting a film at the school. It was to be an historical epic.

Villagers passing by the schoolyard could see rabbit pelts on curing frames stinking in the sun. In the senior classroom, Mhairi and Hamish were making a cloak. They had a pile of furs, and a sheet of grey sugar-paper onto which Molly had drawn an outline with a thick green wax crayon. Mhairi and Hamish laid out the skins like a furry jigsaw.

Friends were painting each other's faces and donning home-made finery. They were Moors and blacks, slaves and princes; they strutted and preened and the noise was terrific. But above all this, another voice was strong: Mungo was ranting.

'It's a power struggle, just power. All this heritage shite ...'

'Now, Mungo ...!'

'TaBunte politicos despise the Pinwa heritage; they've damn near wiped the Pinwa out! They want to get their hands on the mask so that they can desecrate it.'

Molly's eye was on the children.

'Take the big scissors, Hamish – just Hamish, please. Mind, they're sharp – and cut off all the rabbits' feet.'

Hamish amputated with gusto.

'What will you do?' Molly asked. Mungo folded his arms.

'Nothing. They can't have it.'

'But if the Foreign Office insist…'

'Shall I tell you why they insist? There's a hydroelectric plan, a British consortium bidding. Never mind the massacres: think of the shareholders.'

Molly called to the cloak makers.

'Now, Mhairi, how many skins have you used?'

'Twelve rabbits,' the girl shouted.

'Very good, so, if it takes twelve rabbits to make one cloak, how many will you need for three cloaks? Do the sum. The rest of you: all ready for tomorrow?'

And the darkies chorused:

'Ready! Aye, ready!'

'Imagine, then,' Mungo boomed to the costumed class, now settled at their places. 'Imagine, two hundred years ago: you're Mungo Park, standing at the edge of a huge, unknown country. You've no map, you have no idea of the people, or of what dangerous or beautiful animals live there.'

He moved among the spellbound children.

'You have a native guide – but can you trust him? Maybe he'll rob you, kill you, cut your throat by the campfire. Maybe he'll sell you as a slave, maybe he'll eat you. But maybe he'll lead you safely across half of Africa. And somewhere, perhaps hundreds of miles in front of you, is a mighty river that you must find…'

Eventually, Glenfarron got to see *The Adventures of Mungo Park*. Molly held a screening in the hall.

The earlier shots are a tad wobbly; the camera operator was little Mhairi, and nervous. But it improves. It opens with a panorama of the Braes of Farron, over which there winds a lane. In the distance, two figures lead a pony.

'This is the story of Mungo Park.'

It is Callum who reads the script:

'He loved Africa, loved the animals in all their colour and strangeness, loved the people and their customs. He opened his heart to it all.'

Into the foreground comes Hamish, dressed for exploring the 19th century, with high boots and a broad-brimmed hat from the costume cupboard. Over his shoulders hangs a water bottle, a bandolier and a toy rifle. His companion is a fearsome savage, leading a diminutive Shetland pony which carries well-trussed travel bags.

The filming of these opening scenes was observed from the gateway into the lane. There was Aggie Hulewicz, the bikers, Alec Aitken and Gordon Morrison, and Cameron Geddes minding his pony and his boys.

'Is this school or Bollywood?' Gordon grumbled.

'I dinnae ken,' said the shepherd, 'but they're having a braw time.'

'Mind,' Aggie remarked, 'there's not one as can add up their sweetie money in the shop.'

'They don't steal the sweeties, do they?' Cameron retorted.

The Expedition neared the camera, and Molly called *Cut!*

Mungo took the pony's reins.

'That's grand, Hamish. Go and thank Mr Geddes and ask if we can get through the lower gate to the river.'

◆◆◆

There came another unwelcome visitor to Parkneuk: the British Council was back, with a new friend.

Brian had made excellent progress with the old Harley-Davidson. They were standing about admiring it, and Zippa wanted a go. Her black boot touched the kick-start, then thrust hard – and the motor fired eagerly, shivering with energy. Two blips on the throttle, then Zippa went thumping out of the yard and scudding down the long track towards the road. Her unhelmeted hair streamed; her friends whooped.

Mungo was watching also, but had another claim on his attention. Standing alongside Edwards of the Council stood an altogether cooler specimen who studied Mungo with interest.

'Won't you even discuss the matter, Robertson?' Edwards pleaded. 'Mr Smallbone has come up especially from the Foreign Office…'

'Will you look at that?' Mungo enthused, watching the Harley. 'That's fine, now.'

'There would be full compensation,' Edwards tried again.

'Compensation for what?' Mungo riposted, not turning. 'A priceless example of African art, or the lives of a thousand butchered tribesmen?'

Edwards appealed to his colleague: 'Mr Smallbone…?'

Calm, purposeful, Smallbone stepped forward.

'Mr Robertson, I am here on the personal instruction of the Foreign Secretary. As we see it, the return of the royal mask is a matter of some national importance.'

'To which nation?' Mungo demanded.

'Why, to both Britain and Gabunte,' said the softly spoken official, 'both former employers of yours. We mean to return the mask, Mr Robertson.'

'Mr Smallbone,' parried Mungo, 'it is not yours to return.'

'Arguably, it is not yours either.'

'How so?'

'Imperial plunder, some might call it: the spoils of foreign adventuring.'

'Good, good,' Mungo agreed. 'Then you'll be returning the Elgin marbles, the Benin bronzes and Cleopatra's Needle. That's good.'

'Each case on its merits,' Smallbone replied.

'Each case on its engineering contracts,' snapped Mungo.

Brian, Lewis and friends, awaiting Zippa's return, heard the escalating tone, glanced round and drew closer.

'Africa's domestic squabbles,' Smallbone opined, 'are not our affair. You'd not want us to interfere…'

'You are bloody interfering! You're proposing to hand over the most potent tribal symbol in Gabunte.'

'We judge that to be necessary,' Smallbone breathed.

'You judge poorly.'

'And we shall take whatever steps we consider to be…'

Mungo roared: 'Are you threatening me?'

He loomed over the Foreign Office man. Smallbone was not perturbed, but Edwards was made of feebler stuff. He tapped Smallbone's arm: they were encircled. The bikers, all studs, black leather and oily fingernails, were closing in on them.

Smallbone, not intimidated, pointed with his chin towards Mungo's museum steading.

'You've put a lot of work into this.'

Mungo gestured to the ring of bikers:

'*We* certainly have.'

'It was a barn, I take it,' Smallbone remarked. 'Did you have planning permission for the change of use?' The question was pure rhetoric; he knew the answer. 'We are in touch with the Regional Council, you see.' A mock sigh. 'A pity to take it all apart.'

'Get out of here, before I impale you.'

Mr Smallbone smiled icily at Mungo, then stepped passed Brian to the car. Edwards scampered after, scurrying to the driver's door. Before the bikers could scratch profanities into his paintwork, Edwards took off at speed down the rutted track. Zippa was returning on the stately Harley. The car made no effort to swerve or slow, forcing her through an open gate into the field. Zippa bounced and dropped the heavy machine, staggering clear.

'Zippa! Zippa!' Her lover Fly pelted down the track yelling at the car. 'There is a baby, you bastard!'

'Aye,' said Brian, and he spat into the goat's feed bucket.

◆◆◆

Adventures of Mungo Park, continued:

Under a spreading oak, a Moorish Queen holds court, seated on a green gym mat. Her servants cool her with coloured paper fans on sticks. The Queen's name is Katy. The robe about her shoulders is of rabbit fur, she has a tea towel for a turban, and her followers are armed to the teeth with garden canes and plastic swords.

Callum's voiceover:

'All across Africa, poor simple people invited him into their homes. Even with enemies, with powerful folk who could have killed him, nae bother, he was nice and pally. And so he was able to travel on.'

Katy looks disdainfully at Hamish who stands before her in his explorer's whites. She is regal, cruel, superb.

'So, Mungo Park, I give you permission to cross the Empire of Gabunte to find the Great River.'

'Thank you, O Queen!'

Sweeping off his hat, Hamish bows low.

'But,' Katy continues, 'because you are a foreign pig, you must give me half your money.'

'Who says?' the great explorer protests, turning to Molly (out of frame) in indignation. 'Miss, why?'

'Well, Hamish, she's the Queen,' says Molly, 'so she's allowed.'

Katy waves her followers forward. They seize the saddlebags, tip them out onto the ground, stir the contents and grab the purse of pennies. Katy sticks out a peremptory hand and the minions fill it with coin, which she pockets.

'Only half, Katy,' Molly is heard to say. 'We have to share.'

Katy divides the stash and flings half over the head of Hamish. The tribe pounces.

'Miss!' Hamish wails.

A scuffle breaks out between tribesmen.

'Stuart,' cries their teacher, 'we don't steal!'

'Miss, you said he has to share.'

'But we mustn't touch what isn't ours.'

'Why?'

'Because that's property.'

The little boy dithers, bewildered.

Katy, having concealed much of the cash about her person, stands tall on her gym mat.

'You can go now, Mungo Park.'

Near to tears, Hamish turns away.

Katy turns to Mungo Robertson: 'You can go too.'

He bows low – *Madam!* – then addresses the class:

'On! On to discover the River Niger. Forward!'

And they all go scuttling after, costumes flapping. Katy sees them off, picks up her fur cape and follows.

◆◆◆

'Really, I don't think you need worry,' said Dr Dulce.

Seated in front of him in the surgery, the two young Poles looked at him, at each other, at the doctor once more. They were frightened, they were not convinced.

'Please, believe me,' Charlie urged as gently as he could. 'Zdzislawa was not injured, thank heaven. There's no sign of internal bleeding. Obviously, if you do start to bleed in the next day or two, then we must fear the worst. But this is very unlikely; at this stage, the foetus is a tiny bean in a thick padded pod. Later on, an accident could be more serious, but not yet. We could send you to Inverness for a scan, but it would make no difference to what we do – or, to what *you* should do, which is to carry on as normal.'

He smiled pleasantly at the girl who, he saw, was now half-way to trusting him.

'How long are you staying with Great-aunt Aggie?' Charlie asked.

The Poles looked at each other again.

'We are not so sure,' said the girl. 'Somehow we like to remain. We are very happy here, it is so beautiful and interesting.'

'Except the sausages are bad,' Czcibor added. 'But we must go to school – to college. Even with a baby.'

'Well, yes,' said Charlie, 'you've your futures. But if you do stay, be sure we'll take excellent care of Zdzislawa.'

'How come,' the girl said, 'you can pronounce my name?'

Charlie beamed.

'You haven't heard? My father was Polish, an airman in the war. I never knew him, I'm afraid, but I was brought up by a Polish friend. He made sausages, excellent Polish sausages, right here in Glenfarron. There were a lot of us about. Your family and mine, we were good friends, sixty years back.'

He saw them out, hearing them murmur questions to each other as they headed for their room at the back of Aggie's shop. He thought of how he'd envied their love and freedom, now circumscribed by the common cares. And he realised that he envied them still, but fondly.

Then Julia marched in, thrusting at him some wearisome demand for audit. So Charlie came down to earth.

◆◆◆

A balloon glass swilling with sickly Irish Cream slithered along the bar to Marion. Cameron Geddes wondered: if she spilt that stuff onto her synthetic panda skin, would the mixture ignite?

Gordon Morrison was banging on.

'No, self-sufficiency, that's fine, that's when they mak' their ain videos.'

Marion sipped the liqueur, sticking her tongue like a butterfly's proboscis into the muck.

'But I need Katy to mind her letters,' Gordon persisted. 'I'll need *one* of my bairns' help with the farm.'

His son Brian did not look up from the billiards. Marion sipped again and needled her husband:

'I want Katy to learn so she can get the hell *off* the farm.'

'Say that again?' Gordon hissed, reddening.

Cameron intervened in a hurry.

'Have a malt, Gordon? And Mr Robertson?'

'Much obliged,' Mungo nodded. 'I will.'

'Now, I've heard,' Marion took up, 'that you had bother with some boy from London.'

'Indeed,' Mungo nodded, 'there's an item in the museum; certain crooks and bigwigs in Africa are demanding that I hand it over.'

'Well!' Marion gasped.

'It's in my safekeeping. In Africa it would have been destroyed.'

'They dinnae value their things,' Gordon averred. 'Can they mak' you gi'it back?'

'The Foreign Office is trying.'

'That's terrible!' cried Marion. 'Our own government.'

She gazed at Mungo, appalled and admiring.

'They'll nae be getting it,' another voice interjected.

Everyone looked round: Lewis and Brian were standing as stalwart as redcoats at Rorke's Drift, with billiard cues at high port.

'They'll be takin' nothing frae here, nae chance!'

◆◆◆

Adventures of Mungo Park, continued:

Callum, voiceover –

'He had to catch his own tea, and eat giant lizards.'

The blackamoors watch intently. From a rabbit hole in the dirt slope, a plastic dinosaur is creeping (with the help of invisible nylon thread). Unaware of the digital camcorder and the spectators, the monster inches forward. It spies the bait: a tasty piece of cheddar, such as African lizards like best. The beast wriggles forward into a short section of plastic drainpipe positioned over its hole, in the centre of which there hangs a noose. It hesitates, it nudges a little wooden peg… *Twang!* Up whips a long willow, the noose jerks tight, and strangles that lizard dead as dead.

The camera rolls, the class cheers the trapper's feat. Hamish, triumphant, gnashes on his victim's throat.

◆◆◆

Around the turn of the Millennium, Molly Anderson had bought an old barn which, in the early 1970s, had been converted into a desirable dwelling. It was an interesting building, situated at the edge of the forest near Torbrechan farm. The conversion and sale, detaching the barn from the farm estate, had caused painful scenes between the young Dr Charles Dulce, his mother Joyce and Vladislaw Obremski; there were powerful memories attached to the building. But finally Charlie's view had prevailed: that one had to move on, and not make a fetish of a scene of injustice. Besides which, Charlie had badly needed cash in order to purchase *Mandalay*.

Of this story, Molly new nothing.

To reach her new home, Molly had to pass Torbrechan by a dirt track which then skirted the forest. The barn stood half in, half out of the trees; one end was shaded by old beech and ash while the other looked out into a broad field. At the shaded end, a flight of stone steps had once given access to the farm hands' accommodation above, but now there was an internal spiral of varnished timber, and the former bothy had become a tasteful bedroom with *en suite* bath. Below, what was once the great barn door had been glazed to form a picture window that looked along the edge of the woods.

A while back – and never suspecting any connection – Molly had invited Dr Dulce to tea. She had had no idea that the converted barn was one of the few Glenfarron houses Charlie had avoided entering.

Presented with a simple invitation, however, and by someone as sympathetic as Molly, Charlie had decided that the past was a long time ago, and he had succumbed to curiosity. He had not divulged his reasons for snooping around the house.

She had made it very pleasant. Her kitchen was a neat, well-ordered, feminine room, the walls hung with charts of fungi and crustaceans. There were pulses and pasta in tall jars ranged along a sideboard of solid pine, on which the orange polyurethane glowed. There were cookbooks on Tuscan and Andalusian cuisine, crocks of organic wholemeal flour and a bread-making machine.

She had bustled about with the rooibos and the teapot, and had asked Charlie (indicating a sideboard drawer) to get out a mat. He had opened the wrong drawer, revealing not cork squares but a stack of red-checked dishclouts. He'd lifted these, seeking mats, but what he had found was a photo in a gilt frame. It was a portrait of a young man; he looked a go-getter. He had got to Molly once, before he slipped away to run his Dalmatian sailing school.

Molly had seen Charlie studying the portrait.

'Next drawer along,' she'd said, her voice husky.

Charlie had thought: poor girl, she is terribly lonely.

Not long after, he'd nipped upstairs to the bathroom. Molly's bedroom door had been open, and through it Charlie had glimpsed her bed: an enormous, pink princess bed with flouncy, lacy drapes. It had rung a bell.

'I say,' he'd burbled, 'that's a terrific bed upstairs. Do you mind my asking where you found it?'

Molly had blushed. She'd muttered something about an auction of house contents at Brig o' Farron.

And Charlie had remembered: he'd attended a patient with a failing liver in that self-same bed, his very first house-call in Glenfarron, some thirty-five years ago. It was Gideon Baird's bed, the centrepiece of a love-nest that Gideon never got to share.

◆◆◆

Adventures of Mungo Park, continued:

By the Farron Water, a broad meadow lies. In the warm sun, the sky is loud with craws and corbies, the tall summer grass swaying in the breeze. By the stone dyke, a column marches. Only a white hat and the tops of spears and baggage balanced on childish heads are visible above the grass.

The Farron Water is before them. The microphone catches a liquid rippling over stony shallows.

The expeditionary column comes into full view as it meets the bank and halts there. The pony and the half-naked children in loincloths, sandals and face-paints, all stare into the Water as though for the first time.

Hamish – Mungo Park – sweeps an imperious hand over the view.

'I've found it! I'm the first white man ever to see the great River Niger. Hooray!'

He flourishes his cap pistol, and fires above the rapids. The porters put down their loads and caper, the Moors yodelling and cheering.

◆◆◆

A shame they didn't film the next scene.

Late afternoon, a convoy entered Glenfarron. It consisted of Constable Reid in the police Land Rover, followed by a black limousine with a pennant fizzing on the radiator top and, trailing these, the British Council Rover. In the limo, all three occupants – chauffeur and two passengers – were black. Achule was snappily suited; beside him was a yet finer figure, a woman of enormous nobility and presence. She was swathed in billowing robes of blue and gold with a heap of headdress to match.

She was an Ambassadress.

As they progressed through the glen, Achule deferentially remarked upon the features of the landscape, indicating to left and to right, drawing slight smiles from the regal figure beside him. She was, surely, the first black woman ever to gaze upon the Farron Water.

The convoy swept into Glenfarron village. Three of the most reliable gossips – postmistress, shepherd, farmer Gordon – loitering in the lee of the shop, saw the limo flash its lights at the police; all three vehicles drew to a gravelled halt. Out jumped the chauffeur, spinning upon his heel to open the passenger door. But Achule put up a hand.

'Madam, please! Let the chauffeur fellow manage the shopping.'

'I am doing this, Achule.'

The imperiously beautiful figure gathered up her robes, stepped (with a little duck to preserve her turban) down and, with gracious smiles to the speechless natives, glided into the SPAR. Everyone piled in after.

Behind the till, ringed by onlookers, Aggie Hulewicz stood with mouth agape. The Ambassadress was holding out her purchase: a bar of milk chocolate.

'How much, please?' she asked.

Aggie continued to stare. Patiently, the Ambassadress held the chocolate up between them.

'It is chocolate,' she elucidated. 'How much is the chocolate, please?'

But Aggie was tongue-tied. Gordon Morrison helped out.

'How much is chocolate, Aggie?'

'78p, Your Highness,' Aggie Hulewicz whispered. The Ambassadress smiled pleasantly:

'Thank you, I am merely an envoy.'

Aggie received coin from a hand that was very dark on one side and delicately pink on the other.

The Ambassadress inquired, 'Are we on the right road for Parkneuk?'

She left the shop with the crowd in tow, all of whom pointed her on her way. As the cars departed, the shepherd voiced the general consensus:

'Yon wyfie's no frae hereaboots.'

But Gordon Morrison's shrewd eyes narrowed.

'There'll be trouble at our museum.'

At that precise moment, however, Mungo Robertson was not at the museum. He was at Molly's house, the barn by the woods, sipping at a mug of Fair Trade coffee.

'Explain a puzzle to me, if you will,' said Molly. 'Why did your father name you after Mungo Park?'

'I am indirectly descended.'

'But your father never went to Africa?'

'My father was appalled by the very thought of Africa. He despised foreigners of all sorts.'

'So, why…'

Mungo was smiling.

'He was misinformed. He believed Park to have been an imperial conqueror, a Rhodes, a Clive, a Wolfe. When I left for Africa – to work as a volunteer – my father was outraged. He swore blue murder, said I'd got the wrong idea entirely, but it was he himself who'd planted the seed, with that name. Farcical, no?'

He laughed softly. Then he looked round the room: the pictures, the comforts.

'You have a lovely home,' he said. They were in mellow and intimate mood.

'In the colonies, one becomes conscious of certain perils,' he remarked, standing mug in hand. He was taking in the view of the forest edge curving away, with (Molly dared to hope) approval.

'What perils are those?' she enquired. She'd striven to dress in a manner at once rugged and appealing: cavalry twill slacks and a denim shirt with the collar turned up. 'To life and limb, do you mean?'

'Life,' Mungo affirmed. 'The danger of becoming an eternal expatriate, rootless, no fixed abode, and so on.'

'What's the 'so on'?' Molly prompted, oddly coy. He hesitated an instant.

'No family. As commonly understood.'

She was unable to meet his eye. Oh, she reproved herself, this is ludicrous, I'm grown up!

'I'm pleased you like my home. I love it. I think it would be ideal for a couple.'

'You know the story of the barn, do you?' Mungo parried. 'There was a murder here. Locals shot a Polish airman for seducing village girls. For years the place was synonymous with lust.'

'I hadn't heard that,' she gasped, scrambling to understand him. But Mungo said no more.

'I was wondering if I could tempt you,' she eventually continued, 'with dinner? One of these lovely evenings. Or lunch. Whatever.'

The phone rang. She stepped into the hall – and returned more flustered yet.

'You'd best be away,' she said. 'You've important visitors at home.'

'Good Lord.'

Embarrassment beat between them. All Glenfarron knew, it seemed, when Mungo Robertson was calling on Miss Anderson.

By the time he reached Parkneuk, however, matters had taken a serious turn.

There was a stand-off between a white official in a white Rover, a white policeman in black uniform, two black diplomats, and six white bikers in black leathers. Brian and Lewis, Fly, Zippa and the twins had formed a cordon in front of the museum doors, solid as a regiment.

Constable Reid spoke into his handset: 'He's here just now.'

Mungo was accelerating up the drive.

'Mr Robertson,' Achule jeered, flapping a contemptuous paw at the bikers, 'your security staff are impeding the restitution of stolen goods.'

'And you,' Mungo retorted, slamming his cab door and striding forward, 'you, laddie, are stretching the Highland welcome near to breaking point.'

The Ambassadress interposed her not-inconsiderable bulk to prevent a punch-up. Her tone was gracious and mollifying.

'Mr Robertson, please! I am honoured to meet such a notable friend of Africa. Can we not be friends?'

'Tomorrow,' Mungo replied.

'We can be friends tomorrow?'

'We can talk.'

'I say, Robertson,' Smallbone urged, 'the Ambassadress has come from London.'

'Then she will appreciate a night's rest,' said Mungo.

'The Ambassadress is a very busy person!'

But the Ambassadress raised a hand:

'I am also a flexible person, Mr Smallbones. I am happy to stay in Glenfarron tonight. Did we not pass a hotel in the village?'

'The village, Madam?' Smallbone sneered. 'You mean, the pub?'

'Return to Inverness if you wish; I shall be comfortable, and shall resume my visit in the morning. Ten o'clock, Mr Robertson?'

Her cavalcade departed.

Mungo turned to the bikers.

'Right! On your bikes and round the houses. Get as many folk as you can, here tomorrow for nine-thirty. Tell them their heritage is at stake, tell them the TV is coming, tell them anything. I want this witnessed.'

◆◆◆

Cameron was standing in the yard at Torbrechan, blasting mud from his tractor with a pressure washer that pinged and battered off the mudguards and couplings. From the corner of his eye, he saw his smaller boy Tom emerge from behind the barn, waving urgently to Callum. His sons vanished; Cameron glanced after them suspiciously, then worked on in the long Highland evening, his gaze wandering to the enclosure of Parkneuk downstream…

'Da! Da!'

'Aye loons, fit noo?'

He turned off the jet; his tractor stood glistening in a swill of muddy water. His boys trotted towards him from the steadings, bearing a curious contraption. There was a short length of piping, a whippy garden cane with an arrangement of string – and a dark, smooth tail protruding. The boys were clamouring both at once.

'It's a trap! Mr Robertson showed us.'

'But we made it!'

'In the steading!'

'It works, we caught a mouse!'

They held it up, hugely proud. The trap was exactly like

Mungo's at the filming, but inside there lay not a plastic dinosaur but a real and thoroughly garrotted mouse.

Cameron stared at the mouse, at the contrivance, at his boys. 'Aye,' he said, astounded. He grinned delightedly. 'Aye!'

◆◆◆

There followed a most unusual evening in the Farron Hotel; the bar had never seen such crowds.

Marion Morrison, pleasantly tipsy with her panda draped over a bar stool, looked up as the door opened yet again.

'My word, Doctor and Mrs Dulce too, we are honoured.'

Charlie Dulce looked round, and saw familiar elbows on the beer mats, the usual nips and pints in the usual paws. But a throng packed the L-shaped public bar, and everyone was trying not to stare at something just around the corner.

Aggie Hulewicz stood nearby.

'We told her about the Country Club, but she wouldn't!' Aggie hissed to Marion. 'Claire says you can't get into her room for robes. And she's had a bath.'

They glimpsed a voluptuous swish of magenta shot with gold.

'Good evening, Charlie,' Claire Dulce murmured, ignoring Julia, whom she disliked.

'Claire,' the doctor nodded. 'You've colourful company tonight.'

'I've always made foreign visitors especially welcome,' she returned. 'May I get you something, or are you here to spectate?'

He frowned: 'I'll take a pint of Export, and a white wine for Julia.'

Again, he searched the faces – and at last saw Mungo Robertson.

In a far corner, the farmers were clustered about Mungo, their faces set and resolute.

'They've seized nothing jes' yet?' Gordon was asking.

'We stopped that,' Mungo assured him. 'My young allies prevented them. Tomorrow, we – and the children – shall be ready.'

'They'll be there,' Molly confirmed.

'Grab the headlines,' nodded Cameron.

'Aye!' Gordon snarled. 'Katy'll put the frighteners on this shower.'

Seated across the room, Mr Smallbone had the diplomat's knack of clocking distant conversations while not appearing to pay attention. He scrutinised Mungo, then leaned closer to the Ambassadress who was devouring Claire's sticky toffee pudding and whipped cream with evident enjoyment. Smallbone whispered something, letting his eye rest one half-second upon Molly. The Ambassadress followed his look.

But the next remark that Smallbone overheard he did not pass on. Perhaps he found it merely coarse. It was from Julia Dulce, now joined by Gordon Morrison at the bar. She was saying:

'I am not in the habit of taking orders from Africans.'

'Nae mair Lunnun folk,' frowned Gordon.

'It's unacceptable.'

'Little short of theft, Mrs Dulce.'

'Our educational facilities!'

'Those things belong here.'

'Valued as artefacts, and properly looked after.'

'Not like in Africa…' said Gordon, shaking his head.

'Where they have no notion of Heritage,' said she.

They scrutinised the African delegation.

'However,' Julia opined, 'we must not have it said that the Community Council has been discourteous. I think we should liaise with the Foreign Office. Where has Charles got to? Charles!'

But Charlie was edging away, awkward but determined, across the room towards Mungo. He saw that Mungo had registered his approach, but was stubbornly not looking in the doctor's direction.

I *will* speak with him, thought Charlie. I must.

'Robertson,' he began, as soon as Mungo could not avoid him, 'Mungo! I have to clarify something here. Please, I must assure you, it was no doing of mine that the Embassy…'

Charlie got no further. There was a sudden loud scrape of chairs, and a general stir. The Ambassadress rose from her bar supper, Smallbone parting the way for her.

'I shall call for you, Madam, at 9.30 tomorrow. Edwards and I are lodged in a hideous castle, now a country club, a mile up the road.'

Charlie felt a hand on his elbow; it was the grip of Julia.

He cleared his throat: 'Er, now...'

'Thank you all.' The Ambassadress smiled broadly. 'And good evening.'

She swept past regally, heading for the stairs. The doctor stammered at her retreating back:

'I say... On behalf of the...'

'Not just now, if you don't mind,' Smallbone murmured.

And they were gone.

Julia hastened to Charlie's side.

'Did you see?' he whispered.

'To the telephone, Charles,' she hissed. 'An extra-ordinary Council meeting, this ae nicht!'

So the phone wires of Glenfarron burned.

◆◆◆

The following morning, just before ten, Molly Anderson stood scanning the local paper in Parkneuk yard.

'Crisis Talks in Afro-Glenfarron Rift.'

Molly asked, 'Did you write this?'

'I cannot tell a lie,' said the hack.

'Black leather guards confront officials.'

'Whose side are you on?' Molly demanded.

The reporter ignored the question.

'I've been talking to Smallbone,' he said. 'Do you know why Robertson left Africa?'

'Early retirement,' Molly answered.

'He was sacked – for obstructing development projects. Didn't want British technical advisers brought in. Wanted the savages kept savage.'

Having scored this hit, he stalked off to gaze down the lane.

Molly sighed: 'Just when we think we know the story.'

A voice called across the yard: 'Here they come!'

Half the population of Glenfarron were gathered at Parkneuk, together with the press and crews from television and radio, all squeezing the squashy ends of their microphones and swapping lenses once more for luck. At the sound of drumming, everyone rushed to the fence.

The cavalcade of the Ambassadress had reached the turn-off from the road, and there the motorbikes waited. From each pillion rose two metres of Pinwa battle spear with pennons of blood-red warthog vellum; on each shoulder, a zebra-hide shield; on every jacket, feathers and thongs and copper rings; on every handlebar, skulls of hartebeest. On the Goldwing, Pam perched behind Lewis, facing backwards and slamming at a tom-tom roped to the springs, as the bikes streamed up the track ahead of the diplomats, spraying dust at them. Thus escorted, the Ambassadress entered Parkneuk yard in a rhythmic hubbub.

The chatter stilled. Achule trotted round to open the door, and she stepped down. Today she wore a gown of green and yellow, and a silvered silken headdress that sparkled above her lustrous black forehead. Smallbone, Edwards and young PC Reid hovered in attendance.

Mungo raised a hand: the drumming stopped.

'I do come in friendship,' said the Ambassadress.

Without replying, Mungo signalled again. Now Molly hauled open the steading door as Lewis and Brian began the beat anew, pounding with sticks upon an oil drum. Out from the museum wound a chain of children dressed and ornamented as young Pinwa, dancing, clapping, streaming into the yard to encircle the intruders, stamping in a ring.

The Ambassadress beamed down at them.

'Madam!' Achule spluttered furiously at her elbow, 'this is a provocation!'

'Smile, Achule,' his boss replied, between her teeth.

'Madam?'

'Do it.'

Moments later, the crowd was packing into the steading: children, pressmen, TV crews and diplomats, bikers, and locals who'd not seen Mungo's museum before (not having come to the opening) but were here to defend their patrimony, gawking at the outlandish displays. As they passed by, little Katy stopped to inspect her favourite figurine, the elegant Pinwa lady.

The Ambassadress bent down by Katy, hands upon her knees and her face almost on a level with Katy's own. They gazed at the statuette.

'She's beautiful,' said the dignitary.

'She's Mr Robertson's best.'

'Is that so? A Pinwa lady.'

'She *was* a Pinwa,' Mungo interjected. 'She was murdered with all the usual TaBunte savagery.'

The Ambassadress straightened to face him, a steely glint in the diplomatic eye.

'But that is Africa,' she said. 'Beauty and barbarity. One has heard it so often. Can't we move on, Mr Robertson?'

'The cameras are waiting,' he retorted. 'Say your piece.'

'So.' She smiled and, with the grace of an empress, took the centre in a ring of spectators.

She began:

'For eighty years, my peaceful country was stripped of its riches by colonial masters. We ask only the restitution of our property, just as each one of you would ask for stolen things to be returned.'

Mungo wouldn't have it.

'Her peaceful country,' he guffawed, 'is a nest of warring tribes. Her lot, the TaBunte, are the worst. The Pinwa farmers – the poor bloody farmers who made all these things – are the victims. I will not be called a thief by murderers.'

The Ambassadress did not lose her temper. Molly scrutinised her flock of children, who formed the inner ring; as the elders murmured, the young remained thoughtful. It was to the children that the Ambassadress spoke.

'Children – you know, Africa does not like the British telling us how to be peaceful. Have you heard how the peaceful British killed our chiefs and took our cattle and our farms? How they said they could find nothing in their London files to show that we Africans owned any land at all? Children, has Mr Robertson told you this?'

She crouched again by Katy, and fingered the rabbit-cloak.

'So, you have learned to make clothes out of rabbits. That is fun, for sure. You show me sometime; you know, these fine robes of mine are cold in the snow. But did Mr Robertson tell you about his work? In Africa? What was he doing there, while he was having a nice time collecting his museum? Did he tell you that?'

She fished in her pocket, and addressed Hamish the Explorer:

'Now, you see this: what is this?'

'A bean?' Hamish wondered.

'A bean. What bean is that? A baked bean? You want to eat that bean?'

Hamish took the large nut, sniffed it cautiously like a cat nosing a morsel, then handed it back.

'But that's a cocoa bean,' she cried, 'for chocolate.'

She produced her bar of chocolate.

'You know, when Mr Robertson and his friends were in charge, this was the bean we must grow. In all our best fields, only this chocolate bean: no corn, no fruit, no vegetables – chocolate, chocolate everywhere. We got so sick.'

'You'd starve soon enough if you couldn't sell those beans,' retorted Mungo.

'Oh yes,' she agreed, 'a fine mess now, always a fine mess since you left us blackies on our own. But you know' (she turned back to Katy) 'we like to make our own mess. We don't like to be told to tidy up. And you, Mr Robertson, it's time you gave us back our toys.'

She went to the great royal mask that oversaw the gathering, touching it with one long delicate finger.

'We play our own games,' she mused.

'What games?' Mungo mocked. 'Golliwog Pogrom? Noddy Goes Headhunting?'

He got no further. Achule strode across the floor and swung a right into Mungo's jaw, sending him staggering against the wall, after which there was bedlam. Mungo rose to battle like a great bearded lion.

The children retreated through the hole in the thorn fence.

◆◆◆

This episode united the community.

To a fusillade of approval, Mungo drove into the shop forecourt. From across the road by the Post Office, a knot of locals applauded vigorously:

Mr Robertson! Bravo!

He gave them a nod, but the acclaim did not seem to warm his heart as it should, after such a famous victory.

Inside, the shop was quiet; there was only Alec Aitken waiting to be served, with his long-life bread in its silver plastic bag. He took a Penguin from a box on the counter, and ate it as he gazed through the window at the gathering opposite.

In came Mungo, his face dark.

'Robertson,' nodded Alec, 'you won that round.'

Mungo did not reply. He seized *The Scotsman*, slapped a pound on the counter and marched out to face his fans.

'Bravo, Robertson,' someone again applauded. 'You're entirely vindicated.'

'Utterly disgraceful!' someone concurred.

'We're all behind you.'

'Thank you, yes.' Mungo forced a smile.

'We'll be pressing for Planning,' the Council Secretary informed him. 'With immediate effect.'

They crowded at the door of the Land Rover.

'We'll not have Scotland's birthright…'

'Pillaged by looters from Africa!'

'Thank you,' Mungo acknowledged. And he left them.

The scene was observed by Dr Dulce from his window.

With a surgery to run, Charlie had not been present at the Battle of Parkneuk, but he did have to tend to the casualities: Achule had twisted a finger in punching Mungo, and it required strapping. Brian, attempting to propel Edwards bodily back into the British Council Rover, had stumbled and both had fallen; Edwards' trousers were torn and so was Brian's upper lip.

As he returned the orange antiseptic to the lotions cupboard, Charlie wondered if this was his opening, his chance for redemption in Molly's eyes. Could he not present himself as a figure of moderation, of disinterested calm? Could he be a go-between, perhaps?

It was a role he fancied, until it dawned on him that the only thing the visitors wanted was the dance mask, and that there was no possibility of Mungo surrendering that. In such an intractable dispute, an intermediary was liable to end up looking foolishly impotent.

But Charlie was determined to try. He would offer his good offices, and he would do it through Molly…

The opposition, however, got there first. Smallbone went to the school, and stood by the classroom window.

'Your friend Mr Robertson has been presenting a somewhat bowdlerised version of African history, Miss Anderson.'

After the violence of the morning, Molly found this visit

unnerving. In the car park, she saw Edwards on watch, and Achule pacing up and down. They made Molly think of secret policemen.

Smallbone turned to her.

'The career of the estimable Mungo Park is not without its question marks, you know. His journey of 1796 was a triumph, certainly, but the 1806 journey was frankly a debacle.'

Molly did not respond. She was wary – and weary too, though her classroom was quiet. Homemade Africana littered the desks.

Smallbone was smooth and seemingly candid.

'With recent events we are again on treacherous ground. The Pinwa started it, however. Fighting began with their raiding a government outpost in some backwater town. It was full of idle parasitic clerks, and the Pinwa butchered them all.'

He paused, looking out of the window.

'Achule's father was in that office, a minor functionary. He was, I gather, castrated, eviscerated, and decapitated.'

Outside, Achule glanced back at them. Two small children scampered across the playground, almost colliding with him. Achule steered them safely past.

'Not a man one warms to,' Smallbone observed, 'but he has legitimate grievances.'

He turned again to Molly.

'Now, about the Lady Ambassadress. Your thoughts, Miss Anderson?'

Soon after, Molly fled home, feeling cowed and depressed.

◆◆◆

Mungo did nothing to help.

It was suppertime. Molly in her pine kitchen winced as Mungo, on a floodtide of anger, thumped *The Scotsman* onto a worktop.

'This!' he bellowed. 'Behind our backs!'

'Would you like a glass ...' she ventured.

'A trade agreement! Of all despicable, craven acts.'

'The soup will only be ...'

'Training at Sandhurst for hand-picked thugs.'

'Mungo!'

Her tone stopped him short. He stopped ranting. The table was pretty with picnic things ready for the hamper: pies and fruit, French tarts and wine glasses.

'Can you not,' she tried, 'for once,' she pleaded, 'bring the rest of you back from Africa? The Mungo that's still there, roaring about with a sore head? Please?'

He didn't know what to say.

'Let's talk of other things,' she begged. It was a lovely evening; they were supposed to be getting out for some fresh air, an impromptu and light-hearted supper by the Farron. There came a childish knock on the door. Molly composed herself; Mungo looked contrite. They went outside to meet their little guest, and walked half a mile upriver through the warm meadows.

Where the languid stream sang lullabies, Katy Morrison sat upon a rock. She stared down into the water, watching the late sun wavering, till the surface of the pool broke under the impact of a pebble.

Katy asked:

'Could you really go by boat from here to Africa?'

'If you don't mind a few rocks and rapids and storms at sea.'

Mungo, puffing a cigar, scraped up a handful of small stones. One by one he tossed them into the water just in front of Katy. The child jumped to her feet and scampered along the bank.

Molly asked, 'Now what are you thinking?'

'Walter Scott,' Mungo replied, 'once met Mungo Park tossing stones into a river. Park said this was the way that he gauged the depth of African streams, by the bubbles. Scott believed that Park was pining for Africa.'

'And are you?'

Mungo remained silent a moment, studying Katy who had found the skull of some small rodent and was mounting it on a stick.

'Strange,' he said. 'Why have I made this a matter for public debate? The mask, I mean.'

He flung the last stones in a broad fan across the water.

'Isn't that what you wanted?' Molly probed. 'To talk about all the massacres and so on?'

Mungo frowned.

'That mask is in my safekeeping, legitimately given me. I should tell them all to go and jump in the Farron.'

He stopped, distracted and troubled. Katy was filling the eye sockets of the skull with moss.

Molly asked:

'Are you perhaps thinking it should go back?'

'I am thinking: that TaBunte woman is no fool.'

'No. In fact, the children want her at the school.'

'What's that?'

'Would you believe, Marion Morrison dug out some old Nigerian cottons. Marion! She had a missionary uncle, she said, and thought we might like dressing up. Then Hamish said no, he wanted the real African lady. Well, Mungo, I believe they should hear all sides in this.'

'All sides? Sides of what? All sides of slaughter? All sides of the bloody corpse? Damn her!'

'Mungo, please…'

Katy, crouched on the grass with the fetish she had made, looked up at them. Molly felt that she and Mungo were standing on opposite banks of a river that rushed between, breaking, eroding, carrying everything away.

Katy squinted up into the watery sun, and asked:

'What's safekeeping?'

◆◆◆

The blow fell.

How did he discover it? Sunk in thought among the Pinwa artefacts on their pedestals, in their sanctuary, Mungo drifted, touching his favourites. He came face-to-face with the portrait of Park, whose expression was unhelpful. Mungo sighed, and knew that he could not expect enlightenment.

He felt his heart turn sadly. He was drawn to the plinth of his dearest piece, the little terracotta figurine. He glanced down, even as his hand went out for the familiar rough-baked clay…

And found nothing. Absence only; the plinth vacant. The kneeling Pinwa girl was gone.

◆◆◆

'When something gets broken in your house,' the lady asked the class, 'and your papa is so angry, who gets the blame? Maybe your big brother says you knocked it over.'

'Mhairi always tells…'

'I don't!'

The Ambassadress laughed aloud.

'You say it was the cat! And the cat says no, no: it was the dog broke it. The same story can be told many ways; all depends who's telling.'

In their little seats, by their low octagonal desks in the classroom that smelt of gum, the children gazed up at the monumental black woman. From beside the door, Achule observed.

'So it is with the story of Mungo Park,' she continued, 'who walked alone across Africa. Oh, that's very fine. But in Africa, why should we care about one young man walking? We walk miles every day! We remember how Mungo Park came back, seven years later. I want you to imagine how it was then – so very different.'

She moved among them, letting her glowing, billowing fabrics brush against each child, letting them breathe the deep wood-oil fragrances that followed her.

'This time he came with soldiers, thirty-eight redcoat soldiers with rifles and pistols. No, this time it was not peace and friendship, this time he came with orders from the King of England who wanted the gold, the ivory, the land and all the glory. So, this little army marches across Africa and soon there is fighting, and stealing from the villages, and shooting, and Africans die and British die and robbers attack them and they kill anyone who comes near. And they fall sick in the rains and die some more. Next, they are building a boat upon the great River Niger and calling it His Majesty's Ship *Joliba*, though it's nothing but a rowboat, and down the river they go, shooting, shooting, and Africans shooting back. Well, you know, one thousand miles later they are nearly all dead, all but this Mungo Park and his lieutenants. And they come to the rapids of Bubaru. It is the end, the finish of them, drowned. And I have to tell you, we in Africa are not sorry, not one little bit. We are happy.'

The Ambassadress stood tall and straight in the midst of the little children, and repeated, loudly: 'We are happy!'

At which, the door was thrown open by a furious, cinder-bearded figure.

'Welcome to our history class, Mr Robertson,' said Achule.

Mungo stood in the doorway, studying the Ambassadress with loathing.

'Yes?' Achule snickered.

Mungo was not to be intimidated by the likes of Achule. He strode into the classroom.

'I have just one question. Someone has stolen something very precious to me, and I mean to have it back. You, Madam: did I hear you say that Park neglected common civilities in Africa? That he took things without a by-your-leave? Did you say that?'

The lady regarded him with frosty calm.

'Do I understand that you accuse me of something?'

But Mungo nodded at Achule.

'No, I daresay you sent your slave. Perhaps you thought it would serve an old colonial right. Perhaps, if you took my dearest treasure, I'd give in?'

'Now, you be very careful!' Achule snapped, jabbing a finger. Mungo ignored him, and thundered:

'Well, Madam? Shall I summon the Police? Do I call PC Reid?'

'I warn you now!' Achule yelled. The Ambassadress did not move, as Mungo roared:

'Speak up, woman. Or shall we strip off those fine robes?'

'I've got it,' said a little voice.

An instant's disbelief – then all eyes turned to Katy.

'Is it the wee statue? I've got it.'

Molly advanced rapidly across the room.

'Katy, you're to give me that now.'

'I'm looking after it.'

'Did Mr Robertson say you could take it?'

'But I want to look after it.'

'How could you do that? Give it to me now.'

'I can mind it as well as anyone.'

'Katy Morrison, do you hear me?'

'It's at home. It's safekeeping…'

'It's nothing but theft, young lady!'

'It's not – he said!'

Mungo regarded Katy with pain and tenderness. Over the little girl stood her teacher, screeching with mortification, while the Ambassadress looked round for explanation – but the door was near slammed off its hinges, as Mungo left the building.

◆◆◆

The light was failing, the wind getting up. A quiet, persistent drumming throbbed in the dusk. On the slopes above Parkneuk, the bikers were building a bonfire, dragging together a few shattered pallets, debris of wind-felled pines, and old tangled gorse.

Mungo observed a moment, then turned to stare down Glenfarron towards the village. He sensed someone near him, and glanced to his left: it was the doctor's son, Lewis. Mungo returned to his watch over the river, musing.

'I showed little Katy all that I have: my collections, and my tired heart. But what have I taught her? To steal, and call it something nicer.'

Lewis said: 'There's a car coming. I know those lights: it's my Da.'

Mungo bristled. Lewis added: 'He's not so bad, my Da. He was for the museum really, ye ken?'

Mungo looked at Lewis with affection – and at the friends nearby who stacked up the dry gorse, scrap lumber and dead boughs.

'Maybe,' he said, 'but others won't be far behind. We must get a move on. I'm away for petrol.'

He walked back to the motorbike shed, and found a can beside the Harley. Then he entered the museum. He turned on all the lights, flooded the room and walked directly down its length, scarcely glancing at the portrait of Park. He stopped before the dance mask, which smiled its spiral smile at him.

Mungo said, 'I shall never send you back there. But I can no longer keep you here, either.'

He lifted the mask from the hooks on which it hung. His arms around the soft barkcloth, he hugged it gently, pressing his face into its soft fringes, sniffing the residue of Africa. Then he moved towards the door.

Before he could leave, a silhouette appeared against the dusk, framed in the doorway.

'Robertson? It's me, Charles Dulce.'

Charlie took one cautious pace into the steading, looking with surprise at Mungo with his burden of rustling mask.

'What's this? What are you doing?

'You'll see in due course,' Mungo replied stonily, 'if you'll step aside.'

'I've something for you,' said Charlie. 'I had a phone call...'

He held out an untidy ball of newspaper; it was a gift of reconciliation that fortune had put Charlie's way. Because Mungo had his arms full, Charlie began unwrapping.

'A call from Miss Anderson, was that?' Mungo prompted.

'Oh no,' Charlie replied. 'No, from Marion Morrison. She found this in little Katy's room; she was sure it was yours.'

The paper fell from the terracotta statuette.

'I ... I can't precisely explain,' Charlie said, in agonies of embarrassment, 'why she called me, exactly. She mentioned thinking I was possibly someone you might trust...'

He gazed at Mungo with so much hope; at last, the latter nodded. Encouraged, Charlie looked again at the figurine, and breathed:

'Was she ... I mean, I did wonder ... she wasn't your ... wife?'

'Not my wife, no. She was my daughter. I have no need of a wife.'

He gave Charlie a piercing look, and a half-laugh.

'Put her on that table for now, Doctor. And then, perhaps you'll oblige me by bringing that fuel can.'

On the hillside beyond the gate, petrol was sluiced over the heaped brushwood.

Charlie asked, 'Are you not going to regret this?'

'Doubtless,' Mungo replied.

Away down the glen, lights flashed, hurrying towards them: headlamps – two pairs, three – turning off the road and up the Parkneuk track.

'Quickly now,' Mungo cried.

Lewis heard him, and shouted to Zippa: 'Go on!'

With her gas lighter, Zippa ignited a rolled newspaper, tossing it onto the bonfire that *whoomphed* into flame. The wind had gathered force, and now streamed off the inky, bleak highlands down Glenfarron, whipping up a storming heat.

'What do you think, Doctor?' called Mungo. 'An end to all these old loves and hauntings?'

Brian and Fly hefted two long poles into the air; between them swung and swayed the dance mask, and in the surging orange light the black spirals of its eyes spun in a fury. They raised it and bore it forward, high over the blaze.

The flames leaped to grab their prey. The mask took fire.

THE END

Fiction from Two Ravens Press

Love Letters from my Death-bed: by Cynthia Rogerson
£8.99. ISBN 978-1-906120-00-9. Published April 2007

Nightingale: by Peter Dorward
£9.99. ISBN 978-1-906120-09-2. Published September 2007

Parties: by Tom Lappin
£9.99. ISBN 978-1-906120-11-5. Published October 2007

Prince Rupert's Teardrop: by Lisa Glass
£9.99. ISBN 978-1-906120-15-3. Published November 2007

The Most Glorified Strip of Bunting: by John McGill
£9.99. ISBN 978-1-906120-12-2. Published November 2007

One True Void: by Dexter Petley
£8.99. ISBN 978-1-906120-13-9. Published January 2008

Auschwitz: by Angela Morgan Cutler
£9.99. ISBN 978-1-906120-18-4. Published February 2008

The Long Delirious Burning Blue: by Sharon Blackie
£8.99. ISBN 978-1-906120-17-7. Published February 2008

The Last Bear: by Mandy Haggith
£8.99. ISBN 978-1-906120-16-0. Published March 2008

Double or Nothing: by Raymond Federman
£9.99. ISBN 978-1-906120-20-7. Published March 2008

The Falconer: by Alice Thompson
£8.99. ISBN 978-1-906120-23-8. Published April 2008

The Credit Draper: by J. David Simons
£9.99. ISBN 978-1-906120-25-2. Published May 2008

Vanessa and Virginia: by Susan Sellers
£8.99. ISBN 978-1-906120-27-6. Published June 2008

Senseless: by Stona Fitch
£8.99. ISBN 978-1-906120-31-3. Published August 2008

Piano Angel: by Esther Woolfson
£9.99. ISBN 978-1-906120-34-4. Published October 2008

Short Fiction & Anthologies

Riptide: New Writing from the Highlands & Islands: Sharon Blackie & David Knowles (eds)
£8.99. ISBN 978-1-906120-02-3. Published April 2007

Types of Everlasting Rest: by Clio Gray
£8.99. ISBN 978-1-906120-04-7. Published July 2007

The Perfect Loaf: by Angus Dunn
£8.99. ISBN 978-1-906120-10-8. Published February 2008

Cleave: New Writing by Women in Scotland. Sharon Blackie (ed)
£8.99. ISBN 978-1-906120-28-3. Published June 2008

Non-fiction

The Sam Book: by Raymond Federman
£9.99. ISBN 978-1-906120-29-0. Published June 2008

Poetry

Castings: by Mandy Haggith
£8.99. ISBN 978-1-906120-01-6. Published February 2007

Leaving the Nest: by Dorothy Baird
£8.99. ISBN 978-1-906120-06-1. Published July 2007

The Zig Zag Woman: by Maggie Sawkins
£8.99. ISBN 978-1-906120-08-5. Published September 2007

In a Room Darkened: by Kevin Williamson
£8.99. ISBN 978-1-906120-07-8. Published October 2007

Running with a Snow Leopard: by Pamela Beasant
£8.99. ISBN 978-1-906120-14-6. Published January 2008

In the Hanging Valley: by Yvonne Gray
£8.99. ISBN 978-1-906120-19-1. Published March 2008

The Atlantic Forest: by George Gunn
£8.99. ISBN 978-1-906120-26-9. Published April 2008

Butterfly Bones: by Larry Butler
£8.99. ISBN 978-1-906120-24-5. Published May 2008

Meeting the Jet-Man: by David Knowles
£8.99. ISBN 978-1-906120-30-6. Published October 2008